monsoonbooks

THE FLIGHT OF THE SWANS

Born in Malaysia, D. Devika Bai is a retired school administrator. Her short stories and articles have been published in print in Singapore and Malaysia, and online in several North American e-publications. She is the great-granddaughter of one of the earliest Tanjore Maratha immigrants to British Malaya.

Devika Bai lives with her family in Rawang, Malaysia. This is her first novel.

T0159434

THE FLIGHT
OF THE SWANS

D. Devika Bai

monsoon

monsoonbooks

Published in 2005
by Monsoon Books Pte Ltd
Blk 106 Jalan Hang Jebat #02–14
Singapore 139527
www.monsoonbooks.com.sg

ISBN 981-05-2367-X

Copyright©D. Devika Bai, 2005

The moral right of the author has been asserted

Front and backcover photographs: Swans©Edmund
Fellowes; Fort©Nitin M Kelvalkar/Dinodia Photo Library;
Author photograph©Oscar Colour Lab & Telecommunication
Sdn Bhd, Rawang

Printed in Singapore

10 09 08 07 06 05   1 2 3 4 5 6 7 8 9

For my parents
R. Devaji Rao Bhonsle (the late) and R. Rajendra Bai Mohite
and my brothers
Murahari, Puranath,
Dushwant and Nanjun

When night comes I bury my face in my arms
and dream that my paper boats float on and on
under the midnight stars.
The fairies of sleep are sailing in them,
and the lading is their baskets full of dreams.

—Rabindranath Tagore, *The Cresent Moon*

Contents

PART ONE

Ramdas Rao Bhonsle	15
Killa	30
The Flight	42
Champakapur	60
Of Rice Planting and Goat Testicles	84
Vrishabha	111

PART TWO

Tara Bai	135
The Arsa Mahal	141
The Rich Citizen	150
Refuge	160

PART THREE

Madhav Rao Bhonsle	171
Revelations	180
Married Life	191
The Neighbourhood	198
The Falling into Place	212

PART FOUR

Arundhati Bai Bhonsle   225
The Crossing   229
In a New Land   239
An Oversight   259
Prospects   276

PART FIVE

The Third Eye Opens   293

EPILOGUE   315

ACKNOWLEDGEMENTS   319

BIBLIOGRAPHY   320

PART ONE

Ramdas Rao Bhonsle

Ramdas hardly noticed the phenomenal flight of swans overhead as he marched purposefully across the battlefield. Even flying elephants would not have distracted him. So preoccupied was he by the dreadful thing he was about to do.

Behind him lay Killa Fort, licked for the first time in centuries. It was suffering the painful rasp of the tongue of Defeat. Ahead was the city of Killa, bombarded beyond recognition. Milling around him was an army of battlefield ghosts: armless, legless, headless. The ghosts screamed. They tore at Ramdas, jealous because he lived. And above was Lady Night Sky, flaunting her star-sequined gown as if to mock Ramdas and his loss.

He had just lost queen and country. But that was only the first of his losses. Before the death god, Yama, came to take him, he was to lose much, much more. For Ramdas was one of those unfortunate beings doomed to suffer hell on earth to enter paradise.

He felt strangely naked, stripped of his patta. The long-bladed weapons had carved human flesh, splintered bone and bathed in blood. They had been so much a part of him that now his hands kept roving to his hips to grip them, only to grip air. The ultimate humiliation he suffered that afternoon still rankled—the surrendering of his swords to the British. They had even confiscated the bank tucked at his waist. The sickle-shaped dagger had served him well in hand-to-hand combat. He could still see the humiliating scene of surrender: himself, Captain Ramdas Rao Bhonsle, at the head of a snaking line of sepoys laying down their arms in separate heaps for swords, lances, daggers and muskets. It felt like being emasculated.

As his long legs erased the miles, Ramdas thought of his family.

His aging parents were agitated when he left the fort. They could not understand him. For the first time in his life, he was disobeying them. His wife was whimpering, terrified at the prospect of never seeing her new groom again. And all three were afraid for his life. But they did not say so in case the very words they uttered spelled his doom.

"Whatever you do, you can't bring the Rani back to life. It's over, Ramdas," his father had said after a short argument, just before Ramdas left.

"Over? Not for me. I know I can't bring the Rani back to life but by God I won't let her death go unavenged!"

The family saw that anger, frustration and despair had settled like a fossilised twin in his chest. They knew Ramdas to be neither a man of mantra nor of tantra. If he were the former, he would be praying now, as many of his countrymen were. If he were the latter, he would be cloistered in the Shakti shrine, unconcerned about the fate of his country. But he was a man of the sword—a Kshatriyan—and in his book, loyalty and revenge were the sides of the same sword.

Ramdas' comrades had not nicknamed him 'Ranidas' for nothing. 'Ramdas' meant 'Servant of God'. And since Ramdas volunteered for every action, overt or covert, ordered by the Rani against the British, his friends teasingly dubbed him 'Ranidas'. He was her true servant. Even now he was on this self-imposed mission, knowing he might not return alive.

But then, who wouldn't die for one such as the Rani? Many had volunteered to accompany him but he decided there had been enough death all around to last a century, and so had set out alone.

*   *   *

When the gods want a great rajah's or rani's death to be remembered with awe, they show a sign by creating strange phenomena. So the Marathas of Killa believe. Years after the royal personage's ashes have floated down the mighty Ganges and mingled with the waters of the ocean, people will gather around fires on winter nights and talk of these phenomena. In hushed tones, they tell their grandchildren how, when such and such a rajah died, the god Indra suddenly javelin-ed lightning and hammer-threw thunder out of a blue sky. Or how Yama made the healthy royal elephant suddenly keel over and die; how Agni turned a green banana orchard black overnight; how Bhumi Devi aborted a centuries-old banyan tree in perfectly calm weather; or how Shiva petrified a standing teak grove.

One such phenomenon occurred in the central Indian kingdom of Killa after its rani died.

That night, the people heard a sudden whisper in the sky. At first they thought a swarm of locusts was approaching. They were used to the uninvited guests dining on their crops. But when the whisper became a clamour, they realised it was the flapping of hundreds of wings accompanied by ululating cries.

In Killa Fort, every Maratha rushed out to see. They were astonished, having never seen such a sight in Killa before.

There, appearing out of the north sky, were flocks of white, wild swans. They were flying in giant 'V' formations. The swans flew so low the people could see their pink bills. What astonished them even further was: the swan leading the foremost flock was thrice the size of the others. As the swans flew overhead, their cries black-holed every other nocturnal sound. The swoosh of their wings blew dust into the pop-eyes of the spectators and sent dry leaves cartwheeling on the ground. Wave after wave flew by. Still ululating, the birds arrowed south, leaving the night air quivering like a plucked bowstring.

A momentary silence fell over the fort. Then everybody started talking at once.

The religious and superstitious were agog.

"It's the Hamsa swan!" they cried.

"Goddess Saraswathi's vehicle!"

"Rani Meera Bai's come to us as the Hamsa!"

"She was the largest one leading the flocks!"

"Did you hear how forlorn her cries were?"

"She's come in spirit to protect us."

"Quick! We must offer oblations."

Shaking their heads in wonder, the citizens hastened to pray, their grief and battle-weariness forgotten for the moment.

The few sceptics among them put the episode down to a freak winter up north in the Himalayas. The havoc must have panicked the swans into migrating four months earlier than usual, they reasoned.

Whatever the explanation, the occurrence would remain a topic of conversation for years to come in Killa.

*   *   *

The scent of stale battlefield blood choked Ramdas. He had to keep swatting at bluebottles that mistook him for a corpse, their lure being his bloodstained uniform and the superficial cut on his arm. They buzzed greedily around the cut. Ramdas' ears still rang with the boom of cannons, the clash of steel and the roar of sepoys, all silenced since early afternoon.

As Ramdas had expected, wolves, jackals and dholes had invaded the battlefield. The night was savage with their snarls. Lammergeiers and crows had joined them. The scavengers were fighting their own battles over morsels of human and horse flesh: a severed thumb or a finger; a toe or an ear; a scrotum or a penis ... In their frenzy, the canines snapped at Ramdas but he warded them off with his staff.

Just as he was thinking, Thank God the bodies and carcasses have been removed, he caught sight of the dead elephants. The thrashed sepoys had left their cremation till the next morning. There was not enough wood and they would have to range far to look for it. (The Rani was clever. Before the siege, she had made sure all trees and bushes in a five-mile radius around the fort were cut and the wood stored in the fort. That way the enemy would have no place to hide, no wood for their fires and no fodder for their animals. She only left the thorn trees around the fort standing.)

The enemy had used the elephants to pull gun-carriages. Now the elephants' stiff legs jutted out amidst upturned cannons and formed macabre sculptures against the sky.

Scavengers were half-buried in the elephants' bellies. Ramdas retched. Not that he was squeamish about gore. He had seen more than his share in his twenty-five years, especially during the past month's siege. His nausea had more to do with the Rani's death, and the loss of Killa. The gore just drove home the point with finality. Wanting to exit the battlefield fast, Ramdas broke into a lope. But his feet squelched in the blood-soaked ground and made his nausea worse.

He reached the zigzag trenches the enemy had dug outside the city. In the dark, they looked like abysses. But Ramdas crossed them without incident.

Soon, the bombarded city of Killa loomed before him. It looked like a pile of bricks smashed by a Danava giant. Sounds of wailing flew out of the city like bats from a cave.

Inside the city, Ramdas saw women tearing their hair and beating their faces and breasts. Many were looking at the empty sky and chanting. They were still awed by the flight of the swans. The newly widowed had gone mad with grief. They were screaming as the flames of self-immolation gobbled them. Orphaned toddlers were bawling for their parents. They bawled even louder when strangers tried to console them.

In contrast, the men were quiet. The shell-shocked sat staring amidst their smashed homes. Those salvaging their possessions were dragging themselves about, as if shackled. Though they had taken the side of the Raj and had won, they knew deep down in their hearts that the true winners were the colonisers.

Ramdas paused to look at the Rani's dreams, now dead like her: the half-built Moorish-style State Library, collapsed in rubble; the Phool Bhaag so full of orchids, roses, lilies and dahlias, ploughed up; the largest deul, masjid and church in the land, flattened; the new hospital, demolished; and the modern drainage systems, damaged beyond repair.

He ran past the Rani's city palace. Travellers said it rivalled the Taj Mahal. Now it was a black cavern. The British had made it a point to raze the palace as soon as the Rani took refuge in the fort. To Ramdas, every burnt column was a prod, goading him to seek revenge.

Ramdas passed through the city unaccosted.

From the fringe of the city, all he had to do was take the shortcut across the smashana to reach his destination.

*   *   *

The smashana was a hellhole. In the aftermath of battle, the crematorium was dotted with mounds of burning corpses. Ramdas gagged as the odour of barbequed human flesh hit him. And the heat was so intense, he felt he would leave the grounds half-tandooried.

Ramdas saw sweating priests chanting mantras at the fires. A few men, either relatives of the dead or undertakers, were in their company. The priests looked half-dead. The siege had exacted its toll on them. It showed in the way they croaked, swallowed syllables and even whole sloka. Now and then, melting fat from the dead exploded in the fires, drowning their chants. 'Fat' salutes in lieu of gun salutes for my queen, Ramdas thought bitterly.

Normally, people dreaded going near the smashana at night. They were frightened off by tales of the skull-garlanded Shiva dancing on the ashes of the dead. They said the skull cup he held in his hand contained fresh human blood.

Besides Shiva, there were the vethaala that haunted the crematorium.

Ramdas recalled that, as boys, he and his friends had dared each other to spend a night in these very grounds. Armed with sticks, they huddled under a monstrous banyan tree, hoping to catch sight of a vethaala—an ashen entity that enters a corpse and makes it rise and walk like a zombie. Once the vethaala clutches anyone, it never lets go. It devours him. First, it nibbles off the ears; then, it chomps on the nose; next, it sucks out the eyes. As it turned out, another apparition scared the shit out of the boys: that of a wild-looking undertaker wielding a cutlass. Ramdas and company ran helter-skelter.

They tripped and fell into ashes and went home looking like vethaala themselves. They abandoned the idea of vethaala-watching after that.

There was an ancient Shiva temple on the outskirts of the crematorium. Its granite edifice, polished for centuries with gingelly oil, gleamed like a sea serpent in the night. Inside this temple were the Shaktas who petrified ordinary folk. For Shaktas practiced black magic and sacrificed humans. They could put a curse on you and ruin your life; they could make you vomit blood or go mad; they could have you possessed by evil pisasu; and they could chop off your head and offer your blood to the blood-thirsty goddess, Kali. Cocooned in their cult, the Shaktas were not touched by the war, except for individuals who craved money and power.

As Ramdas neared the temple, he heard the sudden jingling of anklets. It reminded him of tales of the ghostly, white-garbed temptress, Mohini pisasu, who wore anklets and roamed at night to seduce unsuspecting mortals. But he made out a very mortal woman running out of the temple. She was naked from the waist up, her cascading black hair veiling one milk-white breast. Part of her underskirt was hitched and tucked at one hip, sensuously revealing a thigh. Laughing, the wanton rushed up to him.

Ramdas recognised her. But that still did not prepare him for the shock of seeing her half-naked and on the prowl.

She was Kausalya, the traitor Hanumant Rao's wife. Husband and wife belonged to the Shakta cult. They frequented a shrine dedicated to Shakti (also called Kali) in the Shiva temple. There they invoked Shakti's spirit with offerings of wine, fish, meat, grain and sex.

The woman's possessed by a spirit all right, Ramdas thought; that of the country-wine kind; how she reeks of the stuff!

Still laughing, Kausalya caught Ramdas' hands.

The next thing Ramdas knew his hands were cupping her breasts. He felt their temple-statue voluptuousness: firm, round, inviting. The rage he was in he felt like throwing her to the ground and ravishing her to death.

"Come! Come with me, my handsome," he heard Kausalya croon. "Let me give you the Shakti, the Power! You'll be a god among men once you've tasted of it!" She was referring to the ritual sex after Shakti worship.

Ramdas found Kausalya bewitching, even in the starlight. Her cat eyes jabbed green fire. Her body glowed. It looked like she had been carved out of ivory and then polished. As she purred and rubbed against him, Ramdas sensed in her the combined strength of the Gir lion and the

21

Bengal tiger. He also sensed the danger.

Her grip was vice-like but Ramdas tore his hands away and strode off.

The lioness-tigress trotted up, pleading, "Don't go, priykar. Don't leave me!"

"Silence, woman! How dare you call me priykar. I'm not your lover!" Ramdas growled, glaring at her. "Your lover and husband is at the British camp, worshipping the Shakti *they've* given him. You can worship it, too, when he brings it home. *If* he brings it home, that is!"

When Kausalya tried to clutch him again, he broke into a sprint.

Kausalya shrieked: "May your sons be cursed!! May you never live in peace!!"

Still cursing, she scooped up handfuls of sand and threw them into the air to make her curses potent. For a second, the air was painted with her sinister sand art. Then the sand settled, each grain shot with the power to reduce Ramdas to dust.

Ramdas did not look back at Kausalya. As he dashed past the temple, he heard the beat of drums. The drumbeats signalled the start of festivities. He knew that inside the shrine, scores of Shaktas were dancing naked and coupling in frenzy, even before the blood had dried on the sacrificial stone.

*   *   *

Kausalya stomped into the Shakti shrine.

Two stone lions, their fangs bared, stood guard at the entrance. Their amber-embedded eyes looked frighteningly real in the night. Inside the shrine, the gargantuan statue of Shakti, in all her ten-handed glory, presided over the Shaktas. At her feet were heaped yellow and orange marigolds. She was surrounded by statuettes of dwarf demons, just as ferocious-looking as her.

The smell of ghee, burnt sacrificial wood and sweat greeted Kausalya. There was a trace of fresh blood in the air, too. But the body of the recently sacrificed virgin was nowhere in sight. Only her head, fringed by marigolds, rested at the goddess's feet. The death-frozen, contorted features on the victim's face told their own tale.

Through the flickering golden lights of the ghee lamps, Kausalya saw the mass of thrusting, heaving bodies locked in an orgy. Every level of society was represented here: from prince to pauper to red-robed priests in scalp locks.

Her warped need for Ramdas too much to bear, Kausalya grabbed the nearest single Shakta. She did not care that he was of the lowest caste—a Shudra—and a night-soil carrier.

The horny man was only too glad to oblige. It was only in the Shakti shrine, where there were no caste distinctions, that he could take a woman of higher caste, even a Brahmin like Kausalya.

As they joined the orgy, Kausalya fantasised the Shudra was Ramdas. She saw Ramdas' black-opal eyes looking down at her; she touched Ramdas' crinkly hair, his aquiline features; she traced the centipede-like scar on his cheek; and felt his powerful muscles. Like she had once, ten years ago.

Afterwards, shoving the Shakta aside, Kausalya hurried to skinny-dip in the tank behind the shrine. She wanted to cleanse herself not only of the Shudra but also of the memory of Ramdas.

The tank was a carpet of stars. She plunged into it, melting the stars. When she resurfaced, she realized she was not alone. There was a lone white swan cruising on the water. It was huge and was gazing steadily at her, but that did not register. For, like Ramdas, she had only revenge on her mind.

Wrapping a strip of black voile around her glistening body, she ran towards an adjacent tenkdi. The tenkdi was a group of basalt rocks and boulders that looked like giant moles on the face of Mother Earth. She made a beeline for the only boulder with a crevice. The boulder was as big as a house and light pulsed from its crevice.

Kausalya found what she wanted in a cage next to the crevice. Inside the cage were half a dozen black cockerels. Outside were a chopper and a stack of coconut shells.

The place stank of rotting flesh and chicken droppings.

Kausalya opened the cage. The cockerels squawked. They fell over each other in alarm. She whisked one out. The bird fought her in a flurry of squawking, flapping wings and flying feathers. She held it to the ground with one foot. Her hands sure, Kausalya chopped off its head. She collected the spurting blood in a coconut shell. Cockerel blood would have to do in the absence of tomcat's, he-goat's or man's blood.

Blood-filled coconut shell in hand, Kausalya slid through the crevice and stepped into a cave.

Shakta lore had it that the cave had been chiselled inside the boulder during Vedic times. Since then, Shaktas had used it for their darkest deeds.

The cave could seat at least fifty Shaktas. Its black walls and floor were streaked with thick olivine veins. The olive green of the veins made it appear as if serpents were writhing everywhere. And the floor had a shine, polished by the bottoms of countless generations of Shaktas.

A sacrificial fire illumined the cave. Shaktas had lit it earlier to cast spells. A rough-hewn image of Shakti sprang from one wall. Only the goddess's protruding eyes and tongue were painted, the tongue blood red. Against another wall lay a pile of human-skull cups, bones and an urn full of ashes from the smashana. Camphor-fume choked the cave but Kausalya was used to it.

She stood still for a moment, listening. The uninitiated would only hear silence. But Kausalya's trained ears picked up the ancient voices that filled the cave—voices that whispered tantric verses. Even as a child she had put her ear to the crevice to listen to the voices, when other children her age put their ear to the conch to listen to the sea.

Kausalya poured the cockerel blood into a skull cup and scooped ashes from the urn with another. She set both near the fire. Other paraphernalia she needed were already in place: ashoka twigs, camphor and a potion of crushed rose apple, plum and nipa flowers. The potion gave off a sweet-sour scent.

Sitting cross-legged in front of the fire, Kausalya smeared her forehead and arms with the human ash. She dipped her thumb into the cockerel blood and marked her forehead with it. Then she began casting her spell. Whispering incantations, she threw the twigs and a handful of camphor into the fire. The fire crackled in response. And its flames leaped devilishly. Next, she tipped in the potion she believed would begin

Ramdas' downfall. Then, the fire dancing in her eyes, she whip-cracked the words that would finally destroy Ramdas and his sons:

> *Kl-e-e-m! Hr-e-e-m! Shr-e-e-m!*
> I who am a Brahmin witch and devourer of my young,
> I command Thee, O Thousand-Eyed Curse,
> To come forth in your Chariot
> and deliver this curse that I shall utter:
>> *May he who spurned me consort with crones,*
>> *May he befriend she-devils and ogres,*
>> *May he and his progeny live their evil dreams,*
>> *May he and his progeny suffer a thousand calamities!*
> Accept my offerings of Ash of Man and Blood of Cockerel
> and go forth, O Thousand-Eyed Curse,
> over Kala they call Time,
> over hills and mountains, rivers and seas,
> and deliver my Curse!

Later, on her way back to the shrine, Kausalya noticed the swan was still gliding in the tank. It followed her along the edge until she climbed the steps to the shrine. Strange why the lead swan alone has stayed back, Kausalya wondered, having witnessed the flight of the swans. She did not for a moment imagine that, the next morning, Shaktas would find her mysteriously dead, one hand clutching a bunch of white feathers.

*   *   *

By the time Ramdas reached his destination—the British camp—his uniform of white salwaar, quilted tunic and red cummerbund was glued to him with sweat. (His pagri had been knocked off his head during the battle.)

He tied a black kerchief below his eyes to mask his face. With body slung low and one hand on the hilt of his kitchen knife, he crept through the elephant grass towards the tent city before him.

Campfires hissed in front of the occupied tents, their flames snake-dancing. More than half of the British sepoys were at the captured Killa Fort. The rest had stayed back to wrap up operations. While low-ranking British officers occupied the fort, the high-ranking were still at the camp. They proposed to move in the next morning. More comfortable accommodation would be ready by then.

A sudden movement in the grass startled Ramdas. In a flash he had his knife in his hand, ready to slit the throat of whoever it was. But it was only a shrew. He saw its dark form scuttling away in a hurry.

There were hardly any sentries guarding the camp. Those few who were on duty were lax to the point of chatting or smoking beedi. Their commanders ignored the misdemeanour. After all, they reasoned, there'll be no more resistance from the Maratha wretches as we've confiscated all their weapons; we tigers needn't fear kittens, need we?

Ramdas' heart drummed as he slipped through the grass to the largest tent. He was sure that was where the British top brass would be. And his quarry, too.

Sepoys were eating and drinking around the campfires. There was an air of celebration as two nautch girls whirled and gyrated in front of them to the music from pipes and drums. The stitched mirrors in the dancers' billowing skirts picked up the campfires and showered them like sunbursts in the night. Some sepoys clapped to the beat of the music. Your casualties may have been high, but when you defeated a formidable foe like the Marathas, you celebrated.

Some sepoys were snoring in spite of the revelry.

Around the fire in front of the main tent, a company of British officers belted out 'Greensleeves'. Then they launched into 'Loch Lomond' and 'Homeward Bound'. The strains of 'Blue Danube' (all the rage then), met Ramdas as he made an easy dash to the back of the main tent.

The men swayed to the mouth organ melody. Some grabbed partners and dragged each other around in a drunken waltz.

There were voices coming from the other side of the canvas.

"... To Her Majesty," a sonorous voice said.

"To Her Majesty!" a group chorused.

There was a clinking of glasses as the top brass toasted Queen Victoria. A scraping of chairs signalled their sitting. There followed a murmur of voices.

An acrid smell seeped out from under the tent. Cigars, Ramdas thought. The thick odour tickled his nose and made him feel like sneezing. So he ran a few steps away from the tent. He remained there, fearing a sneeze would give him away. After that, he could only catch snatches of conversation.

Ramdas had a smattering of English. He learned it in the compulsory night classes organised for her military officers by the far-sighted Rani. From what he heard it was clear that a fête was in progress for the traitor and his three accomplices. The traitors had lowered the drawbridge and opened the North Gate that morning.

He heard Hanumant Rao crow as he accepted flattery from his bribers. There was the unmistakable heavy ring of sovereigns as the British threw Hanumant and his cohorts their reward. The beggars get their pickings, Ramdas thought.

He crouched in the grass and waited for Hanumant to come out. It galled him to think that Hanumant, his subordinate and an unintelligent one at that, could have duped him into complacency. How innocent and sincere Hanumant and his accomplices had seemed. It just goes to show you never know which viper lurks in which pit, Ramdas concluded.

He felt like kicking himself for not keeping an eagle eye on Hanumant. Especially since he had witnessed Hanumant's depraved childhood in the village where they grew up together.

Hanumant came from a poverty-striken household. Contrary to the Maratha grain, his parents were too lazy to work. They stole food. His weaker siblings died from starvation. Driven by Hanumant's constant clamouring for food, his parents beat him. They even scalded him once. He still bore the massive scald-mark on the left side of his chest. He was unschooled and wore the skimpiest of loincloths. And he was always begging for food and clothing. So it came as no surprise to anyone that he grew up vowing to become rich one day—by hook or by crook. "He'll eat shit even for a single paisa!" people said of him. By the time the British arrived in Killa, Hanumant was prime material for bribery.

Ramdas knew that it would have been safer if he had waited for Hanumant in the city of Killa, where the traitor lived. But Ramdas suspected he would flee to another city, leaving Kausalya to her own fate. Though the British promised Hanumant protection, Ramdas was sure the traitor knew that his own people would lynch him in the city.

After what seemed like an interminable ten minutes, Hanumant staggered out of the tent. He looked like the *Ramayana* simian he was named after. His accomplices followed. They took a lighted torch each, hollered their goodbyes and came in Ramdas' direction.

Delirious with joy, they held up their money pouches and shook them. Hundreds of jingling gold coins made music in the night.

The four did not notice Ramdas as they passed a couple of yards from him.

They did not stink of alcohol as Ramdas had expected. High on bhang, Ramdas decided. The British were known to satisfy every craving their stooges might have, be it for money, women, wine or drugs.

When Hanumant fell behind, Ramdas grabbed his chance. He pounced on him like a panther and caught him in a stranglehold. Then he slit his throat.

"Die, you jackal! Die!" Ramdas said vehemently. He felt a strange satisfaction as Hanumant gurgled blood and fell dead.

Hanumant's torch set the dry grass on fire. Before Ramdas could stamp out the flames, the accomplices turned around to check the sudden glare. They saw Ramdas running away and raised the alarm.

In no time, the entire camp was chasing Ramdas. Dozens of torches turned night into day. Someone close enough made a flying tackle and floored Ramdas. In the struggle that followed, his mask tore off.

"It's Captain Bhonsle! I'd know that scar anywhere!" one of Hanumant's accomplices shouted.

"Kill him before he kills us!" another brother-at-treachery screamed.

Ramdas, alert, fought off the sepoy and British officer who were upon him.

Another officer lunged at Ramdas. As Ramdas fell supine, the officer fell on Ramdas' up-turned knife. He hissed his dying breath into Ramdas' ear.

If it had been only Hanumant that Ramdas had killed, the British would not have pursued the matter further. Of that Ramdas was sure.

After all, they had given the traitor his promised reward. Their collective conscience was clear on that count. "The bloke is dispensable," Ramdas could hear them saying. "Blimey! The money-worshipping rascal might just about betray us as he has his queen!" But then, a British officer was dead and that warranted immediate action.

As Ramdas fled for his life, he heard an officer bellowing, "Don't let him escape! Search the city! Search the fort! And bring him back dead or alive. *Jaldi! Jaldi!*"

Killa

When the Moghul hordes of Genghis Khan poured through the Himalayan passes and swept across northern India, they set the seal on the course of the subcontinent's history for the next six hundred years. That was during the thirteenth century.

By the time of the death of the last Moghul emperor, Aurangzeb, in 1707, Moghul rule extended from Delhi in the north to Haidarabad in the south.

But not all principalities and kingdoms fell to the Moghul sword. There were pockets of resistance to the very end of Moghul rule. The Cholas and Nayaks to the south, the Sikhs to the north and the Rajputs to the west were untouched by Moghul reign, thanks to their fighting spirit. So were the Marathas.

The Marathas of Central India are engraved in history as the greatest freedom fighters India has ever known. Fiercely independent, they fought to the death any group that threatened their sovereignty.

During pre-Moghul days, the Marathas lived in scattered, self-contained agrarian communities ruled by their own chiefs. Even then they clashed against each other at the first sign of incursion. Then, Maratha religious leaders like Tukaram, Eknath and Vaman Pundit brought about radical reforms during the sixteenth and seventeenth centuries.

Besides preaching universal values, they brought down the axe on the caste system by declaring all men equal before God. So the Marathas fought the high-and-mighty Brahmins and won social equality for themselves. But they were still a scattered people, easy prey for the designing Moghuls. Until the greatest Maratha of all—Chatrapati Shivaji Bhonsle—appeared on the scene. He united all the Marathas. He traversed the Satpura Range, the Western Ghats and the Deccan collecting able-bodied men. Then he transformed them from simple farmers tilling their land and tending their herds to a vast fighting force. Under his kingship, the Marathas fought the Moghuls. The all-conquering Akbar, Shah Jehan and Aurangzeb found their match in Shivaji. The Moghuls toppled, the Maratha stood like a colossus over India, with one foot planted firmly in Delhi in the north and the other in Tanjore in the south.

Then Shivaji died. His successors were not as capable as him. Absence of a strong leadership and centralised government coupled with poor economy and internal dissensions among Maratha chiefs served to produce disastrous results. Fine cracks started to appear in the Maratha Empire. The shrewd British, watching from the fringes under the mantle of the East India Company, obtained not only more trading concessions from rival chiefs but also concessions to govern vast regions. The chiefs, greedy for power, gave these concessions in exchange for help in waging war against each other. And the downward slide began.

During the Anglo-Maratha Wars from 1779 to 1806, Governor General Lord Wellesley wrested Delhi, Agra, Laswari, Cuttuck, Ahmednagar and Argaon from the Marathas.

A crushing blow fell when prominent Maratha rulers succumbed to the British onslaught. Daulat Rao Sindhia of Gwalior was routed in 1803, Yashwant Rao Holkar of Indore in 1806 and Peshwa Baji Rao of Poona in 1817.

But all was not over, as the British thought. They did not count on the tenacity of the Marathas. Fierce resistance continued even from the smallest kingdoms and principalities. Tatya Tope, Rao Saheb of Kalpi, Nana Saheb of Bithur and the Raja of Banpur were some of the scintillating stars on the Maratha firmament then. So was Rani Meera Bai of Killa.

Maratha history brims with Maratha queens and ordinary women who either fought Indian tyrants or foreign invaders. They were highly emancipated women who, ahead of their time, learned to read, write, ride, fence and shoot with arrows and firearms. To name just a few: there was Savitri Bai of Belvadi who held her besieged fort for a month; Rani

31

Tara Bai Mohite of Marathawad who crushed the Moghuls; Rani Ahalya Bai Holkar of Indore who fought the British; and the firearms-trained Rani Lakshmi Bai Moropant of Jhansi who was another nemesis of the British. Rani Meera Bai of Killa was the last of these titans.

Killa was just as illustrious as its Rani. Illustrious because of its unconquered fort. (If there was any single factor that helped perpetuate Maratha rule in India for almost four centuries, it was the more than three hundred and fifty forts that dotted the land. Most were natural forts on rocky hills and were impregnable.)

An interesting story is told of Killa's beginnings.

In the year 1400, a splinter army of the Moghul Tamerlane swept down the slopes of the Ajantha and started invading peaceful Maratha lands. One of these lands, Morgaum, with a population of thirty thousand, was ruled by Raja Sonaji Jadhav. A kind ruler, he was much revered and loved by his subjects. But the Moghuls sacked Morgaum in a lightning raid. They killed the palace guards, plundered the palace and sent the Raja fleeing in the middle of the night. They ransacked every home and slaughtered dwellers who resisted. Then they did something they learnt from Tamerlane: they built a pyramid, in the city center, with the skulls of the twenty thousand people they slaughtered. They considered it a grand monument to themselves.

But still the Moghuls did not leave Morgaum. An epicurean delight made them stay. Morgaum abounded in peacocks. And the invaders had acquired the taste for peacock meat from their raids into China where the meat was considered an exotic delicacy. So the Moghuls stayed until they hunted the peacocks to extinction.

The Raja and the survivors among his family, courtiers, nobles, sepoys and subjects trekked day and night through thick forests to escape the Moghuls.

One evening, they walked into a swirling fog. The further they advanced, the poorer visibility became. When the fog swallowed their surroundings and they could not even see their hands in front of their faces, they decided to stay put till the fog lifted.

It was then that they noticed there was something uncanny about the fog. All night, the people heard strange hissings, as if the ground was crawling with snakes. And yet they felt no such creatures on the ground. Where are we, they wondered; are we on magical or malevolent ground? They found out the next morning.

When the fog lifted, they saw before them a brooding basalt hill. The rocky hill rose steeply from its surroundings of thorny kanta trees. A circle of rocks sat on its crest like a crown.

Raja Sonaji was struck by the hill. He liked its defiant, craggy slopes and its shield of thorn trees.

"Why, it will make an excellent killa!" he exclaimed.

Everybody agreed with him. The hill had the ideal features for a fort: height, isolation and natural protection. A little strategic construction and it would become impregnable. The Raja sent out reconnoitrers to check out the hill.

It was while they were waiting for the reconnoitrers to return that something extraordinary happened.

The Raja was resting, leaning against a rock.

"Snake! Snake!" a courtier shouted and pushed the Raja away from the rock.

The snake that had half slid out from under the rock had the Raja and his people shocked. It was nothing like they had ever seen before.

For a start, it was double-headed. And its body was as thick as a man's thigh. It had neither the diamond-shaped markings of a python nor the yellow-and-black bands of a krait. Neither was it green like a tree snake nor spotted like a viper. The nearest the people could compare it to was the king cobra. And yet it was not deep green or wholly pitch black like that species. It was black but pulsated with a royal purple sheen in the sunlight.

The Raja immediately consulted the Swami, his spiritual advisor.

"Maharaj, we stand on hallowed ground," the learned man said. "This snake bears the sign of Vasuki."

Everyone gasped. They knew that Vasuki was the mythical thousand-headed serpent that guarded the netherworld treasures of Pathaala. They watched spellbound as the snake inched back into its pit.

"The treasures Vasuki guards include the Navratna gems, Maharaj," the Swami continued. "This is a good omen. Henceforth, Your Highness should wear the Navratna. They'll bring good luck and prosperity to you, your successors and your kingdom." The Navratna were the nine most precious jewels: diamond, sapphire, emerald, ruby, topaz, red coral, cat's-eye, pearl and hessonite.

When the reconnoitrers returned with favourable reports, the Raja decided to set down roots in the new land. He ordered his people to build a fort on the hillcrest. Later, a city sprouted around the fort.

That was how Killa got its name. And how Rani Meera Bai came to wear the Navratna Crown.

The night after the battle, Killa Fort was knocked out from exhaustion.

The British Central India Field Force slept from the exhaustion of victory. The Marathas slept from the exhaustion of defeat. But regardless of how they slept, the next morning many would say they dreamt of a white swan.

For the Marathas, sleep was a short respite before the new day; a day that would see the rigor mortis of their spirit as they, for the first time, bowed to the British.

Only a few sepoys assigned to sentry duty were about. But they, too, were being courted by Sleep.

The daylight hours had been spent dousing fires and clearing the fort of the dead.

Dead people and dead horses had been stacked high. But Death still lingered. The dying tried to shoo it away but it would not leave.

All the Rani's functionaries, including her wise chief advisor, the Diwan; the battle-scarred commander in chief of her army, the Senapati; and her fatherly mentor, Lakham Rao, had been captured and sent to the temporary gaol in the administrative block. Everyone knew what *their* fate would be.

There was nothing for the Marathas to salvage in the fort. They had donated most of their gold jewellery and money to The Cause. Whatever trinkets and loose change remained had been looted. Even the statue of Saraswathi in the Mandir had been ripped of its ornaments.

To the defeated Marathas, even their normal surroundings suddenly seemed unreal in the night: the bombarded magazine, the provisions store, the mint, the forge, the sickbay, the communal kitchen, the fort temple—all these looked like misshapen hulks from a nether ocean; the gutted fort palace, its white marble floors and walls now marred with patches of soot, was a colossal piebald from another world; the flag poles were serpents pointing to a godless heaven; the maidan was a sea of scum; and the haathi tal, where elephants bathed, was a molten tar-pit. But the wells were havens, tempting the weak-willed to jump in and end their great sorrow.

The only comfort the Marathas had was that their Prince Dilip had escaped the slaughter. One day, they told themselves, he would return to take up arms against the Raj, and win back Killa.

Meanwhile, they relived the horrible day in their dreams.

*   *   *

Morning, 17 June 1869.

Killa Fort wrapped its defenses about itself, crouched, and waited for the attack.

The fort looked down from the hill, like an all-seeing eye, on Killa. Its turrets and towers had defined the Killa skyline for five centuries. Its loftiest point was the Saraswathi Mandir, built by the Rani. An avid reader and collector of ancient palm-leaf texts, she had dedicated the temple to Saraswathi, the goddess of learning. Inside the temple was a golden statue of the goddess seated on her Hamsa swan. From this temple tower, one could take in the fort, the city of Killa and the vista beyond: the sweep of the Ajantha hills to the south, the tributaries rushing to join the Narmada to the north, the tilt of the Deccan to the east, and the dip of the Tapti River valley to the west.

Besides the Tophkhana House (for storing ammunition), forges, stables, sickbay, administrative block, living quarters and communal kitchens, the fort also housed two shrines, the Saraswathi Mandir and a palace.

The fort's defenses were rock solid.

Razor-edged scarps were its first line of defense. Split skulls wedged in the crevices below were proof.

Kanta trees with spikes that ripped flesh like tiger claws were its second.

A moat infested with gavials was its third. Four drawbridges over the moat at the North, South, East and West Gate offered safe passage from the gavials.

The fort's fourth line of defense were its walls. They were of masonry—red, white, grey and black stones—twenty feet thick and more than forty feet high. Even earthquakes had not been able to shake them. Hundreds of loopholes in the walls were ready to blizzard bullets on the enemy.

Guns were its fifth line of defense. Forty mortars secured the battlements. Four cannons, mounted on towers at the four corners of the fort, promised hellfire to approaching enemies. Of these, the cast-bronze monsters Indra Shakti and Mahisha Mardini were deadly, each with a range of five thousand metres. But deadlier still were the Megh Garjana and Agni Astra, reputed to devastate.

The sixth line of defense were the twelve thousand Maratha men, and women, garrisoning the fort. They were wizards with lances, sabres and muskets.

And the fort's final and most important line of defense was the Marathas' legendary spirit, courage and tenacity.

At precisely eleven thirty that morning, the British Central India Field Force fired its first salvo at Killa Fort. The shots fell short of the South Gate. So did the following shots.

Intelligence reports the Rani had received were accurate. The British were first attacking the superficially breached South Gate, hoping to capitulate on its weakness. But the breach had been shored up overnight and was stronger than ever.

About a fifth of the British troops were advancing towards the South Gate, scaling the precarious slopes. But the sappers did not stand a chance. Many fell on the kanta trees below and were impaled or disembowelled. The rest were closing in fast on the North Gate, leaving the East Gate and West Gate free. It was a complete change from the previous days' strategy when they had stormed all the gates.

The Marathas bided their time for the enemy to come within range. Then, at a signal from the Rani, they opened fire.

Volleys raced each other to welcome the enemy in their fiery embrace. The explosions were so deafening it seemed as if the god Indra had released all the thunderbolts from his arsenal.

First to fall were the sepoys of the British army. The infantrymen, mere cannon fodder to their white officers, were mowed down by the barrage from the bastions, battlements and loopholes. But they kept coming. Waves of redcoats advanced like a red tide. Scores fell, but they were gaining ground, inch by bloody inch. Their cavalry, meanwhile, waited out of range, like a frozen red sea waiting to be thawed.

The shots from the British artillery were ineffectual against the fort. They were like pebbles hitting a monolith. Some shells blasted the gavials in the moat. The gavials thrashed, painting the air with blood-tinted watercolour.

Making no headway at the South Gate, the regiments from that target moved to join the assault on the North Gate. They swelled the red tide, creeping up the slope to the gate.

Suddenly, the cavalry erupted into action. It came thundering across the battlefield. As if on cue, the infantry closed ranks and dashed forward.

The Rani's ace gunners opened fire with the Megh Garjana and Agni Astra. Living up to their names, the cannons exploded thunder and streaked lightning. Together, they quaked the air and the ground. Men and horses rocketed before crashing into the craters made by the cannons' impacting shots.

The British cannons boomed in quick reply. But they were no match for the Rani's twin gods of death, and her other batteries. The women servicing the Rani's cannons rammed the gunpowder and shots down the muzzles so fast, and the gunners fired so rapidly, that the enemy had no time to duck their heads. Continuous firing made the battlements look like they were on fire.

The ace-gunners were demolishing the British batteries one by one. As more enemy guns and soldiers went down, it looked like the Marathas were well on their way to victory.

From high up on the Saraswathi Mandir tower, the defiant Rani observed the attack. A frown of anxiety marred her good looks. Her advisors nearby looked anxious, too.

The British sepoys were advancing in tight formation, even with most of their guns down. The whole army continued heading for the North Gate.

During the past days' battles, the British had set a pattern of retreating as soon as their guns were silenced. But today, guns did not seem to matter. Neither did the lives of their men. They seemed bent on a suicide mission.

The Rani and her advisors were puzzled. What, exactly, were the British up to?

The answer came within a few seconds.

To their horror, the observers saw the spiked doors of the North Gate open and the drawbridge come crashing down. A skirmish had broken out among a small group of Marathas inside the gate. Shots were being fired. Maratha soldiers were falling. Those nearby were too stunned to move. The Rani, looking through her telescope, recognised Captain Bhonsle lashing out with his swords in the mêlée.

By the time the onlookers came to their senses, it was too late. The British Central India Field Force was a tsunami.

The Senapati gave a signal from the tower. All the guns around the fort were turned inward. Gunshots and cannonade rocked the fort. The reek of sulphur and saltpetre invaded the fort and spiralled sky-high.

The Rani's infantry and cavalry leaped into action, roaring "Long live Rani Meera Bai!" and "Killa *ka Jai!* Victory to Killa!" In their white salwaar and tunics, the sepoys looked like a gigantic cotton cloud come down to earth. They engaged the enemy with a fierceness the Rani had never seen. The guns, meanwhile, concentrated on sections of the red deluge that were breaking away like lagoons to swamp the components of the fort.

The Megh Garjana and Agni Astra fired just a few shots before an elite company of snipers killed the ace gunners and their teams. Their replacements were also killed. With that, the great guns were silenced.

The Rani's army fought with valour. But as the snipers scored bulls-eyes with the Maratha batteries, the enemy started gaining ground.

"Maharaj, it's no longer safe for you to remain in the fort. You must leave immediately!" the Diwan urged.

"Leave? And surrender the fort to Inglistans and traitors? Never!"

The Rani was dark with fury. It had taken her a minute to realise that her own sepoys had betrayed her.

"There's a trap door behind the Saraswathi statue. You can escape through the underground tunnel," the Senapati suggested. "Quick! The Inglistans will be here any minute!"

"I don't think the tunnels are safe anymore. The traitors would surely have laid traps there."

"My child, your life's what's important to the kingdom now. Your bodyguards will see you through safely," Lakham tried persuading her. "Don't worry. We'll rout the Inglistans yet." The old man's tremulous voice failed to convince the Rani.

"Forgive me, Lakham-ji. I must disobey you. I will not desert the fort. And I will not give up Killa!" The Rani dashed down the steps of the tower, leaving her advisors gawking.

As soon as they gathered their wits, the others clattered down after her.

Below, Mumtaz was already waiting with the Rani's Arab stallion. Mumtaz was the Rani's faithful Mohammedan companion. She and the Rani's guards had seen the mayhem below. Knowing her queen, Mumtaz knew exactly what her decision would be.

All of them mounted their steeds and were off.

The Rani galloped, her raised sword a streak of silver lightning. Her advisors and Mumtaz rode abreast of her.

Like avenging angels, they plunged into the raging battle.

The sight of their monarch gave the Marathas fresh inspiration. They fought like demons. The British fought back doggedly. They had already seized the administrative block, magazine, munitions factory and provisions store, the element of surprise working in their favour.

The ground floor of the palace was on fire. The maids had formed a bucket brigade to battle the flames. Not used to drawing water from the wells and carrying buckets (the water bearers usually did that), they toiled with hitched skirts and uncovered heads. And they got no help from the soldiers assigned to the palace's defense. The soldiers were falling like dominoes.

The living quarters, too, were ablaze. Old men and women were fleeing, hugging infants and dragging toddlers. For them, there was no place to hide. Those who escaped the enemy's blades and bullets jumped into the wells for refuge. They were searched out and shot dead.

Invalids in the quarters were charred where they lay.

The Rani fought like a wounded tigress. Holding her horse's reins in her teeth, she swished her twin swords right and left as she engaged two hussars. The white men were like birds in a tiger's paw. In no time she had pierced one through the heart and slashed off the other's arm.

Mumtaz fought next to her. She had not left the Rani's side, ready to die for her queen. All the Rani's advisors and bodyguards were nearby, too, giving the enemy hell. As the Rani was parrying another attack from three sepoys, Mumtaz saw a sniper taking aim at the queen. Screaming, Mumtaz rode straight towards him. In putting herself between his aim and the Rani, she took the shot full in the chest and fell dead from her horse.

The man's next shot bored into the Rani's left thigh, just as she had dispensed with the three sepoys. Ignoring the excruciating pain and gushing blood, she whipped out her pistol and shot him in the head. His brains splattered on the nearby sepoys. By then another man, a white officer, was upon her. He thrust his sword into her belly. Then he yanked it out and knocked the pistol from her right hand, cutting it. With a cry, the Rani used the sword in her left hand and sliced off his head. She had the satisfaction of seeing it trampled into the ground. But, by then, she had lost a lot of blood.

In the eternal seconds before the end, she saw the blurred faces of the Senapati and Lakham hovering before her. They clutched her to prevent her from falling off her stallion. Their cries of "Maharaj! Maharaj!" seemed to come from another planet. Far beyond them, she saw shadowy figures taking down something from the dome of the palace. In a flash of clarity, she saw that they were tearing down her Tiger Flag.

Then they started raising the Union Jack in its place.

Beyond the flag, she saw flesh-hungry lammergeiers circling the fort in such great numbers as to almost blot out the sun.

Then, she sank into the strange darkness that was beginning to envelop her.

The Flight

Mukta Bai tossed and turned on the bare floor of her home in Killa Fort. Sleep had decided to play hide-and-seek with her.

Her day had been long and hellish. As an assistant nurse in the fort's sickbay, her time was spent dressing wounds, applying tourniquets, administering chloroform and staunching blood flows. She had never seen such gruesomeness. The screaming of pain-racked soldiers coupled with the nonstop firing of artillery drove her to the brink of collapse. Only two things kept her going: her sense of duty and the thought of her husband, whom she loved more than herself.

At first, the maimed had only trickled in. But as the British advanced, broken bodies flooded the sickbay. Hundreds were laid outside where they did not stand a chance. They either bled to death or were massacred by the enemy.

Now, during her tortured sleep, Mukta saw only wounds spewing blood or mummies with bloodshot eyes. But she also saw a white swan serenely gliding by. On its head sat the Navratna Crown of the Rani.

Nearby, Mukta's mother-in-law snored softly. Her father-in-law, a mat's length away, was rending the bedroom with his snores.

They were lucky. They slept amidst the rubble of their partially bombarded quarters whereas hundreds slept in the open. Only their living room had caved in. Their bedrooms and kitchen stood intact.

The bedrooms provided much-needed shelter to four mothers and their newborn babies born during the height of the day's battle. They were alive only by the grace of God. From where she lay, Mukta could see another woman in a corner of the kitchen. The stove fire the woman had lit to keep herself warm threw into relief her gaunt features. She wa rocking to and fro and crying silently. There had been no ayah to help birth her baby and her first-born had been strangled by his umbilical cord. Someone had left a newly orphaned infant next to her. The baby whimpered. She looked at it, then turned away. The baby started to cry. Again she looked at it and turned away. Twice. Then the distraught woman could not stand the torture any longer. She grabbed the baby and suckled it at her engorged breasts, closing her eyes in pain and pleasure.

What beauty amidst ugliness! Mukta thought, watching the woman. There are new beginnings even in carnage, she mused. At sixteen, Mukta was beginning to learn one of her first lessons in life.

Mukta's in-laws had escaped the carnage. As they had no grandchildren to look after, Raghunath Rao Bhonsle and Ganga Bai had been assigned duties in the sickbay. There, they helped the kitchen staff prepare light meals, pepper soup and goat trotter broth. Sometimes, Ganga even helped the nurses spoon-feed patients.

When the slaughter started, Mukta had propelled the couple towards the firewood stack at a corner of the sickbay wall. There was just enough room for the three of them to squeeze in, with others, between wall and stack. There they had stood sandwiched for hours until it was safe to emerge. By then they were stiff as poles. And, in their fear, the old had soiled themselves like babes.

Mukta sat bolt upright when she felt someone shaking her violently.

"You're back, nawra! Thank God!" she said as she saw Ramdas standing before her.

"Sshh …" Ramdas signalled. "Quick, we must leave now! Wake Ma and Bah," he said, panting.

Raghunath and Ganga got up and looked around, like little children lost.

"What? What's happening?" Raghunath's voice was half-asleep.

"The Inglistans are after me. Hurry! We must leave."

Ramdas chucked some clothes, candles and matchboxes on a blanket and tied it into a bundle.

Mukta did likewise.

Ganga would not be hurried. Or silenced.

"What have you done, Ramdas?" she cried, wringing her hands. "We told you not to go after Hanumant (may he rot!). But you wouldn't listen. Did you kill him?"

Ramdas nodded. "Scum like that don't deserve to live. And an Inglistan officer died in the scuffle."

"One calamity is hardly over and you bring another upon us?" Ganga's face contorted with sadness and fear.

"Let him be, Ganga. This isn't the time for histrionics," came Raghunath's sober advice. Understanding immediately his son's predicament, he said, "Are you sure you want your Ma and me to go with you? We'd only slow you down, you know."

"Bah, they'll search you out and break your bones. Then they'll throw you into the dungeons. Both of you must come with us."

"Then lead the way, son."

Still aflutter like a startled mother hen, Ganga gathered her sari about her and followed Raghunath. "Deva! Only you know what lies ahead. You're our only hope," she mumbled to her god. Her severe features appeared even more severe with her centrally parted and oil-plastered hair.

Mukta did not raise a murmur. She had knotted her tresses into a chignon and tucked in her sari securely. When Ramdas made a move to carry his clothes-bundle, she waved him aside. "I'll carry it. You'll need to keep both your hands free to protect us."

Ramdas took a kitchen knife and tucked it at his waist. He also grabbed a staff. Raghunath, too, carried a staff besides his and Ganga's clothes-bundle.

Just before leaving, Ramdas rummaged in the living room rubble. When he caught sight of something glinting, he pulled it out. It was a framed picture of Rani Meera Bai. "Thank God! I thought it was destroyed. Here, Mukta, tuck this into my bundle."

As the family left, Ramdas hurriedly instructed the other women in the house to leave and shelter elsewhere to avoid being grilled by his pursuers.

"May Allah be with you!" one of them called.

Led by Ramdas, the family headed for the fort palace, picking their way around sleeping loyalists. Unlike the turncoats in Killa, the loyalists did not wail. The loss of their Rani was too numbing. Only some babies and the old whimpered in their sleep. And a few of the injured groaned softly.

As the family neared the palace, they heard hoofbeats in the distance. They began to run. Ramdas and Mukta were swift on their feet. Raghunath had to drag his wife. Ganga could not even remember when she last ran. Her joints creaked as she waddled after Raghunath, her double chin trebling with the effort.

The hoofbeats grew louder. People began to stir.

"Search the living quarters!", "On the double to the kitchens!", "... the wells!", "... every inch of the sickbay!", speared through the night.

The fugitives rushed into the palace.

Mukta lingered for a second. She had never stepped into a palace before. Her round eyes rounder in the dark, she strained to see the palace's scarred beauty. To her, even the gutted palace, lit by the stars, was awesome. Ramdas' pulling her hand catapulted her into a run.

The group stumbled after Ramdas to the palace kitchen.

Ramdas went to the largest wood stove. He knew of a secret passage under it. All the captains had been briefed on escape routes from the palace, in case they had to smuggle out royalty.

A copper cauldron, half-full of dhal curry, stood askew on the stove. Curry was spilt all over it. The place reeked of scorched dhal. Underneath the stove was an arched compartment for storing firewood. The wood had already caught fire in the morning. Only warm ashes remained.

Ramdas put his hand under the arch and turned a concealed knob. The floor of the compartment fell, raising an ash cloud. Everyone coughed. When the ash cleared, they found a rectangular hole yawning before them. Mukta and Ganga gasped in surprise.

"Let's go. *Jaldi!*" Ramdas said and jumped down the five-foot-deep hole. He helped his parents down, then his wife.

Ramdas lit a candle. Holding it up, he looked for the knob to close the trap door. He found and turned it. The trap door shut with a bang, making them all jump.

They were in a tunnel.

The candlelight revealed black basaltic walls. If walls could talk they would tell of ancient rajahs and ranis who escaped death by fleeing through the tunnel; of assassins being smuggled in; and of secret lovers being smuggled out.

"We must hurry. The Inglistans will surely find the trap door, now that there are no ashes covering it," Ramdas said.

At first, Ramdas and Raghunath had to stoop as they sped along the tunnel. But as the tunnel grew larger, they were able to bring their six-foot frames erect.

Luckily, there were no obstacles. The tunnel had been readied for emergencies. It first dipped in a series of chiselled steps, seemingly to the bowels of the earth. Then it levelled off, and finally rose in a gentle gradient for a distance of three miles. The fugitives felt cool air brush their faces from concealed ventilation shafts.

Ganga puffed like a goldfish, straining to keep up with the others. She was tiring fast. Deva, please give me strength, don't let me be a burden on the others, she prayed in her heart. Just when she thought she would collapse, they reached the end of the tunnel.

A few steps led up to the trap door in the ceiling. Ramdas opened it. When they climbed out of the tunnel, they found themselves in a forest. Ganga was the first to flop on the ground. Seeing no immediate danger, the others joined her to catch their breath. The chill night air was balm on their hot bodies. The orchestra of forest creatures filled their ears.

Ramdas told Mukta to light a candle.

Outside the periphery of the candlelight, everything was black. Except for the eyes. The forest had a thousand luminous eyes: grey, green, yellow, orange and red. They peered at the family unblinkingly from all around, looking like miniature twin planets suspended in space. The family shivered. Would a pair of eyes suddenly leap at them and materialize into a predator?

"Where do we go from here?" Raghunath asked.

"We'll follow one of the forest paths." Ramdas looked anxiously at his mother. "Ma, are you ready? We've a long way to go before daylight.

The more distance we put between them and us the better."

Ganga got up from the ground. Her legs felt like logs. "I'm ready, Ramdas," she said, hiding her pain. Ramdas hugged her. Ganga felt strength surge into her.

"Mukta, light another candle and give it to Bah," Ramdas instructed. Mukta did as she was told.

With the help of the candlelights, they found a narrow forest path. They walked single file with Raghunath leading, Ganga behind him, Mukta next, and Ramdas bringing up the rear.

Fear stalked them like a forest beast.

Under her breath, Ganga chanted litanies: to Ganesha, the elephant god, to protect them from elephants; to Govinda Krishna, the cowherd, to protect them from gaurs; to Durga, she-who-rides-a-tiger, to protect them from the big cats; and to Shiva, the original hunter, to protect them against all the other forest creatures.

They trudged silently, except for Ganga's fervent litany.

When they heard muted voices coming from the direction of the tunnel, they quickly blew out their candles. They started to run. As they ran, the women's saris ripped, caught in twigs and thorns.

The path forked. Ramdas had been briefed that the path on the left first led to scrubland, then to forested mountains inhabited by cannibals. The path on the right also led to mountains, but of the bare, rocky kind. One would need ropes to negotiate the slopes. To Ramdas, the second path was out of the question. They had no ropes. And even if they had, the women could not rappel.

"We'll take the left path," Ramdas decided.

As they rushed forward, the sound of voices diminished. The family felt relief. But they kept to a trot. Thankfully, there were no leeches, the ground being dry, but clouds of mosquitoes bothered them. Once, they heard a snake hissing but missed being bitten. They froze when a tiger coughed in the distance. Or was it a leopard?

Ganga's litany became more fervent.

The path was winding. It led up gentle slopes. But Ganga tripped once and hurt her ankle. After that she started to limp and had to be helped along by Ramdas.

Hours later, when they could make out the teak, ebony and blackwood standing in ranks like sepoys, the family knew that it was dawn.

The fugitives emerged from the forest edge. Here, the mood was joyful, challenging theirs. The forest displayed its skirts like a nautch girl, the sun smiled down on the family and birds filled the morning with happy operas.

Looking around, the family realised they were standing on a crest. Before them lay an expanse of scrubland—hot, dry and uninviting.

They looked at each other, wondering how they were going to survive in the wilderness.

*   *   *

They camped a mile from the forest edge where a rivulet gossiped to stones and rocks about the ancients who had passed by, on their way to or from the tunnel.

Here the trees had given way to scrub and grass. Ramdas knotted the corners of his blanket to shrubs so that it became a canopy. Clearing the ground underneath of bushes, he spread another blanket under the canopy for resting.

They gulped palmfuls of the sweet rivulet water. It was breakfast time but they were so tired their appetites had already gone to sleep. So they stretched out and slept. Until sunset.

Ramdas was the first to awake.

He looked with pity at his parents and wife. He could not bear to see them sleeping on the rough ground. And they were curled up, as if it was winter. He had never seen them sleep this way in summer. Then it struck him they were grieving.

His body ached. Not from the night's exertions but from the horrendous fight for Killa. He had mastered the art of fighting with two swords at once to emulate his queen. Now his arms felt as if they would drop off his shoulders.

He went to the rivulet. He washed his face. Then he rinsed out the bitterness in his mouth. But he could not rinse out the bitterness in his heart.

Ramdas remembered he had to find food for his family. He hastened to the forest fringe so he could return before dark.

It being June, the trees were sagging with wild summer fruits.

Mango trees were about to collapse with their burden. The mangoes were so ripe that, at a touch, they fell into your hand like a plump golden gift. Many carpeted the ground. Oversized jackfruit looked like they would crash to the forest floor and shatter any minute. Their burst seams flashed tantalizing yellow flesh that beckoned man and bird alike. Fruit flies danced dizzily around the fruit. Clusters of overripe red plums dripped juice as their skins cracked in the heat. Ramdas stuck out his tongue and caught a drop. It was heaven. He felt tipsy just smelling the fruit wine in the air.

Monkeys and birds were making a din all around. For Ramdas, it was a welcome change from the din of battle.

Something hit Ramdas' head with a thud. It was a mango. He looked up and saw a leaf-monkey grinning down at him. It had a distinguishing bald patch on one cheek. Ramdas ducked just in time to avoid its next mango-missile. The monkey screeched to his mates to complain about the miss. They did not pay any attention. They were too busy gorging themselves with mangoes.

Parrots, cuckoos, larks, sparrows, mynahs and bulbuls jetted from tree to tree and quarrelled around the fruit.

Ramdas gathered fruit for his family. Making a cradle of the front of his tunic, he heaped as many mangoes and plums as he could into it, ending up looking pregnant. As he left, another mango landed on his head. He saw the same monkey grinning at him. He grinned back.

On the way to the shelter, he picked bunches of wild basil growing along the way.

He found his father awake when he returned. Raghunath informed him the women were bathing downstream, behind a bend. They could hear them splashing water and talking.

When the women returned, looking refreshed, the men went off to bathe.

Mukta and Ganga spread their wet clothes over the bushes to dry. Then they sat in the dying sunlight and dried their wet hair, combing their fingers repeatedly through the strands.

Mukta set about pounding the basil her husband had collected. She pounded it with a stone on a flat rock. During normal times she would have relished the mint scent the leaves gave off. But times were far from normal. Mukta burnt a twig. She spread the mash on a sari-strip, heated the mash over the flame, and bandaged it around Ganga's sprained ankle. The poultice would reduce swelling and pain. "There you are, Mami. Your ankle will be as good as new in the morning," Mukta reassured the old woman.

The men returned, bathed and changed. Mukta draped their wet laundry on the bushes. Then she washed the plucked fruits in the stream. Their appetites now wide awake, the family sat together and devoured the succulent feast.

"It's getting dark. Let's build a fire," Ganga suggested.

"No, Ma. We're still too close to the forest. A fire in the dark will be a sure giveaway," the military man in Ramdas spoke. "Tonight, we must endure the dark."

"And tomorrow?"

Ramdas did not answer. He felt stung. But he understood why his mother was being so pointed.

"I wonder where we are," Raghunath broke the cannon-blast silence. "Have you been here before, son?"

"No. I'm just as lost as you are." They had covered more than ten miles during the night. "But I do know that the forest edge is part of the Killa border. We're now out of Killa. We could be in the Bhuranpur or Jalgaon district."

"But they're Inglistan strongholds!" Mukta pointed out. She felt the situation warranted the brushing aside of etiquette to join a conversation between her husband and father-in-law.

The men looked surprised for a moment. Then they nodded acquiescence.

"That's why we've to leave first thing in the morning, when Ma has rested enough." Ramdas peered at his mother in the gathering darkness.

"You see, because of me you've to leave tomorrow. Otherwise you'd be leaving right now." Ganga was remorse itself.

"Ma, you know we'd never leave without you."

"I must've done a lot of good karma in my previous life. That's why I have such a good husband like your Bah and a son like you." Looking at Mukta, Ganga added, "And a daughter-in-law like you."

Mukta smiled shyly.

Ramdas beamed at the compliment his mother had paid his wife. It was a lot coming from her. With Ganga, fault finding and tongue-lashing came first, compliments a distant second. How the siege has changed Ma, Ramdas thought.

Suddenly, Ganga crumbled. It was as if a monsoon cloud had burst.

Mukta put a consoling arm around her. "Hush, Mami. Don't cry. You're going to be all right."

"I'm not ... crying ... for myself. It's the ... Rani." She wailed louder.

"Quiet, Ma! Somebody might hear us."

Ganga could not control herself. The fatty rolls ringing her body shook as she sobbed. "She has died so young. It's not fair! And we didn't even give her a decent funeral."

The Rani had been hastily cremated in the fort grounds. (While alive, she had expressed repeatedly, "I will not have even my dead body sullied by British hands.")

Mukta's lips quivered. Her eyes became twin pools. The men bowed their heads and clamped their jaws.

"And her poor soul will not rest in peace," Ganga said, wiping her tears. "Our scriptures say it takes four hours and forty minutes for a soul to journey to Deathland. A body should be cremated only after that time. But she was cremated too soon." Ganga paused thoughtfully. "No wonder she returned ... Did you see the flight of the swans, Ramdas? Mark my words, she was the Hamsa leading the flocks."

Ganga fell silent for a moment. Then, "Deva, why do you keep old ones like me alive and take away one so young?"

Her Deva did not answer.

The next morning, they washed, bathed, changed and breakfasted on fruit. Ramdas and Raghunath collected more fruit for their journey.

They were pelted by the same monkey. Mukta's poultice had worked overnight. Ganga said all she needed was a short rest now and then.

Ramdas decided to follow the direction of the rising sun. West was Killa. North and south were perilous mountains and forests. Only the east looked viable with its scrubland that rose gently and levelled off in the distance.

As they were about to leave, Mukta gasped and pointed at the sky.

They saw a great white swan circling overhead.

"It's her!" Ganga almost choked on the words. She joined her palms above her head in salutation.

Mukta followed suit.

The men watched the swan in silence.

It flew in concentric circles until it was directly above them. It hovered. Then it streaked off in the direction of Killa.

"Shall we go?" Ramdas said gruffly.

*   *   *

They trudged for many days, pitching their blanket-tents every evening near pools of water.

Their fruit supply lasted only two days. After that they gathered food they found along the way. Their earlier fear of starving in the scrubland was unfounded. Wild cassava and yam roots they dug from the ground; plantains they plucked from the scarce trees; and pennywort they picked from the creepers on the ground.

At night, they roasted the cassava and yam in their campfire. The tubers were fluffy and filling. The plantains were mushy and sweet and the pennywort crisp and bitter.

Ramdas put to good use the survival skills he had learnt in the army. He knotted sticks with vines to make a cage with a trap door. With this contraption, he trapped fat kabutar. The pigeons were succulent when roasted. But before that, Ganga massaged her ankle with the slaughtered birds' fresh blood. "It's a cure for sprains and aching joints," she explained.

To quench their thirst, they drank from the pools of clear water they saw animals drinking at. Where no water was to be found, Ramdas once again used his army know-how: he looked for pitcher plants that held rainwater in their cups; bamboo that stored water in their hollow stems; and fleshy aloe leaves filled with juice, though the last was bitter and made the family purge.

Weeks passed. They did not even once meet a single human; which, in a way, they were thankful for. They were not ready yet to satisfy other people's curiosity. Ramdas, especially, feared being recognised. As for the absence of humans, the family put it down to the lack of a river.

Hundreds of farmers would have cultivated the scrubland and turned it into a green belt if water was readily available. As it was, the sandy soil only sported the rare tubers and banana plants, dwarf bushes and tufts of yellow grass. Isolated thorn bushes made up the rest of the sparse vegetation. Squirrels, iguanas, bandicoots and beetles darted in and out of the scrub.

Once, the family stood rooted at the sight of a combat between a mongoose and a cobra.

The cobra hissed and spat venom as it tried, again and again, to bite the mongoose. (Mukta had goose pimples just watching the snake slithering and looping.) The mongoose had its own tactics. First, it tired out the snake. It dodged this way and that many times, making the snake strike. But the mongoose stayed just out of reach. Then, when the snake's reflexes slowed, the mongoose attacked. Screeching and with fangs and claws bared, it went in for the kill. A dash, a skull-crunching bite on the head, and the snake was in its death throes.

"So, its true, what they say. Mongooses and snakes do fight to the death," Ramdas observed. But as a military man, he was fascinated by the mongoose's clever tactics. It reminded him of the British.

Before the family knew it, one full moon had followed another. But without much event.

The days, unable to bear their hot burden, passed their heat to the night, so that sleep became a stranger to the family.

Days, the family plodded, ignoring protesting legs and feet. To protect their heads, the men turbaned their towels. The women covered their heads with their sari ends. There was no whisper of complaint even from Ganga. She remained strangely silent.

Nights, they built a fire and sat around it to eat. Then they talked of many things, including their future. It was uppermost on their minds.

"What do we do once we get back to civilisation?" Ganga asked her husband.

Always the practical man, Raghunath answered, "Why, we go back to farming of course! That's what we were born to and that's what we'll do now."

"You're right, Bah. Soldiering's not safe for me anymore," Ramdas joined in. "Not as long as the Inglistans are looking for me. Farming in a remote village seems to be our best option."

"You shouldn't have killed those men ... And I hate this running away," Ganga said.

"Ma, if I had the chance, I'd have killed Hanumant during the battle. It's just that the viper escaped in the confusion."

There had been a dozen traitors. All the others were killed in the fort. Only four, including Hanumant escaped. A dying traitor had confessed Hanumant was the ringleader.

"How is it that when I killed so many in battle it's right and killing just one traitor a few hours later is wrong?"

No answer.

"As for the Inglistan officer, it was only an accident. Now consider the subject closed, Ma. And don't keep harping on about it!"

Ganga felt miffed. But then, she had always known her son would stand by his convictions.

Other nights, they talked about Killa: their peaceful life on a paddy farm away from the fort; the annexation of Killa by the British; Ramdas' answering the call-up; their move to the fort three years ago; Ramdas' training under the great Maratha masters of war; his marriage to Mukta; the siege; and the final battle for Killa.

"More than half our people died in the fort," Raghunath observed. "It will be easy now for the Inglistans to herd the rest and crush them."

"Bhagia Bai is dead." Ganga remembered her nextdoor neighbour. They had been like sisters. "I saw her with a hole in her breast. You could put your fist in it."

"Whole families were wiped out. Did you see how the dead lay everywhere, like spilled mustard seeds?" Raghunath shuddered in spite of himself.

"Old Kantha told me all the women in her family were raped," Mukta said with horror. The thought that she could have suffered the same fate terrified Mukta.

"I wonder what'll happen to the Diwan and the other advisors." Deep down, Raghunath already knew the answer.

"You can be sure they'll be executed on cooked-up charges of treason," Ramdas confirmed the family's fears. "The Inglistans don't favour spirited Maratha queens and ministers."

"What hell the Rani must have gone through," Raghunath reminisced. "Killa annexed, her royal inheritance confiscated, her religious obligations not respected ..."

"Killa will never be the same without the Rani," Ganga said. "Who but she could have inspired a whole generation of Maratha women to fight?"

No Maratha woman could forget the Rani's charisma. Once they had seen and heard her, they downed their ladles, sickles and handlooms. They converged from all corners of Killa to the fort. There they brought up their sari hem between their legs and tucked it behind, so that the sari became trousers. Then they took up the sword.

Ramdas thought of his last meeting with the Rani. It had been just before the final battle. She was inspecting the troops in the maidan. Twenty-five thousand swords made a blinding flash as they were raised in salute. And when she gave her rallying call of 'Killa *ka Jai!*', her sepoys roared in response. The British camp heard the roar and went weak in the knees.

Ramdas and his fellow captains looked at her with adoration. They hero-worshipped her. They were all, as a matter of fact the whole army was, a little bit in love with her.

The Rani was fair and full-blown. A firm chin augmented her intelligent looks. Her face was unlined in spite of the rigours of her life. Ramdas remembered she cut a fine figure, even in plain battledress, like those of her warriors: white salwaar gathered at the waist, matching long-sleeved tunic of quilted linen, and a pagri on the head. Around her waist, the Rani wore her favourite black leather belt. The belt had a gold thread filigree pattern. It had two ruby-studded scabbards for her swords. The Rani treasured the belt. It had been presented to her by her father, a maharaja, when she won a duel against him at seventeen. So were the twin kirach swords encased in the scabbards. Their gilded hilts flashed dangerously in the sunlight. The swords were heavy and their thirty-three-inch blades made mincemeat of the enemy. A kattari was tucked at one hip. The dagger was decorated with gold koftgari work and the Rani's name was emblazoned on the hilt. The kattari's tip was so strong she had pierced the foes' armours with it. A flintlock pistol was tucked at her other hip. The Rani was renowned for shooting moving targets at full gallop.

While she was having a private word with her captains—she called them 'my angry lions'—Ramdas was given special mention by the Senapati.

"Maharaj, Captain Bhonsle wiped out five of the enemy's batteries under heavy fire yesterday. His was the decisive blow that sent the Inglistans scuttling from the breached South Gate."

"Well done, Captain Bhonsle! I hope to see more of your good action today, too."

"Have no fear, Maharaj. Today, the Inglistans will not know what hit them!"

"How is your bride? Well, I hope." The Rani smiled kindly.

Her question surprised Ramdas.

"With your blessings, she is keeping well, Maharaj," Ramdas replied, bowing. He glowed with happiness because the queen remembered attending his nuptials five months ago.

"Senapati, remind Captain Bhonsle to me after all this is over. He deserves a gold medal and a promotion," the Rani said in Ramdas' presence. Then she galloped off, looking as if she had been born to the saddle.

That was the last he saw of his queen.

"Even the British admired her," Ramdas said in recollection. "Our spies said they admired her organising ability and wondered how she, a woman, could command an army. Above all, they admired her courage."

Then the family would take out the Rani's picture and gaze at it with sadness.

The picture was done in oils. The Rani wore battledress. With head held high and shoulders thrown back, the beautiful Rani sat astride her white stallion. A drawn sword was in one hand, her Tiger Flag and reins in the other. And on her face was a look of calm determination.

On yet another sultry night, they talked of the *Ramayana*.

Raghunath started the topic.

Ramdas was all ears. He loved to hear his father speak of the *Ramayana*. It reminded him of his childhood days. Back then, Raghunath had entertained him with many tales from the epic.

"It must've been like this for Lord Rama, Sita and Lakshmana when they were banished from their kingdom." Raghunath began as he whittled a palm-sized wedge of wood. He liked whittling. In Killa, his expert hands used to produce little tigers and bullocks, boats and carts, and rajahs and ranis. He used to give them away to the village children. The looks of delight the children gave him were his only reward.

The *Ramayana* was Raghunath's favourite epic. From the way he talked, it was clear to Ramdas that the campfire was not the only light illumining his father's face.

"They, too, must have wandered like us through forest and scrub and trod rough, stony paths."

"Only worse," Ganga joined in. "They wandered for fourteen years!"

"And they had to fight wild beasts."

"And rakshasa and rakshasi. These male and female demons were vicious and blood-thirsty."

"And ugly, too."

"But some rakshasi are beautiful." Ramdas' statement startled the others. "I mean that rakshasi Kausalya. She tried to tempt me the night I went after Hanumant."

"*Are Deva!*" Ganga clapped her hand to her mouth, alarmed. "What did you do, Ramdas? What did you do?"

"I rejected her, of course!"

57

Ganga gasped with relief. So did Mukta. For a moment, they thought the worst. Too many times they had heard of the best of men falling for the enchantress and abandoning their families. The men had even contracted the dreadful disease women of her kind carried.

"Even Lord Rama was tempted by the rakshasi, Surpa-nakha," Raghunath pointed out to assuage Ramdas. "The fanged demon appeared to him in the form of a ravishing beauty. But Lord Rama spurned her."

Then Ramdas told his family of how Kausalya had cursed him.

"Not surprising, coming from her," Ganga said. "But may the curse backfire!" A pause. Then, "The slut has not got over her crush on you, has she? Remember her passionate love letters to you until you got married?"

Ramdas remained silent. He was thinking of a secret he would carry to his grave: a mango-flower-scented afternoon, a decade ago, when he had lost his boyhood innocence to Kausalya. But that was before he found out she was a picker-of-men. After that he had avoided her like leprosy.

"I'm grateful that so far we've been safe here, even if it's from demons and curses," Raghunath's voice broke into his thoughts. "Let's pray that we'll remain safe."

Raghunath had had friends who disappeared without a trace while out hunting. Yawning tiredly, as if he had worked in the paddy from dawn to dusk, Raghunath fell off to sleep. The whittling lay beside him, shapeless.

The family noticed. It was the first time he had left a piece unfinished. And they understood why.

That night, before going to sleep, Ganga offered a special prayer to the fire god, Agni, who purified all things profane. She hoped to reverse Kausalya's curse with the prayer.

Sitting before the campfire, she closed her eyes and chanted:

> O Agni! Slayer of Demons,
> Send forth your Winged Missile
> to seek the Curser, like the eagle seeks its prey;

Send forth your Winged Missile
to return the Curse to the Curser.

O Agni! Protect my son,
and protect his progeny,
save them from harm and sorrow, I beseech Thee.
Accept, O Agni, my offering of wood ash
in place of sacrificial ash
and answer my prayer.

Ganga threw a handful of ash into the fire. Then, she marked Ramdas'
forehead with a dot of ash.

Later, she told Mukta how Kausalya would have gone about casting
her spell. Ganga had heard of such matters from her grandmother who
had heard it from her grandmother.

Ramdas did not listen. He did not believe in curses.

Some nights, they did not talk much. Each was occupied with his or
her private thoughts.

They thought of Killa; of a new home; of paddy farming; of hearing
the patter of tiny feet ...

But they mostly thought of Killa. Killa had been a paradise, until the
British arrived.

As the weeks passed, the shock of losing queen and country
diminished. The faraway look, the quick move to tears, the freezing on
hearing unfamiliar sounds, the knot of fear in the chest, the racing
heart—these wore off. A semblance of acceptance replaced total denial.

When, at last, they emerged from the wilderness, they were prepared
for any rigour that lay ahead. After Killa, nothing could be worse.

But they were to find out otherwise.

Champakapur

The family was standing on tableland. It had taken them thirty-five days to cross the scrub. Before them lay the endless Deccan Plateau.

Like a mythical dining table, the red-brown plateau was laid with chunks of hills, draughts of rivers and cornucopia of chestnuts and magnolias. Prettifying it were arrangements of tall bamboo, sweet-scented sandalwood and tanbark. And the distinguished company at table were tigers, leopards, cheetahs, monkeys, deer, wolves, hogs, snakes, small birds and peacocks—all dressed in their jungle best.

Another day's journey from the edge of the plateau brought the family to the first village.

It was a cluster of bamboo huts with thatched palm-leaf roofs. Wisps of smoke curled from a central outdoor pit. A hog was roasting on the pit. Its sizzling juices made the family salivate.

Their hearts leapt at the sight of humans. But the family was wary. They hid behind bushes and looked for signs of cannibalism or head-hunting. There were no carelessly tossed human bones about or shrunken human heads on poles. They were safe.

The people were almost ebony and short. They radiated the robustness of outdoor living. Ropes of saga seeds, or beads carved from sandalwood, almost strangled them. For the women, the beads did more to cover their breasts than did the strips of bark they used. Beads encircled their wrists and ankles, too. Black-and-white hornbill feathers stuck out from beaded headbands.

The village was filled with a rotten stench. It came from the pelts of the big cats, deer and foxes laid out to dry. The pelts looked like an exotic quilt on the ground. Shrunken fox heads grinned everywhere.

Ramdas and his family knew they were amongst tribal hunter-gatherers.

The chieftain was wild-looking but kind. Gesticulating and speaking in a mix of broken Marathi and Telugu, the potbellied man said he was of the Chenchu tribe.

"You're now in Haidarabad State," the chieftain informed, on Ramdas' enquiry.

When Ramdas asked where the family could meet up with farmers, he replied, "You wish to till the soil? You'll have to travel further south. South is where the nadi flows. And that's where farmers live."

The smelly but generous women proffered a tiger pelt and bunches of wild plums to the family. The family declined the pelt. But they accepted the plums.

When they left, there was a spring in their step.

Maybe it was the word 'till'. Maybe it was the word 'nadi'. But the family was galvanised. They squeezed every ounce of their reserve strength to drag their bleeding feet over the last leg of their journey.

Looking like underfed refugees (which is exactly what they were), they arrived two mornings later in what, to them, looked like paradise.

Having just lost one paradise, Ramdas wondered if the paradise before them would last.

"*Paradesi yet ahe! Paradesi yet ahe!*"

"Foreigners are coming!"

A group of children screamed their announcement when they saw the Bhonsles limping into the village. Having abandoned their game of kabadi, the scared but curious children were torn between running away and standing and staring at the newcomers.

A pack of mongrels barked their heads off.

Mothers with toddlers on their hips came rushing out of their huts. They blinked at the spectre of strangers in their village. The last time they had seen strangers was a year ago when zemindary officials of the Nizam of Haidarabad had visited. The women drew their sari drape over their heads as they approached the family.

The Bhonsles joined their palms limply in greeting. Ramdas spoke first.

"Sisters, we come from distant Killa. May we speak with the patel?"

"Sure. The headman lives down the road," a chestnut-brown old woman answered through a mouth full of paan. She squinted in the sunlight. "Come, I'll take you to him." She was the only one wearing her hair in a kona-konde—a bun knotted at the side of the head. She wore no choli. Her sari covered her pendulous breasts. And she smelled of a perfume the family could not identify.

Ramdas was relieved the woman spoke Marathi. He assumed he was in a Maratha village.

A motley crowd of curious women, children and mongrels followed the family. The women wore plain, handloom cotton saris. The boys skipped along in salwaar and short-sleeved tunics. The girls sported ghagra skirts and short cholis. They wore their crow-black hair in plaits.

The more daring of the children tugged at the family's clothes. They wanted to check whether the strangers were living beings because, dust-coated, the family looked like ghosts.

Ramdas' assumption was right. When their guide introduced him to the headman, he welcomed the family in Marathi.

"*Yea! Yea!* Welcome to Champakapur! I'm Patel Bhima Rao," the headman boomed.

A flock of pittas scattered at the sound of his voice.

His name suited him. He was a Bhiman of a man. Like the strong-man, Bhima, of the *Mahabharata* epic, the headman seemed capable of throwing men, horses and chariots high into the air. Even his teeth were big. They reminded Ramdas of harmonium keys.

"Who are you, brothers and sisters? Where do you come from?"

Ramdas briefed him.

A spark of enlightenment lit the man's face.

"From Killa, you say? The same Killa where the Rani died fighting for her kingdom?" The man looked from one to the other. When they nodded in unison, "Oh! How I've wanted to meet someone from Killa! I heard a lot about Killa on my last visit to Haidarabad. The city was afire with news about our people's stand against the Inglistans. Come, you must tell me more about it." Then, looking them up and down, "But first, a bath and victuals. You look famished!"

Bhima led them into his brick house. The doorway was so low they had to stoop to get in. Bhima had to bend almost double. Women and children crowded outside the open door and windows. They stretched their necks like geese to get an eyeful of the strangers—especially since they were from the now famous Killa.

"Kasthuri Bai! Come here. We have guests!" the patel called his wife.

The middle-aged woman came in through the back door. She balanced a full brass water-pot on her hip. Putting down the pot, she came to meet the newcomers. She looked dwarfish standing next to her husband. Her eyes said she was pleased to meet the Bhonsles.

"Hurry, woman! Get the stove going. Our guests are famished. They've been in the wilderness for more than a month. And travelling on foot at that." Turning to the Bhonsles, "You can use the room at the back. Follow me."

The house was palatial by village standards. There was a roofed terrace outside. The reception hall inside led to three rooms and a kitchen. The hall was sparsely furnished: two wooden straight-back chairs, a canvas deck chair, a side table and a bureau. The lower half of the plastered walls was decorated with a continuous wavy line of slaked lime, with dots at the center of each rise and fall.

Bhima showed the family to the third room. It was empty except for a rice bin in one corner.

"The nadi is behind, if you're ready to bathe."

"Bathe? I'm just waiting to drown myself!" Ramdas joked.

They deposited their bundles on the floor. The men stripped to their longuts. The women knotted their long underskirts above their breasts. Then they shuffled to the river.

Bhima dispersed the villagers. "You can go home now. We'll meet in the evening."

Ramdas and his family had to pass magnolia trees to reach the river. They marvelled as their feet sank into a carpet of fallen purple blooms. Nowhere had they seen such a profusion of magnolias. After treading rough ground for weeks, the flowers felt like velvet under their feet. Weak, they felt oppressed by the flowers' powerful scent. Suddenly, they realised that the old woman who guided them earlier had smelled of these flowers.

They ran to the Lahan Nadi and jumped in. Ganga made the biggest splash. They found the water only waist-high. But it flowed swift and silent.

Soon, they were luxuriating in the nadi's satiny caress. They scrubbed away every bit of caked dirt and grime with tufts of coconut husk. Ganga scrubbed Raghunath's back. Mukta scrubbed Ramdas' and Ganga's back. No one scrubbed Mukta's back. She had to contort herself to get the job done.

Sighing with contentment, the family lolled in the water. It seemed ages since they had a decent bath. The river was oceanic compared to the pools and puddles that had paraded as baths during the past weeks. Like little children, they were reluctant to leave the river.

When at last they emerged, they were raw and red like Kashmiri tomatoes. They felt the river had washed away not only dirt and grime but also some of their exhaustion and grief. A fraction of their lost happiness was returning to them.

*   *   *

If you approached the village of Champakapur from a distance, you would first notice a strange, light-purple mist concentrated at a single spot. As you neared the spot, the mist would expand and intensify. At the outskirts of the village, you would gasp as the mist solidifies into a mass of champaka flowers. The magnolias choke the trees on which they grow. Their sweet, overpowering scent vaults to the heavens. Then it descends in an invisible cloud to drench you. On the ground lies a carpet of the fallen magnolias.

Ankle-deep. Inviting. The type of carpet you would associate with great lovers: Shakuntala and Dushyanta, Nalan and Damayanthi, Mumtaz and Shah Jehan. Surely, you would think, they lay on such a carpet, raining purple showers on each other in acts of mutual worship.

Even the Lahan Nadi flowing by the trees shimmers purple. It tricks you into believing the riverbed is covered with a million and one amethysts.

The villagers put the fallen champaka to good use. They produce an attar from them.

Every morning, you can see children with baskets skipping to the champaka stand. They fill the baskets with freshly fallen magnolias. The magnolia oils are strongest in the morning. The children deliver the blooms to a shed next to the village temple. The attar is made in the shed. Old Chenggamma of the kona-konde takes delivery of the flowers. She heaps them on the floor. Then she starts the attar making.

The process is simple. First, Chenggamma plucks the pointed petals from their calyx. Then, she places the petals in knee-high wooden tubs. Next, she pours in spirit of gooseberry wine till the petals are immersed. Lastly, she seals the tubs with tight-fitting lids. She allows the magnolias to steep for a month. It takes fifty magnolias to make one drop of attar.

Batches of attar stand in the shed. The attar keeps for years. It is so strong a couple of drops are enough to impregnate a room. Champakapuris help sell the perfume in the city of Haidarabad. Even the memsahibs buy vials of it. They say once you have used Champakapur's Attar of Magnolia, your nose becomes immune to all other perfumes.

The founding fathers of the village did well to name the village 'Champakapur'—Magnolia Country.

A hundred village huts embraced the magnolia stand and the Lahan Nadi. They were built of mud bricks and thatched with straw. The thatch harboured fat scorpions. The huts were so close they rubbed roofs. Lanes between the huts were the haunts of little boys. When the fancy took them, they challenged each other to a contest of who-can-shoot-piss-the-highest-on-the-wall.

To the west of the village stood a Kaliamman temple. Its gateway and sanctum faced east to greet the rising sun.

To the east was an open ground. In its center stood a death-defying pipal tree. After the magnolia stand, the pipal was Champakapur's second landmark. Pittas and mynahs nested among its branches. The village Methuselah remembered it existing in a mature state even during his childhood. He recalled that then it was the meeting place of Buddhist monks. The shaven, saffron-robed monks, on pilgrimage from Ceylon to Nepal, would sit meditating in the lotus position under the tree.

Now, the tree's ample shade was where children chased each other in abandon; where men exchanged news about their crops or gossiped (their wives gossiped at home); where the village barber simultaneously yacked and shaved so fast it was a miracle he did not slit his customers' throats; where travelling jatakwallah read the lines on eagerly extended palms or had a parrot pick astrology cards; where wandering ascetics, with matted hair and spiralling nails, rested; where passing tribals sold their charms, potions, pelts, beads and necklaces of tiger claws; where a travelling gondhali brought respite with ancient ballads and the soulful twangs of his sarangi; where delinquents (juvenile and adult) loafed or gambled; and where the panchayat met, like it did on the evening of the Bhonsles' arrival.

The panchayat was the village court. Five men dealt justice in this court. There was Patel Bhima Rao who was the chief judge. Assisting him were an English-dabbling secretary, a patriarch of a twenty-member extended family, the resident temple priest, and the schoolmaster.

The five sat on the mud platform built around the base of the pipal. Ramdas and Raghunath sat with them. The rest of the villagers sat on the ground. Men and women sat in separate groups. Children joined the women. So did Mukta and Ganga. They sat at the front of the group with Chenggamma. The air was thick with Attar of Magnolia.

The court had convened not to hear a case, but to hear the tales of the newcomers. The village-crier had done his job well. All the thousand-odd Champakapuris were present.

The women who had met Ramdas and his family earlier, stared at them. The four were unrecognisable, now that they had bathed.

Ramdas looked ruggedly handsome. The centipede-like scar running down his right cheek added character to his good looks. His gaze met frankly the gaze of the villagers. On his face was a smile of friendship and hope.

Raghunath was a faded copy of his son, his crinkly hair greying at the temples. It was obvious from whom Ramdas got his good looks and hefty build.

Mukta, fair and nymph-like, gave the impression of wilting if touched. Her oval face was framed by long black hair. And her round eyes only enhanced her natural beauty.

Ganga, square-faced and thick-lipped, was a freshly washed version of a baby elephant. It was a wonder how her tiny feet supported her bulk. You're like a sack of tamarind, Raghunath used to tease her.

The family looked pinched. But their spirits were high. The good Kasthuri Bai had filled their bellies with chapatti and dhal. Then she had tended their sore feet. They were comfortable now as they sat with tulsi-leaf paste bound to their soles. The basil paste felt cool and stopped the throbbing.

Introductions over, Ramdas and Raghunath began their tale. The chatter of birds coming home to roost, the lowing and bleating of home-bound cattle, goats and sheep became a distant murmur as the Champakapuris, as one, listened to the tale.

The men first described their early life on a paddy farm and their move to Killa Fort.

"Now tell us about the Rani," the patel said.

Everyone moved closer to hear.

*　　*　　*

The Rani's story:

I, the Rani of Killa, went through ten layers of Hell before I decided to take up arms against the Raj.

Through all these hells, my escort was neither Lucifer, for I am no Christian; nor Shaitan, for I am no Mohammedan; nor Mara, for I am no Buddhist. Nor was he Yama, though I am most certainly Hindu. My escort was the Raj: white, blue-eyed, powder-wigged, tail-coated, wellington-ed, and very innocent looking. He did not ride an ugly black buffalo like Yama but a handsome black mount that was so sure-footed it did not even once trip over the treacherous path that linked all the hells.

There is no saying which layer of Hell was most tortuous. What is for sure is that, in these hells, I was in turn boiled, roasted, flung, pierced, dunked, metamorphosed, crushed, torn, blinded and scorched.

THE FIRST LAYER OF HELL: They who enter KUMBHIKA shall be boiled in oil.

It all started with the annexation of my kingdom of Killa.

"My dear Rani Meera Bai, we do not recognise your adopted son," the Raj sneers as he shows me into Kumbhika.

"But my late husband adopted him lawfully," I protest. "Even you witnessed the rites of adoption."

The Raj was present at the ancient sacrificial ceremony of homa when the Maharaja and I threw offerings of gold into the sacred fire. He heard the reciting of the sloka from the Vedas as the Maharaja sat Dilip on his lap and proclaimed the boy as his son. "You even received part of Prince Dilip's weight in gold!" I fling at the Raj.

"That does not make the adoption any more legal," he retorts.

"It is legal according to the laws of my independent kingdom!" I say, my blood boiling.

"But my dear Rani," the man is smarmy, "Dilip is not your natural heir, only the son of a relative. According to our 'Doctrine of Lapse', states and kingdoms without natural heirs come under our direct rule. So Killa will be annexed."

My ensuing pleas and petitions are brushed aside. I learn the hard way that the 'Doctrine of Lapse' is just a glorified term for stealing another's birthright.

THE SECOND LAYER OF HELL: They who enter KALASUTRA shall be roasted in fire.

The Raj does not prod his mount. He prods me, instead, into Kalasutra. There, I see my military troops disband after the annexation.

Many of my sepoys are lured to join the British Central India Field Force with promises of titles, land and riches. As the traitors slink away, my army shrinks to half its former size of fifty thousand.

The remaining sepoys become unemployed. I try my best to feed them and their families until such times they become adept at other skills. But I cannot meet their upkeep. Not with the beggarly purse the

Raj provides me.

For the first time, I see my sepoys suffer deprivation. They starve. They wear tatters.

They sleep on the pavements. They beg.

There is a fire in my belly as I watch their sores fester, their babies die, their children grovel in the dust with dogs and pigs for discarded food.

THE THIRD LAYER OF HELL: They who enter AVICHIMAT shall be flung down from a great height, hoisted up and flung down again, but shall not die.

The Raj shoves me with all his might into the Avichimat pit.

As I plunge, I see in a frozen moment others falling with me. They are zemindars, the rich landowners of my kingdom.

"Help us, Maharaj! Help us!" they cry.

"The Raj has introduced a new 'law of sale'."

"We don't understand the new 'law'."

"He has used the 'law' to sell off our lands because we cannot repay arrears of revenue."

"Arrears accrued during our grandfathers' times! Why should we be held responsible?"

I see the Raj grinning down at me as I crash to the ground and lie inert.

THE FOURTH LAYER OF HELL: They who enter SUCHIMUKHA shall be bound with barbed wires.

Durga—she-who-rides-a-tiger—is my family deity. We pray to her at the Temple of Durga. The pre-Maurya temple and the villages surrounding it have belonged to our family for ten generations. The villagers are the caretakers of the temple. The Raj has done the unthinkable by resuming the villages and relocating the people.

I see the temple standing desolate. The wind moans through it. Its pillars, that produce musical notes when struck, are strangled by jungle creepers. Clinging ficus obliterate its gateway. And a wall of thorn trees blockades the temple.

It is as if the Raj has driven a barb into my heart.

THE FIFTH LAYER OF HELL: They who are thrown into the VAITARANI RIVER shall be immersed in blood, pus, excreta and boiling urine, but shall not die.

The Raj's mount expertly picks its way over and around the littered carcasses of cows. I trip over one and fall.

I pick myself up and step into a gory forest—a forest of hanging sides of beef.

I choke. I gag. I run this way and that but cannot find my way out of the gory forest.

When at last I do, I find myself bloodied from head to toe.

I see my people go about pinching their noses. There is a stench in Killa.

The Raj has introduced cow slaughter, against the principles of our religion. Beef is sold openly at the marketplaces.

Will the Raj show no respect for our faith?

THE SIXTH LAYER OF HELL: They who enter KIRIMIBHOJA shall metamorphose into maggots that will devour one another.

I see many kaleidoscopic scenes in Kirimibhoja.

"Praying to idols will lead you to Hell. Embrace Christianity and go to Heaven!" a black-frocked padri rants at my people. "Embrace Christianity before it's too late. Save your souls!" he raves. I feel sorry for him. He has a lot to learn.

Money-mad traders are adulterating wheat flour with powdered cattle bones. The Raj rewards them by throwing them coins and they grovel in the dust for the pittance.

My people are queueing to buy salt. They look forlorn. The commodity's price has more than doubled since the Raj imposed a levy on it. "We've never heard of a levy on salt before!" my subjects cry to me.

"Maharaj, we cannot afford to use this kind of officially stamped paper," another group complains. "It's too expensive!"

From high up on his mount, the Raj throws back his head and laughs as he watches the little grievances eat into me.

THE SEVENTH LAYER OF HELL: They who enter SUKRAMUKHA shall be crushed like castor-oil seeds between stone grinders.

The Raj crushes whatever little hope I have left of being friendly to him.

He is supplying my Hindu and Muslim sepoys with cow and pig fat with which to grease cartridges. How he disregards our faiths!

The situation has become explosive. I only have to say the word and the Raj will have a major mutiny on his hands, like the horrific one he has already had in Meerut.

THE EIGHTH LAYER OF HELL: They who enter RAURAVA shall be torn to shreds but shall not die.

Things start to get out of hand as my escort shows me into Raurava.

The Raj is furious with me. Two hundred of my sepoys have rebelled because I counsel patience and will not betray the Raj. The rebels have joined hundreds of mutineers in the neighbouring kingdom of Karampur. But I remain loyal: I still fly the Union Jack in my palace to show my respect and loyalty to the Raj.

I see the mutineers attack the Raj-held Karaha Fort and massacre the soldiers.

Shamelessly, the Raj asks me for assistance.

I hesitate. But only for a moment. I rush my troops and artillery to the fort. I send a week's provisions for the trapped Englishmen, their wives and children inside the fort.

Still, the Raj does not trust me.

"You will help your kind in secret!" he says unkindly.

By now, my loyalty to the Raj lies in shreds.

THE NINTH LAYER OF HELL: They who enter TAMUSRA shall live in a world of perpetual darkness.

By custom, I, being a widowed Rani, must go on a compulsory pilgrimage to the holy city of Varanasi on the Ganges. There, I must perform final death rites for the late Maharaja. But the Raj refuses me permission to go. And he offers no good reason for his refusal.

"Here is your Varanasi! Here is your Ganges!" he mocks as he conjures before me a vision of the city, its Visalatchi Amman Temple, its crowded ghats and the shimmering Ganges.

Excited, I reach out to touch the temple but my hand just goes through the mirage.

I grope for amicable solutions to this and all the other problems I have with the Raj.

But none are forthcoming. Now, even my advisors are hinting at rebellion.

THE TENTH LAYER OF HELL: They who enter VAJRAKANTAKA shall be branded with red-hot metal.

I see my vast personal property lying in jumbled heaps in a corner of Vajrakantaka. The Raj has confiscated my property on the pretext of settling some ancient debts of state.

Devilishly, the Raj makes his mount rear and bring down its forelegs hard on the heaps. The heaps start to tremble. The Raj prods the heaps and things start tumbling: brass and copper pots; palace furniture of ebony and teak inlaid with ivory and mother-of-pearl; howdahs and palanquins; gold and silver ornaments and trappings of my stable of elephants and horses; gold and silver coins; and royal accoutrements and jewellery of gold and every gem under the sun, including my Navratna Crown.

Below the heaps lie my stockpile of small firearms, guns, cannons and ammunition—the envy of the Raj and every neighbouring state.

And crushed beyond recognition under all this is my most treasured possession: a collection of ancient Sanskrit manuscripts from my palace library. They are invaluable Vedic treatises on religion, politics, marriage, sex, health, medicine, astronomy, astrology and the arts. The collection is a labour of love of the late Maharaja and me.

My advisors, shackled and spectral, converge from all corners of Vajrakantaka.

"This is daylight robbery, Maharaj!"

"The Raj is no better than our dacoits!"

"It's clear the Raj doesn't trust Your Excellency with this inheritance."

"After the help you gave him when his kind were trapped in Karaha Fort!"

"The ungrateful dog!"

"The Raj should be thrown out of the country!"

"I say we blow him up with cannons!"

"Just say the word and we'll break out of these shackles!"

My goodwill dies.

All the teachings of restraint, diplomacy and tolerance I have imbibed from the Vedas and Puranas now come to nought in the face of British supremacy.

I am forced to embrace a new dogma, a new god, whose principal teachings are rebellion and revenge.

*　　*　　*

Ramdas and Raghunath related the catastrophic events that followed the annexation.

Nods of approval and utterances of *"Changla! Changla!"* punctuated the narration as the men recounted the virtues of Rani Meera Bai and her awesome courage.

Mukta circulated the Rani's picture.

The villagers admired it and shook their heads in regret.

Gasps of shock and anger arose as the men described the treachery and the brutal slayings committed by the British.

When the tale ended, the villagers were silent and deep in thought. They could not imagine how such turmoil had been going on right next door and they had been left untouched. On the one hand, they were glad their ruler, the Nizam, had ceded to the British without bloodshed; on the other, they asked themselves: has Moghul rule made such wimps of us that we have given up our independence, nationhood and pride without so much as a feeble protest? But common sense told them that they, being Marathas, were a minority in the state of Haidarabad. They had to flow with the current. Anything more would be suicidal.

"What will you do now? Where will you go? Especially after killing the white officer," Bhima asked. "Forget about going anywhere near Haidarabad. It's crawling with Inglistans." The patel's concern was genuine.

"It's a good thing you came to Champakapur. This is a remote part of the Deccan. No Inglistan has ever set foot here," the patriarch said reassuringly. He was a corpulent man, overfed by the women of his extended family.

"If you've no objections ..." Ramdas began. He glanced at his father and the panchayat members. Then, looking directly at the patel, "We'd like to settle here. For now, I think this is the safest place for me. Will you accept us?"

Silence.

Ramdas felt hot with embarrassment. Have I asked for too much, he thought.

Bhima addressed the court. "What do you say, brothers? Who's for the Bhonsle family staying with us?"

"I am," the schoolmaster said, raising his hand.

"The great Bhagwan has sent you to us for shelter, so we will give you shelter," the vibhuti-striped temple priest said.

"You're welcome. The more the merrier," the patriarch chirped.

"Any friend of yours is a friend of mine, old chap!" the secretary told the patriarch, showing off the English he had picked up in Haidarabad. That he had used the words in the wrong context did not bother him.

It was Bhima's turn.

Everyone held his breath. Under special circumstances, the patel had the power of veto.

"The Bhonsle name has always been an honoured one among us, from the time of Chatrapati Shivaji Bhonsle two centuries ago. Bhonsles have always been in the forefront of wars against the Moghuls and the

British. Here we are of the Mohite, Ghorpare, Gaekwad, Malusare, Jagthap and Savant clans only. I shall be very proud to have Bhonsles among us, especially ones who have fought so bravely, in their own ways, for the Motherland." Bhima turned to the family. "Brothers and sisters, consider Champakapur your home from now on."

Cries of 'Shabas! Shabas!' and thunderous clapping greeted the patel's speech. The men surrounded Ramdas and Raghunath, shook their hands and patted their backs. The women touched Mukta's and Ganga's head, cheeks, shoulders and hands in a show of acceptance.

The Bhonsles were overwhelmed. It was not easy for strangers to gain acceptance in a village. During these days of political intrigue, one's innocent-looking nextdoor neighbour could well be a spy. Or a mercenary. Or an assassin. They themselves had learnt the hard way how just twelve traitors could topple an entire kingdom; traitors who had paraded as friends and comrades-in-arms.

In retrospect, the family had never dreamt of being uprooted from Killa. But Champakapur seemed a good place to set down new roots. It was, after all, a farmland; a green farmland. With a sweet-smelling purple heart.

That the sweet smell would become putrid one day, the Bhonsles did not foresee.

*   *   *

The family settled in their new home as comfortably as doves settle in their cote.

The patel had been generous. He donated to them his old house. It was a clay-brick house, like the patel's new one. The house faced an empty rice plot at the western fringe of the village. The family was to work the plot for its own subsistence.

It took the family five days to whitewash the house, repair its roof and weed the compound. The villagers gave them their spare brass and copper pots and tin crockery and cutlery. They also donated charpoys, mats and pillows.

Until the family was self-sufficient, the villagers would provide them with provisions and raw vegetables. The family was happy with the arrangement.

One of the first things they did was hang the Rani's picture on the wall. They garlanded it with a string of oval glass beads hung with red tassels. The garland was a gift from the patel.

It was time for Ramdas to dream; to rest; to quell the storm in his breast; to make love; to forget Killa and the crushing defeat.

When was the last time I admired the sky, the mountains, the rivers? Ramdas thought.

It was a week after their arrival in Champakapur. He was lounging on the terrace in front of the house. The setting sun, like a child having fun, was pasting elongated shadows everywhere. Nest-bound birds were rioting in the trees.

Sure he'd looked at nature often enough. He'd looked at the sky, to see if rain clouds were gathering to wash out his military campaigns; he'd looked at the hills and mountains, to identify vantage points for battle; he'd looked at the rivers, to see where his troops could best ford them; he'd looked at the trees, to see if they hid snipers; he'd looked at the flowers, to pluck and lay on his dead sepoys' graves; and he'd looked at animals, to see if they would fill his sepoys' bellies on a long march.

When did I last listen to the sighing of the breeze and the singing of the birds? When was the last time I enjoyed the sight of a glorious sunrise or sunset? Ramdas could not remember.

For almost two years life for him had been an endless round of training sepoys, drills, marches, mock-battles and sporadic skirmishes with British forces. We don't even have time to shit, his men had complained.

When was the last time I touched my wife?

After his marriage, he was away months on end. When he did come home on short furloughs, it was in exhaustion. He slept like the dead most of the time. Mukta remained invisible. She suddenly materialised, like a jinnie, to serve him his meals and attend to his bath. Then she disappeared into the realm of the kitchen. By the time she finished her chores and materialised again, he was in another's arms—the arms of Morpheus.

This state of affairs got his mother worried. And, characteristically, she was as direct as ever about it.

"*Are* Ramdas! Don't sleep like a Kumbhakarna!"

"Who's Kumbhakarna?"

"He's a demon in the *Ramayana* epic. Kumbhakarna used to sleep for six months at a stretch. And it took them days to shake him awake."

"But I don't sleep for six months at a time!"

"You sleep long enough. At this rate, how am I going to be a grandmother? I want my grandchild to play on my lap before I die. Look at your wife, she's as pretty as a parrot!"

Mukta must think I'm a pervert, the way I've been neglecting her, Ramdas thought as he watched the sun, tired of pasting shadows, duck below the horizon to play another game.

But his conscience was clear. He belonged to that breed of men to whom king and country came first, family only second. He had not told his wife of the secret vow of abstinence he and his fellow captains had taken (you didn't discuss sex with your wife). They had sworn off women and wine until the British were driven out of Killa. Indeed, the majority of his countrymen were like him.

Ramdas went inside the house. It was a replica of the patel's new house. There was the verandah, the hall, three bedrooms, an anteroom and the kitchen. For bathing and washing, there was the sparkling Lahan Nadi. Ramdas could hear its soothing sounds from the house.

He saw Mukta and Ganga emerging from the anteroom after prayers. The room served as a prayer-cum-storeroom.

The temple priest, Prohitar Goswami, had presented them with an image of Lord Ganesha. He had moulded it from clay. It was a shade of dark ochre and stood two feet tall. Ganga thought the trunk too long and the eyes too large, but was grateful to the priest for the favour.

Raghunath came in after his bath. Ramdas noted his shoulders sagged. Poor Bah, Ramdas thought, our plight is telling on him. In his heart, Ramdas prayed his father would emerge from their nightmare unscathed.

Father and son had spent the day clearing their plot. It was thick with gavat. The tall weeds played host to quails, grasshoppers, frogs, mice and a couple of cobras. The bunds had crumbled and the narrow nullahs were choked with earth and grass. After their long break from farming, the men found the scythes heavy and unfamiliar. They came home with chafed palms.

In the late afternoon, they had gone to see Bhima about a plough and cows for pulling it. The implement and animals now stood in the lean-to behind the house. The cows would also provide milk for the family.

"We start work early tomorrow, Ramdas," Raghunath said, towelling his wet hair vigourously. It was natural for him to take the lead when it came to farming. He had, after all, seen forty more annual harvests than his son. "We still have some weeding to do. After that we can start ploughing."

"The rice seeds are in the anteroom. Ma said the patriarch's son came by earlier to deliver them," Ramdas informed.

"Good. We have to procure some manure, too. Deccan soil is light and infertile. Not like the dark, rich loam we have back home. We have to pamper the soil here."

"That shouldn't be too difficult, seeing how green the other zaga are."

"Yes, but remember fertiliser alone isn't enough. Water, my son, is the crux. It's the life-pulse of farming." He paused to secure his dhoti. Then he combed his hair with a coconut-shell comb. "We're lucky the rains have been copious this year. But the villagers tell me the rains fail sometimes." Raghunath's brows creased with concern. He had never tasted drought in Killa.

"Let's not worry about that now, Bah. It's not going to change the whims and fancies of the rain god."

"You're right. Please forgive the straying thoughts of this old man."

"You're forgiven, old man!" Ramdas said, tongue in cheek. "Come, let's eat. Ma, is jewan ready?"

"In a minute. Be seated."

After washing their hands in the kitchen, the men sat on square straw mats below the Rani's picture. It was a place of honour in the house. And being men of the house, they would eat first, their wives last.

Ganga bustled in with plates and a pot of cooked parboiled rice. The hall at once filled with starchy fragrance. She sat in front of the men and ladled out the rice. Mukta placed tumblers of water beside the men's plates. Then she brought in the curry and vegetables. Ganga served them. She dished out the choicest bits of fish, drumsticks and pumpkin on her husband's and son's plates.

The men ate heartily. The rice was hot and fluffy; the fish curry pungent with wedges of sautéed brinjal; the drumsticks and pumpkin rich with mustard seeds, onions, garlic and shredded coconut; and the chutney sweet-sour with sliced green mango, red pepper and jaggery.

When he finished eating, Ramdas could not help licking every finger. Raghunath belched with satisfaction. Ganga and Mukta preened.

"Shall we soak the seeds?" Raghunath asked as the women cleared the plates and pots.

"Yes, Bah. I'll get the seeds and the tray."

They went to the lean-to. A sputtering oil lamp lit its confines. Ramdas placed a shallow, rectangular wooden tray on the ground. Raghunath emptied a bag of rice seeds into the tray. The sun-browned seeds were dry and hard. He shook the tray to spread the seeds. Ramdas filled the tray with water till it stood three inches above the seeds. The water was enough for the seeds to absorb.

"Let the seeds bloat. They'll be ready to germinate in four days. By then, we shall have finished preparing the nursery," Raghunath said. He preferred the Killa way of sowing seeds in the nursery first and then transplanting the seedlings, rather than broadcasting the seeds directly into the plots. He knew his method was more tedious, but it was orderly and made use of every available space.

The two white cows in the lean-to were chewing their cud. They stared marble-eyed at their new masters. Seeing their dull hides, Raghunath made a mental note to scrub them down after the ploughing.

The men blew out the lamp and left, carefully side-stepping dung on the floor. The reek of cow urine followed them into the house.

They joined Ganga and Mukta on the verandah. Mukta sat in Ganga's shadow.

Ganga had a paan tray before her. The tray was of brass, donated by the village barber. It could not compare to the sterling silver one the family had in Killa. The donated tray was oblong and had compartments. Each compartment held a different ingredient: paan, areca nuts, lime, cardamom, cloves, nutmeg, camphor and saffron. Another compartment held an areca-nut slicer, no longer than a betel leaf.

"Please let me work a corner of the rice plot. I wish to plant vegetables," Ganga announced as she spread lime on a paan.

The others looked at her, surprised.

Pretending not to notice, she placed flakes of areca nuts, two cardamom seeds, a clove, three silvers of nutmeg, a pinch each of camphor and saffron on the paan. Then she folded it into a triangular wad and handed it to Raghunath.

Raghunath popped the paan into his mouth and started chewing it. A look of bliss came over him as the flavours married in his mouth. Their progeny lulled him and banished his tiredness.

"Did you hear what I said, nawra?" There was a hint of impatience in Ganga's voice as she saw Raghunath's half-closed eyes. "I said I wish to plant vegetables."

"Plant vegetables?" Raghunath concealed his surprise. Ganga planting vegetables? She has always shied away from the sun, he thought. I wonder what has brought about this change.

Ramdas could not hide his surprise.

"What! Really, Ma?" he burst out.

"And just what vegetables do you propose to plant?" Raghunath asked.

Ganga was preparing another paan.

"I was thinking of tomatoes and brinjals."

She offered the prepared paan to Ramdas. He declined it, not fancying his parents' stained teeth. Ganga then gave the paan to Mukta. The men noted Ganga had waived aside family protocol and not taken the paan herself. Another welcome change, they thought.

"They're easy to grow and need only minimum care. Isn't that right, Mukta?"

Ganga looked knowingly at her daughter-in-law.

"Yes, Mami," Mukta was quick to reply. "We grew them on our vegetable farm at my village and they always yielded bushels. Occasional manure and daily watering is all they need."

"We can even sell the surplus to the villagers," Ganga enthused, stuffing the next paan into her mouth.

"But you've never done any outdoor work! How can you stand the sun now, Ma?"

Even during his childhood, Ramdas noticed that while other women planted, harvested, thrashed and winnowed rice in the open, his mother desisted. She only deigned to husk and mill the grains in the cool shade of the terrace. Before his soldiering days, he and his father managed all the outdoor work.

"I'm no longer afraid of the sun, Ramdas. Not after our recent flight. We baked in the sun for more than a month, remember?"

It suddenly struck Ramdas what his mother must have gone through. He had been too preoccupied to think of her ordeal. And she had not once complained about the blistering heat.

"I've learnt I'm not a wax princess. I won't melt in the sun. Anyway, I'll have Mukta helping me."

"You mother-in-law and daughter-in-law have got it all worked out, haven't you?" Raghunath looked amused. It augured well for the women's relationship. He knew that his wife, while being a good mother, was not the best of mothers-in-law. He also knew that Mukta was a gem.

"All right, then. You shall have your vegetable corner."

Ganga and Mukta beamed.

Raghunath winked at Ramdas.

The family spent the next half-hour talking of Champakapur, the villagers and such topics that interest farmers: the climate, the local weather, crops, pests, yields, revenue, etc.

Three times Ramdas caught Mukta staring at him with one big round eye. The other was blocked by Ganga's massive shoulder. When Ramdas caught her eye, she quickly lowered her gaze and slowly withdrew her face behind Ganga's back. How lovely! Like the moon disappearing behind a cloud, thought Ramdas. He felt the first stirrings of a long sidetracked passion as she peeped at him from behind Ganga.

That night, Ramdas rediscovered Mukta.

He gave his enforced celibacy a one-way ticket to oblivion. All the passions of his youth were set free in a healing deluge as he explored Mukta's every curve, every mole, every dimple, every cleft, every mound, and made passionate love to her. Mukta responded with her all, bursting as she was with pent-up love for her husband. That night, it was as if they were Kama Deva and Rathi Devi, the love god and love goddess themselves.

So it was every night.

Ramdas was whispering into Mukta's ears as they lay in each other's arms.

They were in the magnolia stand. At midnight, it was an arbour dripping perfume, enchantment and sensuality. Even the chirping crickets could not break its magical spell.

"Give me a son. Give me two sons."

"Mmm ..." Mukta answered. She was dreamy, luxuriating in Ramdas' embrace.

"What exactly does that mean? Mmm ... yes, or Mmm ... no?"

"Yes! Yes!" came the more alert reply. "And daughters, too."

"But sons first," Ramdas insisted.

They were in deep shadow. Even the moonbeams were unable to pierce the flower-dome overhead. A single magnolia fell on Mukta. Ramdas whiffed it. The perfume was intoxicating. Then he drew the magnolia along Mukta's arms and around her face.

"I want my sons to be great soldiers."

"Soldiers? And leave their wives for months as you've left me?" Mukta teased, tracing the scar along his cheek.

"Yes. Even years. No war is too long for the sake of the Motherland."

He tucked the magnolia in her hair. Then he entwined his fingers in hers.

"My sons shall not be captains like me. They shall be generals. Of great armies. Their fame will spread to the far corners of India, and ..."

"And what?"

"And all the maharajahs will hold the svayamvara competition. Princesses will vie each other in archery, fencing and horseback riding to win my sons' hand in marriage."

Mukta shook with laughter at Ramdas' suggested reversal of roles.

"Oh what dreams you have, my nawra!"

"This isn't just any dream. It's a dream that will change our fate. And I'll make it come true one day. But give me sons first."

As Mukta listened, Ramdas spun his dream: the Maratha army would rise again; Prince Dilip would lead it; his sons would be the Prince's right-hand men; and, together, they would wipe out the Inglistans.

"I sincerely hope your dream will come true." Mukta sounded more serious. "For all our sakes."

"And for Killa's sake," Ramdas added.

They were lost in their own thoughts for a while. Then, they nuzzled each other and were soon lost to the world. Kama Deva. Rathi Devi.

Of Rice Planting and Goat Testicles

Father and son cleared the remaining patches of weeds in the rice plot. Weeding done, they emptied the nullahs of soil. The soil they used to rebuild the crumbled bunds. After their exertions, the plot emerged a patchwork of neat, rectangular parcels of earth delineated with bunds.

The nullah ran along a side of the plot. From one end of the nullah, Ramdas and Raghunath cleared another narrow and deeper watercourse that connected the nullah to the Lahan Nadi. It was back breaking, digging the hundred-yard stretch. But at the end they were rewarded when the waters of the Lahan Nadi gushed in and filled the nullah, ready to give new life to the fallow plot.

The next morning, it was time to plough.

After an energising breakfast of steamed ragi puttu with coconut and banana, and a tumbler of coffee with fresh milk, the men set out to their plot with the plough and cows.

Ramdas bore the plough on his hefty shoulders. It was a primitive wooden affair with a new metal share. All the Champakapuri farmers were using ancient ploughs, too.

Raghunath led the cows. Ganga had waved burning camphor and vermillion in front of them for good luck. So they all wore vermillion dots: the men and cows on their foreheads and the plough on its share.

The rice field was fifty yards from the house. A bullock-cart path led to it. As they walked along the path, a villager shouted greetings from the neighbouring plot. Like the other rice farmers, he, too, had started ploughing. He was dressed like Ramdas and Raghunath. His dhoti was brought up tightly between the legs so that it reached halfway between groin and knee. His short-sleeved shirt was collarless. He had a thundu wrapped around his head for protection from the sun.

Ramdas and Raghunath hollered their greetings to him. Then they entered the first sub-plot nearest the path.

The sub-plot was fifty strides long and twenty strides wide, a third of the size of the other nine sub-plots. This was to be the nursery.

Raghunath yoked the cows to the plough. "*Hai! Hai!*" he shouted as he slapped the animals' hinds and got them moving.

The cows were sluggish at first. But with more Hai Hais and prodding, they got into their act. Soon, they were plodding up and down the length of the plot, Raghunath steering them. Ramdas followed, using a hoe to break up the sods the share turned up.

In their wake came flocks of pittas. They feasted on the bugs, worms and seeds in the broken sods.

After two rounds, Ramdas took over. He led the cows along the width of the plot. This time around, the cows crushed the remaining clods of earth as they trod on them.

It took the men the whole morning to plough the compacted soil. In between, they stopped to drink water.

The patel came by at midday. He strode like a colossus down the path to the plot. "How's work progressing, Bhonsle?"

The pittas scattered.

"Through your kindness, it's progressing well, Patel. We start sowing tomorrow," Raghunath answered. He and Ramdas came to stand with the headman.

"Good. The other farmers will be sowing, too."

The landscape was dotted with rice farmers driving their ploughs and cattle-teams across their plots. On the rise in the distance grazed cattle, sheep and goats. But the wiry grass did not meet their needs. It was on the farms that these animals had their bellyful of hay.

"Gokul says you can collect manure from his farm whenever you wish," Bhima informed the men.

Gokul was one of two cattle farmers in Champakapur. The other was Shankar, his cousin. They were the village dudhwallah. Between them, they supplied the villagers with milk. They also supplied manure and dung patties. Shankar reared Sangamneri goats and Barbary sheep, too.

They produced excellent lean meat.

"We'll need only four bucketfuls for the nursery now," Raghunath said. "When we've ploughed the whole field, we'll need a few cartloads at least."

"That shouldn't be a problem. Gokul and Shankar are generous. Is there anything else you need?"

"No. Not for now," Ramdas answered.

"In that case, I'll be off. But first, here's something for you." Bhima fished out half a pumpkin, a cabbage and a handful of red peppers from his sling bag. "With compliments of the wife," he said.

"Patel, you and your wife are generosity personified. I don't know how to thank you," Raghunath said.

"*Are* Bhonsle, it's I who should be thanking you for cultivating this rice field of mine."

Bhima explained that he and his wife were too old now to work. But they used to, during their younger days. And before he became patel. Now his patel duties didn't allow him time in the field.

"If only we had a son like you, Ramdas." Bhima said, looking fondly at him. "He'd be helping us now as you are your father."

Bhima had long accepted his wife's barrenness. And he did not take a second wife. Most of his countrymen would have. You must have a son at least to light your funeral pyre, his departed parents had urged. His contemporaries had said the same thing.

According to the villagers, Bhima loved his wife even more because of her fate. He had never once pointed the finger of blame at her. "Being a woman, the burden she bears must be heavier than mine," he said understandingly. Filled with longing, he looked with a fatherly eye on all the village's young men. He thought of them as the sons he never had.

Raghunath admired the patel's fortitude and good humour in accepting what the gods had ordained.

"I'll go-and-come, Raghunath, Ramdas," Bhima took leave.

"Go-and-come," the men echoed.

After another round of ploughing, father and son surveyed the nursery. It was to their satisfaction: long furrows of crumbly soil devoid of weeds and pests.

Then they went home for lunch and a nap.

In the afternoon, they carried two tin buckets each and went to Gokul's cattle farm. Along the way, they saw housewives preserving food for the coming winter months. The women laid rectangular pieces of cloth or cartwheel-sized straw trays along the road. On these they spread mutton slices coated with turmeric and salt, rice-paste nuggets flavoured with cumin, freshly rolled black-gram pappad, and curd-soaked green chillies and sundakkai. The food would be sun-dried daily. When crisp, they would be stored.

Gokul's farm sprawled at the eastern fringe of the village. The reek of dung and urine spiked with Attar of Magnolia plumed over the farm.

A group of villagers was just leaving, carrying milk or dung. Father and son exchanged greetings with them. They found Gokul in the milking shed.

Gokul was a squat, brown man. He perpetually smelled of his four-legged charges. His only lament in life: No matter how much gingelly oil, shikakai and water I use, I can't get rid of the cow smell; even Attar of Magnolia doesn't work!

"*Are* Gokul, how do your two wives put up with that stink?" his friends poked fun.

"It couldn't bother them much. He has ten children to prove it, hasn't he?" they teased.

Gokul left his milking to attend to Ramdas and Raghunath.

"Come, come. I was expecting you. The patel told me you need manure," he said, leading them to the dung shed.

They walked past his herd of milch cows. They were white brahmins, well fed and clean. Two milkmaids were milking them. Under their expert fingers, the milk spurted into a frothing mass in the buckets below.

Ramdas stopped to get a whiff of the fresh milk. He loved it. It was years since he had last seen so many buckets of milk. Not since moving to Killa Fort.

To Ramdas and his people, there was no liquid more propitious than fresh cow's milk: for nourishing the body; for bathing temple icons; for the new bride to offer her groom on their marriage bed; for immersing the nuptial-string of a woman on the death of her husband; and for sprinkling on the warm ashes of the cremated. So-and-so has a heart as white as milk, people said of a good man. The villagers said it of Ramdas and Raghunath.

They passed the crammed cowsheds. A boy was catching urns of urine gushed by a cow. The warm urine overflowed, wetting the boy's hands, before splashing on the ground.

"What's the gomutra for?" Raghunath asked.

"Two families need it. Nanda will be sprinkling it to cleanse his house. It's the last day of his wife's confinement. And Mitun will be doing likewise. His father died last night and was cremated this morning."

They arrived at the dung shed at the far end of the compound.

A green hillock of dung stood in the middle of the shed. The damp beetle-ridden mass emitted a gas so overpowering that Ramdas and his father thought they would be smothered. Gokul just wrinkled his nose. Two old women were busy making dung patties.

In less than a minute, Gokul finished shovelling the dung into the buckets.

"*Dhanyavad*, Gokul," Raghunath thanked him.

"Never mind the thanks," Gokul said. "I wish you a bountiful harvest. May Sita Lakshmi rain her blessings on you."

He gave them a dozen rati. He had rows and rows of the cow-dung patties slapped against the low walls of the cowsheds. They looked like green chappatis. The dried rati was fuel. Gokul would sell them to the villagers at five paisa each.

As Ramdas and Raghunath were leaving, another group of villagers was entering the farm, carrying empty urns and buckets.

Milk, gomutra, dung, rati—life does seem to revolve around cows, Ramdas thought.

That they would save him from certain death, he did not dream.

That night, on the eve of sowing the first seeds of the season, Ramdas led Mukta to the nursery, in deference to an ancient fertility rite; as had his father taken his mother, his grandfather his grandmother; and as had all his ancestors since the dawn of their farming culture.

It was the custom in the land that on the eve of sowing the first seeds of the season, the youngest couple in the family should lie in the furrows of the prepared seedbed. Their ensuing act of love would be dedicated to the earth goddess, Sita Lakshmi.

Every farmer worth his salt knew that Sita was the goddess of the crops (rice, wheat, millet, barley and corn in Champakapur). She was goddess of the pastures where farm animals grazed. And she was goddess of the soil from which she had sprung. The furrow made by the ploughshare was also called 'sita'. Since Sita was an incarnation of the goddess Lakshmi, the gods called her Sita Lakshmi. The fertility rite dedicated to her ensured a bountiful harvest.

As Ramdas and Mukta lay in the seedbed, they knew that other couples, too, would be making sweet love in one or the other of the surrounding rice fields.

A soft breeze drizzled magnolia scent on Ramdas and Mukta. It fired their sensual mood. Soon, they were one, seeking the dizzying heights of their desire. And high above, the stars jostled for a better view and winked at each other, at the show of such raw passion below.

In the cool of the next morning, Ramdas and Raghunath brought the soaked rice seeds to the nursery. The grains were bloated and ripe for sowing.

They first distributed the dung evenly over the plot. Then they dug a channel in the bund. Water from the nullah rushed in and flooded the seedbed.

When the water was shin-deep, the men plugged the channel. They brought the cows into the plot for one more round of ploughing. For an hour, man and beast sloshed in the water. They took one plodding step after another, to incorporate the dung into the soil.

To Raghunath, it was euphoria to once again sink his feet into the mud and feel its cool, soothing grip. It sent invisible messages up his legs to tug at the very core of his heart.

Ramdas, whose first love was soldiering, willed himself to re-learn the ways of the rice field. This is only temporary, he told himself; the time will surely come when I'll once again be on the other field—the battlefield.

Mukta came to help with the sowing. The sight of the seedbed made her blush with memories of the previous night. She lowered her head, hoping her husband and father-in-law would not notice her red face.

They each filled a small basket with the germinating seeds. Standing close to each other, they started sowing the seeds, bending almost double. Their hands worked like pistons—in, out, in, out—punching the seeds into the mud. Their dripping sweat mingled with the soil, enriching it, entreating it to give life.

"Drops of sweat. They're like drops of blood," Raghunath used to say. "You shed both to keep your country alive."

During the weeks that followed, the first green blades of rice grass pierced their watery roof. As the seedlings grew taller in the nursery, Ramdas and Raghunath ploughed the rest of the field. Their cows, having seen years of toil, were steady and reliable.

Mukta came out to the field with their lunch every day. One day it was curd rice with lime pickles; another day tamarind rice with gram-dhal chutney; yet another day lime rice with potato masala; or just rice gruel peppered with green chilli, onion and mustard seeds. The meals were washed down with body-cooling lassi.

After a month, the rice shoots had grown a foot tall. The nursery looked like an emerald on Mother Earth's brown breast.

Then it was time to irrigate the field. Only the plot next to the nursery was left dry for Ganga's vegetables. When flooded, the rice field looked like a grid of rectangular mirrors reflecting rectangular patches of blue sky and cauliflower clouds. The clouds would bring crucial rain during the growing season.

Once again, Mukta came to lend a hand, this time with the transplanting.

They uprooted the shoots and gathered them in bunches. Holding two or three shoots in a clump, they pushed the roots into the mud. The next clump, they planted a stride away. They repeated the process until the whole field was filled with neat rows of rice shoots.

The transplantation took three days. At the end of it, the men were moaning aloud of backaches. Their wives had to give them warm-water fomentation. Being a daughter-in-law, Mukta could not complain openly about her aches. But Ramdas, aware of her mute forbearance, secretly massaged her back in the privacy of their bedroom. "Don't tell Ma," he said.

The transplanting was done in mid-August. The rice would be left to grow until January. It would be ready for harvesting then. During this interval, all the men had to do was spring water into the field when the water level dropped, as rice shoots are guzzlers; add cow dung from time to time; pull out the inevitable weeds; and keep a sharp lookout for signs of the rice-stalk maggot. The creepy-crawlies could ruin an entire crop by boring into and devouring the juicy young stalks.

After the transplantation, life took on a leisurely pace for the family. While Ramdas and Raghunath occasionally checked the rice field, Mukta and Ganga tended the brinjal and tomato they were growing.

Ganga was an eager beaver novice farmer. Covering her head with the end of her sari, she would spend an hour in the morning or evening watering the plants, weeding, and pruning. Sometimes she would add cow dung or goat dung as manure.

When the yellow flowers of the tomato and purple flowers of the brinjal unfurled and the heads of the fruit burst into the world, there was no end to Ganga's joy. She ground turmeric roots to a paste, diluted it with water and sprinkled the yellow solution on the flowers. "The turmeric will prevent fungus attacks," she declared knowledgeably to her husband and son. She had taken great pains to learn about growing the vegetables from Mukta and the other vegetable farmers of Champakapur.

Ganga was happy watching her vegetables grow from day to day; as happy as she had been watching her own son grow. But her happiness was not complete. There was a nagging thought at the back of her mind all the time.

It was precipitated by her cronies in Champakapur. There was Old Chenggamma, the attar maker. There was Manglamba Bai, dudhwallah

Gokul's mother. And there was Saroja Bai, wife of the village cobbler. Together, they shared an affinity brought about by their similar ages.

The old women sometimes sought each other out on long evenings. During such times, they delved into various topics of interest to them.

Which was the better cure for their grandchildren's cold—getting them to drink basil juice or fomenting with heated betel leaves and lime? How best to cook goat blood and brain. When should saffron be administered to their daughters and daughters-in-law—during the seventh or eighth month of pregnancy? Is turmeric paste really effective in minimizing crow's feet? The advantages of eating millet. What's the best course of action when your aging husband's dead sexual drive is suddenly rejuvenated: do you plead a headache or a stomachache? You can't very well plead a vagina-ache, can you? Because that's what you get when your other pleas fail. Which brings us to the next question: which oil is the best lubricant for alleviating painful intercourse?

It was on one such occasion that, while talking about barrenness, Ganga's cronies broached a certain subject. Though private, it was customary to inquire about such matters.

They were sitting on Chenggamma's verandah. Nearby, young boys were shouting while playing goli. The glass marbles shot out of their hands like crystal balls as they caught the sunlight. A group of young girls was practicing henna-drawing on each other's hands. Another group was alternately chatting and whispering and filling the air with high-pitched laughter as they shared secret jokes. Little children were playing catch or making vain attempts to catch the pigeons on the ground. And the evening sun was peeping on the happy scene through the cloud-slats in the sky.

"What, Ganga, isn't there any bug or worm in your daughter-in-law's womb yet?" Chenggamma raised a hairless eyebrow as she prepared paan for the women. Her kona-konde, sleek as ever, jutted like a black cone behind her right ear.

"Not yet, Chenggamma," Ganga spoke sadly. She was neither surprised nor offended by the question. "There's no god I've not prayed to, to ask for the gift of a grandchild."

"How long has your son been married?" Manglamba asked,

finger-combing her freshly washed jet-black hair. (If there was any single trait the women of Champakapur shared, it was jet-black hair, because they all nourished it with coconut oil steeped with magnolias.)

"Oh, for eight months now."

"That long? I wonder what's wrong with Mukta. Look at my daughter, she conceived the very next month after marriage. And my daughters-in-law, they have babies every year." Manglamba was very proud of her ten grandchildren.

"Does she menstruate regularly?" Saroja asked, chewing paan like a cow chewing the cud.

"Like clockwork! If only her periods would stop."

"Some women conceive late," Chenggamma tried to look on the bright side.

"You all know Sarsu's daughter. She conceived only after twelve years of marriage."

"Twelve years! I'll be dead and gone by then!" Ganga moaned.

"Make her eat bittergourd every day," Saroja tried to be helpful. "The dark-green unripe ones, you know, not the yellow mature fruit. It will clear her system of impurities. Perhaps then she'll conceive."

Spitting betel juice into a spittoon, Manglamba leaned closer to Ganga and started whispering, so that the young girls nearby could not hear. Chenggamma and Saroja craned their necks to hear what was being said.

"It seems things can go wrong with men, too. I've heard say of the seeds of men being weak, especially if they're old or prone to illness."

"But my son's a healthy colt!"

"Yes, but what about the injuries he's suffered from battles? Who knows, he might've had a few knocks in the unmentionable place. That could affect his bed-sport, couldn't it?" Manglamba speculated.

"Oh-h-h!" Ganga wrung her hands. "I don't know about that. But I do hear their bed creaking every night."

"Creaking! It should've collapsed by now, woman!"

Ganga was a picture of dejection.

"Why not do this?" Chenggamma suggested as she controlled the betel juice threatening to spill from one corner of her mouth. "Fee im go icles."

"What? I can't understand what you're saying. For goodness sake, spit, Chenggamma!"

Chenggamma spat. Then she spoke clearly.

"Feed him goat testicles. I swear by the deities Ramdas will become as virile as a young ram." She paused for effect. "And he'll be able to father a dozen children, too."

"Dudhwallah Shankar rears goats. You could place an order with him to send over the testicles on slaughter days," Saroja suggested.

"Well, it looks like it's going to come to that," Ganga conceded.

"Try it. It may just do the trick," Chenggamma urged.

After that, Ganga's mind kept returning to the conversation. Cooking goat testicles would be one thing but getting Ramdas to eat them would be quite another.

When Mukta secluded herself for yet another time of the month, Ganga panicked.

"What's this, Ma?" Ramdas inquired one day, on seeing unfamiliar, shiny cubes of curried meat on his dinner plate. The meat cubes were beside his normal helping of fried mutton and his favourite: leg of goat. He loved to suck the marrow from the open ends of the leg bone. Nothing could beat the buttery taste and melt-in-the-mouth texture of the marrow.

"It's mutton," Ganga replied, her heart skipping a beat, "a new recipe I learned from Old Chenggamma. Taste it. You'll like it."

Ramdas pressed a piece between his thumb and forefinger. It did not disintegrate into fibres as cooked lean meat would. Instead, it remained spongy.

"But it doesn't look or feel like mutton, Ma. What *is* it?"

"I'm telling you, it's meat of a goat," Ganga hedged. "Chenggamma said it's good for you." Pause. Then, addressing the floor, "Only if you eat this will Mukta have a baby."

"What!" Ramdas was incredulous. Then he softened as realisation dawned on him. "Oh, I see ... But wouldn't it be better if Mukta ate it?

She's the one who's going to have a baby, not I." He could not help pulling his mother's leg.

" *Are* Ramdas!" Ganga slapped her forehead in exasperation. "How do I make you understand? Advise him, nawra, advise him!" Ganga dragged Raghunath into the subject. "Don't sit there like a rock!"

Raghunath was eating beside Ramdas.

"All right, Ma, all right. I'll eat it." A twinkle came into Ramdas' eyes. "See?" he said as he daintily picked up a cube, showed it to Ganga and, with a flourish, popped it into his mouth.

Ganga waited with baited breath.

Raghunath continued eating as if nothing unusual was happening.

Mukta fled into the kitchen in embarrassment.

"Mmm ... Feels spongy and tastes like cooked goat blood. Not bad."

The verdict was enough for Ganga. From then on it was goat testicles for Ramdas. Curried. Fried. Broiled. Or steamed. In between, he also had to drink a concoction of goat testicles boiled in milk with sugar. "It's recommended by the ancients," Chenggamma had said.

The whole episode brought satisfaction all round: to Chenggamma because her advice was being heeded; to Ganga because, at last, she was doing something about getting a grandchild; to Ramdas because he was making his mother happy; and to dudhwallah Shankar because he was making an extra rupee out of selling goat testicles which he usually threw to the dogs.

But Ganga was not about to leave Mukta alone either.

After consultations with her friends, it was bittergourd for Mukta, day in and day out. The gourd remedy was accompanied now and then with sips of neem-leaf extract. Mukta did not know which was more bitter. But she humoured her mother-in-law.

One evening, Ganga insisted on taking Mukta to the village Kaliamman temple. Mukta was surprised. It was not a Friday, the day they usually went to temple.

The small temple housed a central shrine surrounded by a high, whitewashed wall. It was alive with devotees, bell-tolls and the scent of sandalwood, incense and camphor. Attar of Magnolia wafted from Chenggamma's shed next door. Two ancient trees dominated the compound—a pipal and a bael.

Under the pipal stood a small shrine with the image of Lord Ganesha. Ganga propelled Mukta towards it. Ganesha was the remover of all obstacles. So he would remove whatever stood in the way of Mukta conceiving.

Next, they prayed to the main deity, Kaliamman—the black goddess. She sat in an equally black shrine lit by the single flame of an oil amp. Her round silver eyes bored them. But they seemed benevolent to the faithful, terrifying only to the uninitiated. To Ganga, they were questioning: What is your wish, my daughter?

Mukta and Ganga placed a tray of bananas, betel leaves and areca nuts at her feet. Then they threw handfuls of camphor into the camphor urn outside the shrine. The camphor burst into flames. To Ganga, they were flames of supplication.

Finally, Ganga led Mukta to the strange bael tree. It stood in one corner of the temple compound.

The tree was old, skirted with buttress roots and hung with hundreds of bael fruit. When the hard, brown fruit fell to the ground, the temple priests dried and strung them into necklaces, for want of the preferred rudraksha seeds of the blue marble tree. They wore the bael-fruit necklaces, or used them, like a rosary, for counting mantras.

The tree looked strange because its top half was green with leaves and its bottom half was a riot of red, yellow and saffron. This was because the leaves on the bottom half were obliterated by hundreds of pieces of coloured silk hanging from the branches.

The narrow strips of silk were tied, cradle-fashion, to the branches. Each cradle had a thumb-sized clay image of a baby in it. They were silent pleas to Kaliamman from childless couples. People swore that she had granted them their boon soon after the cradle-tying. The poor, who could not afford silk, made do with turmeric-coated string with a pebble hanging on one end to represent the baby.

Some of the old silk cradles hung in faded tatters, the clay babies having long fallen and melted into the ground. The recent additions were brilliant.

"Come, Mukta. Knot this cloth to the branch." Ganga said as she produced a strip of saffron-coloured cotton. They could not afford silk. Ganga had purchased it, together with a blessed clay baby, from the temple priest.

Mukta knotted the cradle securely. Then she placed the nondescript baby-image into it.

"Now pray hard, Mukta. Ask Mother Kali in earnest for a child. Besiege her to open her eyes to your plight as she has to the plight of others."

Mukta brought her palms together, closed her eyes and prayed dutifully. She was eager to please her mother-in-law. And she knew that it would please her husband that she pleased his mother. As Mukta saw it, life was all about pleasing others.

Mukta did not know it then, but almost three decades later, she was to tie another bael knot, in another land, and ask another boon of Kaliamman.

A month later, when Ganga announced that Mukta had conceived, the old women could not agree on what did the trick.

"See, I told you the bittergourd will do her wonders," Manglamba was the first to take credit.

"I think it was the goat testicles that did it!" Chenggamma exclaimed, not wanting to concede to the ever-boasting Manglamba. "They're a hundred times more potent than bittergourd, you know."

Saroja would not be left out. "I see the hand of Kaliamman in all this. Don't ever doubt *her* powers."

"Whatever the reason, I'm going to be a grandmother at last," Ganga said contentedly. "That's enough for me."

"Thank God! No more goat testicles for me!"

"And no more bittergourd for me!"

Ramdas and Mukta giggled like children as they cuddled each other soon after Mukta learned she was pregnant.

"But don't be surprised if these old mhataris come up with a new list of must-eat foods, now that you're in the family way."

"If they do, I'm sure they mean well. So long as it's not bittergourd.

W-a-a-ck!" Mukta pretended to be sick.

As it turned out, the old women did not compile any new list. But they did insist that Mukta not touch pineapple and papaya during her pregnancy. They are very 'heaty' foods and can trigger a miscarriage, they explained. Not that pineapple and papaya were easily available in Champakapur. One had to travel much further south, where there was abundant rainfall all year round, to buy the fruits.

*   *   *

Two major events occurred from the beginning of Mukta's pregnancy to the birth of her child. The first was the harvest and its attendant festivities. The second was the eclipse.

The harvest was in mid-January, when Mukta was in her fifth month of pregnancy; the eclipse, three months later.

The rice fields of Champakapur had produced gold.

When the peacocks in the temple spread and shivered their trains at the start of their mating season, the farmers of Champakapur knew they signalled the coming of the monsoon rains. Sure enough, the rains screened Champakapur like shaken silken tresses screen a woman's face. The rains, crucial to the growing stages of the rice, kept the Lahan Nadi flowing and the rice fields well watered, so that the stalks soon drooped with heads of green rice.

Ramdas and Raghunath were kept busy getting rid of pests. Rats loved to nibble the rice stalks. So did the small crabs that scuttled among the plants. The frogs the men left alone. The amphibians, flicking out their tongues in lightning strikes, ate the bugs and insects that threatened the crop.

Silver nethili swam in the waters of the rice plots. They were a boon. Ramdas scooped the anchovies in a home-made fishing net. Mukta coated the fish with turmeric, red pepper and salt and deep-fried it to a crisp for the night meal. Occasionally, rice-field crabs took the place of anchovies for dinner.

As soon as the rice grains showed the first signs of ripening, father and son opened the bunds and allowed all the water to drain out to the nullah. Fully grown, the rice would thirst no more. Instead, it would hunger for strong sunshine, to ripen.

The rains petered out as expected. Heavy rains during the ripening stage spelt disaster. The roots of the rice plants would rot and the whole crop would die a premature death.

With the sun's rays beating down on them daily, the rice heads first turned yellow. Then they turned a rich gold, the colour of the earth goddess, Sita Lakshmi.

The golden grains attracted pests of the feathered kind, from clouds of little brown sparrows to flocks of orange pitta to squadrons of white egrets.

Raghunath drove man-high stakes into the ground at the points where the bunds intersected. On top of these stakes, he inverted variously painted earthenware pots. Ramdas had painted them. Most of the pots bore garish, grinning faces. The others were soot black, marked with white, anna-sized dots. These scarecrows were largely effective, but there were still some elements of the feathered kingdom that were bold enough to swoop down and pick at the grains. To counter them, Ramdas and Raghunath erected a platform in the middle of the rice field. The high wooden structure was sheltered with palm leaf. Little tin cups were strung from the platform to a stake thirty yards away. Raghunath manned this post in the mornings and Ramdas and Mukta in the afternoons and evenings. As soon as they spotted avian intruders, they shook the string so that the tin cups knocked against each other and clanged resoundingly. The alarmed birds instantly took flight.

Only the kawdaa did not. They were old hands at the game and the family welcomed their presence. The reddish-brown partridges nested in the dry paddies. They helped farmers by feeding on bugs, beetles and weed seeds. Sometimes, Ramdas trapped a kawdaa or two. Then the family enjoyed a meal of fried or roasted kawdaa, a juicy treat.

Flushed with pregnancy, Mukta loved lazing away the afternoons on the platform, sometimes reclining against Ramdas, at other times dozing on the floor.

Ramdas felt a new tenderness for Mukta. He fed her slices of the sour mangoes she so craved for these days. The way she smacked her lips with every bite made Ramdas feel like eating the fruit, too. Sometimes, when Ramdas least expected it, Mukta would playfully nip at his fingers as he fed her. Then he would put on a great show of pain and they would both dissolve into laughter.

There was another of Mukta's cravings Ramdas was party to. He smuggled out handfuls of rice grain from the bin at home to satisfy Mukta's strange pregnancy-induced fancy.

At first, Mukta had popped a few grains at a time into her mouth, at home, when the urge overcame her. But, one day, Ganga had spotted her.

"Don't eat raw rice, Mukta. You'll become anaemic. And they say, if it's a girl, it will rain buckets on the day of her marriage!" Secretly, Ganga was glad that Mukta did not have the shocking cravings that some pregnant women had for ash, charcoal and sand, like some of Manglamba's daughters-in-law.

After being found out, Mukta's munching became furtive. But on the rice-field platform, she was as free as a bird. Aided and abetted by Ramdas, the rice grains seemed all the more sweet, like stolen kisses. But Ramdas was at a loss as to why she found the raw grains so tasty.

One hazy-lazy month followed another. Soon, January was upon them. The sun, having bestowed its golden kiss upon the rice crop, was already losing its warm magic to winter's cold grip.

"The sun god will start his northward journey to the summer solstice soon," the farmers of Champakapur said. "Let's harvest the crop and give Surya a good sendoff in return for his favours."

Cresent-shaped sickles in hand, the farmers descended upon the fields. The mood was euphoric as sickles crunched through the Three Thirds. In rice farmers' parlance, the fully grown rice plants were of Three Thirds: the Bottom Third, the Middle Third, and the Top Third.

The Bottom Third, the stubble, was for the earth goddess. After the harvest, the stubble would be burnt and the ashes returned to the soil to enrich it. The Middle Third, the stalks, was for herbivores. The stalks would be turned into hay to feed grazing farm animals. And the Top Third, the rice heads, was for man. The rice would feed people.

Ramdas and Raghunath reaped their harvest with deep satisfaction.

Mukta laid out the sheaves to dry in front of the house where a waist-high cane basket stood by. It was equipped with a wooden slab for threshing.

When the rice had dried, Ganga and Mukta took turns to thresh it. Ganga lifted the sheaves high over her head with both hands and brought them down hard on the slab. The grains rained from the stalks into the basket. Mukta, her belly already bulging, laboured at the task. When she stopped to catch her breath, Ganga commented, "Go on. All this bending and stretching is good for you. The more you toil now and in the months to come, the easier your childbirth will be." After a pause she added, "Manglamba told me her daughters-in-law have such easy labour. It seems all they do is squat and the baby slithers out. If you ask me, it's all due to their hard work on the farm."

Ramdas and Raghunath helped with the threshing once they had done reaping. In two days' time, the basket was overflowing with rice grains. Then they waited for a windy day to do the winnowing.

When the wind tickled the magnolia trees of Champakapur and they shook with laughter, so that the magnolia fell in purple showers, Ramdas showered trays of rice in the open air so that the wind blew away the empty husks while the pregnant grains fell in a mound below. He spread the grains on the ground. In a couple of days, the sun crisped the grains.

Then the men fetched the grains to the verandah. Mukta and Ganga were waiting with a pestle and mortar borrowed from the patel. The women took turns pounding the grains to split open the husks. What with cooking and housekeeping, it took them the better part of a week to mill all the rice.

Finally, they sieved the milled rice and stored the long white grains in a bin in the anteroom. By then, it was almost the end of the Indian month of Pausha. On the first day of the following month of Maaghah, on the auspicious day called Ponggal, the sun god would start his journey. It was time to celebrate the harvest.

But first, on the eve of Ponggal, all the households in Champakapur observed the rites of Bhogi.

During Bhogi, the houses were spring-cleaned. There was much fetching and carrying of water from the Lahan Nadi as the villagers scrubbed and washed their homes. The washing away of dirt symbolised the cleansing of the spirit.

Small boys climbed on each other's shoulders to whitewash their homes. They spattered themselves with lime and loved every white splotch of it on their grinning faces.

The womenfolk scrubbed their clay stoves. Then they coated the stoves with a thick layer of fresh cow dung. When the dung dried, they drew rangoli of curliewurlie lines with rice flour around the stoves.

Little girls, all excited over the impending festivities, chattered shrilly on the way to the outlying jasmine grove, boasting about their new clothes and accessories. At the grove, they filled their baskets with the heady blooms. On their way back, they picked fresh magnolias at the magnolia stand. At home, they strung the jasmines into garlands. The garlands their mothers hung around the images of deities. A few arm-lengths they kept aside for the women and girls to decorate their hair the next day.

The menfolk went to the vegetable farmers' plots to cut sugar cane. They returned, balancing on their shoulders bundles of the yellow stalks, complete with their crowns of long, sword-like leaves. Then they tied sugar cane stalks on either side of their front doorways, so that the canes formed an arch. 'May the rest of the year be as sweet as the sugar cane at your doorway', the good wish went.

All rusted and disused utensils, broken furniture and torn clothes were thrown into a bonfire that could be seen from miles around. Every last seed of old stocks of pulses was used to make a pulse and vegetable stew—khendhotta. The khendhotta was made flavourful with spices and crunchy with sugar cane cubes.

Rice bins were cleaned out. The rice grains were ground into flour between millstones. The rice flour the women used to make patties to be eaten with the khendhotta.

The bins were then filled to the brim with the newly harvested rice. It augured well to have full rice bins.

Empty storage pots were cleaned, whitewashed and dried. Using ochre and viridian, the women decorated the pots with curly lines, dots and geometrical and floral motifs. They then refilled the pots with fresh pulses and stacked them, one on top of the other, in a corner of the kitchen. The largest pot stood at the bottom while the smallest stood at the top, in a delicate balance. Like life.

At the crack of dawn on Ponggal day, all the Champakapuris were up to greet the sun god as he started his journey north.

They gathered around the makeshift stove built with new bricks under the ancient pipal tree. All the villagers were freshly bathed and dressed. They were drenched in the magnolia-scented morning mist and Attar of Magnolia. The women and girls smelled extra sweet with jasmines in their hair.

Earlier, the temple priest had placed a small image of Surya near the stove. The clay model of the god had him riding a chariot drawn by seven red mares. The mares were sculpted in a radiating pattern, symbolising the rays of the sun.

Young girls drew an intricate rangoli around the stove. The lads built a wood fire in it. The flames blazed and crackled merrily, sending up showers of sparks. The fire lit up the faces of the villagers that were already shining with an inward flame of joy.

The patel was given the honour of placing a newly made clay pot on the stove, his wife that of pouring fresh cow's milk into it.

Temple musicians struck up an auspicious tune. Awakening birds in the trees sang their own mantras while the temple priest chanted his. But they were drowned by the 'dum-dum' of the drums, 'pee-pee' of the clarinets and 'ching-ching' of the cymbals.

Everyone waited expectantly for the auspicious moment: the moment the milk boiled over. The children, especially, waited with baited breath for they would be called upon to chant at that moment.

In the gathering light, they watched as a layer of skin formed over the heated milk. A ring of bubbles formed around the rim. It looked like a transparent pearl necklace. Slowly, the milk started to seethe under its skin. Unable to contain itself any longer, the milk gathered its skin from the rim and sent the shrivelling mass down its eddying vortex. The white mass simmered for a few seconds. Then it boiled over the pot in a thousand bubbles, marking the overflowing joy of the Champakapuris.

At the moment of the boiling-over, the music reached a crescendo and a great shout went up from the villagers. "*Ponggal-o-ponggal! Ponggal-o-ponggal! Ponggal-o-ponggal!*" they shouted three times. Some children could not stop shouting. They cried themselves hoarse repeating "*Ponggal-o-ponggal!*" while clapping and jumping around the fire. Like the boiling milk, they could not contain themselves.

As they watched, Ramdas saw tears well in his father's eyes. He knew they were not caused by the smoke.

Ganga and Chenggamma tipped large measures of newly harvested rice into the milk. Mukta and two other women added jaggery and small cubes of sugar cane. Then they let the rice cook, stirring it now and then and re-stoking the fire.

While the ponggal rice was cooking, a group of girls danced the kolattam around it: they skipped, twirled and beat short bamboo rods against each other to the rhythm of folk songs sung by the women. Then they did a dhangari number, spinning around the drummers while waving multicoloured scarves. The men watched appreciatively while the lads carried on a hot debate as to who was the most beautiful dancer.

After the dance, a group of toddlers had fun trying to mimic the dancing girls. They provided laughs for the adults. Some little girls stood frankly examining each other's new clothes and jewellery.

When the ponggal was almost ready, Chenggama stirred in handfuls of ghee-toasted cashew nuts and spoons of powdered cardamom. She also added a tub of home-made ghee donated by Gokul. The temple priest threw in a few squares of camphor for added fragrance and flavour. Soon, the ghee-spices-camphor aroma was fighting with the Attar of Magnolia for dominance.

"Come! Come everyone!" the patel called when Chenggamma informed him that the rice was done. The congregation gathered again.

The priest placed a banana leaf full of the ponggal in front of the sun god's image. Women set trays of banana, lime, coconut and magnolia around the rice. The priest then rang a silver bell and chanted sloka of thanks as he dedicated the offerings to Surya.

After the prayers, the villagers were served the ponggal. Many asked for a second helping. Mukta, eating for two, gorged herself till she was breathless. The old women who observed her said, "The poor thing. Let her eat her fill for she is pregnant. But she should eat in private or some may caste the evil eye on her."

The festivities reached a climax the next day. On this day, the farmers paid homage to their cattle that toiled with them in the fields.

The day began with the men and boys leading the animals to the Lahan Nadi.

Like the other farmers, Ramdas and Raghunath bathed their cows in the river. Then they painted their horns in bands of green, red and yellow. The tips of the horns they covered with goldleaf. They hung brass bells around their necks. Ganga garlanded the cows with magnolias, draped them in shawls and waved oil lamps around their faces. Then, together with the other farmers, the men led their cattle in a parade around the village.

Village musicians came out with their chipla clappers, daf drums and pipes to make cheerful music. They led the parade with somersaulting and cartwheeling boys, and men dancing the puliattam. The prancing men, wearing only loincloth, were painted from head to toe like tigers.

Youngsters skipped along with the parade. All the way, generous householders set bucketfuls of rice conjee, a treat for the animals, outside their doorsteps. The farmers would later collect the conjee and their four-legged wards would lap it up. But during the parade, some of the farmers had to coax their animals back into line as the bovines, casting sidelong glances, veered off the path to the tempting buckets.

After the parade came the day's highlight: the annual jallikattu or taming of the bull.

Young and old could not wait for the sport. They went en masse to the arena just outside the village. The still-green bamboo slats attested to the arena's recent construction.

Ramdas stood in the front row with his family and the patel. He felt he was in the Killa village of his childhood once again.

Every year, the fiercest bull in Champakapur was used for the jallikattu. This year, Gokul's prize bull was to be used.

There were gasps as Gokul released the beast from its pen in the arena. It had taken three stalwarts with ropes to lead the snorting and balking animal from Gokul's farm to the pen.

The massive black beast, a Brahmin, thundered into the arena and the people fell back in fear. But it stopped short at the centre. The people gathered their courage and milled around the arena again. The bull stood like a rock, turning its great head right and left. It stared malevolently at the crowd. As its muscles rippled, the sunlight danced on the sheen of its hide while the crowd's eyes danced on its enormous horns, dewlap, hump and scrotum. Every lad present imagined himself to be as strong and virile as the bull. And every father seeking a bride for his son twirled his moustache and boasted to prospective in-laws: My son, too, is like this jallikattu bull.

The event was about to begin. Gokul, as owner of the bull, was master of ceremonies.

"Young men of Champakapur! Come, subdue my bull!" Gokul's voice rang out like a ringmaster's. He was dressed in a silk veshti and jippa and dripping with Attar of Magnolia. "Come! A hundred silver pieces to you if you dare catch him by the tail! And the bull to you if you take him by the horns! Come, if there are any bulls among you!!"

A scrawny fellow rushed into the arena. One look from the bull and he turned tail and rushed out again, drawing hoots and laughter from the crowd. Half a dozen hopefuls dashed in but also chickened out, drawing more laughter. The village idiot tore straight towards the bull screaming, "I'll tame the bull! I'll catch him by his balls!" Gokul's men promptly bundled him out.

"What, are there no bulls among you?" Gokul cried. "Come on! Let's see who's the bravest and strongest young man in Champakapur!"

Another batch of hopefuls came forward, more to impress the girls than to wrestle the bull. The bull tossed them the minute they touched its horns or tail. They flew like scarecrows through the air and thudded on the ground. They were lucky to escape with minor cuts and abrasions. Those who had bet on them lost.

Then, a promising stalwart stepped into the arena. He was Giridhar, the son of the village barber.

No one had paid much attention to him until now. Giridhar had arrived in Champakapur only at dawn that morning. He had spent most of his boyhood at his uncle's house in the next village. He had stayed there expressly because that village had a yoga, bodybuilding and martial arts guru under whom he wanted to train. And did.

When the dusky six-foot Giridhar removed his tunic, the villagers' jaws dropped. They could not remember when they had last seen a man with such a broad chest and such stout muscles. None of them had expected the lanky lad to grow into this magnificent specimen of a man.

"Why, he looks like a young bull himself!" they said.

"Bull against bull. What a match this is going to be!"

"I bet my last paisa Giridhar will win!"

Raghunath, watching from the ringside, was temporarily lost in another dimension. His was remembering the occasion during his youth when he had once stood in the arena, just like Giridhar. After all, that was how he had won Ganga's hand in marriage—by fighting a bull. Ganga's father, a patel, had offered her as prize to the one who subdued his favourite bull. Ganga had been slim and lithe then, Raghunath recalled. And the bull had been only half the size of the monster that faced Giridhar now. The cheering of the crowd snapped Raghunath out of his reverie.

Standing next to him, Ganga was having pleasant thoughts of her own. The spectators' applause as she garlanded the victorious Raghunath rang in her ears now.

Earlier, when Raghunath had jokingly asked, "What, Ganga, shall I fight the bull?", Ganga had replied roughly, "What's come over you, old man? Don't you want to live to see your grandson?" But Raghunath had not missed the tender look in her eyes.

Ramdas and Mukta were thinking what all Maratha fathers and mothers-to-be of those trying times thought: that their sons would grow up to be as strong and intimidating as a jallikattu bull—to take up arms and rid the Motherland of the British.

A silence fell upon the crowd as Giridhar strode towards the bull, flexing his muscles.

The bull snorted and started to paw the ground with its hoof, stirring up puffs of dust. Then its snorting changed to a guttural moo-roar and, with a sudden dip of its head, the bull charged.

The crowd screamed as the bull picked Giridhar up by his narrow waist and, with a toss of its head, flung him yards away. The youth lay stunned for a second then leapt to his feet.

Giridhar did not wait. He charged the bull. As the spectators cheered, he caught the beast by its horns but was tossed away again. The bull stood triumphant in the middle of the arena.

Unfazed, Giridhar rushed at the bull again. The bull, too, lunged towards him.

This time around, Giridhar neatly side-stepped the animal. Surprised, it stopped in its tracks. That was enough for Giridhar. He caught the bull's horns from behind and, with a powerful jerk, twisted the animal's head to one side. Disoriented, the bull was slow to react. There was perfect silence as the crowd watched in suspense.

Muscle strained against muscle as man and beast pitted their strength against each other. After what seemed to be an interminable minute, Giridhar slowly, but surely, started to bring the bull's head down, inch by strenuous inch.

Summoning all his latent strength and breathing his yogic prana vahyu, Giridhar gave one final push downwards on the horns. And it was over. The bull went down on its forelegs. Then it toppled over.

The crowd went wild. Cheering men flooded the arena and smothered Giridhar with garlands. They swept him off his feet and threw him into the air, catching him as he came down. Through the cloud of petals the women threw, they carried him in a victory lap around the arena. The women ululated. The boys whistled while the girls screamed their heads off and almost swooned over their newfound dream-boy.

For the moment, Giridhar was the people's god.

The bull, subdued, allowed itself to be led away by Gokul's men.

So ended the festivities of the harvest. The Champakapuris were satisfied that they had given their sun god a fitting sendoff.

But much as he admired Giridhar's feat, Ramdas went home feeling sorry for the bull. He could not understand the sentiment but he felt there was something vulgar and undignified in forcing a proud beast to come down on its knees.

Ramdas had no idea that, in time to come, the bull would suffer the same indignity, at *his* hands.

Three months later, a most feared phenomenon occurred. There was a total solar eclipse. The temple priest had pre-warned the villagers about it.

"Go into your room," Ganga ordered Mukta well before the start of the eclipse. "Sit still. And don't even begin to think of anything unpleasant. Otherwise you'll have a shaitan for a child."

Other elderly women of the village were shooing mothers-to-be likewise. One didn't fool around when the monster deity, Rahu, was about to swallow the Sun.

It is said that Rahu (of the dragon-head and comet-tail) once displeased the gods. He saw the gods drinking soma, an ambrosial beverage, reserved only for them. Envious, he took on the appearance of a god and joined in the soma-drinking. But the Sun and Moon found him out. They reported the matter to Vishnu. And Vishnu sliced off his head with his spinning disc. Rahu fell to the Earth. But his severed head, still alive, rose to the sky.

Since then, he took revenge on the Sun and Moon by occasionally swallowing them. And woe betide anyone who dared look upon the sight.

"Make sure you don't pinch your ear," Ganga told Mukta. "If you do, your child will be born with a nicked ear. And don't pinch your nose either or he'll have a crooked nose."

All over Champakapur, similar taboos were flying right and left.

Don't chop vegetables or your baby will be born without limbs.

Don't clip your nails or your child will have no fingers.

Don't tear cloth or cut anything with scissors. If you do, your child will have a harelip.

Don't look out the window. Better still, close it. Otherwise, you may see a monkey and your child will look and behave like one. Look at the village idiot. While his mother was carrying him, she saw a baboon during a solar eclipse!

And it went on. Don't sew. Don't eat. Don't drink ...

As the day turned to unnatural night, the men in the fields downed their tools and returned home, careful not to look up at the sky. They did not eat nor drink for the duration of the eclipse. Neither did they make love. Children conceived during an eclipse would be born blind, deaf or dumb.

There was a strange stillness in the land. Even the animals and birds, by some primordial instinct, restricted their movements.

Mukta suffered herself to be sequestered in her dark room. She paid heed to all the Don'ts and just lay on her bed. She thought only of her unborn son and all the motherly things she would do for him. Mukta was sure it would be a boy. After all, had not the all-knowing Chenggamma herself predicted a boy-child? The old woman's keen eyes had just glanced at Mukta's bare belly and she had announced, "Notice how her wide belly spreads to her hips, Ganga. It's going to be a boy. If it's a girl, the belly will be narrow and more pointed to the front."

After Rahu regurgitated the sun, the people cleansed their homes and bathed. Then they offered prayers and ate only vegetarian food for the day.

Satisfied with the list of taboos she had imposed on Mukta, Ganga believed that her grandchild would be born without any defects.

Mukta shared her mother-in-law's belief.

Ramdas remained a detached observer of the goings-on during the eclipse. As with curses, so with superstitions: he did not believe in them. With a faultless mother like Mukta and a father like him, he was sure his son would be born whole—physically, mentally and spiritually.

Vrishabha

Mukta gave birth to a spanking boy-child at twenty minutes past nine on the morning of 20 May 1870, five months after the harvest.

Ganga, Chenggamma and Manglamba helped with the birth.

Ganga and Chenggamma played dai. As midwives, they got ready the bricks on which Mukta would squat to deliver the baby. They also helped massage her back and rubbed ghee in the birth canal for easy birth. When the time came, they delivered the baby and wound a band of cloth around Mukta's waist for her to regain her shape.

Manglamba was present to give a helping hand. She prepared two drinks. First, she boiled the milk-and-jaggery drink that would dilate Mukta's uterus. Then she extracted the juice from the Indian mulberry that would shrink the uterus after birth. Later, she would bury the neem-leaf-wrapped placenta in the farthest corner of the compound behind the house.

As soon as the baby was born, Manglamba ran to the doorstep with a brass tray and a metal ladle. She held up the tray and beat it like a gong. The clanging noise could be heard all over the village. It sent the birds flapping away in fear and little animals scurrying for cover. Not only that, its clamour, the people believed, scared away evil spirits like preta and bhuta. The spirits, attracted by the scent of warm blood, were hovering to enter the newborn's body and devour him from within.

All the villagers stopped in their tracks when they heard the beating of the gong. Then, they went about their business, knowing a baby had been born.

The baby was jambu-pink. (It was not in vain that Ganga had got Mukta to drink a tumbler of milk mixed with a generous pinch of saffron every night since the eighth month of pregnancy, to give the baby a lovely complexion.) A shock of black, curly hair and round eyes were his most distinguishing features. Until Ganga made her discovery.

"Ten fingers ... ten toes ... everything's there," Chenggamma announced through the piercing cries of the infant.

Mukta sighed with relief. Her sweat-drenched face portrayed calmness completely opposite to that of the contortion just before the birth.

"Look!" Ganga exclaimed, pointing to the infant's crown as she washed his hair. "He has double whorls!"

Chenggamma and Manglamba peered in the semi-darkness of the room to see for themselves the two adjacent whorls. It could mean only one thing.

"He'll have two wives," Chenggamma stated matter-of-factly.

No one refuted her statement.

When the baby had been bathed, Ganga presented him to Ramdas and Raghunath. The men had been pacing outside the room like cats with litters.

Ramdas swelled with pride. All he could say was, "My son!" Then he felt an unfamiliar lump in his throat. It prevented him from saying anything further.

"He's come right out of his father's mould," Raghunath commented as he stroked the baby's plump cheek. "And look how well hung my grandson is. Ramdas, your son's going to father an army!"

"All the better to oust the Inglistans!"

"At last, I'm a grandmother," Ganga said and sighed with contentment.

"Yes," Raghunath said. "And now that I've seen my grandson, can I go out and fight that bull?"

Ramdas wasted no time in buying sweetmeats at the village sweet shop. He distributed the sugar-encrusted laddoo and syrupy jelebi to every Champakapuri household as he went about announcing the birth of his son.

"*Ashirwaad!*" the villagers blessed Ramdas and his son.

On the same day, Ramdas went to the temple on a very important errand: to find out the baby's star sign, but only at the insistence of his parents and Mukta.

Told the exact time of birth, the priest went through his astrology charts. His self-importance was evident. He knew he was the only person for miles around who could decipher the ancient Sanskrit codes stylus-ed on sheaves of dried palm fronds. He was the Champakapuri authority on births and deaths.

"Vrishabha," the priest announced. "The baby was born when the sun entered the House of Vrishabha. It's associated with the sign of the bull."

"Is it a good sign to be born under?" Ramdas asked. No one in his family was a Vrishabha.

"It all depends. He can grow up to be hefty, strong and physically commanding, like the bull. These qualities, coupled with intelligence and spiritual strength, will take him far. But if his spirit is weak, his physical strength will only be a bane on him," the priest explained. "On the other hand, he could be of small stature but his inner strength will make him a giant among men."

Then, he delved into the shashtras and pronounced, "You may name him using one of the sounds beginning 'Na', 'Ne' or 'Ni'. They have the most affinity with his star and augur well for him."

Enlightened, Ramdas thanked the priest and presented him with sweetmeats and a comb of bananas. On his way home, Ramdas was full of dreams: his first-born would be as powerful as a bull and grow up to be a warrior.

They named the baby Nilkanth Rao Bhonsle, on the sixteenth day of his birth. 'Nilkanth' was an epithet for Lord Shiva meaning 'blue throat'. Shiva had done the stupendous by holding in his throat the poison that would have destroyed mankind. While holding the poison, his throat turned blue ('nila'). Hence 'Nilkanth'. Ramdas hoped that, like Shiva, Nilkanth would save, not the world, but the Motherland from the British.

It was sunset, an auspicious time for the naming-ceremony. Lakshmi, the goddess of wealth, visited homes daily at sunset. She would bestow fortunes on the infant and his family.

Before the ceremony, Ramdas had carried his son outdoors. He had lifted him high above his head and, facing the direction of the setting sun, had said, "Killa, on this day I offer you my son. May he take up the sword for you."

Ganga, being the paternal grandmother, had to name the infant. That was the custom. Holding the baby in her arms, she whispered "Nilkanth! Nilkanth! Nilkanth!" three times into its ear, and the baby was considered named.

The baby, disturbed by the whispering in his ear, stirred and stretched, farting with the effort. "My, what a grand fart!" Ganga commented and everyone within earshot laughed.

The baby's eyes wandered, not focussing anywhere in particular. The orbs crossed. This made Mukta frantic with worry.

"Is my son cross-eyed?" she asked Ganga. "Please God, don't let him be!"

She worried in spite of Ganga's reassurance that it was only a temporary occurrence in newborns.

All of Mukta's friends and Ganga's cronies were gathered in Ramdas' house for the ceremony. The patel and his wife were present, too. The patel's booming voice lent an extra air of festivity to the occasion.

Ramdas had purchased a turmeric-coloured cotton sari (he could not afford a silk one) from a travelling merchant. This sari the men now tied into a hammock hanging from the rafters. By right, Mukta's silk nuptial sari should have been used. But that had been looted in Killa.

Ganga passed the infant to Mukta. As Mukta stood with the baby, three young women, their sari ends draped over their heads as custom demanded, waved ghee lamps around the child. "May the Evil Eye be kept at bay. May you live to be a hundred," they blessed.

Then, all the women held the hammock on either side, swung it gently, and sang 'Jojo re Bala', a lullaby. As if on cue, the baby fell asleep.

"How Krishna-like he looks!" commented one of the guests.

The whole family preened at this ultimate of compliments.

For a moment, Mukta caught Ramdas' eye across the room. The rest of the world ceased to exist. Both of them were thinking the same thing: how they loved each other.

Proof of just how much they loved each other came a month later. Before Ganga and her cronies had time even to think of another round of goat testicles and bittergourd, Mukta announced she was with child again.

The family was elated.

"Give me another son!" Ramdas demanded. "I will turn him into a great —"

"General!" Mukta interrupted, laughing. "A great general in the Maratha army. Yes, I know all about that. And what if it's a girl?"

"Then, she too will fight alongside her brothers!"

Ramdas' second son was born three months after the family's second rice harvest, in April 1871. Ramdas named him Madhav Rao Bhonsle. "Madhav Rao was a famous seventeenth-century Maratha general," he explained.

Mukta sighed in resignation.

A shade darker than Nilkanth, Madhav had Mukta's oval face and wavy hair. He was not as robust as Nilkanth but his cries, at times, were lusty enough to wake up the whole neighbourhood.

Mukta settled into her role of motherhood as gracefully as a swan settles over its brood.

During the day, she was very busy. She divided her time equally between her household chores, helping out at the rice field and vegetable garden, and breast-feeding her children in between. Which was why she sat awake late into the night and watched her sons' Krishna-like faces as they slept.

At times, Ramdas joined her vigil. Together, they would gaze down at their offspring, thrilling when they smiled or cried soundlessly in their sleep.

During the afternoons and evenings, Ramdas played with Nilkanth. Nilkanth was over a year old now and could toddle around the house. Ramdas alternately trumpeted or roared as he gave Nilkanth an elephant-ride or lion-ride on his back. And Nilkanth rode him as if he were born to ride elephants (like a king), or ride lions (like a god).

Sometimes, Ramdas walked him to the rice field. There he pointed out to Nilkanth the birds, the butterflies and the beetles; he rolled blades of rice grass into reeds and blew 'pee-pee' sounds on them, much to Nilkanth's delight; he tickled him with rice stalks; and tumbled with him in the hay.

One of the moments Ramdas cherished most was watching Mukta handfeed Nilkanth at night.

Sitting in the verandah, she would coax Nilkanth to eat while reciting in her singsong voice the age-old nursery rhyme 'Chaand Mama', inviting the moon to sail over the mythical Mandra mountain and partake of a whole onion and half a roti.

Ganga, cradling Madhav in her ample lap while Mukta fed Nilkanth, would coo to the infant. She would carry on a one-sided conversation with him, calling him every endearment from batcha to sona to Gokul Das. (They meant 'young one', 'gold' and 'Servant of Vishnu' respectively.)

Grandmotherhood mellowed Ganga. Gone were the last traces of the grumpy and taciturn ways which gripped her during the cessation of her periods. Ganga devoted herself to her grandsons, proudly calling them 'my rajahs'. And she revelled in her grandmotherly duties: drawing along the baby's gums with the point of an unhusked rice grain to facilitate the emerging of milk teeth; coating the baby's tongue with honey daily, for clarity of speech; and tracing the first letter of the Maratha alphabet on the baby's tongue, with a miniature spear, so that he would grow up studious.

Some evenings, she would hoist the children on her hips and waddle down to Chenggamma's hut. There she would allow them to play with the latter's grandchildren. Both grandmothers would then exchange boasts about their wards while the wards exchanged blows in their rough-and-tumble games.

Raghunath relived his own early fatherhood through his grandsons. He recounted every moment of anxiety and joy Ramdas' birth had brought. He remembered how, on the day of the naming-ceremony, he, too, had lifted his infant son high above his head and offered him to Killa.

"The future of Killa lies in hands such as theirs," he remarked of his grandsons to Ganga.

The sun god had made four northward journeys after Madhav's birth. Nilkanth turned five. Madhav was a year younger.

Ramdas did not waste a moment. It was time to start making his dream come true.

He fashioned his sons a toy sword each from a sturdy magnolia branch. They were just like his patta that he surrendered to the British, down to the last vine carving on the hilts. Then he started them off on swordplay.

"Let's play sepoys," he said one day.

"What's 'sepoys', Bah?" Nilkanth asked.

"Sepoys are men or women who fight for the raja. Or rani."

"Like those who fought for Rani Meera Bai, whom you are always talking about?"

"Yes!" Ramdas said, happy that the child was observant. "I, too, am a sepoy, you know." He looked into the distance, remembering.

"Then why aren't you fighting?" The question broke into Ramdas' thoughts.

"Because, son, this isn't the right time. But a time will come soon when you, Madhav, I and many others will rally under the Rani's Tiger Flag and fight our enemy."

"What's 'enemy'?"

"A person who takes what's ours and tries to harm us."

"So who's our enemy?"

"The Inglistan. You haven't seen him yet. His skin is white but his heart is black."

"And what has he taken from us?"

"Our country."

Nilkanth already showed signs of being a born swordsman. For a child, he was lightning-quick at his thrusts and parries. Madhav, however, had to be guided by Ramdas. Ramdas held his hand over the child's and helped him to parry Nilkanth's thrusts. The boys enjoyed their make-believe duels immensely. They liked it best when they lunged at each other, thrust their blunted swords at each other's hearts and fell down 'dead'.

When it came to playing Marathas-and-Inglistans, Nilkanth, taller and stronger, would assume the role of the villain and Madhav would always be the brave sepoy killing the Inglistan.

Ramdas taught his sons to march.

"*LASH-K-A-A-R! Kuch kara!* Left, right! Left, right!" he would bellow and Nilkanth would lead Madhav in a quick march across the front of the house. Madhav mostly fell out of step. It made his watching mother and grandparents laugh but Ramdas impatient.

Then, at Ramdas' command, the boys would charge the rice-field scarecrows, sword-arms extended. Sometimes, they pretended their swords were rifles and 'shot' at the scarecrows, imitating the loud 'toph! toph!' rifle sounds their father made.

Very soon, 'military training' became part of the boys' daily routine. A typical day went like this: washing and bathing at the Lahan Nadi; breakfast; household chores; calisthenics; running three times around the rice-field bunds (anyone who slipped and fell into the mud had to do an extra lap); swordplay; lunch; afternoon nap; tea; climbing up and down a hill; swordplay; bath; dinner; sleep. A year later, the boys' schooling (under the pipal tree) was fitted in between household chores and calisthenics.

As boys will be boys, Nilkanth and Madhav played pucks sometimes. They dallied in the Lahan Nadi, stood to watch egrets or catch crabs while running on the bunds, and strayed to chat with and help their pals herd sheep and goats down the hill. After such escapades, only Mukta's interceding saved them from punishment.

One day, Ramdas, gathering all his courage about him after five years of hiding in Champakapur, ventured to the nearest Deccan city, Haidarabad. It was the capital of the state of the same name. Ramdas aimed to gather news, any news, about Killa. He left disguised with a false beard and moustache. The village natakwallah were kind enough to lend him the items from their stage-drama wardrobe. They even concealed his scar under skin-toned make-up. "Put on a silk outfit and turban and you'll look like the Nizam of Haidarbad himself!" they joked, happy to see Ramdas taking the initiative.

Ramdas returned to Champakapur all fired up.

There were two reasons for this. The first was the natural outcome of visiting the exotic Mohammedan city. Ramdas was ebullient about its Char Minar with marble minarets and domes; its colourful bazaars; its veiled women; and its rows and rows of bangle shops which the city was famous for.

The second reason was, however, more important, as far as Ramdas was concerned.

As he mingled with the crowd at a bazaar, he had overheard a group of men talking in Marathi. He edged closer to the group and picked up snatches of conversation, all the while pretending to examine the stacks of glittering bangles in front of him.

"Prince Dilip lives! Prince Dilip lives!" Ramdas burst out as soon as he reached home. "Ma! Bah! Mukta! Our prince lives! I heard it in the city!"

There was stunned silence from the others.

Ganga was the first to react. Looking up at the Rani's picture she said, "Did you hear that, Rani Meera Bai? Your son lives!" There was a catch in her voice.

"*Dhanyavaad Deva! Dhanyavaad!*" Raghunath thanked God. "I thought he was dead!"

Hearing no word about the prince all these years, the family had presumed that he had been killed after his escape from Killa. Such assassinations were common. Even the occasional passing travellers in Champakapur said that they had not heard any news about the prince and that they feared the worst.

"Where's he now?" Mukta asked, gathering her sons about her.

The boys were wide-eyed. They looked from one elder to the other, puzzled. They had never seen such animation in their faces.

"In a secret hide-out. That's what they said. Somewhere in the forested valleys of the Godavari River."

"At last, there's hope for Killa," Raghunath said.

"And you know what? The Diwan is alive, too. He's with the prince."

"I think the Diwan will start marshalling the troops now," Raghunath speculated.

"Not so soon, Bah. I heard he's training up the prince first before making any major move."

"The prince must be eleven now. Poor thing! How he must be missing his mother,"

Ganga was all sympathy. "May the day come soon when he will avenge his mother's death and be enthroned as Maharajah of Killa."

The whole night, they talked of nothing but Killa.

From the Haidarabad trip onwards, Ramdas became like one possessed. He drove his sons over the limit, in the name of Killa.

The boys protested.

"But Bah, today we want to catch butterflies," they would chorus.

Or, "It's windy. We want to fly kites."

Or, "We want to play marbles with Pravin."

"There'll be enough time for all that later," Ramdas answered gruffly, "but for now, Killa comes first."

"Killa! Killa! Killa! Is that all you can think about, Bah?" Madhav chided in his childish way, a smile hovering behind the mock glare he gave his father.

"The child is too young to understand your fervour, nawra," Mukta interceded. "Give him some time. After all, he's only five! And look at Nilkanth, he sulks all the time."

Nilkanth was staring balefully at his father. It shocked Ramdas that a child could look that way.

"Say what you will," a miffed Ramdas said. "But hear this. A mollycoddled boy will not a general make!"

Brushing aside even his parents' protests, Ramdas continued with his sons' training. And every session inexorably ended with the victory cry, Killa *ka Jai!*

Ramdas carved his sons wooden rifles, almost like the originals, and taught them how to 'handle' the firearms. He made them catapults and honed their aiming skills. They progressed from large paddy-field egrets to small rooftop sparrows. The boys soon became crack shots. Ramdas fashioned toy soldiers from clay. Then he placed them on a map of Killa which he drew on the ground, and taught his sons war games. When a travelling fair came to Champakapur, he hired one of the horses for a full week to let the boys get the feel of the animal and the saddle. Emboldened after his Haidarabad trip, he started taking the boys to the nearest town for riding lessons. In the meantime, the swordplay lessons continued at home.

Inevitably, other children joined the boys' training. At first they were curious onlookers, turning up daily to watch the brothers being put through their paces. Then, one by one, they asked to participate. Ramdas was overjoyed. He welcomed them and soon Champakapur had an army of child sepoys with Nilkanth and Madhav as their generals.

A perceptible change came over Ramdas and Raghunath after the Haidarabad trip. There was a sudden squaring of the shoulders, a proud tilt of the head, lightness in the stride, and an expectant look in the eyes (as if the prince would ride into Champakapur any minute).

The Champakapuris noticed. And they understood. As the wise patel put it, "Steal a man's wife, you wound his pride; steal a man's money, you wound his money purse; but steal a man's country and you wound the very depths of his soul. Such a man is like an empty rice husk. He'll not rest until he regains his birthright. Then his soul will heal and he'll become whole, like the full-grained husk."

Ramdas made more incognito trips to Haidarabad in the hope of gathering more information. He expected to hear any time that the Diwan had ordered a secret call-up in the Godavari Valley. But he heard no such news. However, he did glean that Prince Dilip was raring to fight, youngster though he was. But the Diwan prescribed caution as the British were still alert for any sign of rebellion.

Back home, Ramdas spent the long evening hours telling his sons heroic tales of Rani Meera Bai: how she fought in the thick of battle with two swords, one in each hand, and struck down her enemies; how she shot her targets accurately while riding her horse at full gallop; how she, disguised as a man, led daring raids into British strongholds to save her imprisoned sepoys and dignitaries; and how she rallied Maratha housewives and changed them, almost overnight, into fighting machines. The boys listened, savouring every morsel of information about their father's, and therefore their, queen.

Ramdas told them how he got the centipede scar on his face.

"I got it protecting the Rani. She did not know me then. It was just after the annexation. A representative of the Raj had invited her for talks in his residence. At first, the Rani did not want to go as she was afraid the invitation was a trick to kill her, as the British saw her as their enemy. However, she went against her instincts and decided to meet the representative. For the sake of her people. She hoped some good would come out of the meeting.

I was one of the captains assigned to escort her. We waited just inside the towering doors of the durbar hall. And you know what? The Rani was right.

When she disagreed with his conditions, the Inglistan drew his pistol, saying, 'I will not put up with a rebellious native!' But he was too slow for our Rani. She leapt at him and gauged one side of his face with her bagh nakh."

"What's bagh nakh?" the boys asked in unison.

"The bagh nakh is a set of steel claws worn inside the fist. The wise Rani had taken the precaution of wearing it."

"What happened next?" Nilkanth asked.

"We rushed to her aid and fought the British sepoys. There were ten of us against thirty. That was when I got the cut." Ramdas paused, remembering. The bleeding had been profuse, the suturing a torture. "Anyway, the Rani escaped in her waiting carriage. And we escaped without losing any lives. The siege of Killa began soon after that."

From then on, the boys looked with awe at the scar and told all their friends about its history.

Raghunath, on his part, spoke of one greater than Rani Meera Bai—Chatrapati Shivaji Bhonsle, the Maratha monarch who had been the nemesis of the powerful Moghuls. He engaged the boys with tales of

Shivaji's daring exploits and conquests, his fairmindedness towards Hindus, Muslims and Christians, his kindness and his piety.

Shivaji especially forbade his sepoys to molest the enemy's women and destroy temples, mosques and churches. Those caught doing so would be hanged. "How much Rani Meera Bai resembled Chatrapati Shivaji," Raghunath said.

Ganga and Mukta described to the boys the magical flight of the swans after the Rani died. The boys listened, engrossed. They had never seen a swan. They ran to the schoolmaster's house and had him show them a picture of swans in flight. After that, they made paper swans (with one larger than the others) and ran holding them above their heads, imagining the swans were flying in the sky with the Hamsa swan leading.

"Tell us more about the Hamsa," the boys said.

Ganga and Mukta told them.

"It was the bird that laid the First Egg. And inside the Egg was the World."

"The Hamsa has the power to separate milk from water."

"And it can change into a beautiful maiden whenever it wants to."

"It's intelligent, and can distinguish good from bad. That's why Saraswathi, the goddess of learning, chose it as one of her symbols."

"You can recognise a Hamsa easily. When other swans take off from a pond, you'll see water dripping off their bodies, wings and legs. But the Hamsa never gets wet."

The boys were amazed.

Thus, as the months flew by, Ramdas, Raghunath, Ganga and Mukta imbued the boys with a deep sense of their heritage and impressed upon them the urgent need to rid Killa of the British.

"Killa, my boys, is only a dream away," Ramdas used to say.

The sun god made yet another journey to the north but still the Haidarabad grapevine yielded no positive word from the Diwan.

Nilkanth turned seven. "He's going to be a heart-throb when he grows up, Mukta," the village women predicted, seeing his increasing fairness, thick eyelashes and perfect proportions. In size, he was a jallikattu bull-calf compared to the other Champakapuri boys of his age. At any test of strength—wrestling, barbell lifting, club-swinging—Nilkanth would win. He could even win a tug-of-war singly against his playmates.

What a general my son's going to make, Ramdas thought. But something disturbed him. Twice he caught Nilkanth bullying his playmates. On one occasion, Nilkanth wrestled down his friend, snatched his marbles and ran away. On another, for no reason he kicked and destroyed the sandcastle a girl was building by the river. Ramdas had to force Nilkanth to apologise to the children.

When some parents came complaining about Nilkanth, Ramdas became alarmed. They variously said Nilkanth had punched or bitten their son, pinched their daughter, dunked their boy in the Lahan Nadi, drowned their cat, and scalded their cow. "Could you please discipline your son?" they said.

Ramdas was chagrined. He could not fathom Nilkanth. Why's he so different from Madhav? he thought. After all, I shower equal love on both of them. He knew his wife and parents, too, doted on Nilkanth. Could it be just a passing phase, he wondered.

Ramdas took Nilkanth aside on the occasions parents complained and gave him good, fatherly advice. But Nilkanth continued with his bullying. One day, he even clobbered Madhav on the head for not following his orders during a game. This resulted in Madhav losing consciousness for a moment. Ramdas took Nilkanth aside again but this time he gave him a sound thrashing.

After that, Nilkanth watched his behaviour and complaints from parents ceased. But the episodes left a niggling worry in Ramdas.

Once in a while, Ramdas allowed his mind to stray to the killing of Hanumant Rao. But the thought did not trouble his conscience. He remembered the tense night in the fort, the cheery singing and laughter in the British camp. Obscene singing, obscene laughter, Ramdas thought, an obscene celebration of the death of my noble queen.

Gentle Mukta watched as the boys went through their daily grind of drills and swordplay. But sometimes she remonstrated with Ramdas for taxing their stamina and humour.

"But do you know that your sons are now the best child sepoys around?" Ramdas countered.

"And the best child horsemen, too!" Mukta answered. "But they are children first. Keep that in mind, nawra."

Madhav's parents yearned for Killa. Mukta told him how they eagerly awaited his return from trips to Haidarabad. The trips had become more frequent of late. The old couple clung to every word about the prince and the Diwan. They lost themselves when they described Killa to their grandsons: the magnificent Fort with its Megh Garjana and Agni Astra cannons; the marble palace with its fabulous treasures and secret passages; the city of contented Hindus and Muslims; the grand royal processions when elephants and horses were decked just as ornately as the royals; the annual gymkhana and country fair so filled with acrobatics, juggling, wrestling, music, dance, snake-charming, the cloying smell of attars and sweetmeats, fabrics the colour of the rainbow, and baubles and jingling bangles.

"Let's go to Killa now, Ajjibah," Madhav would say to his grandfather, jumping up and down with excitement.

"Yes. When can we go?" Nilkanth would ask.

"All in good time, my batcha. All in good time. As sure as the sun rises, one day you will see Killa."

When the boys asked where Killa lay, the couple pointed in the direction of the setting sun.

*　　*　　*

Champakapur prospered.

The rains came like clockwork and continued giving life to the land. At times the rain was so torrential it looked like a wall, blocking out the surroundings. During such times, the Lahan Nadi roared its way out of Champakapur. But it never burst its banks. After the rains, the land reciprocated by giving bountiful harvests. Champakapuris knew no hunger.

Ramdas managed to stash away a tidy sum from the sale of surplus rice from his harvests. Unlike the lean times when he had to buy a cotton sari for Nilkanth's naming-ceremony, Ramdas could now afford to buy silk clothes for his whole family. He even bought Mukta a pair of gold bangdi from Haidarabad.

Mukta did not waste any time showing them off to her friends. The rope-patterned bangles were studded with red crystals. The friends, in turn, showed off their newly bought bangles, rings and nose studs. Their husbands, too, had rupees to spare.

Now that he had the means, real swords for his sons were next on Ramdas' agenda. He had in mind single-edged patta with curving blades of wootz and with, perhaps, a little silver inlay on the hilts.

For Ramdas, Champakapur was still a safe haven. A few times, he thought he had almost been recognised when some sepoys looked at him twice in Haidarabad. "Haven't I seen you somewhere before?" one even asked. "Now let me see ..." Before the man could finish, Ramdas vanished into the crowd, his heart pounding like a kettledrum. Though he heard no new word from the prince or the Diwan, Ramdas was confident that the call-up would come soon. And he was prepared for it. What better place to train his sons than in the company of the Maratha masters of war in the Godaveri Valley.

The population of Champakapur multiplied.

Chenggamma, Manglamba and Saroja all boasted of more grandchildren. So did the other old folks. There was talk of setting up a school building for the children as they were still studying under the trees. The patel was relegated the task of finding another schoolmaster to assist the present one.

As the people multiplied, so did the cattle. And goats. And ducks. And chicken.

Gokul's herd expanded, thanks to his jallikattu bull. He had to build four new cow sheds.

Dudhwallah Shankar would, from time to time, tease Ramdas good-naturedly: Ramdas, my goats have more than trebled. Would you, by any chance, want to purchase some goat testicles?

The magnolia grove lengthened along the Lahan Nadi. Children frolicked under the grove's shade by day. By night, it continued harbouring romantic young couples, Ramdas and Mukta included. And the demand for Chenggamma's Attar of Magnolia spread from Haidarabad to Secunderabad.

Life was happy and peaceful in Champakapur. As far as the Bhonsles and Champakapuris were concerned, it was the most beautiful place on earth: a verdant oasis wearing a lustrous purple crown in the semi-arid Deccan.

Then disaster struck.

*   *   *

By the time the Sinister Sisters—Drought and Famine—had had their way with Champakapur, it was nothing but an ugly brown scar on the face of the Deccan.

Drought, the elder sister, came first.

She came in the form of a searing wind, cartwheeling in powerful gusts over the plateau. Devoid of moisture, she moaned her barrenness as she swept across the land, embracing everything in her path as if they would give to her the moisture she so craved.

Champakapuris gaped as her bone-dry fingers touched the pregnant rice heads, the lush vegetables and fruit, the sweet white jasmine and the magnificent purple magnolia and shriveled them all into horrible brown masses; they gaped as she forced the plants and trees to suck up every molecule of water from the soil to stay alive, and then die; they gaped as she stripped naked the magnolia trees of their flowers, leaves and barks; and they gaped as she made the Lahan Nadi disappear, leaving a marriage bed of hot stones and pebbles for the mating of Thirst and Hunger.

Drought stayed. No, she overstayed. She watched gleefully as the earth of Champakapur fissured into giraffe-spots and the desperately dug wells dried up. She sniggered when the Champakapuri women made supplications to Indra, the rain god: the first year the rains failed, they held marriage ceremonies for frogs all over the rice fields; the second year, they paraded a naked virgin in the dead of night around the village; and the third year, all the women descended to the rice fields at midnight, stripped, ploughed a token patch and planted germinating seeds in it.

127

Nothing worked.

Delight filled Drought as she saw the Champakapuris walk about with their tongues hanging out, like their dogs. She danced when the buds of life in women's wombs withered and died. She waited patiently for her younger sister, Famine, to join her.

Famine, uglier than Drought, arrived the following year and completed the havoc her sister had started.

Famine grinned like a devil as the level of rice in Champakapuri rice bins dropped day by day. She cackled when the haystacks shrank and the farm animals started tottering about. She revelled at the 'death' sign stamped on every face in Champakapur.

Their missions completed, the Sinister Sisters waited for their lord and master, Yama the death god, to visit. In the meantime, they gloated over their victory.

Finally, ugly Yama visited. Dressed in blood-red and bile-green robes, he rode into Champakapur on his buffalo. *His* harvest was bountiful.

*   *   *

The Champakapuris were gathering for the last time.

They stood under the lifeless pipal tree. It looked like inverted black lightning against the sky. Had it been just a year ago that the tree had afforded such cool shade, or had been the hub of their lives? To the befuddled villagers, it seemed more like ten years.

Hollow-eyed, hollow-cheeked and hollow-bellied they waited like zombies for the patel to address them.

"My dear Champakapuris," the patel rasped. The couple of surviving pittas pecking around his ankles did not fly away. "The time has come for us to part. I know I speak all your minds when I say that we leave Champakapur with leaden hearts. It will be difficult to find another Champakapur on the face of this land." The gaunt patel paused to catch his breath. "Soon, Champakapur will become just a memory. But wherever we go or whatever we do, let us not forget the peace we enjoyed in Champakapur, the kindness and cooperation we practiced, and all the little blessings Bhagavan has given us, though why He chose to punish us this way escapes me." Another pause as he looked at the haunted faces before him. The faces were partially hidden as the people held their towels or sari ends to their noses to block the stench of the putrid carcasses of farm animals and birds littering the village; a sickening stench to replace the heady perfume of their magnolias. "Let us each plant a little piece of Champakapur in the new places we go to. Then, Champakapur will live forever. What is lost is lost. Let us set out with hope for a better tomorrow. May Bhagavan be with all of you."

Too weak with emotion, the patel sat on the ground. The people nearest to him hovered around in concern. But he regained his composure soon and stood up.

"Come, my fellow Champakapuris," he managed to say aloud, "let us leave."

The sun was setting with a brilliance that mocked ravished Champakapur and its people.

Ramdas looked one last time in the direction of the setting sun; the direction of Killa. For a moment, he thought he saw a lone white swan flying across the orange orb of the sun. Or were his eyes playing tricks on him, hunger-crazed as he was?

A crushing sense came over Ramdas. Champakapur had been his closest link with Killa, offering hope, even if it was only a glimmer. He felt as if Drought and Famine had squashed his dream into a bundle, chucked it in his face and said: Here! Take your dream and get out! We care not for noble dreams.

Ramdas carried his invisible dream-bundle. And it weighed him down more than the rice sack he was carrying.

He remembered the occasion when they were forced to flee Killa. But they had fled with hope of returning. Now, hope was lost within a sphere of cracked earth, burning winds and a cruel blue sky.

Sure I've a full money purse at my waist, Ramdas thought, but what good is it? It can't wring water from stones nor pop rice from cracked earth. Only God can. And He's dead.

He turned away from the setting sun and joined the exodus.

The villagers parted four miles out of Champakapur where the single trail diverged into three. The trails lead north, east and south.

No one was going north as they heard that the Sinister Sisters were playing havoc there, too. Most were going far east to the coastal belt called the Coramandel where, travellers said, the rains never failed. Haidarabad in the east, too, was closer. But news had trickled in that people were killing each other for water in the drought-stricken city.

Ramdas and his family had decided to go far south, to the Maratha enclave of Tanjore. They had no choice. The Great Famine was sweeping across all of Central India. And the regions untouched by famine were teeming with the British. So Tanjore it had to be. They heard the city was drought-free and had only a token British presence. It would be another safe haven for Ramdas. But the journey would be long and dangerous.

The patel and his wife had thrown in their lot with the Bhonsles as had Manglamba, Gokul, his two wives and their children.

Chenggamma was dead. Parched and shrunken, she had been the first victim of the calamity. Dozens of old men and women had followed her. So had infants, including two of Chenggamma's grandchildren. In all, half the Champakapuri population had been wiped out.

There were only a few sniffles as farewells were said. Most were too weak to cry. The village idiot created a small diversion, insisting that he wanted to follow Nilkanth and Madhav whereas his family was going east. He had to be dragged away by his parents.

"Ganga Bai, I'll go-and-come," Saroja tried to sound optimistic as she took leave. Her voice was steady as she took her friend's hands in hers. "I'm sure we'll meet again some day."

"Go-and-come, Saroja Bai. Let's hope we all survive our journeys." Ganga's tone was flat. It held no hope.

As the groups separated, there was only one thing on their minds: survival.

How long will our rations last? Ramdas thought. A sack of rice, a packet of salted mutton, the last few flasks of water, milk from Gokul's decimated herd, and meat from a dozen straggling goats. What happens when we finish the rice? No, we'll eat the goats first and keep the rice for last. What happens when we finish the water? We'll not drink the water first. We'll drink goat blood as we slaughter them for food. When we run out of blood, we'll drink cow's milk. We'll keep the water to the last for cooking rice and drinking. What happens when all the goats have been eaten? We'll eat the salted mutton. What happens when the salted mutton finishes? We'll eat the rice. And when the rice finishes? We'll eat the— No! We can't eat the cows! It's unthinkable!

Ramdas watched the eastbound group ghost in the distance. Then, Ramdas' group set forth into the vast silence. There were no birdcalls, no insect chirps, no dog barks. Not even the moan of the wind. Around him, Ramdas heard the shuffling of feet and hoofs and the ding-dong of the bell on the jallikattu bull. To him, the bell sounded like a death knell.

Out in front, he saw Nilkanth and Madhav, his little generals, lead the band of children. All the children, grimy even at the start of the journey, carried their own bundles of clothes.

Nilkanth and Madhav carried their clothes-bundles over their shoulders—hung on the blades of their toy swords.

PART TWO

Tara Bai

"Tara Bai! Will you move your bottom off that swing and come in at once! It's time you bathed and dressed!" Mother shrieks from inside the Mahal. "Be warned, this is the last time I'm calling you!" Pause. Then, "If you don't come in now, I'll come out with a dildo and shove it up your c#*t!!"

Mother's shriek jolts me out of my reverie.

Violent words. Violent woman. How many times has she been calling me, I wonder. For the past half-hour, my body has been on the swing but my spirit has been in another world: that ordinary yet enticing world that lies beyond the Mahal's prison-like walls.

In that ordinary world, I live with an ordinary husband in an ordinary house.

We make ordinary love and have ordinary children. We wear ordinary clothes and eat ordinary food. We go to ordinary places and mix with ordinary people. We experience ordinary joys and ordinary sorrows. We even have ordinary diseases and die ordinary deaths.

Oh for an ordinary life! What I wouldn't give to live an ordinary life.

I don't flinch at my mother's words. Dildo. C#*t. They're part of my mother's vocabulary and trade, not mine. She has flung the words at me so often they roll off me like water droplets from a lotus leaf. But Mother has not always been this way. Only of late.

I smile as I stroke the ruffled feathers of the cockatoo perched on my wrist. Startled by Mother's outcry, the bird raises its crest and squawks in alarm.

"There! There! My popat," I coo. "Don't you be scared by Mother's shrieks. You know how she is. Her shriek is worse than her shove."

The cockatoo, calmed, lowers its sulphur-yellow crest and makes a throaty sound. The bird's an exotic gift to Mother from a maharajah. They say he brought it back from his travels to the distant land of Malai Nadu.

I remain on the swing. It's hung from a branch of the spreading gul mohar tree in a corner of the Mahal garden. Thick jute ropes support the swing. I've been playing on this swing since I was four. Now, at twenty, I still thrill as I swing, my eyes half-closed and my tresses flying behind me.

I cuddle the fidgety cockatoo to my breast. Around me, the garden is alive with bird-twitters and the scent of musk roses. A pair of peacocks struts about, showing off gay plumage. The whole garden is bathed in the rays of the setting sun. Which is precisely why I'm drawn to the garden every evening. I love the touch of gold on the gul mohar and cassia, begonias and balsams, parrots and peacocks, fountains and ponds, and the marble facade of the Mahal.

Of particular charm to me is the play of gold on the displayed trains of the peacocks. At sunset, their iridescent blues, purples and greens shimmer with a fine mist of gold. The fans of the gods must look like this, I think.

There's a slamming of doors inside the Mahal. The next minute, the door leading to the garden is thrown open. Mother fills the doorway. She is about to ruin a perfectly lovely evening. And not for the first time.

She's flanked by two hijra. Compared to her, the eunuchs look puny. She can haul me (people say I'm wispy) all the way into the Mahal by herself but has thought the better of it (people also say I'm spirited); hence the extra help.

She charges down the tiled garden path, her breasts—big as pomeloes—knocking against each other. She looks diabolic, walking between the hijra: like the *Ramayana* demon, Surpa-nakha, flanked by her brothers.

I get up from the swing and carry the cockatoo to its gilt cage hanging from a branch of the gul mohar. Depositing the bird inside, I whisper, "I'm sorry I have to return you to your cage. If you'd been mine,

I'd have set you free long ago." I bolt the cage door. "You know, I'm also a prisoner like you. But don't worry. One day, you and I, we'll both be free."

Mother stands glowering at me. Her square shoulders, thrown back to their full extent, hint at the ox-like strength in her. In her hands she brandishes what, to me, is the most dreaded of objects: the dildo. The solid gold phallus reflects the sun's rays. The rays are golden darts of terror piercing my heart.

"Pin her down!" Mother orders the eunuchs.

The sari-clad hijra, one fair and the other dark, are only too glad to obey. They have me floored in a second. Grinning, the masculine lines of their faces showing through their thick face-powder, they bear down on me. They can't wait to see the coming action.

In a flash, I remember another incident when I was thus pinned down: two old courtesans holding me and squeezing onion juice into my eyes. They were punishing me for refusing to play with the sex gadgets they offered as part of my initiation into the world of the courtesan. Good courtesans start young, they said. But I insisted on playing with the Indian prince and princess dolls one of my mother's paramours had bought for me. I remember how my eyes stung with the onion juice and how I screamed. I was six then.

Will Mother really carry out her threat now? She has not on many previous occasions, always stopping short before the moment of violence. Amid the crusted layers of lust, greed, ambition and frustration in my mother, I know there is, trapped somewhere in between, the molten lava of love for me, her only child. So I call her bluff.

"Go ahead, Mother. Take away my virginity! That's all you've been wanting to do all these years, haven't you? Go on, violate me. After that find a good explanation to give to the Rich Citizen." Then I give her a shock. "He's paid you a hundred mohur to deflower me, hasn't he?"

Mother looks stunned. She thinks her business transaction of a hundred gold coins a secret, carried out as it was in the dead of night, in the garden, with only a nightjar for witness. But she made the mistake of confiding in an old courtesan who is sympathetic towards me.

"My child, why can't you be like the rest of us? Why are you so different?" Mother neatly sidesteps my question.

I make no answer. How do you explain being different? How do you explain hating alien hands touching your most private parts in a place where private-part touching is as ordinary as brushing your teeth or having a cup of coffee? Perhaps it has something to do with my accidental discovery of the secret Kaala Kothri (Black Cell) deep under the Mahal. I was twelve then. I shivered and remained feverish for days after seeing the vision of 'retired' courtesans: they were ghoulish, smelling of putrefaction, screaming, groaning, crawling, their bodies were oozing puss, and bits of their flesh were dropping to the floor. It made me determined never to be a courtesan.

"Why are you giving us so much trouble?" Mother's looks soften as she kneels beside me. She signals to the eunuchs to release me.

They spring away and I sit up. The hijra pout in disappointment, cheated out of their fun.

"We're courtesans, Tara, courtesans! We're born into this ganika profession. Nobody can change that."

"I can."

"Look, we've been through this umpteen times —"

"Just give me a chance, Mother. Find me an ordinary husband beyond these walls and I'll prove we can live and love like all those women out there."

"But we're not those ordinary women, Tara. We're the Koh-i-noors of society. Even kings and princes seek us out. Not to mention pundits, brahmans and poets. And we serve them. It's our karma."

"Yes, Tara," the fair eunuch interjects, knowing Mother will not mind. "Surely you remember the law of dharma?"

The dark eunuch speaks, emboldened by his companion's words.

"The law says if you are born a prostitute you must remain a prostitute all your life."

I slap him.

He starts to snivel.

"Be off with you, hijra!" Mother dismisses him. "I hate sniveling men." Turning to me, she says, "What's to become of me, Tara? Are you going to leave me destitute in my old age?"

"Destitute? Mother, the wealth you've fleeced off men will last you two lifetimes!"

"Pah! It won't even last a couple of years, considering my lifestyle." Pause. "Just think of all the things I've done for you." She tries to make me feel guilty. "I've given you the best of everything. The best of food. The best of clothes. The best of jewels. The best of tutors —"

"Only to one end!"

Mother ignores me.

"I'd have even given you the best of lovers, if only you'd let me. Why, the late Maharajah offered a thousand gold pieces for a single night with you. Be grateful he was an honourable monarch. He respected your excuse that you weren't ready for him yet.

Anyone with such power could have bundled you off to the palace with a snap of his fingers. Goodness child! Don't you know how devastatingly beautiful you are? You could be the lifelong mistress of any king!"

"And end up like you? Discarded like an old rag because of the disease you carry?" (I wonder how long it will be before she is thrown into the Kaala Kothri.) "Can't you see, Ma, were're just exotic moths attracted to the fire that will consume us?"

"That, too, is part of our karma."

"I'm not interested in maharajah or merchant. All I want is an ordinary husband who will love and care for me for the rest of my life."

"And will your ordinary husband give you all that you're accustomed to? Silks? Gold? Diamonds? Ghee sweetmeats? Lavender perfumes? Goat-milk baths? Why, I'm sure the ordinary man can't even afford cheap rose-water baths, let alone goat-milk baths!"

"I can learn to live without all these luxuries, Mother. I've read that if we're prudent with our money, we can lead a comfortable life anywhere."

"So that's it! You've been reading too much. I was wondering where you got your notions from." Mother is silent for a moment. Then, "It's my fault. I shouldn't have given you all those books to read. I should've limited you to the Kama Shastras and Vedas only." Another pause as she examines her deeply grooved fingernails. "What about those ordinary people out there? Do you think they'll accept you? I doubt it. They act holier-than-thou and are ignorant to boot. They know nothing of the respect accorded to us in high circles. And you know what a marriage between a courtesan and an ordinary man will look like? Like a marriage between a peacock and a crow!"

Then she plays her trump card.

"And what if the outside world asks you who your father is? You wouldn't be able to answer! I suppose you never thought of that."

The stalemate that follows is punctured by the clanging of the bell from the nearby Brihadisvara Temple. It signals the time for the temple's sunset puja.

Dusk, like a pimp, is knocking on the doors of the Mahal to stir my sister courtesans into motion. After their languorous slumbers of the day, it's time for the women to get ready for the delights, carnal or otherwise, of the long night ahead.

"I'm asking you for the last time, Tara. In fact, I'm begging you." There's desperation in Mother's voice. "Be reasonable and accept my arrangement. In the long run, it will benefit both of us."

"It will definitely benefit you, Mother. You'll be able to continue leading your cushy life, on my earnings. But it will be hell for me."

"Take up the offer, Tara. Secure your future. The man's willing to keep you for the rest of your life." She strokes my cheek tenderly, hoping to win me over. "Rich Citizens are not easy to come by these days, you know. Not with the British levying such heavy taxes. Look how they've impoverished even royalty! And there's talk the British want to stamp out our time-honoured profession. Come, Tara. All I want is for you to be the richest woman in the city. Now, is that so wrong?"

"I'm sorry, Mother. No."

"Then I'm sorry, too. You give me no choice."

Saying "Quick! Hijra!", Mother pounces on me. So does the eunuch.

Between them, they drag me—screaming and kicking—into the Mahal.

The Arsa Mahal

The district of Tanjore in South India is so antiquated it is even mentioned more than two millennia ago in the history of the Indian Mauryan Empire and in the AD 80 periplus of the Greeks. Both praise Tanjore civilisation to the skies.

Successive South Indian dynasties shaped Tanjore into an eminent kingdom. Not only did Arab and Malay Archipelago seafarers frequent its ports but also Chinese from Cathay. And by the time King Rajaraja Chola of the Tamil Chola Dynasty came to power in the tenth century, Tanjore was poised for even greater fame.

Rajaraja Chola was the most luminous of the powerful Cholas. He had great dreams. Amongst the first was to build a new capital for his Chola Empire. The empire encompassed almost the whole of South India, Ceylon, the Nicobar Islands and many islands beyond.

So, while the Fatimids of Egypt were building an academic powerhouse in the Al-Azhar Mosque in Cairo and while the Incas of Peru were building their capital in Cuzco, Rajaraja Chola set about building a sprawling temple-city as his new capital. He would call the city Tanjore. He chose for its location the right bank of the Cauvery where the river began to fan out into the flood-plains of the delta.

When built, Tanjore rose to be a centre for religion, the arts and industry. Its fortified walls protected monumental temples, lavish palaces, exquisite frescoes and invaluable bronze icons. Libraries and music academies flourished. And the most classical of Indian dances— the Bharathanatyam—was born in Tanjore.

Under Rajaraja Chola and his son, Rajendra Chola, Tanjore's fame burgeoned. It became well known not only for its promotion of the

Hindu religion, scholarly enterprises and performing arts but also for its ambitious naval expeditions to Bengal and Southeast Asia. The Cholas even had China in their sights.

If the Chola Dynasty developed Tanjore arts and culture, then the Maratha Dynasty honed them. The Marathas were the last rulers of Tanjore from the seventeenth to the nineteenth century. Under Maratha auspices, especially during the reign of Maharaja Sarabhoji Bhonsle, the unique gold-leaf Tanjore painting, pottery, sculpture, silk weaving and the collection of ancient Devanagari manuscripts reached an apex. Bharathanatyam, too, peaked in the Tanjore Maratha Court.

It was during a very brief stint of Moghul control before Maratha rule that the Arsa Mahal joined the silhouettes of Tanjore temples, towers and palaces.

After the Brihadisvara Temple and the Palace, the Arsa Mahal was the most outstanding structure in Tanjore. It was an oddity amidst the Chola architecture. Its Moghul-inspired domes contrasted starkly with the many-tiered gopuram, or entrance towers, and vimhana, or deity-shrine towers, of the city's temples. But it more than made up for the difference with its striking beauty.

The Arsa Mahal had been built by a sixteenth-century sultan for his favourite begum.

After their deaths, it had fallen into disuse until a maharaja with exotic tastes chose it to house his exotic harem. It is said the harem dazzled with prized beauties from Turkey, Arabia, Persia, Burma, Kashmir and even Mongolia. These beauties were inducted into courtesan life. The present residents were descendents of these courtesans.

The Mahal was set far away from the palace zenana where queens and other female members of the royal family were secluded.

The Arsa Mahal was, in effect, a small palace.

The pink-marble edifice featured two cavernous halls (the Shastra Hall and the Nautch Hall) separated by an open courtyard, a kitchen, a servants' and slaves' quarters, a common bath, a stable, and gharri and palanquin bays. All these were on the ground floor.

The top floor boasted forty apartments: ten apartments set against each wall of the square-shaped Mahal. Courtesans lived in these apartments. The common balcony running outside the apartments looked upon the central courtyard below. There were no balconies along the outer walls for fear commoners would lay eyes on the courtesans. The courtesans were that jealously guarded. Only small, rectangular windows opened to the outside world, but even these were screened by intricate marble latticework. The rooms were ventilated by the long windows facing the balconies and courtyard.

From each corner of the first floor of the Mahal, a staircase curved down to the ground floor. Another short flight of steps led up to the four domed towers of the Mahal.

Armed guards stood at these towers and also at the gates below.

The uniqueness of the Arsa Mahal lay in its exquisite cut-mirror—arsa—motifs and panels. The sultan who built the Mahal had fully exploited the talents of the pool of local craftsmen called netti. They lived along the artists' street called Chitrakar. These craftsmen were famed in the land for their cut-mirror work.

Using a home-made glue of cooked tamarind kernel powder that could withstand the tropical heat, the craftsmen embedded in the walls of the Mahal myriads of hand-cut mirrors. The mirrors were no bigger than a pea. They were cut into triangles, diamonds, squares, rectangles, circles, pentagons and octagons. The craftsmen created the most breathtaking motifs with the mirrors. Here a flower; there a fruiting tree; here again an animal; and there again a bird. Each motif was delineated and bordered with precious stones, pearls and mirror-tiles. The motifs adorned the inner walls of the Mahal.

Not only that. The fountain in the courtyard was embellished with cut mirrors, too.

The fountain was in the form of a circle of five life-size elephants showering water on the images of the apsaras, divine courtesans in the heaven of Indra. These ravishing nymphs—Rambha, Urvasi and Menaka—stood in various stages of undress in the middle of a water-lily pond. The elephants' shawls and head decorations, the apsaras' robes and the edges of the pond were all done in cut mirrors. They said that

143

if you looked hard enough at the fountain at midnight during the full moon, when the mirrors reflected a thousand moonbeams, you would see Indra himself cavorting with the apsaras in the fountain.

The pillars of the halls and balconies were embellished with entwining vines and grapes of the same cut mirrors. Even the ceiling of the halls and rooms glittered with huge lotus motifs, the lotus being favoured by Saraswathi, goddess of the arts; for what was the Arsa Mahal but a learning place of the arts. The Sixty-four Arts, eroticism included.

"Let me go! Let me go!" Tara screamed as she struggled and kicked to free herself from her mother and the hijra.

In her terror, she did not hear the gush of the courtyard fountain that was usually music to her ears.

Tara did not see the gurus and their courtesan students drop their scrolls and come rushing out of the Shastra Hall to see who was causing such a ruckus.

She did not see or hear the dance and music teachers and their charges in the Nautch Hall falter in their steps or miss their beats and stop in alarm.

The scintillating cut-mirror motifs of a peacock, a cheetah, a basket of rose flowers and a bowl of mangoes along the walls, and the curious courtesans who came out of their apartments were only a blur to Tara as she was dragged to her apartment and dumped on the floor.

Dismissing the eunuch with a brusque "Get the palanquin and the guards ready!", Sundari banged the door shut.

Tara's screams ceased.

Shaking their heads, the gurus (all of them male) herded their students into the Shastra Hall to continue with their rudely interrupted studies. "Will she never learn?" they said. "And so ungraceful, too!" Too many times they had seen her screaming and kicking as she was hauled to her room.

The Nautch Hall once again began to fill with the jingling of dancing-bells, the staccato beating of drums and the lilting notes of flutes.

"Ah well! The day had to come!" the courtesans commented as they returned to their apartments to continue dressing for their night engagements.

"How long did she think she could run away from her fate?"

"Poor Sundari! Still supporting her good-for-nothing daughter. Forever reading and playing on the swing! Look at my Champa. She's only fifteen and has already earned a fortune!"

"It's high time Sundari Bai showed her daughter her place in this Mahal."

Like all the other courtesans' apartments, Tara's, too, was spacious and well appointed.

The bedchamber housed a monstrous teak bed with a swan-shaped headboard and a matching teak dressing table and cupboard, all inlaid with ivory and brass; a carpet with cushions and bolsters; a low white-marble table with gilt lion-head legs; and a crystal chandelier and satin punkah hanging from the mirror-studded ceiling.

An attached marble bath and toilet complemented the bedchamber.

Tara's favourite piece of furniture was a Sawantwadi lacquered almirah. The glass-doored almirah held all the literature that was closest to her heart: bound volumes of the Vedas, the Puranas, the epics, the Shastras, and a set of tales on the famous women she so admired and wanted to emulate. There was Sita of the *Ramayana* who epitomised the virtuous wife; there were the ancient Rani Ahalya Bai Holkar, Rani Manggamma and Rani Padmini who had valiantly fought for their kingdoms; there was the Princess Damayanti who remained true to her prince-turned-pauper husband; and, above all, there were Manimekhalai and Vasantasena. The last two were courtesans who, defying their caste, had thrown off their mantle of prostitution. Manimekhalai had spurned a prince to become a Buddhist nun; and Vasantasena had given her body and love to only one man.

Whenever Tara was not dreaming of her ordinary husband, she read and re-read the stories about these courtesans, especially that of Vasantasena.

Sanjna and Sandhya, two jaded courtesan sisters, were already in Tara's room to assist Sundari. Of the two sisters, Sanjna had been Tara's nursemaid.

While Sundari pretended to make a last-minute check on Tara's garments and jewellery, the hefty sisters ripped the clothes off Tara and propelled her into the toilet chamber. They gave her a few minutes alone. Earlier, on Sundari's instructions, they had removed the chamber-door bolts so that Tara could not lock herself inside as she had on previous occasions. When Tara dilly-dallied, they barged into the chamber and hauled her out. They plumped Tara down at the edge of her bath-pool, next to silver pots and jars. The pots brimmed with musk oil, the jars with sandalwood-scented water.

The women massaged Tara with the musk oil. Uncaring whether they hurt her, they rubbed, kneaded and pummeled until they felt Tara's tense muscles relax and saw her body turn luminous. Then they plunged her into the pool and scrubbed her with soap.

During all this, there was not a whimper from Tara, only apparent submission.

Sundari sobbed quietly in a corner of the room, unable to pretend to examine Tara's accoutrements any longer. Determined as she was to have Tara practise her profession, she could not bear the sight of her daughter being roughhoused by others.

Tara reminded her too much of how she had been during her younger days—refined, alluring and single-minded. That she herself had been part of the rough-handling a little earlier mattered none.

Sanjna and Sandhya gave Tara a final shower with the sandalwood-scented water. After rubbing her down, they led the glowing Tara into the bedchamber. There they found Sundari waiting at the bedside, the turmoil within her breast concealed.

Laid out on the bed was the most exquisite ghagra suit. The pleated skirt, narrow at the hips and flared at the hem, and its matching choli were of Chanderi silk gauze. Tiny pearls dotted the gauze. When Tara was dressed, the pink gauze picked up the pink of her skin. And left little to the imagination.

"Child, you could tempt Saint Vishwamiter!" Sanjna could not help remarking as she pressed a sunburst diamond stud into Tara's exposed navel.

Sandhya styled Tara's henna-dyed hair into a coiled bun at the back of her head and decorated it with a string of Burmese pearls.

Sundari pampered Tara's face and hands with cream of aloe and dabbed her with lemon scent. As for make-up, Tara did not need much. She, like all the other courtesan girls in the Mahal, had been nourished from the inside and out with milk, curds, honey, herbs, fruit, berries and juices since the age of five. All Sundari had to do was dust Tara with a light touch of talc, and line kohl to accentuate her green eyes which sparkled like the cut mirrors of the Mahal. Then she embellished Tara with a set of Kolhapur silver jewellery, the best in the land: nose stud, earrings, choker, bracelets, rings, anklets and toe-rings. A matching diadem set off the ensemble. On Tara's feet, she slipped on Kolhapur chappals. Then she stood back to admire her daughter.

"You look like a bride, Tara, if I may say so myself."

"A bride who'll never be. You should know that more than anyone else." Tara was stung by her mother's insensitivity.

Sundari looked at Tara through the dressing-table mirror. She did not know whether to trust or suspect her daughter's docility.

"Come now, Tara. Leave all your silly notions in this room. You go to serve our money god Kubera himself. Never mind if he walks about in the form of a mortal. Remember, if you've no money, even a dog will not look at you. Now be your mother's daughter and do what you're destined to do."

Sundari kissed Tara on the cheek. Tara did not respond.

The women shrouded Tara from head to toe with a red-and-gold dupatta.

As they led her to the door, Tara caught her reflection in the cut-mirror bird of paradise on the wall. The thousand fractured images she saw of herself described exactly the state of her feelings.

Outside, night was waiting like an illicit lover for Tara.

As Tara was led along the balcony, courtesans once again came running out of their apartments, the word of her departure having spread faster than kerosene-fire.

Tara's estranged friends were glad to see her go. Somehow, she had given them a feeling of inadequacy, what with her different convictions and stubborn will. What riled them even more was that she was described as the only padmini, or sacred lotus, among them: fair, slim, doe-eyed, delicate, graceful, wise, modest but proud, and with a vagina of the right size (not-too-deep-not-too-shallow). In other words, she was the perfect woman. The rest of them were either shankhini (fairylike), chitrini (whimsical) or hastini (elephantine)—all uncomplimentary terms that described their shortcomings.

"Before the night is out, she'll be toppled from her ziggurat," the estranged friends said with glee. "Then, perhaps, we can meet her on an equal footing." Young and too mature for their age, they gave Tara knowing looks and sniggered behind her back.

The older courtesans were all for Sundari. They understood the panic and anguish she was going through, having lost her only means of livelihood to the dreaded disease.

They knew she would soon start wasting away. And they thanked the money god for their conforming daughters, their insurance against poverty.

All the courtesans followed Tara down the stairs to the palanquin bay. On the ground floor, even servants and slaves stopped in their tracks to stare at the spectacle of the soon-to-be-deflowered Tara setting out for her first engagement with a man. Eight years late by courtesan standards.

The group crossed the courtyard. It was dotted with the handiwork of young courtesans practicing some of the Sixty-four Arts learnt during the day. There were rangoli of flowers and coloured rice flour; mosaics of chipped rubies, amethysts and emeralds; a half-finished stool and carpentry tools; rattan strips and woven rattan baskets; and potted plants and gardening tools.

In the Shastra and Nautch Halls, girls were learning more of the Sixty-four Arts: music, dance, languages, storytelling, recitation, gaming, chess, deportment and good manners.

On seeing Tara and the other courtesans, parrots and mynahs called out from their cages hanging round the periphery of the courtyard.

"Tara!", "Sonali!", "Champa!", "Rakhi!", "Urmilla!", "Meenu!", "Deepa!" … they called their mistress's names, having been trained by them. Training the birds to talk was part of a courtesan's accomplishments, too.

Like Tara, the other courtesans called were richly dressed. They wore Paithani saris or skirts and glittered with gems and gold. All were ready for their appointments in various parts of the city: Sonali was to dance at a temple; Champa was to give a greenhorn prince his first lesson in sex; Rakhi was to teach a princess the finer points of playing the veena; Urmilla was to discourse upon the Vedas, the *Mahabharata* and the *Ramayana* at court; Meenu was to rejuvinate a rich old merchant's failing sexual powers; and Deepa was to sing and recite poetry at a nobleman's wedding reception. A fleet of palanquins and gharries waited to take them to their destinations.

Some of the courtesans ribbed Tara about the Rich Citizen as she was about to get into her palanquin.

"Suck him dry, Tara!"

"… of his money, we mean."

"If you know what's good for you, you'll get him to marry you!"

"… even if he has two wives already!"

"… both older than him!"

For the first time in her life, Tara felt orphaned. She had been alone most of her young life but then she had her many books, some pets, her now estranged friends, half a dozen servants and her nagging mother for company. But at this moment, she felt utterly abandoned by all in the Arsa Mahal. Only her dream, like a ghostly twin, accompanied her into the palanquin.

The Rich Citizen

There was a small commotion on the way to the Rich Citizen's mansion. Tara heard shouts. The palanquin bearers stopped. Tara peeped from behind the curtains. By the light of the torches, she saw a scuffle between a well-dressed man and a group of men, including some of her guards. A guard bludgeoned the man on the head.

The man collapsed. Two men carried him away into the darkness. Tara resumed her journey, feeling sorry for the assaulted man. Must be a drunk unwittingly creating trouble, Tara thought.

There was no further incident during the rest of the journey.

They looped through the winding streets and alleys of the city. Through the gauze curtains, Tara saw the Brihadisvara Temple, the Sangeetha Mahal, Tanjore Fort and the Schwarz Mission Church. The night lent such magic to the ancient streets and monuments that, on previous occasions, Tara had felt she would suddenly see Lord Shiva doing his cosmic dance outside the Brihadisvara Temple; hear heavenly nymphs playing the harp and singing the *Gita* in the Sangeetha Mahal; thrill at Maratha sepoys galloping down the streets; or witness Jesus Christ carrying his cross. But Tara felt no such thing tonight. She was too busy thinking of the terror that lay ahead.

The men set the palanquin down at the gas-lit terrace of the Rich Citizen's mansion. The guards quickly surrounded the palanquin so that Tara could not escape.

Four matronly women came running out to receive Tara. They were devoured by curiosity. Not in all their years (they were in their fifties) had they seen a virgin courtesan beyond the age of twelve.

The women led Tara into the mansion.

"Come, my princess," the most handsome among them said, "our Master awaits you."

To Tara, the welcome sounded like an invitation to hell.

Tara found herself in shockingly different surroundings.

All the palaces and mansions she had danced or sung in until now had been of brilliant white or pink marble. But this mansion seemed to be entirely of black marble, or so Tara deduced by the black-marble entrance hall in which she was standing. The thin swirls of grey veining the marble did nothing to soften the starkness of the black.

Tara hated black. She feared it. It was the colour of night. The night-coloured Kali could only be appeased by human sacrifice. It was the colour of sorcery that could make a sane man mad. That Kerala mantravadi had worn black: the one her mother had hired to 'exorcise' the non-existent spirits from Tara when she was a child. Her mother believed the spirits made Tara rebel. The shaman's incantations, potions and whippings had had no effect on innocent Tara. Even his whip was black. She could still remember it snaking towards her in quick succession and sinking its fangs into her tender flesh, like a cobra.

The black-marble surroundings confirmed what Tara had heard: the Rich Citizen was a man of different tastes.

From the dim entrance hall, the women led Tara towards a closed room. The black periphery of the light seemed to suck in and swallow the jingling of Tara's anklets.

As she walked every reluctant step towards the room, her mind worked at ways of escaping.

"My child," she heard the handsome matron say, "not just any woman walks in through these doors. Countless have tried and failed."

"Our master is very discerning," another woman chipped in. "If you're smart, you'll harness the wind that's blowing your way."

Tara was struck by the women's Benares-silk saris and silver ornaments. The man's generous to his servants, she thought.

The muted sounds of music and laughter came from behind the massive teak doors.

At a knock, the doors were opened from inside. The maw of debauchery opens, Tara thought. Her heart hammered in her chest.

Laughing, the women gently pushed Tara into the room and closed the door.

"At last, the padmini meets the stallion. Tonight, even the gods won't sleep. So engrossed will they be in the union of lotus and stallion," the handsome woman remarked.

"Is it true what they say, Bhanu Bai," a newcomer in the group asked, "that his linga is twelve fingers long?"

"Twelve fingers. And not a finger less. It seems like only yesterday that I had all of him in me." She paused, remembering. "But that was years ago, when he was a frisky colt and I an older mare."

Tara stood in a room brilliantly lit by Ottoman chandeliers.

From the setting and goings-on, Tara knew she was in the reception hall of the mansion.

Her earlier guess had been right. Black marble shone on the walls, floor and the sturdy pillars supporting the high ceiling. With the strong lighting from the chandeliers, the place was not as oppressive as the entrance hall. But that was no consolation to Tara.

As she entered the hall, everyone before her froze. The nautch girl, just stripping off the last bit of her flimsy clothing, stood in mid-gyration, one hand raised gracefully over her head. The sitar, sarod, tabla, flute and percussion players—all women—stopped in mid-tune. And the audience of four men looked as if they had seen an apparition.

The men were reclining against white satin floor-cushions and bolsters and holding tumblers of mead in their hands or smoking the hookah. The hall was awash with their attar-musk-sandalwood perfumes, wine scents and hookah vapours.

As soon as they recovered themselves, the men ogled at Tara and licked their lips.

"So, the lotus has arrived!" one of the men said as he sprang from the cushions.

He was the most stunning man Tara had ever seen. He reminded her of a god. He came to stand towering above Tara, blocking her view with his broad chest. His gold-trimmed black dhoti and kurta and his shock of black curly hair set off his fair skin. And his mesmerising smile almost made her swoon.

"Welcome! I've been expecting you," the god-of-a-man said, his baritone voice adding to his attractions.

So this is the Rich Citizen, Tara figured.

"I'm Nilkanth Rao Bhonsle. I'm sure you've heard of me."

Sure, your reputation precedes you like the elephant precedes the sound of its bell, Tara thought but said nothing.

Seeing her head bent, he tilted her chin. Then he stepped aside, making Tara blink in the chandelier light as he unblocked her view.

"Friends, this is Tara Bai. From the Arsa Mahal."

"*Vah-re-vah!!*",

"A padmini if I ever saw one!",

"It's not fair! The gods always favour you, Bhonsle!"

— the men responded variously to the introduction.

Like their host, they were dressed in silk. Like their host, too, they flashed diamond rings on their fingers. The diamonds were of the Panna and Wajrakarur variety.

The nautch girl, miffed by the attention turned on Tara, wrapped her dupatta about her podgy, hairless body, picked up her strewn clothes from the floor, gave Tara an icy stare and disappeared into an adjacent chamber.

The musicians stared at Tara with frank admiration. And the flautist, a lesbian, positively drooled.

"Tara must dance for us, Bhonsle. Tell her to dance," an all-excited guest said, twirling his moustache to show his virility.

"Yes, Bhonsle. Be generous! Allow us, too, to feast our eyes on her," another guest, dark and piggish, said. The lecher felt a certain part of his anatomy rising in tandem with his excitement.

"Dance for you, my friends? Yes. But fully clothed. Her nakedness is for my eyes only."

The guests groaned in disappointment. But they knew Nilkanth too well to press him any further.

"Look how red she's turned. Like the flesh of the ripe guava!" the moustacheod man quipped.

Tara had turned dark with shame and rage.

"How much redder she must be in her secret place!" came the crass rejoinder from the third guest, an old man with diamond ear studs and the chandelier beams dancing on his bald pate.

Tara closed her eyes. God, please help me! she screamed within, as the men groped and clutched her with their eyes.

"Come, Tara, perform a Kathak for us," Nilkanth's voice cut into her prayer. He was lounging again among his friends. "But first, a drink. Some mead? Or maireya, perhaps?" As he held up a crystal jug, the diamond rings on all his fingers winked seductively at Tara.

At a glance, Tara knew they were Golconda rocks, the whitest and most expensive in the land. They said he had a collection of them stashed away in his bedchamber.

Tara declined the drink with a shake of her head. She had seen on her Arsa Mahal mates the intoxicating effects of the mead and maireya. As a matter of fact, she had learnt to make the liquors herself. The mead was made from honey and the maireya from fermented plums, ginger peel, pepper and molasses. It had all been part of her courtesan training.

"A teetotal courtesan? Well, I'm amazed!" Nilkanth exclaimed. "That's another petal in your Lotus-Crown. All right. Dance."

The musicians struck up a Kathak number.

Tara stood still.

"Dance, I said!"

Tara still did not move.

Nilkanth's face turned ugly.

Suddenly, the crack of a whip sundered the air.

Tara's eyes widened with shock. She felt a burning sting around her calves.

There were loud gasps from the guests as Nilkanth's next whiplash ripped off her dupatta and exposed her goddess-like beauty under her gauzy garment.

The piggish man with a hard on ejaculated immediately. He looked around sheepishly, hoping no one had noticed his shudder of pleasure.

For the next ten minutes, Tara danced. She was a blur of rhythmic footwork, eye and hand movements and pirouettes, her ankle bells adding music of their own to that of the musicians.

The men reached out to touch the hem of her skirt as it flared about her ankles. All the time they raked her with their eyes.

Tara danced with desperate abandon. Not with the gay abandon she always danced in the temples. Absent were the smile and expressive eyes that made the dance whole (which the sex-hungry men did not notice). As her feet worked at the steps, her mind worked at ways of hoodwinking her patron-cum-would-be-rapist.

The men applauded volubly when the Kathak ended. They threw fistfuls of gold coins at Tara's feet. Tara did not pick up the coins. Neither did she bother to give her audience the polite salaam at the end of the dance. The men chose to overlook it. Her great beauty atoned for her impoliteness.

At a signal from Nilkanth, the musicians left the hall. Nilkanth showed Tara into an antechamber. Tara heard the ominous click of the lock as he imprisoned her. Her heart plunged into her belly.

Nilkanth left to show his reluctant guests out. The trio left, once again grumbling at Nilkanth's good fortune at procuring a padmini, and a virgin at that.

The antechamber was vast enough to host orgies. Tara felt small in it.

Everything in the antechamber was as she had been taught it would be. There was the king-size divan bed covered in white satin. On either side of the divan were marble stools with amaranth garlands, pots of scents including eucalyptus, sweet orange, peppermint and lavender, and bunches of herbs and citrus leaves. Taking up space on the floor were Persian rugs with cushions and bolsters. Books, drawing materials, a veena and a chess set also lay on the rugs. An assortment of tidbits filled little silver bowls on a table. The tidbits were drops of powdered aphrodisiacs coated with honey, lime, salt and bitter herbs to stimulate sexual ardour. Large mirrors, alternating with paintings of nude women, lined walls and covered the ceiling. Outside the windows, mynahs, parrots and partridges flapped about in gilt cages, their calls mingling with the tinkle of fountains in the flower garden. It was obvious to Tara the Rich Citizen followed the advocates of the Kama Sutra to the fullest.

Such a man aimed to be a conqueror of women.

He would burst into the chamber freshly washed, perfumed, garlanded and fortified with a concoction of palm wine mixed with milk, honey, ghee and madhuka flowers. He would have also anointed his penis with a mixture of honey, crushed peppers and datura seeds to charm the woman into submission.

Such a man would not accept resistance from any woman.

If the initial gentle approach failed, he would rip off her clothes, throw her on the divan and ravish her till she bled and fainted. Then he would call in his servants to clean up the mess. Later, he would ravish her again. And again ...

Tara knew exactly what she was in for.

Like a captive deer, her eyes darting this way and that, she looked for ways of escape. There were none. All the windows were barred and the only other door, leading to the garden, was padlocked. Her hopes soared when she saw a bowl of grapes, apples and pomegranates. Surely there must be a paring knife somewhere, she thought as she searched frantically around the bowl and the rest of the chamber. She did not find any knife. And she knew screaming for help was futile. The women in the house would only laugh at her.

Her sweat-soaked clothes clung to her. There was searing pain where sweat mingled with the cuts on her calves. She ignored the pain and looked around for a heavy object with which to attack her captor.

The door opened.

Nilkanth burst into the antechamber. And locked the door.

All's not lost, Tara thought, at least the key's still in the lock.

The man was just as she had imagined: freshly groomed, reeking of patchouli and wearing a jasmine garland around his neck and wrist. There was no trace of the earlier anger on his face, only a disarming smile.

Nilkanth looked directly at Tara.

"I think you need a wash and a change of clothes," he said, eyeing her damp garments and the tear in her skirt where whip had met gauze.

With a magician's flourish, he turned a camouflaged knob on the wall. One of the paintings slid aside to reveal a brightly lit bath chamber. A cloud of rose and lavender perfume engulfed Tara and Nilkanth.

"Come, let me do the honours." A wolf-grin slashed his face as he caught her by the wrist and tried to lead her to the bath.

Tara had learnt about the sensualities of such a bath. But she was repelled by the thought of being bathed by the notorious specimen before her, even if he was a god-of-a-man.

"Let me go, scoundrel. Let me go." Tara's voice was dangerously low.

She wrenched her hand free and ran towards the door. But Nilkanth was faster. He stood like a rock in front of her.

"Ah! So the doe wants to flee," Nilkanth said in a sugary voice. "You know something? I enjoy hunting. Even if it's only inside an antechamber!"

"You can only have my dead body. But a man like you will even defile a corpse, just for the experience!" Tara said and ran from him.

Incensed, he chased her around the divan. Tara picked up a brass vase and threw it at him. It landed, instead, on a mirror panel and shattered it. Nilkanth lunged at her and caught her in his arms. Tara tried kicking, but he had her pinned to him. She could hardly breathe.

"Your mother didn't tell me what a vixen you are. But what a sweet little vixen!" Tara felt his hot breath on her face. "I'm sure you're going to give me innumerable hours of pleasure."

Tara spat in his face.

"Why, you she-devil! You spit at me? You who live off pickings?"

The god-of-a-man turned into a brute-of-a-man. He ripped her clothes and punched her until she fell to the floor, senseless.

Then, still heaving with anger, he strode towards the door, roaring, "Bhanu Bai! Bhanu Bai! Come here at once!"

Bhanu already had her inquisitive ear to the door. She was with a crony, Vanaja. On hearing their master, they ran pell-mell out of the reception hall, made an about-turn and, walking calmly, pretended they were just coming from their room.

Nilkanth flung open the door.

"Bhanu Bai!" he shouted. "Oh there you are," he toned down on seeing her. He ordered in his sweetest voice, "Attend to that she-devil, will you? I want her up and about in half an hour." Then he stalked out of the antechamber.

"What have you done to her, Nilkanth?" Bhanu exclaimed after him, as if she did not already know.

Between them, the women revived Tara. They sponged her gently, tutting at the sight of the angry welts on Tara's face and body.

"Poor child! If only you'd not resisted him!" Bhanu said.

"Someone should have warned you about the Master's temper. Anyway, you should have expected this for going against the grain," Vanaja opined. "No man paying in solid gold is going to be cheated out of his fantasy!"

Tara winced as the courtesans dabbed salve on the cuts on her calves. They dressed her in a white voile garment embroidered with roses at the neck and sleeves. The garment looked strangely familiar. With a shock, Tara realised that it was her own. And she saw a pile of her clothes in the open cupboard nearby.

My clothes must have been sent soon after I arrived, Tara thought. So, it was not to be a one-night engagement, as I was led to believe. How thoroughly mother has betrayed me!

Being fully alert, Tara thought of making a run for it immediately. But she had second thoughts. She had to contend with two women who could easily overpower her in her weakened state. Then she had another idea. She used one of the oldest tricks known to womankind: she pretended to swoon.

"*Are!* She's fainted again!" Bhanu squawked. "Quick, get the smelling salts, Vanaja!"

They tried to revive Tara. As the minutes ticked by, they became more frantic. But Tara carried on with her ploy, keeping her eyes shut and flopping this way and that every time they tried to sit her up.

"What will the Master say?" Vanaja said desperately. "The time he's given us is running out," she said, looking at the clock on the wall.

"I guess I'll have to tell him to wait a while longer," Bhanu said, getting up. "Rub the soles of her feet with eucalyptus oil," she instructed Vanaja as she left the antechamber, leaving the door wide open in her hurry.

Tara pretended to stir.

Vanaja breathed a sigh of relief. "Thank Bhagavan you're coming to! The Master will skin us if you didn't."

While the woman was busy massaging her feet, Tara saw the open door and grabbed her chance.

She kicked the woman aside (Tara was an expert in the kicking department, having been dragged screaming and kicking too many times in the Arsa Mahal.) She bolted through the door, ran across the empty reception and entrance halls, opened the front door and dashed out into the street.

Tara expected to be pounced on by guards. But there were none. The Rich Citizen had not counted on her trying to escape. So sure was he of his catch.

There were shouts in the house. Tara grew wings. She flew down the dark, empty street. But she did not get far. Suddenly, from out of nowhere, a masked figure grabbed her. He held a hand over her mouth, muffling her screams.

"Shh! Don't scream. I'm here to help you," the man whispered urgently.

This time around, Tara really fainted.

Refuge

When she came to, Tara found herself in the presence of two others. In her foggy vision, she saw the ghostly figures of a man and a woman on either side of her. Snatches of what they were saying floated to her as if from a great distance: "Look Ma ... conscious ...", "Thank ... get ... some broth."

The woman floated away. The man brought his face nearer. Tara's vision distorted it like an image in the local tamasha's House of Mirrors.

Slowly, her vision cleared and brought into focus a man with dishevelled hair and rumpled clothes. One sleeve of his kurta was torn at the shoulder. Apart from his questionable appearance, he was most average-looking. He was neither an Adonis nor a Krishna; neither bronze nor ebony; neither midget nor giant; and neither obese nor thin. Just ordinary. The type you would not look at twice.

Tara saw no distinguishing features, until she saw him smile. Then something sublime welled up from deep inside him, shone through his eyes and reached out to touch her tenderly.

Tara was struck by the intensity of his look and smile. For a moment, she was mesmerised.

Then, reality gripped her. She cringed. Where was she? In another vice den? Was the woman a procurer and the man another Rich Citizen? Had she fled from one demon into the hands of another?

"Don't be afraid, Tara Bai," the man said. His voice was gentle. "You're safe here."

He touched her hand reassuringly but Tara snatched it away.

"Who ...who are you?" Tara asked, not sure whether she should trust him. He had mentioned her name. How did he know it?

Out of the corner of her eye she saw another figure in the room. It was an old man.

She could not see his face as his back was turned towards her. He was rocking to and fro on a chair near the window.

"I'm —" the young man was about to introduce himself when the door opened and the woman entered. She held a copper bowl in her hands. Like the old man, she, too was grey at the temples. But her walk was brisk.

"Dear child," she said, coming to the couch on which Tara was sitting, "here, drink this broth hot-hot. It will make you feel better."

She must have looked beautiful once, Tara thought, seeing the hints of beauty still lingering on the woman's careworn face. "But first tell me who you are."

"I'm Mukta Bai. That's my husband." She nodded towards the old man. "I know a wife shouldn't mention her husband by name. But circumstances are such I have to ignore convention. His name is Ramdas Rao Bhonsle." Then, turning to the young man, "And this is our son, Madhav Rao Bhonsle."

Bhonsle. That struck a chord in Tara. It was the name of the ruling clan of Tanjore. Were these people related to the royals? Then, with a shock, she realised that Nilkanth, too, bore the same clan name. Was he related to this family? Her head spun.

"I know what you're thinking," Mukta said, seeing alarm on Tara's face. "No, we're not related to the royals. And yes, Nilkanth is related to us. He's our elder son."

Tara gasped and recoiled.

"Don't be afraid, Tara. You're safe here. This is the last place he'll come looking for you. You see," a quiver came into Mukta's voice, "we disowned him a long time ago." She bent her head and was silent for a moment. "But that story can wait. Now drink up the broth and go to sleep. We'll talk in the morning."

Mukta left to make Tara's bed.

Tara felt a pinch of relief. At least she was not in immediate danger. She gulped the broth. She asked Madhav for water. When he brought her a tumblerful, she gulped that, too.

"Come, I'll show you to your room," Madhav said, leading the way out of what looked like the reception hall to Tara. She noticed that the old man was still rocking in his chair. He had not, even once, turned to look at her.

There were two rooms on either side of the passage from the hall. Madhav took her to the second one on the right. The first door was padlocked. She learnt later that the room had been Nilkanth's.

They entered the second room. Mukta was fluffing up the pillows on the bed.

As soon as she saw the bed, a deep exhaustion came over Tara. She started stumbling. Madhav caught her. He lifted her in his arms and laid her on the bed.

"Sleep as long as you like, Tara. And Madhav will watch over you, just in case."

By the time Mukta drew the blanket over her, Tara was fast asleep.

Mother and son looked down at her. Mukta laid a hand on Madhav's arm and said,

"The gods have sent her to you as you wished, Madhav. Care for her as you would your mother." She gave him a meaningful look and left the room.

Madhav opened the windows to let in the cool night breeze. He left the room to wash and change. Then he had a tumbler of milk and settled into a couch near Tara. He gazed at her for a long time. After midnight, he dozed off.

Once, during the night, Tara woke Madhav.

"No! No! Let me go!" she said as she thrashed about on the bed. When Madhav tried to calm her, she lashed out at him. He held her tightly and whispered consoling words until, finally, she crumpled into sobs. After that, Tara felt better, her pent-up emotions released.

Tilting up her face, Madhav looked deeply into her eyes and said, "Tara, as long as I'm alive, my brother will not touch you."

Tara heard the reassuring words and fell asleep in Madhav's arms.

Tara woke up mid-morning. The day was so bright it hurt her eyes. She heard the comforting sounds of banging pots and pans and sloshing water from the kitchen. The aroma of tomato chutney tickled her nose. Nadaswaram and mridangam music filtered into the room from a street procession. A pair of sparrows streaked in and out of the open windows. Things seemed so normal, until she tried to move. Then her battered body protested. She fell back on the pillows. Memories of the previous evening came flooding back: the events in the Arsa Mahal, at Nilkanth's mansion, and her escape.

Alarming thoughts assailed her. Had Nilkanth reported that she had absconded to her mother? Had he sent out his thugs to look for her? Would he beat her mother, too, in revenge? The last thought terrified Tara. Surely Mother is not to blame for my actions, she agonised, but then she shouldn't have got mixed up with the likes of Nilkanth.

The young man who had whisked her to safety was nowhere to be seen. Tara tried to recall his name. Madhu? Madhan? Madhi? She could not remember. Something beginning with 'Ma' anyway, Tara thought. Then she remembered him holding her tight against his chest. She blushed. Had she been dreaming or had he really held her? How secure she had felt in his arms!

Tara looked around the bedroom. By Arsa Mahal standards, it was as plain as plain could be. A teak double bed, a bedside table, a cupboard, a dressing table and a couch were its only furniture. The chestnut lacquer on them had faded. There were neither pictures on the walls nor flowers on the table.

Tara had lived in opulence in the Arsa Mahal. She had seen the ornate grandeur of palaces. She had, the previous night, even glimpsed the plushness of a rich citizen's mansion. So the house she was in had to be an ordinary house, Tara reasoned, and she had to be among ordinary people. After the royals, nobles, courtesans, priests, pundits and rich citizens, there were only the ordinary folk who lived in ordinary homes. (The hovel-dwelling Shudras did not count. They were less than people. So she had been instructed.)

There was a soft knock at the door. The door opened and Mukta peeked in.

"Ah, you're awake." She stepped in and came to Tara. "Do you feel rested enough to have a bath?" Mukta gasped when she saw the blue-black marks on Tara's face and hands. "You poor child. How could he have done this to you! If it's of any help, I apologise for my son's brutality."

Poor woman, Tara thought. Does she apologise all the time for her son? What a cruel fate!

"Yes, I'll have a bath," she said aloud, "but I've no clothes to change into."

"I've sent Madhav to buy you some clothes. In the meantime, you can wear mine."

So that's his name, Tara thought. Madhav.

She followed Mukta down the passage to the bathroom at the back of the house.

It was a thatched cubicle attached to one of the kitchen walls. Two brass cauldrons shone dully in the dim interior. A scrub of mung paste, thumbs of turmeric and a palm-sized stone turmeric-grinder stood ready by the cauldrons.

Mukta had prepared her a hot bath with margosa and basil leaves. The herbal bath soothed Tara's aches. It made her almost forget the beating she had taken. She noticed the cuts on her calves had closed, too.

Tara got into Mukta's choli. It was too baggy for her as Mukta was stout. But she made do by knotting it tightly under her breasts. Wrapping Mukta's cotton sari about, she went into the kitchen with Mukta.

The maidservant in the kitchen was thunderstruck. She dropped the steel pots she was carrying with a clang. She had seen Tara dance in temples. But courtesans, especially battered ones, did not materialise overnight in ordinary people's homes. Still in shock, the maid picked up the pots. She went back to work, stealing glances now and then at Tara.

The kitchen was spacious. It had twin wood-fire stoves on the floor. A pot of milk was frothing on one of the stoves. The wood smoke stung Tara's eyes. Clay jars lined the shelf next to the stoves. In one corner of the kitchen stood a stack of clay storage pots.

"Come, eat. You must be starving." Mukta sat with Tara on the floor and served her tiffin. Tiffin was idli rice cakes and coffee with fresh milk. Mukta served generous portions.

Ravenous, Tara almost gobbled the idli. She liked them. They were as fluffy as cotton. The tomato chutney dip was chilli-hot. The combination went well with the aromatic, home-ground Arcot coffee. But she could not eat beyond three idli, trained as she was to eat dainty portions.

"You eat like a bird, Tara!" Mukta commented, surprised. "Is the food not to your liking?"

"No, Ba—" Tara hesitated, not knowing how to address Mukta.

At the Arsa Mahal, she had addressed everyone other than her mother as Bhai or Bahen, meaning brother or sister.

"Call me Mami, child," Mukta said, beaming at her.

Tara was puzzled. The term was used to address a mother-in-law.

"No, Mami," Tara felt as embarrassed as she looked. "The food's delicious. It's just that I'm used to eating small portions."

"I see. I'll keep that in mind the next time I serve you. Now, let's have a chat."

Mukta gave instructions to the maid. The girl was still in a daze. As Mukta led Tara to the hall, she knew that the maid would be out in a jiffy through the back door to convey the juicy morsel of news to the neighbour's maid. Mukta also knew that before the sun went down, the whole neighbourhood would have savoured the morsel. It would have relished the juice, then spat with self-righteousness the indigestible fibres. Just when the neighbourhood would start spitting in her face was only a matter of time. Mukta mentally braced herself for it.

Tara noticed the hall was almost as stark as the bedroom she had slept in. It was white, like the rest of the house. A single couch, two wicker armchairs and a low table took centre stage. A bunch of organza red roses in a brass vase graced the table. The flowers added much-needed colour to the hall. A coat hanger stood like a sentry near the front door. There was a bureau against one wall. On the wall facing the front door was what attracted Tara most. It was the first thing that would catch a visitor's eye on entering the house. But in her groggy state the previous night, she had missed it. The object that attracted her was a picture: that of a queen riding a horse, her sword held high in one hand, her Tiger Flag in the other.

Tara was transfixed by the noble looks of the queen.

"That's our rani. Rani Meera Bai," Mukta said. "I'll tell you all about her later."

Tara tore her eyes away from the picture. Then she saw Ramdas.

He was sitting at the same window, rocking to and fro. He looked fresh. His clothes had been changed.

Mukta led Tara by the hand to Ramdas.

"Nawra, this is Tara Bai."

Ramdas stopped rocking. He looked directly at Tara, through sunken eyes.

Tara saw a man who still bore traces of a past handsomeness. His creased face had a creased centipede-scar. But his eyes held no expression. What once were black opals were now glassy, like that of a dead fish. Tara felt uneasy in his dead-fish stare.

"You remember Tara Bai, don't you?" Mukta stroked his back and talked to him as if he were a child. "You know, the girl I've been telling you about. The dancer?"

Ramdas made no response. Then he looked out of the window and started rocking again.

Mukta drew Tara away.

"Don't mind him, Tara. He doesn't mean to be rude. But there are some things the man of the house must be told, even if he's dead to the outside world."

Tara wondered what great misfortune had befallen Ramdas.

"Come. Sit next to me, Tara. Now tell me all about yourself. Right from the start."

After hearing Tara's narrative, Mukta went to the kitchen to see if the maid had followed her instructions. Tara sat alone. She divided her gaze between Ramdas and Rani Meera Bai's picture.

A loud knock at the front door made Tara jump.

It must be someone looking for me, she thought, and was about to flee to the kitchen when Madhav looked through the window.

Tara unlatched the door. She hovered, not knowing whether to stay or go to inform Mukta her son was home.

"These are for you, Tara Bai." Madhav deposited four parcels on the table. He untied them and offered Tara the clothing he had bought her. The saris and cholis were of cotton and not the gauzes and silks of the Arsa Mahal.

"Thank you. But I'm sorry for all the trouble ..." Tara hung her head in shame.

"Don't apologise, Tara Bai. It just so happens you've been caught in an adverse tide." Madhav spoke like a sage. He produced pen and paper from the bureau. "Now if you'll give me a handwritten message saying you're safe, I'll have it delivered to your mother. At least she'll worry less."

Tara liked his sense of responsibility. But she frowned and hesitated.

"Worried they'll come and get you? Don't reveal your whereabouts for now. I'll make sure the courier doesn't either." He explained that they were at the opposite end of the city from the Arsa Mahal and Nilkanth's mansion. So it would be weeks before her mother and Nilkanth came searching for her at his house. That would buy Tara some time.

An alarming thought struck Tara.

"What if they report to the authorities that you have kidnapped me?"

"Kidnapped you? There's no question of that. Remember, it's 1896 and we're under British rule now. Under their law, you're no longer a minor. You're free to stay at home or leave."

Tara chided herself silently for not keeping abreast of developments outside the Arsa Mahal.

"You and your mother are very kind to me. I don't know how I'm going to repay you."

"Forget the repayment. You're welcome to stay for as long as you like." Then, Madhav's voice became husky. "You've no idea how welcome you are, Tara Bai."

He looked deep into her eyes and gave her that intense smile that had so struck her the previous night.

At that instant, as he claimed her with his eyes, Tara knew she had found her ordinary man.

PART THREE

Madhav Rao Bhonsle

I don't have one dream but three dreams.

Let me tell you about my first dream. It has everything to do with my brother, Nilkanth. Nilkanth, who's a fabulous Rich Citizen, a wayward son, a bully and a conqueror of sluts, but, whom I love dearly.

Since his childhood he's been the bane of my parents. Our arrival, as refugees of famine, in the great city of Tanjore only served to seal his twisted fate.

Like most great cities, Tanjore, too, has its underworld with its attendant crime, profligacy and intrigue. In this proud, ancient city that could have given him the highest of education and the noblest of cultures, Nilkanth chose to associate with criminals, fraternise with drunks and sleep with sluts.

To this day, my parents and I are still unclear how he became a Rich Citizen. What we do know for sure is that it was by fraudulent means (he has neither the education nor the skills to earn an honest living). There were rumours about rich merchants being kidnapped and forced to sign over their riches to him; his name was linked to the robbery at the temple treasury; some of his thugs were seen at the site of a plundered, gold-laden ship at the mouth of the Cauvery Nadi; he was even suspected of having a hand in the matter of a Mysore prince being held to ransom. But all this was just talk. The authorities could not lay a finger on him. He's that wily.

When we first arrived in Tanjore, Nilkanth was eight and I a year younger. Even at that tender age, he started playing truant from the

English school Bah sent us to. (Hate though he did the British, Bah wisely decided that an English education would stand us in good stead in the future.) When he played truant, Nilkanth went with his delinquent friends to swim in the creeks of the Cauvery; to steal and eat mangoes from orchards, although Bah bought basketfuls of the fruit for us; to throw stones at passing gharries; and to follow street processions. At ten, he began to smoke beedi, play cards and gamble.

A number of times, he forced me to play truant, too, threatening to beat me up if I didn't. When Bah heard about our escapades, he would give us a sound belting, my share being bigger as I wasn't supposed to emulate my brother.

When he reached puberty, Nilkanth started visiting the slut house in the next neighbourhood. Horses could not keep him away, let alone Bah. "He's like a cat that has tasted fish," Bah said.

When Nilkanth came home and we were alone in our room, he would boast that the dark, foul-mouthed women fought over him as he was such a stud. And I must say he had the physique and looks to match. He was big for his age (almost like a man), fair, and handsome beyond words. Compared to him, I was plain.

Once, peeved at my ignorance in matters concerning sex, he did something brothers never do. He listed out in his chicken-scratch writing the Sixty-four Positions of Copulation. "Here, read this and start acting like a man!" he admonished me, though he himself was not out of boyhood yet.

By the time the down above his lips changed to a coarse moustache, he considered himself a man of the world: well schooled (in the erotic and black arts), well heeled (with ill-gotten money), and well bedded (with every slut in the city, and beyond).

Like a rogue elephant, he set himself apart from normal society, living in a black marble mansion. He fondly refers to it as 'my Black Taj Mahal'. There, it seems, he has the trappings of cultured society: books, musical instruments, art materials and board games. But these are only for appearance. Actually, what goes on inside, I hear, are nefarious business deals, drinking bouts, gambling and kinky sex.

To top it all, Nilkanth married two women (Ma says this has

something to do with the double whorls on his crown). Both his wives are old enough to be our mother. The women live together in another mansion. Comfortably.

Where did we go wrong? our parents asked. We've brought him up the same way we have Madhav, yet why is Nilkanth so different. They tell me of the time in Champakapur when they posed a question to my brother and me: "How do you think the moon came to be?" Even the answers we gave, they say, showed a marked difference, hinting at our future. I had answered, "A child drew the moon, coloured it carefully and sailed it like a kite into the sky. And it got stuck there ever since." Nilkanth's answer had been, "An angry boy trampled on his tin dinner plate and flung it into the sky."

We showered equal love on both of them, yet why did Nilkanth stray? We've tried advising and cajoling him, my parents told friends and neighbours, but he will not change. Why has God punished us so?

"Could it be Kausalya's curse?" Bah wondered. "*May your sons be cursed! May you never live in peace!* That's how she cursed," he said, remembering the fateful night in Killa. "Do curses really come true?"

"Or, could it have been the eclipse?" Ma speculated. "But I observed all the taboos during the solar eclipse, when I was pregnant with Nilkanth. How's it possible that Rahu could have damaged him? And spiritually, too!"

The next question was, who among our ancestors had Nilkanth's traits? Bah and Ma jogged their memories. There surely must have been someone in the dim past. Could it have been Roshan Kaka, Bah's great-granduncle, who was reputed to be a violent, thieving womaniser? Yes, Nilkanth must have inherited his bad traits from that great-granduncle, Bah and Ma concluded.

> Go straight to school.
> Come straight home after school.
> Study hard.
> Don't gamble.
> Don't smoke.
> Don't steal.

> Don't fight.
> Don't lie.

That was the daily litany drummed into me during my childhood. When I became an adolescent it changed to:

> Don't follow your brother to the slut house.
> Don't fraternise with thugs.
> Do an honest job.
> Don't make money your god.
> What's important is self-pride and family name.
> Make sure you marry a virgin.
> Don't ever become like your brother.

And so the burden fell on me to be everything my brother was not.

I dream of bringing back the smile on Bah's and Ma's face. But my resolve to conform did not go down well with Nilkanth. Until he left us, he taunted and ridiculed me for my forthright ways, to the point where I felt like punching him in the face. But one just does not hit an elder brother.

*   *   *

To satisfy my parents (well, Ma at least, from the look of things), I agreed to marry a girl of Ma's choice. That was when I first laid eyes on Tara. I was twenty-three then.

I remember the occasion very clearly.

Ma and I were at the Brihadisvara Temple. The day was auspicious, it being the festival of Shiva Ratri or Night of Shiva, when devotees keep vigil throughout the night. Ma had specially chosen this day to point out my intended bride to me. As prearranged, her family would be bringing her to the temple.

The devotees, dressed in bright Tanjore and Kanchipuram silks, were sitting or standing about in groups, waiting for the puja to begin. Being Saivites, they had traced three horizontal bars of holy ash across their foreheads and placed a round dot of sandalwood or vermillion above their noses.

The air was imbued with religious fervour. The music from the temple's double-orchestra of mridangam, nadaswaram and cymbals only served to heighten the mood.

Ma steered me towards a small group in the temple quadrangle.

"There's the Gaekwad family," she said, indicating the group.

The family comprised three elderly men and women, four boys, two girls and a child. They looked well bred and well fed. We stopped at a respectable distance from the family.

"The girl in the green sari," Ma whispered. "Do you see her? She's the one!"

"Which green sari? The emerald-green or the parrot-green?"

"What parrot-green? I don't see any parrot-green!"

"She's hidden by that obese woman." I'm two heads taller than Ma, so I had the advantage of seeing beyond the woman.

"Well, I can't see her. Anyway, I distinctly remember being introduced to the girl in the emerald-green sari." Ma was flustered. "She has a distinguishing black mole on her cheek."

"So has the other girl."

"Madhav! Don't play games with me! This is serious business."

Ma looked so distressed I wanted to laugh.

"Ma, don't you know it's fashionable for young girls to sport a black dot on the cheek? It's a beauty mark. The black dot, too, looks like a mole."

"But I tell you, it's the girl in the emerald-green sari. I remember her face. Oh Madhav, how you confuse me!"

Just then, a matronly-looking woman in the group caught sight of us. She broke away from the group and waddled towards us.

"There you are, Mukta Bai. I was afraid you'd miss us in the crowd."

Ma introduced me to her. The woman respectfully covered her head with her sari drape, seeing I was her son-in-law-to-be. I gathered she was a widow as she wore neither nuptial string around her neck nor vermillion dot on her forehead.

"What, does your son like the nawri?" the woman asked boldly.

"My liking your daughter is the same as Madhav liking her. He's an obedient son. He'll not override my choice."

"What a relief! An obedient son is a rarity these days, what with British influence and all that. Once they're English educated, they want to pick their own brides."

"Don't include my son in *that* category. I'll choose an auspicious day and come to your house to make a formal proposal."

"That's settled then. My daughter must be blessed to receive such a proposal."

Just then, the temple bell rang.

"Hear that? It's a good omen," the woman said smugly. "Nothing can stop this marriage."

The ringing bell signalled the start of the puja.

My prospective mother-in-law excused herself and rejoined her family. Ma and I started walking towards the shrine.

"By the way, Ma, you still haven't told me exactly which girl it is. The one in the emerald-green sari or parrot-green sari?"

Ma gave me a murderous look.

After the puja, the devotees adjourned to the nautch-girls' platform at a corner of the temple quadrangle. There were to be some diversions before nightfall when the vigil proper would begin.

First, some pundits took to the platform which was actually a low stage. They read and explained the Shiva Purana to the gathering. Next, singers and musicians rendered Carnatic songs and music. Then came the highlight, a Bharathanatyam recital by a much-touted courtesan called Tara Bai. Rumour had it that she was so expert in the dance form that the maharaja had summoned her over and over again to dance in his palace for him and his European guests. This was to be her first appearance at the Brihadisvara Temple.

The minute she came on stage, the crowd fell silent.

Everyone giraffed their necks to catch the rare sight of a courtesan gracing the nautch-girls' platform. Even the regular devadasi temple-dancers looked awed.

I was so deeply smitten by the vision of Tara that it was as if I were a feather in a gust. Eros (thanks to my English education, I am more well versed in Greek mythology than Indian mythology) had scored a bull's-eye in my heart.

This maroon- and gold-costumed vision before me: was she Aphrodite? Or Cassandra? Or Venus? Or a heavenly ambrosia of all three? To be frank, I did not expect to be swept off my feet like that. Least of all by a courtesan.

For the next hour, she wove her magic spell over me; Bharathanatyam gesture over gesture, expression over expression, step over step:

> *thakkatharikittathom,*
> *thakkatharikittathom,*
> *tharikittathom,*
> *tharikittathom,*
> *kittathom,*
> *kittathom.*

After the performance, she was veiled from head to toe in a dupatta and escorted out by a well-built woman. I overheard people say the big woman was her mother.

Later, as we left, I spotted Nilkanth in the crowd. We caught each other's eye. But he looked through me and did not return my wave. A familiar, matronly figure passed by and a cloud of emerald green and parrot green sailed past me. But, by then, I had forgotten the significance of those colours. Only maroon and gold mattered.

Marrying Tara became my second dream. More so after I heard about her from friends who had contacts in Arsa Mahal circles. She was, against all the odds, still a virgin, was fighting to keep her virginity, and wanted to live outside the Arsa Mahal.

I heard, too, that her mother was biding her time to sell her daughter to the highest bidder.

That put me out of the race. I was only a merchant's clerk. I earned a monthly wage of one hundred rupees, enough to run an average household. But then, I was wildly in love. That gave me the impetus to wait for an opportunity to declare my love for Tara. Never mind if she spurned me. At least I'd have the satisfaction of knowing I'd tried.

Through a close friend, I tipped Tara's old nursemaid, Sanjna Bai, to inform me of anyone who had won the bid for Tara. I was prepared to risk my life and spirit her away.

I told Ma about my dream.

She was aghast.

"Are you mad? Do you realise what you're saying? She's not a sweet-shop laddoo you can buy and bring home, you know!"

There followed the expected tirade about further tarnishing the family name and earning social stigma.

"Courtesans and ordinary society are like oil and water. They don't mix." Ma ended her barrage.

But finally, Ma consented, the magic words that did the trick being 'young' and 'virgin'. I gave her a big hug. Brave Ma. Making all the decisions ever since Bah started rocking.

"But think very deeply about it," she cautioned. "She lives in a world far-removed from ours. She's used to the best things in life. Will we be able to provide for her? Assuming, that is, she agrees to marry you. No matter how good or innocent she is, she'll surely miss the luxury she's used to. Love will fly out the window once discontent sets in. Do you see?"

I did not see. And I did not hear.

Love had turned me blind and deaf. And as stubborn as a mule.

As with all things of moment, we told Bah about Tara. There was not even a flicker in his eyes. Only nothingness.

After that, I attended for a full year every Bharathanatyam performance by Tara at all the temples in the Tanjore principality. (I even wangled invitations to the palace for the privilege of watching her dance not only Bharathanatyam but Kathak as well.) And at each of these performances, Nilkanth was present, making a big show of understanding the dance of the gods.

My greatest fear was that he would bid for Tara. And win.

*   *   *

Now about my third dream.

My third dream was actually my first dream. But it took a back seat because of Nilkanth and Tara.

I haven't told Ma about this dream. She'd be devastated.

During my adolesence, my favourite haunt used to be the Brihadisvara Temple, the largest in the land. I loved (and still love) its antiquity, its ampleness, its pure lines, its tall gateways, its mammoth bull called Nandi and its gilt chariots. Most of all, I loved the sense of peace and security it gave me. I would escape to it to forget the hurricanes at home caused by Nilkanth.

That was when I learnt about the inscriptions. Rajaraja Chola was the architect of the classical Tamil inscriptions on the temple tower. He was an art lover and devout Saivite as well.

With the help of a scholar, I deciphered the Vettezhuttu inscriptions and found myself transported into many other worlds.

The inscriptions spoke of the great Chola Empire and the conquests of Rajaraja Chola and his descendents. They had on glorious record how these Tamil rulers had vanquished (besides Bengal, Ceylon and Burma) hundreds of ancient islands of the sea, east of the Coromandel Coast of India. They also mentioned other exotic places, native peoples, and enchanted me with names like Suvarnabhumi, Kadahram, Ayuthia, Kembhoja and Madura, their great rulers friendly with the Cholas.

I was besotted with the writings and soon yearned to see for myself these far-off lands. The only thing that held me back was the thought of Bah and Ma being left alone.

*　　*　　*

What absurd dreams Madhav Rao has, you must think. I completely agree with you.

But then, with life, you never know.

179

Revelations

There were only six people at the marriage ceremony in Madhav's house: the bride and groom, the temple priest, Ramdas, Mukta and Mukta's close friend and nextdoor neighbour, Laxmi Bai.

The bride wore a Kanchipuram silk sari of maroon and gold, Madhav's favourite colours of late.

The ceremony was short and simple. The priest threw oblations into the sacred fire, recited the Maangalyam mantra and within half an hour Madhav tied the turmeric-coated nuptial string, strung with gold and black beads, around Tara's neck. Then the priest collected his gifts of ten rupees, a dhoti, a bunch of bananas and a coconut, and left.

Ramdas did not watch the nuptials though he had been seated facing the bride and groom. He turned in the direction of the window he always sat at, and rocked to and fro, much to everyone's chagrin. When Mukta came to stand next to him so that the newlyweds could touch their feet for blessings, Ramdas did not turn around to face the couple. Only Mukta blessed them.

Laxmi Bai, a small woman with a big heart, also gave her blessings. "May all the gods keep you well."

"I leave with mixed feelings, Mukta Bai," she said as she was about to go home.

The women were alone at the door. Laxmi Bai carried a banana leaf filled with laddoo and jelebi for her seven children.

"I feel so happy for Madhav. I've seen him grow from a seven-year-old to a responsible young man. At the same time, I'm afraid of the reaction of the neighbourhood. You're a strong woman, Mukta Bai, to have made the decision to marry Madhav to a courtesan. I remember how timid you were when you first came here. Why, you wouldn't even look out the door without your husband's permission."

"I have to be strong, Laxmi Bai. For my husband and my son. Madhav is the only child I have left and I would see him happy. Look at him now. I've never seen him this ecstatic."

They looked at Madhav and Tara laughing and feeding each other jelebi. The newlyweds were oblivious to the women.

"Like my husband and I, Madhav has been carrying the yoke called 'Nilkanth' around his neck for too long. And I think it's time he threw it off and got on with what he wants to do in life. Just as long as it's not sinful."

"Be wary, just the same. There are many Kaikeyis in our midst." Laxmi Bai was referring to Lord Rama's stepmother in the *Ramayana*. She schemed to get him banished to the forest for fourteen years.

"Don't worry, Laxmi Bai. With a friend like you, I can face a thousand Kaikeyis."

Laxmi Bai left. As Mukta closed the door after her, she heard whoops of delight from Laxmi Bai's children as they rushed out to get the sweetmeats.

*   *   *

"Tell me, how did you know Nilkanth had won in his bid for me?"

It was night. Tara and Madhav were sitting on the couch in Madhav's room, now their bedroom. The place was sparsely furnished like all the other rooms in the house. It was the second day of their marriage and the second week after Tara's flight from Nilkanth and courtesan life.

"Sanjna Bai. Remember her? Your old nursemaid? I kept a tab on developments in the Arsa Mahal through her."

"Sanjna Bahen?" Tara was surprised. "She was the one who helped dress me for my appointment with Nilkanth. But she was so harsh. I remember how she and her sister ripped the clothes off me."

"She had to pretend, Tara. Otherwise, your mother would have become suspicious. Believe me, she told me in her letter she loves you and how she regrets being rough with you. 'In a way, I was more of a mother to Tara than Sundari Bai ever was,' she said."

"That's true. She understood my feelings."

"Knowing your feelings and my intentions, she secretly prayed that you would be free of the Arsa Mahal and Nilkanth."

"But how's it you didn't rescue me on the way to Nilkanth's mansion? I dread to think what would have happened had I not pretended to faint."

"I'm sorry about that. But Nilkanth outsmarted me. He had set his thugs to trail me. Seeing I was present at your every performance, he must have had his suspicions. Anyway, were you aware of any commotion on the way to Nilkanth's mansion?"

"Why, yes. A lone man was fighting my guards and some other men."

"Well, that man was none other than your humble servant." Madhav gave Tara a mock salaam.

A look of horror came over Tara's face.

"You? *Are!* You must've been hurt terribly!" She felt his head all over looking for bumps.

"The bump has long-disappeared. But thanks for the concern, anyway," Madhav winked mischievously.

Tara gave him a noisy kiss on the cheek.

"They tied my hands and feet and left me lying in a dark alley. Luckily, a drunk came along and set me free. Only after I promised him money for toddy. Well, you know the rest."

"But still, what if Nilkanth had …"

"Raped you?" A look of deep tenderness came into Madhav's eyes. "I would still have rescued you and married you. As long as the heart and mind remain pure, a violated body is of no consequence."

Madhav drew Tara close and they affirmed their love for each other.

The next night, they talked some more. Mukta was with them.

They were sitting on the verandah, eating Ootacammund grapes, after the night meal. The grapes were a luxury Madhav allowed only because of Tara. He knew her palate was more accustomed to grapes than banana, which was the ordinary man's fruit.

A gentle breeze wafted from the Cauvery, carrying with it the fishy smells of the river. The street in front of the house was quiet. Only the wailing of a baby disturbed the night.

The Bhonsles lived in the Maratha quarter of the city. The street on which they lived had no noisy bazaars, gambling dens or nautch halls but only a teashop, a sweet shop and a potti kadei selling provisions. The family lived in the last house in a row of whitewashed brick houses with tiled roofs.

I wonder how many eyes are peeping at us from behind the curtains right now, Mukta thought. The neighbourhood was just beginning to drop little hints of hostility, like drops of bird shit, against her family.

"Sanjna Bai has sent word that your mother's glad you're safe. And it looks like Nilkanth wants his money back. You know, the price he paid for you," Madhav told Tara.

"Repay him and be done with it. That's my advice," Mukta said. "Otherwise, the 'daaktar' will have another battered woman on their hands." Mukta sighed in resignation. "What to do, one son is a Rama, the other a Ravana."

"So that makes you Sita," Madhav teased Tara.

"Yes. As good and as pure, I believe," Mukta added to the comparison.

"But Ravana carried Sita off to Lanka!" Tara ribbed.

"Not to worry," Madhav said in mock reassurance. "If anyone's going to take you to Lanka, it's I!" He did not realise then how prophetic his words were.

Then they talked about Madhav's job and his salary and discussed balancing the household budget. Tara was one more mouth to feed.

Madhav had decided earlier that his parents' and his standard of living ought to be raised a notch to make Tara feel at ease. He would not suffer her eating plain meals and wearing plain clothes like themselves. Meals had to be more elaborate (a mutton briyani or fish tikka thrown in once a week with a fruit sherbet, for example), and clothes had to be upgraded (from rough khadar to fine cotton for themselves and silks for Tara). Therefore sacrifices had to be made.

"Two-thirds of Madhav's salary goes towards the house rent, groceries, the barber, the dhobi, the maidservant and Madhav's father's medication," said Mukta, counting the items on her fingers. "The remaining third we use for clothes, Temple pujas and ..." Mukta looked hesitantly at Madhav.

"And my craze for travelling," Madhav said, feeling a little guilty. "I spend quite a bit on that."

"So we save very little," Mukta continued. "Just enough for emergencies. And for sweets and new clothes for Divali."

"I could cut down on my trips," Madhav offered.

"And I could reduce the temple pujas from a weekly to monthly affair. Buying coconuts, fruit, flowers and camphor as offerings every Friday adds up to a tidy sum. I'm sure Sri Brihadisvara would not mind if I pamper my daughter-in-law at his expense," Mukta said, smiling at Tara. "And the servant, I could do without her."

Tara was touched. She had not expected her mother-in-law to go to such lengths to accommodate her.

"That's a wonderful idea, Mami! I mean about the servant. I was about to suggest it myself. I could help you with all the housework. That way, I won't be idle as I've been the past weeks."

"I won't have you soiling your hands, Tara," Madhav protested, thinking of her velvety hands. "Anyway, what do you know about housework?"

"More than you'll ever guess. I've learnt everything in theory and only need to put it into practice. Just give me a chance."

Mukta vouched for Tara. "I don't doubt your prowess, Tara. I know courtesans are brought up to be accomplished in every field, leaving us women outside the Arsa Mahal sadly lacking. I'm sure you'll adjust to ordinary life without any problem."

"But what about things like carrying water from the well and ... and ... milking the cow?" Madhav asked, cringing at the thought of Tara doing these chores. "Even you, Ma, have not carried water from the well. Only the servant has been doing that until now."

"I can learn. If other women can do it, so can I. As for milking the cow, look at these hands, Madhav." Mukta extended her rough hands.

"These hands have not only milked cows but herded them as well, back home in my village."

"What about you, Tara? Are you sure you can cope?" Madhav asked worriedly.

"If I've the strength and stamina to dance Bharathanatyam for an hour without a break, then housework is going to be as easy as carrying a sack of cotton."

"All right. We'll dismiss the servant. But I still have my reservations. The sacrifice both of you are making ..."

Mukta remembered a moment just like this before.

"You know, Madhav, there was a time like this in Champakapur when your father, his parents and I discussed family matters. I shall never forget the great sacrifice your grandmother, Ganga Bai, made. She offered to plant vegetables to help support the family even though she hated working under the sun. My sacrifice is nothing compared to hers." Mukta was silent for a moment. Then, "Do you remember your grandmother, Madhav?"

"Very well. And Ajjibah, too. I remember how sharp-tongued Ganga Ajji was. Poor Ajjibah. He suffered silently."

"But deep down, she had a heart of gold. If not for her, and your Ajjibah, we may not be alive today." Mukta's voice turned husky at the last sentence.

Tara listened intently, lapping up every bit of information about her new-found family, a family she was beginning to love.

Between them, Mukta and Madhav acquainted Tara with their life in idyllic Champakapur, their flight from the village due to famine and their consequent trek to Tanjore.

"I remember, during the trek, when Bah and Ma were not looking," Madhav told Tara, "Ajji and Ajjibah would call Nilkanth and me and give us part of their rations. 'Eat, children, eat,' they would say, 'you're young and must live.' And my brother and I gobbled their food because we were ravenous all the time."

"When they saw our rations dwindling and the end of the trek nowhere in sight, they must have made a secret pact between themselves to die, so that we may live," Mukta said. "When they died, we found a large portion of uneaten rations on them. Their rations went a long way in sustaining us."

"Bah did find out one day," Madhav recalled, "about us eating our grandparents' food. But he didn't have the strength to get angry with us." Madhav paused, deep in thought. "It's funny, how Bah lost his strength when you didn't, Ma."

"But you told me he was an army captain," Tara said to Madhav, "and the tough one in the family. So he, too, must have secretly not been eating, like his parents."

"It was not because he was not eating," Mukta enlightened Tara. "It was because something was eating him."

"Killa?" Tara guessed.

"Right. And Rani Meera Bai. For him there was no other place as mighty as Killa and no other monarch as mighty as the Rani. They were his universe. 'Might as well be dead than live elsewhere,' he used to say."

"By the time we arrived in Tanjore two months later, he was already half-dead, inside," Madhav recalled. "He even forgot about our sword-fighting lessons."

"But I remember how anxiously he waited for news of Prince Dilip and the regrouping of the Maratha forces. When there was none, he became more and more despondent. But he carried on. For me and the children. He worked very hard as an instructor and advisor to the Tanjore Palace troops."

"And he did not take it out on anyone, as some people do when they suffer great loss," Madhav observed.

"Except once. Do you remember, Madhav?"

"Yes, Ma. It was the day Queen Victoria declared herself Empress of India. To him, that was the ultimate insult. It meant the end of his dream for Killa. He almost went beserk with his ranting and raving. He told us this much later, but that night he went out, hired some thugs, had them collect the Union Jack from every possible public place, and had the great satisfaction of burning the flags. He said other dissidents, too, joined him. He also had the thugs splash night-soil on the Queen's statue in the city centre. From then on, he went about with a haunted look on this face."

186

"But there were other things too," Mukta said for Tara's benefit. "Things that could have increased a hundredfold the turmoil within him."

"What were these things?" Tara asked in her direct way, glad for the opportunity of learning the cause of her father-in-law's present state.

"There was the murder of Hanumant Rao and the death of the British officer, to begin with," Mukta answered. Seeing the question mark on Tara's face, Mukta told her all about Ramdas' rash act in Killa. "But he insisted his killing the traitor was justified. The British officer he killed by accident. So he could not have felt that guilty about it."

"Then there was Nilkanth," Madhav said.

"But before Nilkanth there was ..." Mukta hesitated. She took a deep breath. "There was the matter of the beef."

"Beef?" Tara looked puzzled.

"Yes, beef. You see, Tara, during the trek to Tanjore, he did something unthinkable to Hindus. He ate beef, to keep himself alive."

Tara gasped.

"We were already on the last leg of our journey. Our rations were fast depleting. The rice had gone. The water would disappear in a matter of days. For food, we only had left with us salted mutton which stung our cracked, bleeding lips and blistered mouths and made us even more thirsty. My husband, the patel, the cowherd Gokul, his wives and I tried to dig the soil with our bare hands for water. But, weakened by thirst and hunger, we couldn't dig deep enough to the water table. We had only one recourse left to us—to slaughter Gokul's prize bull." Mukta paused in recollection. "From the time we set foot in Champakapur, that was the bull used for the jallikattu during the Ponggal festival."

"I remember Bah carrying me on his shoulders to see the fights. That bull was a monster. It could toss two men simultaneously into the air, as if they were matchsticks."

"All Gokul's cattle and goats died along the way. We drank the goat's blood and dried their meat. Only the bull survived, thought it was a spectre of its former self. All skin and jutting bones. It started tottering about and that was when the men started eyeing it. 'It's going to die, anyway,' they reasoned." Mukta paused. "Who are we to judge whether they were right or wrong in doing what they did? Does imminent death from starvation absolve the sin of eating beef, for a Hindu?"

The three mulled over Mukta's questions, Tara for the first time.

"Anyway," Mukta continued, "wanting to save us women and children from God's wrath, the men gave us their rations of goat meat. Then they set about slaughtering the bull."

"Can you imagine the blood shooting out of the bull's neck, Tara?" Madhav said. "I still remember that scene. It was like a tableau: Bah and the patel holding down the bull; Gokul bending over it to sever the artery; and a fountain of blood splashing on the men."

"Gokul caught the blood in a vessel. Then the men drank the blood," Mukta said.

Tara shook her head in pity.

"After his first draught, Madhav's father retched. And retched and retched. Then, afraid his share of blood would congeal, he quickly gulped down the rest of it. This way, the men saved the last drops of water for a couple of days. The meat they roasted over a fire and ate. But not heartily. They dried the leftover meat for later use. And for the rest of the journey, Madhav's father did not look me in the eye."

"But I remember him doing penance," Madhav said.

"Yes. He consulted the chief priest in the Brihadisvara Temple. He found out that beef-eating is punishable by beheading. After that, he turned vegetarian. A big sacrifice for someone who relishes bone marrow."

"Who knows, maybe the beef episode is one of the things he thinks of when he rocks to and fro," Madhav said.

"Or he could be thinking about Nilkanth," Mukta said. "It was the son who brought about the father's final doom."

Mukta related to Tara the ways of her cruel, dishonest and philandering son. Madhav added to the narration now and then.

"Madhav's father resented Nilkanth as he did no other, except the British. For years he controlled his resentment to maintain the semblance of peace in the house. But their relationship was as dry as tinder and any small affront could ignite rage. Then, the inevitable happened. Madhav's father exploded. For a trivial reason. Nilkanth was seventeen then. They had a heated argument. And it came to blows. During the fracas, Nilkanth grabbed the pair of wooden swords hanging on the wall. They were the swords the boys had used in Champakapur to learn swordplay. Madhav's father kept them as tokens. They were hanging there," Mukta pointed in the direction of the Rani's picture which they could see through the open window, "on both sides of the picture. We couldn't stop Nilkanth. He was like one possessed. Holding a sword in each hand, he rained blows on his father till he turned blue-black and passed out. That was when I chased Nilkanth out of the house and told him never to set foot here again."

"Bah regained consciousness later. But he was not the same man anymore," Madhav said. "It was as if he had locked himself inside his body and thrown away the key."

"And that was when he started rocking," Mukta informed Tara. "No amount of medicine has been able to cure him. But we continue with the treatment in the hope that he'll recover one of these days."

"Has he ever said anything since the incident?" Tara asked.

"Not a word in ten years. The only thing he communicated to us, by pointing, was to seat him at that window. Since then, we've been seating him there. Other than that, he hasn't communicated with us. Not even to ask for food. And he soils himself. He has become more helpless than a baby. At least a baby cries when it's hungry or in discomfort. And you yourself have seen he doesn't respond when we talk to him." Mukta sighed. "He may be chairbound but he treads most heavily on us. But we don't hold it against him."

"Why do you seat him only at that particular window?" Tara asked. There were four windows in the hall.

"Have you noticed, Tara, which direction the window faces?" Mukta asked.

"No."

"It faces west, the setting sun."

"And Killa lies in the direction of the setting sun," Madhav added.

"So he keeps looking in the direction of Killa every day! How deeply he must love Killa!" Tara said, realisation dawning on her face. "Your poor father. Blow after blow. He doesn't deserve it."

"But then, which good man deserves the blows life deals him?" Mukta observed.

Married Life

Tara settled into married life with ease, a loving husband and a wonderful mother-in-law playing no small role in the happy state of affairs.

Madhav and Tara were deliriously in love. Like all starry-eyed lovers, they swore eternal love for each other. "If I'm reincarnated, I'd have only you as my wife," he said.

"And I, only you as my husband," she said.

After Madhav returned from work and Tara had finished her chores, they would sit together and talk and giggle like children, for hours. When they laughed too loudly and Mukta, distracted, looked up from the scriptures she was reading, they would apologise.

"Don't be sorry. I understand," Mukta would smile and say. "I, too, have been young and in love."

During their togetherness, Madhav and Tara exchanged trivialities about themselves. He said he liked Queen Victoria; she said she liked Rani Meera Bai. He said he liked sandwiches; she said she liked laddoo. He said he liked maroon and gold; she said she liked maroon and gold. And so on and so forth.

They also exchanged knowledge. The attainment of knowledge was an integral part of their individual make-up.

Madhav acquainted Tara with one of his favourite topics: Greek Mythology. Showing her his old reference texts he had used in school, he introduced her to the whole pantheon of Greek gods and goddesses. He spent long hours explaining to her Homer's *Iliad* and *Odyssey*. He told her exciting tales of the adventures of Greek heroes, like 'Jason and the

Argonauts', 'Theseus and the Minotaur' and 'Hercules'.

Tara was especially fascinated by Hercules. She asked many questions about him. She thrilled when Madhav related to her Hercules' slaying of the Nemean Lion and the nine-headed Hydra; of his capturing the Cretan Bull; and of his fetching the Golden Apples from the Garden of the Hesperides. Hercules reminded Tara so much of her Hindu mythological hero—Krishna—who, even as a baby, had killed snakes in his cradle, just like Hercules.

Tara liked, too, the stories about the goddesses Hera, Persephone, Demeter and Helen. But she was drawn most to the legend of Artemis— the daughter of Zeus and sister of Apollo who was a virgin huntress and patroness of chastity. Tara felt she identified with her most.

On her part, Tara verbally painted in rich tones for Madhav the Puranas, the Vedas, the *Ramayana* and the *Mahabharatha*.

She told him of the exploits of the four-headed creator, Brahma; the four-armed preserver, Vishnu; and the human-skull-garlanded destroyer, Shiva.

Madhav learnt from Tara the Hindu version of creation. When Brahma awakes from his cosmic sleep, the universe comes into existence. Then Brahma stays awake for a day which is equivalent to two billion human years. At the end of his day, Brahma goes to sleep and the universe ceases to exist for another two billion years. Then, Brahma awakes and a new universe is born, full of new life forms.

Tara surprised Madhav with the morsel that Vishnu had a counterpart in Greek myth: Hermes. Like Hermes (the son of Zeus), Vishnu, too, appeared on earth frequently in his avatars to help suffering mankind.

She engrossed him with the story of how Shiva came to have his Third Eye. It happened that Shiva's consort, Parvati, while in a playful mood, held her hands over his eyes which were usually open. At once, a frightening darkness spread across the universe. There was no sunlight, no moonlight and no starlight. Only blackness. In order to save the universe, Shiva had to quickly open a third eye in the centre of his forehead so that life-giving light would return and the order of the universe would revert to normal.

On wings of words, Tara flew Madhav to other loka or worlds.

They visited Svar Loka, a paradise, where souls who have led a meritorious life live. They went to Soma Loka, home to the moon and planets. They breezed into Gandharva Loka where they dallied sweetly because they found the male and female spirits of that world most like themselves—irresistible to each other.

After they had heard each other's mythical tales, Madhav and Tara agreed that Greek and Hindu gods were undeniably alike in that they all had human traits: they loved like Hero and Leander, Krishna and Radha; they hated like the matricidal Orestes and Parashurama; they were jealous like Zelos and Rahu; and, as married couples, they fought and reconciled like Zeus and Hera, Shiva and Parvati.

The shashtras were another topic Tara delved into at length: the *Dharma Shashtra* on moral codes; the *Artha Shashtra* on worldly goods; the *Vastu Shashtra* on the science of building; and the *Natya Shashtra* on dance and music (Tara's favourite treatise).

The *Kama Shashtra*—the treatise that was the bible of the courtesans—Tara initiated Madhav into, nightly, in bed. Then she became Madhav's guru and he her eager student.

Madhav was amazed at her erotic knowledge. She did pleasurable things to him that he never dreamed of. In her soft, strong way, she transported him on waves of ecstacy to all the wonderful loka she had told him about.

Is it possible one so young can be so expert in the delights of the boudoir, Madhav asked himself. All the Madame Bovarys and Fanny Hills of his reading pleasure paled in comparison to Tara.

Madhav confided in Tara his dream of visiting far-off places.

"Until now, my wanderlust has taken me only to the cities and towns near Tanjore."

He said he had been to Nagapatnam, Trichinopoly, Banrutti, Madurai and Pondicherry.

"You should see the port of Nagapatnam. It never sleeps. It's as if the whole of India has gathered at a single place. And there's a crush of vessels, and such a forest of masts that monkeys swing from them."

He described the other places to her: the high Rock Fort at Trichinopoly built on a monolith; the vast jackfruit orchards of Banrutti where the fruit hung like a million green lanterns from the trunks; the dazzling diamond nose stud of the goddess Meenakshi Amman, at the temple of the same name in Madurai; and the beautiful spired churches, called Notre Dame Des La Conception and De Sacre Cesur De Jesus, in the French enclave of Pondicherry.

"I specially like the well-ordered streets of Pondicherry," Madhav said. "They're clean and pleasing to the eye. Their missionary schools are of the highest standard. Convents, I hear, have made a name for themselves all over the world. If I have a daughter, I'll educate her at a convent."

Madhav took Tara frequently to the Brihadisvara Temple. There he pointed out and explained to her the inscriptions on the stones. (Though Tara had been to the temple to dance, she had been so closely guarded that she had not been able to explore the place on her own.) Very soon, Madhav had her mesmerised. She listened to Madhav with the curiosity and wonder of a child as he told her of the distant lands where forests kissed the sea, where palaces had golden tiles and ponds golden shores; where the people believed in fairies, spirits and dragons; and where the Tamils of Tamilakam and the Klings of Kalinga met the natives, and merchants from far-off China and Arabia.

"What's Suvarnabhumi?" Tara asked, fascinated by a name Madhav mentioned.

Madhav was only too glad to explain.

"It means Golden Land. A scholar told me it refers to a peninsula, across the eastern ocean, which centuries ago had rivers of gold."

"And Kadahram? What does that mean?"

"It was a coastal city-kingdom in the peninsula. The Chola kings sent emissaries to Kadahram and all the other city-kingdoms in the land. But even before the Cholas, Indian merchants were carrying on a barter trade with the indigenous people there. They exchanged cloth, gems and beads for gold and tin. Many of these merchants settled along the coast and married native women."

"What were the natives called?"

"Malaiyur. That was ten centuries ago. History says they are now called 'Malay' and the peninsula 'Malaya'."

"Malaya. What a lovely name! I wonder if it's like its name? Full of undulating hills, towering mountains and deep valleys. Wouldn't it be interesting to see this land?"

"I'm sure it would be. What with the more than a thousand years of Indian, Chinese and Arab influence it has had."

Like Madhav's, Tara's eyes took on a dreamy look as she tried to imagine the people and places mentioned in the inscriptions.

Madhav showed Tara every nook and corner of the Brihadisvara Temple. He beamed when Tara admired the sculptures, the mammoth bull Nandi (twice the height of a six-foot man and carved out of a single mass of hornblendic gneiss), and the gold-topped dome on the fourteen-storey main tower.

"They say the dome is carved out of a single block of granite and weighs eighty tons," Madhav informed Tara.

"I wonder how they lifted the dome to the top," Tara said as she looked in awe at the structure.

"The ignorant say demons did it. In fact, they say demons built the whole temple, mere humans being incapable of such a feat. But the inscriptions say the Chola king, Rajaraja I, built the temple. The dome was conveyed to the top by means of an inclined plane. It seems it took twelve years of labour to raise the dome. Do you know the base of the dome is so wide a four-wheeled carriage can be driven around it?"

"So how about us taking a ride up there?"

"Good idea. But you may have to wait twelve years, madam!"

Madhav took Tara on a tour of Tanjore during weekends.

They visited the numerous shrines shrill with the sound of bells and pigeons. At each shrine, they offered prayers for Ramdas' recovery.

They walked through the city's labyrinth of streets jammed with people, cows, goats, dogs, pigs, elephants, bullock carts, jinrickshaws and gharries. If you did not look where you were going, you were likely to step on some wretched beggar sleeping on the pavement or a legless person crawling about on his hands. Once, Tara became sick when she saw a leper with half his face eaten.

Tara strolled through the teeming bazaars as if she were in a dream world. The sari shops were heaven to Tara.

At the street stalls of Tanjore, Tara tasted, for the first time, ordinary folks' drinks, like ginger coffee and masala tea. (Madhav steered her away from the palm toddy.) She gorged herself on spicy snacks like pakora and brinjal bhaji , items taboo in the Arsa Mahal as the oily food would ruin her complexion.

They went for excursions on the Cauvery in a parisal, the circular reed-boat that looked more like a basket than a boat. When they walked along the banks, the fishermen's wives came out to admire Tara. She must be from the spirit world, they whispered, no earthling can be so beautiful. Then they touched her to see if she was real.

Madhav and Tara visited the artisans' streets the city was renowned for: one that made and sold moulded, beaten, tooled or filigreed brass and copperware; a second that was heaped with variously shaped clay pots, the fine clay along the Cauvery banks being famous in the region; a third that sold Tanjore's famous thalai-aati-bommai dancing dolls, that, at a touch, bobbed their heads and swayed their hips (Madhav bought one for Tara); and a fourth that produced cut-mirror frames, platters, and elephants. The cut mirror picked up the sunbeams and threw them at each other, as if the gods were at war.

In all these wanderings, they gave a wide berth to the Arsa Mahal and Nilkanth's mansion. Once, Nilkanth passed them by in his carriage. Madhav and Tara froze. The look he gave them was so searing that it could have scorched ice.

"There must be some good in him, after all," Madhav said later. "At least he hasn't pursued you any further. For that, I'm grateful."

"But I'm still not too sure about him," Tara said.

Tara devoted herself to making her presence a difference to the family that had taken her in. She did many things to show her love for them.

She toiled in the kitchen with Mukta. She made the simplest meals scrumptious, adding to them Arsa Mahal secrets. Once in a while, she surprised Madhav with his favourite English teatime treat: scones. The recipe she had learnt long ago during one of her sojourns to the palace library where palace cooks, under orders from Maharajah Sarabhoji Bhonsle, had compiled English recipes to be used when the Maharajah entertained the British Governor.

As with cooking, so with sewing, decorating and gardening.

She filled the empty walls with embroidery and beadwork samplers. Rani Meera Bai's picture she beautified with a beaded frame. And she brightened the front of the house with gay crotons and amandas.

She helped prepare Ramdas' bath, infusing the hot water with mint and eucalyptus, hoping the fumes he inhaled from the bath would somehow unlock his soul. She fed him when Mukta was busy, softly telling him stories of brave rajahs and ranis who won back their kingdoms from invaders. But it was like talking to the wall.

At night she sang kirtan for the family, her voice like the soothing coo of a dove carried on the sigh of a breeze.

Madhav and Mukta marvelled at her.

In return, when Madhav and Tara were alone and intimate, Madhav would romantically promise Tara a garment of a thousand fireflies, a shawl of dew drop-studded gossamer, a necklace of the stars she was named after, and a ring of diamonds from the magical jewel-palace under the earth.

Tara would be tickled pink at his earnestness.

"Give me your love. That's all I ask," she would say.

*   *   *

So passed the dizzying early days of their marriage.

The Neighbourhood

The citizens of Tanjore had their favourite meeting places to discuss their pet topics, whether they belonged to the Maratha-Hindu neighbourhood, Tamil-Hindu neighbourhood, Tamil-Muslim neighbourhood or the Tamil-Christian neighbourhood. The pundits met at the Saraswathi Mahal Library, yogis at the Brihadisvara Temple, merchants at the guildhall, dhobies at the Cauvery ghats, thieves at the thieves' market, and drunkards at the toddy shops.

For the women of Madhav's totally Maratha neighbourhood, their favourite meeting place was the communal well.

The well was old beyond memory. Like all old wells, it had its history: hidden treasure, war-massacred bodies, suicides, secretly aborted foetuses, born-out-of-wedlock babies and unwanted baby girls. Wide, and bottomless as the pits of hell, it was never short of water, like the women who came there were never short of gossip.

The beginning of the end of the Bhonsles' stay in Tanjore started at the well. It began on the day Tara had a shock.

On that day, there were, as usual, a mixed lot of women at the well: young and old, fat and thin, fair and dark, pretty and ugly, clever and stupid, housewives and servants ... But no matter how different they were from each other, most of them had one thing in common—they came to the well to gossip. It was the only place where they could talk without interference from mothers-in-law, husbands or children. In between clanging down buckets and water jars, pulling the ropes, hoisting the vessels and pouring the water, they would exchange juicy nuggets of news about everybody else except themselves.

After their sessions at the well, they would go home knowing which woman had sneaked out of her husband's bed at night to meet her lover in the banana grove; which first and second wife had pulled each other's hair over the husband they shared; which man had contracted the wasting disease from the slut house; which wretched woman had to borrow jewellery to attend a wedding; and which boy was meeting which girl behind the temple walls. The women drew an inexplicable satisfaction from this kind of talk which those not given to gossiping will not understand.

In recent weeks, Tara had been the choice nugget the gossips salivated over. Not that they knew much about her. The only concrete thing they knew was that Tara was a courtesan and had arrived in the middle of the night in Madhav's house. The rest was conjecture. They thought it beneath themselves to seek an explanation from a courtesan or the mother-in-law of one. They tried to pry information from the likeable Laxmi Bai but she remained tight-lipped though Mukta had told her all there was to know. So, not really knowing Tara, the neighbourhood women did not like her.

Many of the gossips were jealous of Tara's beauty.

After her arrival, they went out of their way to learn Arsa Mahal beauty secrets, wheedling the information from Mahal servants who came to the market. Then they pestered their husbands to buy them all manner of beauty enhancers though it could bankrupt them.

They smeared their faces with turmeric and egg white. They almost drowned themselves in goats' milk. They gulped milk boiled with saffron. Like drunkards, they consumed a concoction of crushed pink lotus, blue lotus, saffron and honey. They washed their hair with a paste of henna and mountain jasmine. They blackened their eyelashes with a kohl of burnt camel bones and antimony. Some even went to extremes: they collected drops of sweat from the testicles of a white horse and diluted it with yellow arsenic. They applied this potion to their lips. The lips turned red and inviting. Sadly for them, their husbands only commented, "You look like a whore!" The men were sore their pockets were being emptied.

For some of the women, the beauty treatments worked. But for the majority, they could not enhance beauty where there was none. This irked the women even more. They were waiting for a chance to pounce on Tara. And they did, the day Tara came to the well alone.

The woman talked loud enough for Tara to hear as she approached the well.

"Look how she walks, like a horse."

"And shaking her bum, too!"

"She must be out to snare our men."

"Didn't she have her fill at the Arsa Mahal?"

"I caught my husband peeping at her from behind the window."

"So did I my husband!"

"Goodness! What did you do?"

"I twisted his ear and dragged him from the window!"

"I threatened to throw him out of the house!"

"Your husbands aren't to blame. She is."

Tara stopped and looked at the women. The women fell silent. When Tara started walking again, they continued with their insults.

"At least the dasi in the slut house don't pretend to be paragons of domestic virtue!"

"Who knows what tantra she used to seduce innocent Madhav."

"Sisters, make way for the Maharani!"

The women parted in mock reverence to allow Tara to draw water.

Their words were lances that pierced Tara deeply. But she remained calm. With tremendous effort, Tara smiled at them. But they, in a rude gesture, shrugged a shoulder to the chin and turned away their faces.

A deadly silence prevailed as Tara drew the water.

"Be careful," someone broke the silence, "don't spoil your dainty hands stroking the rope. Your hands were made for stroking more pleasurable things!"

The women laughed derisively. As Tara fled, they spat vehemently after her.

"Slut!" someone called.

"Society can be cruel, unfeeling and very unforgiving," Mukta had warned Tara. "The prince and pariah may forgive you, but it is the ordinary majority in between that is to be feared. This majority has an exaggerated sense of self-righteousness. Make one small mistake and it will brand you, pigeonhole you and never forgive you, no matter how good a person you are. And it judges women more harshly than it does men."

How right my mother-in-law is, Tara thought on her way back from the well. They did not even try to get to know me but here they are labelling me for the misfortune of being born a courtesan. Is this what the ordinary world is like, she asked herself. Suspicious? Quick to jump to conclusions?

During the first weeks of her marriage, when she had gone out with Madhav, Tara had been in such a state of euphoria that her feet hardly touched the ground. She had not even noticed elephants on the streets, let alone the neighbourhood women.

Then, when she and Mukta had started going out to fetch water from the well, she noticed the women whispered to each other and sniggered. A few managed a false smile, only for Mukta. They pretended Tara was not present.

"What, Mukta, you didn't even invite us to your son's marriage," they said. "Some people forget old ties when new ones are forged."

"Even if I did invite you," Mukta invariably replied, "you'd never come. Some people resent new ties, especially if it concerns courtesans."

Mukta's answer angered the women even more.

"Don't antagonise them, Mami," Tara begged in private, "not for my sake. After all, they are our neighbours."

"Be quiet, child. You don't know the outside world yet. Give these women an inch and they'll grind masala on your head!"

As long as she had gone out with either Madhav or Mukta, the women had not dared say anything to Tara's face. So her first trip alone to the well proved to be a sobering experience. The gossips had succeeded in making her feel she did not belong. She was like a white crow among the black.

After the incident at the well, Tara started walking with both feet planted firmly on the ground and so became aware of many things.

As soon as they saw her coming down the street, mothers plaiting their daughters' hair on the verandah quickly whisked the girls into the house and banged the door shut.

Fathers warned their sons as she walked by, "Keep your eyes on the ground. It's bad luck to look at this black flower." It meant Tara was a girl who had severed family ties and, therefore, should not be looked upon.

People made a detour in the temples to avoid her, as if she were a leper.

At the marketplace, the female vendors overcharged her with a take-it-or-leave-it attitude. Their male counterparts pointedly offered her only carrots, cucumbers and snake gourds, with a wry smile on their faces.

The couple of women who were still friendly with Mukta, slighted Tara, too, even when they invited them together for the same function— Tara was conveniently overlooked to bless adolescent girls celebrating their rites of passage; she was not called upon to put bangles on the wrists of a mother-to-be during fertility rites; no one offered her rice to shower on newlyweds; and hostesses 'forgot' to invite her to bless a newborn baby. Worst still were the women who invited everybody else except Tara for functions.

All this was a double blow for Tara.

First, she had to cope with the insults, whether they were direct or subtle. Second, she had to come to terms with the fact that the ordinary world was not going to accept her as a mangalamukhi.

The pundits at the Arsa Mahal had taught her that a courtesan was a mangalamukhi, a bringer of good fortune. Even a king, setting out to war or to visit another state, considered it good luck if he saw a courtesan as soon as he stepped out of the palace. So it was written in the shashtras. But Tara's experience was to the contrary. The neighbourhood behaved as if she would bring a scourge upon them.

For the first time, Tara admitted to herself that her mother had been right in asking whether ordinary folk would accept her. Tara realised there was, indeed, a chasm between the Arsa Mahal and the ordinary world outside it.

But then, I have my husband and my mother-in-law, Tara consoled herself. They stand by me like rocks. And there is the neighbour, Laxmi

Bai. She, too, has shown me nothing but kindness and understanding since I came to this house ...

Seeing Tara's teary eyes daily, Madhav and Mukta could only advise her to ignore the people's taunts.

The matter of Nilkanth made it impossible for mother and son to confront anyone who insulted Tara. Because Nilkanth was a man, the neighbourhood had magnanimously put down his womanising to 'manliness' and the state of his being born a 'double-whorler'. "He's a man. He can do anything he wants," they said. "After all, every family has its black sheep." So the neighbourhood tolerated, to a degree, the presence of the Bhonsle family. But bringing Tara into their midst was an entirely different matter. She was a woman. And no self-respecting woman left the parental home to live with a man, even if she had the intention of marrying him. Moreover, she was a courtesan. And courtesans should stay where they belong.

One man loudly related an allegory to another in Tara's presence and drove home to her the neighbourhood's point: "It seems the snake coiled around Lord Shiva's neck asked Garuda, Lord Vishnu's eagle-vehicle, 'Are you well, Garuda?' To which Garuda replied, 'If everyone remains at his station in life, then all is well.'"

Meanwhile, the taunts continued. They became bolder and coarser.

"Come. Sit at my tea stall. You'll be good for business!"

"Hey! Is Madhav alone enough for you? How about meeting me here at midnight tonight?"

"Exactly what size are you—a cow-elephant, a mare or a doe? I'm a stallion and can satisfy all three types."

Gradually, Tara went out less and less. Madhav rehired the servant-girl to carry water from the well. Even then, Tara was not spared. Things came to a head one day.

Tara and Mukta were at the Brihadisvara Temple. They had arrived too early and had half an hour on their hands before the sunset puja. So they decided to be of service to the temple. Mukta offered to help the junior priest to get ready the brass and copper paraphernalia for the puja. Tara set off to weed the tulsi patch, not dreaming of confrontation in a place of worship. Only a scattering of devotees was about.

The tulsi patch was at one corner of the back courtyard. A total of thirty of the basil bushes stood on the patch. The plants were healthy. Their leaves were a dark green with a profusion of jade-green flowers at the end of each stalk. The sweet scent of the herb was almost overpowering. Though the steeped leaves could be used as a tonic, the temple grew the herb for its flowers. Bunches of the flowers were woven into garlands for the statues of deities.

Tara started weeding between the bushes. The love-grass and touch-me-nots yielded easily in the light, sandy soil.

Chanting a mantra softly, Tara was halfway through when she saw shadows fall across the patch from behind her. She turned and looked up. Three women were looking down at her.

Tara recognised them. They were all from her neighbourhood. The fair one with a coin-sized red dot on her forehead was the barber's wife. She considered herself a paragon of virtue. Tara remembered the woman had called her a horse at the well. The dark one with betel-stained lips was known to be very beauty-conscious. Only problem was, her face was full of pimples. The ugly one was the woman who purposely brushed against Tara on the street, on many occasions, and hissed, "Slut!".

Tara stood up slowly to face the women. Her heart was beating like the temple drums.

Big Dot was the first to speak.

"*Are!* What have we here? A servant of God?" Her tone was sugared.

"How considerate, helping our temple!" Pimples said in the same tone.

"And all dolled-up, too!" Ugly Face said spitefully.

"What right do you think you have to touch these plants?" Pimples asked.

Tara opened her mouth to answer but no sound came out.

Big Dot said, "You contaminate the tulsi with your touch. I swear the flowers will become scorched before the evening is out!"

"And you desecrate our temple," Pimples added, smiling dangerously.

"You're not welcome here. You're not welcome anywhere in our neighbourhood," Big Dot said.

Ugly Face came uncomfortably close to Tara, snorting like a bull. Tara felt a blast of stale breath as the woman began to speak. "I've been meaning to ask you this for a long time, Tara Bai," she was all politeness as she glanced slyly at her cohorts. "What's your father's name?"

Tara's blood curdled. She turned as red as the sari she was wearing. It was the question she most dreaded. For, in truth, she did not know who her father was.

"You're a child of God," her mother had told her when she was five. In courtesan circles, children seldom knew of whose seed they were born. And neither did it matter to them. But ordinary folk put great weight by it. When all is lost, only your father's name remains, they said.

When Tara saw and learnt what courtesan life was all about, she knew she could never really be sure who fathered her. He could have been a rich citizen, a pundit, a poet, a maestro. He could even have been a prince.

"Speak!" Ugly Face said. "What, have you suddenly taken a vow of silence?"

"Can't have," smirked Big Dot, " I heard her crooning to her husband as I passed her house last night."

"Stop it! Stop it!" Tara screamed. "Let me be! What have I done to you that you belittle me so?"

People nearby heard her and started gathering. Mukta, too, heard Tara. She dropped the brass utensils with a crash and ran out to the courtyard.

"Belittle you? How? People who don't know their father's name should not get angry, you know," Ugly Face said and pushed Tara.

Tara fell into the tulsi bushes.

As she was struggling to get up, Mukta arrived and helped her to her feet. Tara's hair was dishevelled and there were bruises and scratches on her face and body.

"Mami, please forgive me for what I'm about to do." Throwing feminity to the winds, Tara tucked in her sari at the waist and did one of the things she did best. She kicked.

She kicked Ugly Face with full force on her hips and sent her sprawling to the ground. Her other two tormentors she kicked in the shins. Pimples' knees buckled and she sat with a thud on the hard stone floor. Big Dot's dot came a notch lower as her face contorted with pain.

The women were stunned. They had not expected such fury and momentum from this fragile-looking woman.

"Walks like a horse, eh?" Tara reminded them of their taunts at the well. "Well, here's more of what a horse does." She kicked them all once again for good measure.

Ugly Face, her face uglier with pain, cried the loudest.

Mukta restrained Tara.

"I may not know my father's name but for sure I'm a hundredfold better than you!" Tara spat at the women as she marched out of the Temple with Mukta in tow.

The crowd was silent. If Tara had silenced them with her great beauty the first time she danced at the temple, now, for the last time, she silenced them with her fury.

As they marched, Tara and Mukta heard a drone behind them. Then they felt the first stones hit them on their heads, backs and legs. They broke into a run, hailed a horse-drawn gharri and sped home to safety.

"We have to leave, Ma. Enough is enough."

"Yes. I agree with you. It's not right that we continue living among people who don't accept us any longer."

Mukta was nursing the deep cut on her head she had sustained from the stoning. Earlier, she and Tara had told Madhav all about the incident in the temple.

Ramdas, as usual, sat rocking in his chair, oblivious to the world.

"Their rancour against Tara I understand. But against you, Ma?" Madhav shook his head disbelievingly.

"All because of me," Tara said with sorrow, more worried about Mukta's injury than the bruises on her own body.

"It's not your fault, Tara. Those women had it coming to them," Mukta said. "As for the stoning, ignorance and ill-will can turn any mob into an unreasoning beast." Mukta paused in thought and then added,

"I just can't believe they hold us in such contempt."

"Well, we can't expect everyone to be like Laxmi Bai," Madhav said.

Even the favourable opinions she had expressed of the Ramdas family failed to sway the prejudice of the neighbourhood.

"If only people would understand!"

"It's too late for that now, Ma. Tomorrow, I'll start looking for a new place to stay. It won't be easy, seeing how overcrowded this city already is. It's difficult to find even a single room for rent."

"Thank God your Bah has been spared all this," Mukta said, glancing at Ramdas.

They fell silent.

Though they had not eaten their dinner, they did not feel hungry. They sat around for a while, Tara and Mukta mentally reliving their horror, and Madhav imagining it.

Then, they went to bed with the same question on their minds: what guarantee is there the next neighbourhood will accept us?

That night, the house was pelted with stones.

Madhav, Tara and Mukta sat bolt upright in their beds. Ramdas continued sleeping like a baby. Next door, Laxmi and her children awoke and started quaking with fright.

There was shouting outside.

"Madhav! Come out!"

"Don't hide behind women's saris!"

"Your wife has attacked our women!"

"If you don't come out, we'll come in!"

Madhav stepped out of the house, raising his hands to protect his head. But the stoning had stopped. Tara and Mukta joined him.

The mob held burning torches and brandished sticks, rods and machetes.

On seeing the weapons, Madhav said, "There's no need for violence. I promise you we'll be leaving soon. Just give us some time to look for other accommodations."

"How much time? We've tolerated you long enough," the barber said, his beady eyes glinting. Big Dot stood beside him, looking like she had three eyes. Her husband continued, "First, your brother brings shame to this neighbourhood, and now you!"

"What next?" a faceless voice asked.

"Maybe his wife'll set up a secret Arsa Mahal here since the white man has already started shutting down slut houses," another faceless voice quipped. Pimples stood in front of the voice.

The crowd jeered.

Incensed, Madhav wanted to lash out. But years of good breeding held him back.

"We're a self-respecting community here, you know. We can't have courtesans and hush-hush marriages in our midst," another man said.

Mukta recognised him as the one whose wife sneaked out at night to meet her lover. A one-time friend had told her so.

"Self-respecting? Hah! You don't know what's going on in your own backyard!" Mukta could not help being vindictive. She felt weak with the effort. Her head wound was throbbing again.

"Madhav, you'd better shut your mother up or I'll do it for you!"

"How can he? She wears the dhoti in the house!" the barber said snidely.

"Look, I know you're trying to drag me into a fight but you're in for a disappointment," Madhav said calmly. "My mother has not bred me to fight with anyone, especially holier-than-thou people like you! You want us to leave, we'll leave."

"We want an apology first!" Ugly Face's husband shouted, twirling his stick.

"All right. I —" Madhav began.

"Don't Madhav! Don't apologise!" a baritone voice rang from somewhere behind the crowd.

The crowd parted as a group of hefty men elbowed its way forward. A woman followed the group closely. A handsome man led the group.

"Nilkanth!" everyone gasped. They looked at each other in fear and panic.

The woman rushed to Tara.

"My baby! My poor baby! I heard what happened," Sundari exclaimed as she hugged Tara.

"Yes! This is Nilkanth!" Nilkanth's voice sliced the air. "I may be a scoundrel but I'm not going to stand by and watch you bullying my mother and brother and ..." Nilkanth clicked his heels and bowed to Tara. "... and my sister-in-law. They have done you no wrong!"

He gave a signal and his thugs drew their pistols and pointed them at the mob. The mob fell back.

"I've eyes and ears all over Tanjore. And beyond. So I know what's been going on here. But I didn't expect things to get this far. Now, who wants an apology? Come forward this instant!" Nilkanth thundered.

No one moved.

"What's the matter? The bhu sandi crow got your manliness?"

Uneasy silence.

"You sons-of-dasi!" Sundari's voice rang. "My daughter was a virgin! A virgin! You hear that? You've no idea how she fought to keep her virginity! And she defied her caste and gave up unimaginable riches to live like one of you. And this is the way you treat her? You didn't even try getting to know her before passing judgement!"

The mobsters were hushed by her voice, her height and bearing.

"'Once a courtesan, always a courtesan'! That's the decree of the world, Sundari Bai," Nilkanth said. "And now," he addressed the mob, "if you're all going to stand there like temple statues, I suggest we disperse. We could all do with a good night's sleep."

When the people still did not budge, Nilkanth instructed his men to shoot. The men fired several shots into the air.

The people ran pell-mell.

"That's better. And remember," Nilkanth called after them, "I'll be keeping an eye on all of you!"

A shrill of whistles filled the air.

"Police!" Nilkanth exclaimed. "Ma, Madhav ..." he looked at them in turn and touched their hands in farewell. Then he and his men melted into the night.

The mothers faced each other, one whose world revolved around her man, the other whose men revolved around her world. Both were wondering what to say to each other.

Mukta spoke first.

"So, we meet at last." She took Sundari's hands in hers. "You must have done much good to give birth to a daughter like Tara."

"Oh how I wish all those nasty people could see you holding my hands. They'd faint!" Sundari rolled her eyes. Ordinary people just did not hold courtesans' hands. "Anyway, I've learnt all about your family from Nilkanth. Don't judge him too harshly, Mukta Bai. There is still some good left in your son. That's why he came running when he heard you were in trouble."

"Hear that, Tara? I told you so," Madhav wanted to dispel the doubts she had of his brother. "Deep down, my brother loves us all."

"I threw him out of this house once, Sundari Bai," there was a tinge of regret in Mukta's voice, "and I thought I'd never see him here again. But now I see the sword has yet to be forged to sever family bonds. That's why *you* came running!"

The women laughed in mutual understanding.

"Won't you come in?" Mukta invited Sundari.

"Not tonight. It's getting late and I must be on my way." Sundari clapped her hands and her carriage came up from the alley in which it had been parked.

Turning to Madhav she said, "Nilkanth has told me a lot about you. From that, I know you'll take care of my daughter like gold. But be wary of the neighbourhood just the same."

"Don't worry, Mami. I promise I'll not let her be hit by stones, or words, anymore." Madhav felt a pang of guilt at not having taken Tara's complaints seriously. "Perhaps if I'd taken these people to task earlier, all this would not have happened."

"But that's not like you, Madhav," Mukta consoled him. "You're good, so you expect only good from others."

"I've learnt my lesson, Ma."

"Both you and Tara have a lot more to learn," Sundari said. "The world is like milk. Not everything is pure cream. There are bound to be some curds, too."

Madhav nodded in agreement.

"And now, if you'll excuse me, I'll be on my way." Sundari held Tara for a long moment. "Come and see me sometime, Tara."

Then, bidding farewell to all of them, she got into the gharri.

"If you need help to find a new place to stay, just let me know," she called as the gharri trundled away.

Mukta, Madhav and Tara mentally turned over the events of the night as they tried falling asleep.

Nilkanth was uppermost in their thoughts.

In a sinister way, Ramdas' dream had come true. How much like a general Nilkanth looked and sounded. How he commanded everyone's attention. Only he was a general of thugs.

Mukta regretted he had to rush off without seeing his father. Would he have wanted to see him if he had the time, she wondered. Suddenly, she wished she had hugged him.

Madhav was glad he had judged Nilkanth correctly.

Tara thanked God that Nilkanth had accepted her as his brother's wife.

The Falling into Place

When you are lost in the black cavern of despair; when you are sinking into the quicksand of sorrow; when you are fighting a losing battle against the demons of the world; and when you are dying but yet cannot die, at such times, if you keep your faith in Bhagvan, He will touch you. And then, everything will fall into place." So said the temple priest when Mukta went to the Brihadisvara Temple to seek solace after the neighbourhood's attack.

For Madhav and his family, three things happened, and, within a month, everything fell into place.

Soon after the aborted attack, Madhav began trudging the streets of Tanjore in the hope of finding a house for rent. He was unsuccessful, as he had expected. Even his acquaintances, whose help he enlisted, could not find him a place.

As a last resort, Madhav decided he would take up Sundari Bai's offer of assistance. According to Tara, Sundari still kept in touch with some of her former admirers and would be able to find them a house through these contacts. So, one evening, Madhav set out to the Arsa Mahal on his way home from work.

There was a large crowd on the next street from the Mahal. Curious, he went towards the crowd. A man was standing on a chair and addressing the crowd. He was almost shouting to make himself heard.

"What's going on?" Madhav asked the waif beside him.

"Job opportunities, brother! Job opportunities! An end to unemployment and hunger!" he answered excitedly, showing a mouthful of rotten teeth.

"Job opportunities? I don't understand."

"See that man talking? He's a kangani. He's come from Malaya to recruit workers for that country. Listen to him."

Madhav's heart somersaulted at the word 'Malaya'. He pricked up his ears.

The kangani was well dressed. Though he was wearing the same dhoti and tunic a few of the other men wore, he could boast of a headdress, a coat and a shiny watch. The watch, worn outside the coat pocket in the manner of the vellaikara dorai or white boss, hung out for all to see. The kangani made a great impression on the half-naked majority in front of him.

"For how long are you going to starve? For how long are you going to remain unemployed?" Madhav heard him say. "You know jobs are scarce in this city. Here's your chance to gain steady employment. The Vellaikara Dorai is laying miles of roads and railway lines in Malaya. He's also opening up rubber estates there. He needs coolies. And tappers. To work in the rubber estates. All you have to do is sign a three-year contract and you'll be on your way to unimagined riches."

The crowd buzzed.

"What about our families?" a man asked.

"Don't worry. You can take your family along. You'll be provided with living quarters."

"What about the pay?" another asked.

"Enough for three bellyfuls a day and decent clothes to wear. As you can see, I'm living proof."

The kangani certainly looked well fed besides being well dressed.

"And what happens after the contract expires?" someone piped.

"You can choose to either return home or continue working in Malaya."

Another buzz.

"Don't be afraid. There are other people seeking better lives there, too," the kangani persuaded. "There are hundreds of Indians from other parts of India there already. Thousands of cheena coolies are working in the tin mines, and many malaiyur people are still coming from the surrounding islands." The man paused to let his words sink in. Then he continued, "If you're interested, you can register yourself with me now. Or you can think it over and register later. I shall be here at the same time for two weeks, starting today."

"What, brother? Are you going? I'm going for sure. Anything to fill my belly," the waif said, patting the cavity below his jutting ribs.

"By the way," the kangani spoke again, "if anyone among you is English educated, you can register at the agent's office in Pookara Street. Malaya needs you, too."

Madhav's heart did a Bharathanatyam number. He abandoned all thoughts of going to the Arsa Mahal for help. He suddenly grew wings and was home in half the time it normally took him.

When he got home, he pulled a bewildered Tara into their room, closed the door and told her all about the recruitment exercise.

On hearing Madhav, Tara became equally excited.

"Going to Malaya seems to be the ideal solution for us," Madhav concluded. "We don't have to look high and low for new accommodation here. And we get to see a new land. You do share my dream of travelling, don't you?"

"I do, nawra. But ..."

"We have to act fast. Such an opportunity may not present itself again."

"What about your parents? They certainly won't leave," Tara voiced her doubt. "And leaving them behind is unthinkable."

"We'll have to find a way, Tara. We must persuade Ma. Bah, of course, will follow her like a lamb," Madhav gushed. "Tomorrow, I'll go to Pookara Street."

"Shall we tell Mami now?"

"No! No! Not till I find out more from the agent."

For the next half-hour, Madhav and Tara talked about what they knew of Malaya from the temple inscriptions and Madhav's old history books.

When they came out from their room, Mukta gave them a quizzical look but they avoided her gaze.

Mukta knew something was up but could not guess what it was.

Madhav had never before grabbed Tara's hand and pulled her in such a hurry into their room. It had to be something important. Then she had an alarming thought: Has it got anything to do with the neighbourhood? God forbid!

The next evening, Madhav made his way to Pookara Street.

Like its name, Pookara Street was lined with florists selling mounds of roses, lilies, marigolds, jasmines and gladioli for use in temples and churches. You could almost float down the street on the cloud of flower scents.

The agent's office was at the end of the street.

The agent sat at a table in what appeared to be a hastily set-up office with a minimum of paraphernalia. A register, application forms in English, a rubber stamp, a stamp pad, an inkwell, a Schaeffer fountain-pen and a blotter lay on the table. A waist-high filing cabinet stood at an angle as if someone had forgotten to push it against the wall. Above the cabinet hung a small portrait of Queen Victoria. It was askew.

On Madhav's inquiries, the bespectacled English-speaking agent informed him that, depending on his academic qualifications, skills and experience, Madhav would be assigned a post in the Railways, the Education Service, the Sanitary Board or the Postal Service in Malaya. Yes, the steamer fare would be subsidised and no, they couldn't travel bunk, only deck. They would have to dish out the whole bunk fare if they wanted to travel bunk. Subsequent trips would be wholly self-sponsored. His salary would be the princely sum of nine hundred rupees (paid in Malayan dollars) and five per cent would be deducted for taxes. No, there was no limit to the number of family members he could take along but would he please leave ill and insane relatives behind (here Madhav's heart plummeted) and would he register within a month. The next recruitment exercise would only take place the following year.

Madhav thanked the agent and left. Leave ill and insane relatives behind? Leave Bah behind? Madhav agonised, his heart torn between going and staying.

* * *

A week later, the Ramdas family had an unexpected visitor: Patel Bhima Rao of Champakapur. He suddenly stood at their doorstep like an apparition.

At first Mukta did not recognise him. He was a wisp of a man now compared to his Champakapur proportions.

"What, Mukta Bai. You look as if you've seen a ghost. It's me. Patel Bhima Rao."

"Patel-ji? I didn't recognise you. You've grown so thin! But please come in." Mukta could not keep the excitement out of her voice.

"Somehow, I never regained the weight I lost during the famine," he said, coming into the house.

Mukta noticed he had not regained the boom in his voice either.

She touched his feet in respect.

"*Ashirwaad* my daughter!" the patel blessed her.

All aflutter, Mukta called, "Madhav! Tara! Come and see who's here!" Mukta was increasingly puzzled at the way the pair had been secluding themselves in their room for hours on end during the past week.

When they came out, she introduced them to the patel. The couple touched his feet and got his blessings.

"*Are* Madhav! How you've grown! You were short as a brinjal when I last saw you," the patel said, looking Madhav up and down as he held him by the shoulders.

Like the cowherd Gokul, the patel, too, had gone to live in a far-flung village after their arrival in Tanjore. He had come only once to visit the family soon after. Then his work in the paddies, his failing health and the death of his wife had kept him in the village.

"And how are things with you all?" the patel asked.

"By the grace of God, everything's well," Mukta lied.

"Madhav, do you remember the tantrums you used to throw because your father wouldn't allow you time for anything but sword fighting?"

"Only too well, Patel-ji. But in spite of everything, there'll never be another Champakapur for me."

"Yes. Those were halcyon days, weren't they? And Nilkanth. How's he? Has he changed?"

The family was shocked that he knew and were lost for an answer.

"I ..." the patel said regretfully, "I heard about Nilkanth. I'm sorry."

"So, his notoriety has spread even beyond the city," Mukta said, bowing her head in anguish.

"Take heart, Mukta. When Bhagvan gives a blow He'll also give an embrace."

"You're right there, Patel-ji," Mukta said, remembering how Nilkanth had suddenly turned up to help the family. "It's just that my husband was depending so much on Nilkanth to take up arms against the British. He insisted Nilkanth, more than Madhav, had the capacity of being a great soldier. 'Nilkanth will make the perfect general,' he always said."

"And Ramdas. Where's he? I've got some very good news for him."

"He's still asleep. I'll wake him up but before that there's something you ought to know."

Mukta and Madhav told the patel about Ramdas' condition and how it came about.

The patel was shocked and bewildered.

"But how could this happen to Ramdas?" he kept repeating. Then, "All the more reason why I've to talk to him. Perhaps what I have to say will bring about a change in him. I pray that it will."

Mukta rushed to get Ramdas bathed and spruced up. Tara prepared his breakfast and a tumbler of steaming filter coffee for the patel. The patel told Madhav about what he had to say to his father. Madhav was filled with hope.

Bathed and fed, Ramdas was led to his favourite seat. His face was expressionless, as usual.

"Nawra, there's someone here to see you. The Patel-ji. From Champakapur. Do you remember him?" Mukta asked gently.

The patel took Ramdas' face in both his hands. "Ramdas, my boy! It's me, Patel Bhima Rao. Do you recognise me?"

If he did, Ramdas did not show any sign.

The patel hugged him in silence. Then, holding his face again, the patel continued, "Ramdas, you must listen to what I'm going to say. Do you understand? Nod your head if you do."

There was no response.

The patel looked at the others. They shook their heads dejectedly.

"Ramdas, listen! It's about Prince Dilip! He has mustered a large force to attack the British in Killa. Do you hear?"

Mukta looked at Madhav, surprised. Madhav nodded to say he knew.

All of them felt their hearts sink when Ramdas showed no comprehension of the patel's tidings.

"Bah, here's your chance to go back to Killa," Madhav tried. "That's what you've always wanted, haven't you?"

"Just think, nawra. It'll be like old times," Mukta said, her heart leaping with fresh hope for her living-dead husband. "Remember how you were rearing to fight for the Prince?"

Madhav said something unexpected, momentarily forgetting his dream of Malaya.

"If you'll teach me how to, I'll fight by your side." Then he ran to his parents' room, opened a locked trunk, took out two wooden swords and ran back to his father.

"Look, Bah! We still have the swords you made for us!" Madhav brandished the twin weapons, hoping they would spark some life in his father.

After Ramdas' fight with Nilkanth, Mukta had locked away the swords so they would not remind her husband of the heart-breaking incident.

"Ramdas, please show us you understand," the patel implored. He was still cupping Ramdas' face.

"Rani Meera Bai. Killa. Killa *ka Jai!* Killa *ka Jai!*" Mukta repeated the battle cry to elicit a response, any response, from Ramdas.

Ramdas wrenched his face from the patel's hands and looked out the window.

The others slumped with defeat. The swords, thudding to the floor from Madhav's suddenly weary hands, accentuated their despair.

Then, Ramdas started to rock.

First, he rocked gently, as he usually did. Then, for the first time, he began rocking fast.

The rest looked at each other, hoping against hope for a miracle.

Ramdas started rocking very fast. He threw himself forward and backward so vehemently that it seemed he would catapult out of the chair.

The alarmed watchers tried to restrain him but he had more than their combined strength.

"Quick, some sedative!" the patel took charge, like in the old days.

Mukta ran to her bedroom to get some laudanum.

With much effort, they forced it down Ramdas' throat. After a while, the laudanum began to take effect and Ramdas slowed down to his normal rocking.

"How many years we've waited to see a change in him," Mukta said, trying hard to conceal her excitement.

"He must've understood!" Madhav thrilled. "Thank you Patel-ji. You've come to us like a god."

"Thank Bhagvan, my boy. All this is His maya."

"I'm sure he'll recover fast if we keep talking to him of Killa," Tara suggested, caught up in the excitement. "Killa seems to be the key."

"How wonderful it would be to see your father alive again, Madhav. I had given up hope," Mukta said.

For the first time in a decade, Madhav saw his mother glow with happiness.

They all sat around Ramdas and talked, for his benefit. Mukta talked about Killa, Madhav and the patel about Champakapur. Tara listened. Ramdas rocked and looked out the window, seemingly unhearing.

The patel stayed for lunch.

In the afternoon, they put Ramdas to bed for his usual nap, but he started rocking dangerously again. A strong dose of laudanum lulled him to sleep.

After tea, the patel said he had to leave in order to reach his village before nightfall.

"I'll return soon, Mukta, to see Ramdas' progress," he promised.

"Yes, be sure to come, Patel-ji. We have to repay our debts to you. You helped us once in Champakapur and now you've gone out of your way to help us again."

"Never mind that. But the important thing is, don't lose hope, Mukta. You, too, Madhav and Tara. Bhagvan has at last opened his eyes to look upon your family."

After the patel left, Ramdas had to be sedated again. At sunset, as he watched the sun go down, he got everybody's hopes soaring by opening his mouth as if to speak while gesturing wildly in the direction of the setting sun. But only a rasping sound escaped his lips. The family's eager prompting had no effect.

"He must be boiling over with excitement inside but just can't express himself in words," Madhav observed as he watched his mother putting his father to bed. Ramdas had been sedated once again.

"That's to be expected. After all, he's not spoken for ten years," Mukta said sanely. "He'll regain his speech only slowly."

"But miracles do happen, Ma. Things can change overnight. I've heard that when the right cord is struck, the paralysed walk, the blind see, the deaf hear and the dumb speak," Madhav's spirit would not be dampened. He suddenly had hope of reviving the cruelly lost father–son relationship he had once enjoyed. "I'm sure he'll talk tomorrow."

On that note, they all went to bed.

*   *   *

Some time during that night, Ramdas died in his sleep.

*   *   *

Besides Madhav, Tara and Mukta, only Laxmi, the patel and Sundari Bai attended Ramdas' cremation. Nilkanth was absent though word had been sent to him.

Ramdas was cremated with the wooden swords.

Mukta took refuge in tears. She felt she had been brave long enough.

When the twelve-day mourning period was over, Madhav and Tara told Mukta about their plans to emigrate to Malaya.

Her first reaction was to protest.

"True sons of the soil don't leave their country to work in another. Tell me, what do other countries have that India doesn't?" Mukta asked proudly. Then, "I can already see the glint of Malayan dollars in your eyes, Madhav. That's dangerous. Don't make money your god."

Madhav was not about to give up.

"It's not about money, Ma. It's about wanderlust."

Together, Madhav and Tara explained, and persuaded Mukta gently. After two days, she relented.

"I'm sure both of you know what you're doing," she said. "And, Madhav, I won't stand in the way of your dream. But why didn't you tell me about it before?"

On thinking back, she realised why and was grateful to Madhav.

The next day, Madhav got himself and his family registered at the agent's office. Even his father's recent death refused to diminish Madhav's joy.

Things had, at last, fallen into place.

PART FOUR

Arundhati Bai Bhonsle

B ah is much taller than my five-feet-two-inches. When I raise my hand straight above, I can just about touch his head with my fingertips. He has sharp facial features. His crinkly hair is always slicked back with vaseline. The vaseline's jasmine perfume tickles my nose. He holds me and I feel his arms are strong, like his voice. Ma sometimes speaks of that intense smile of his and the ocean-deep look in his eyes that had so captivated her when she first met him. He dotes on me. I'm the first person he asks for as soon as he comes home from work every day. And, true to form, he has acquainted me with all his Greek heroes, heroines and villains. Strangely, I'm most fascinated by the villains. Medusa who had snakes for hair. Hades who was the god of the underworld. Centaur who was half-horse, half-man and a drunken lecher. And Charon, the aged boatman who ferried souls across the River Styx. Perhaps it's because like me, they, too, were doomed to live in a different world.

As Bah grows older, he talks more and more about his only brother, Nilkanth, in India. He has told me all about him. He says he has also forgiven him his misdeeds. Funny how time glazes over the events of an unhappy brotherhood.

Ma and I are good friends. That's important. One of our neighbours' daughters is not so lucky. She cries and confides in me that she and her mother don't get along and are constantly arguing. I guess I'm very fortunate.

When Ma holds me close, I can still smell her milk that I sucked from her breast as a baby. I think the lingering smell is a pacifying gift from God to replace another He has so cruelly snatched away. Ma's skin is as smooth as satin, even in old age. I say 'old age' because anyone who's forty-five, like Ma, is considered old. Most women have already become grandmothers at that age. I love to hear Ma sing. Her voice is like the tinkle of the little silver bells on the Penang Thannir Malai Temple door.

Poor Bah and Ma. They yearn to become grandparents. They yearn to see my child. I'm twenty-three but am not married yet; an old maid, by 1920 standards. But, like most young women, I do dream of being married, though there's very little I know about marriage. Bah tells me I'm beautiful like my mother, irresistible to men.

My younger brother, Ashvin, stands shoulder to shoulder with Bah. He was born three years after I was. He has a shock of curly hair. I like to run my fingers through his hair. He good-naturedly allows me to. Bah says Ashvin resembles our Uncle Nilkanth, whom Ashvin and I have never met.

Mukta Ajji, my grandmother, is one in a million. Bah (typically) says that she is the female version of the Greek titan, Atlas. Atlas supports the heavens with his head and hands. Ma says she's Bhumi Devi, the Indian goddess who shoulders the burden of the earth. Like the mythical characters, Mukta Ajji bears a burden, too—the burden of not only Ramdas Ajjibah and Uncle Nilkanth, but also that of my condition. The burden must be unbearable because, sometimes, when I touch Ajji's face, my fingers come away wet.

Bah, Ma, Ashvin and Mukta Ajji feature most in my life. Many people don't. Neither do many things.

For example, colours don't feature at all in my life. They tell me the sky is blue. But what is blue? Or green? Or red? Or yellow? To me, the sweet-smelling rose could be your brown; the large-petalled canna your blue; the round dahlia your grey; and the crepey hibiscus your green. I know cats, dogs and cows all have four legs, two eyes, two ears, a mouth, a nose and a tail. But to me, they might as well be any colour under the sun. However, I do know kittens and puppies are cuddly.

I know some other things, too. Have you heard a little garden pipit as it flies past you? I have. First, there's a soft whir of wings; then, a whisper of wind in your face; and, in a wink, the pipit has flown by. Have you felt a shower of dew drops? I have. I once stood under a dew-laden jambu tree early in the morning and shook its branches. It felt like being pelted with a thousand icy pearls.

Sometimes, I feel the birds are crying and the rain is singing. I wonder what the raindrops say to the ground as they kiss her. Do butterflies (I've felt their silken wings) ask permission of the flowers before they drink their nectar? They must, otherwise the flowers would be angry and refuse to bloom.

Is the intimate touch of a man hot like the touch of the afternoon breeze or cool like that of the night breeze? Will I ever find out? But there's this warm feeling I get when Mr Duncan holds me close and waltzes with me. Mr Duncan is Bah's boss. I've known him since childhood. Of late, he's been visiting me almost every day to chat, to read me stories and poems, to sing with me, or to just hold my hand on my bad days. When he doesn't come, I miss his voice and touch. Is that good or bad? I ask Ma. She says it's neither, it's just youth's quickening, something all girls and boys go through. She says I'll get over it. Mr Duncan is about to retire, anyway, and will soon return to England. I've gathered a lot about men from Ashvin. He tells me, or sometimes reads to me, about great lovers like Casanova, Don Juan and King Henry III (Ashvin shares Bah's passion for Western literature).

I also wonder about dreams.

Do they come true? Do all people dream when they go to sleep? I dream. But not the way you do. You dream what they call images. Sometimes in colour, sometimes not.

I dream sounds. It could be the sigh of casuarinas in the breeze, the bellow of water buffaloes in the paddies, the gaggle of geese in the market or the singsong voice of a Chinaman.

I dream textures. The serrated edge of the lalang, the velvet of a moss-covered rock, the smooth silk of Ma's sari, or the rough striations of tree bark.

I dream smells. The sweet perfume of the night jasmine, the warm blood of a menstruating woman, the damp odour of an approaching storm, or the pungent sweat of a horse.

I dream feelings. The high of happiness, the low of sorrow, the prick of pain, the flutter of hope. Also the hopelessness of loss, the swell of pride, the burgeoning of expectations, the stab of fear, the slap of insults, or the pang of love. But I don't dream of hate. I don't know what it is.

Sometimes, I dream a combination of all four. Once I dreamt of being chased by a buffalo. It was bellowing and its thudding hoofs shook the ground. I could feel its hot breath on my back. Screaming with fear, I ran up a slope. Suddenly, I stood among neem trees. I could tell because of the herbal scent of the clouds of tiny neem flowers. I heard the 'sala sala' of neem leaves in the wind. There was a loud peel of bronze bells. And I knew where I was. I was at the Penang Thannir Malai Temple. It had a neem grove. A sense of absolute peace came over me for I was in Lord Subrahmanya's abode. He would protect me. And he did, for the bellowing stopped.

Sometimes, the dream world is the real world. All the rest is illusion, maya. I know. I live mostly in a dream world. I dream with my eyes open. I dream with my eyes closed. I dream of my parents, my brother, my grandmother, the flowers, the birds, the animals ... I've heard them; I've touched them; I've smelled them. I dream that one day I'll be able to see them.

The Crossing

Do you know how India came to be, according to the Puranas?

Hiranyaksha was a dwarf-demon who was black and ugly. He had a potbelly from drinking too much spirits. But he had the power to change into a handsome man to seduce women. Once, angry with the gods for slighting him, he dragged the Earth, which was then a single mass of land, down under the sea. The gods called upon Vishnu to kill the demon and save the Earth. Hiranyaksha was so powerful it took Vishnu a thousand years of battle to kill him. During this time, the skies were filled with their weapons: thunderbolts, flame-shooting arrows, spark-emitting discs, flying maces and venom-spitting vipers. At the end, when Hiranyaksha died, Vishnu took the form of a cosmic boar and, using his tusks, dug up the Earth from the seabed. That was when the Earth-mass broke apart into continents and subcontinents, including India."

Such was the Puranic episode Tara related as she, Madhav and Mukta watched Nagapatnam Port and the prominent Nagore minarets fade in the distance. They were standing on the bow of the SS *Juggernaut*. It was sailing full steam ahead into the Bay of Bengal.

With her narrative, Tara hoped to cushion the sadness they all felt at leaving the Motherland.

"I have no doubt this very bay was part of the primeval Milk Ocean written about in the Puranas," Tara continued, pretending a bubbliness she did not feel. "I wouldn't be surprised if the thousand-headed Shesha suddenly rises out of the water with Vishnu reclining on its coils. Gosh! A thousand gigantic cobra heads, sparkling with jewel-eyes, joined as a

canopy to shelter Vishnu. Wouldn't that be a sight to behold!" Tara
paused for effect.

Encouraged by the weak smiles on her husband's and mother-in-law's
faces (a weak smile is better than no smile, she thought), Tara gushed on,
the Arsa Mahal in her pouring out. "Just imagine. Vishnu commands
Shesha to uncoil. He gives certain instructions to all the gods and
demons and takes on the avatar of a tortoise. The gods place a mountain
on His back and wrap Shesha around it so that He becomes a churn. The
gods hold Shesha's head-end and the demons hold the tail-end. They
then churn the ocean. From the depths emerge ambrosia (the elixir of
life), the moon, the goddess of wine, jewels, the parijata tree that bears
everlasting flowers, the cow Surabhi whose milk never dries, a bow
whose arrow never misses its mark, Lakshmi the goddess of
beauty and riches, and the most ravishing water nymph, Rambha. These
and many other treasures keep coming out of the water, one by one. Oh,
if only it could really happen now!" Tara let her imagination run wild
like she had in the Arsa Mahal as a child, when she first tasted of the
Puranic tales.

The others remained silent. Having indulgently listened to Tara, they
did not feel obliged to pay attention any longer and lapsed into their own
thoughts.

Mukta wished that, instead of Shesha and Vishnu, other people and
things would emerge from the ocean: her beloved Ramdas, her in-laws,
the Rani Meera Bai (Mukta had the Rani's picture packed in her trunk),
Killa Fort and its brave Marathas, and friendly Champakapur with its
exquisite magnolias.

Has anybody else on this ship taken flight three times like me, Mukta
wondered. Killa to Champakapur; Champakapur to Tanjore; Tanjore to
Malaya. What a long journey! I feel so tired. Mukta, more than the
others, wondered if she would ever see India again.

Madhav largely thought of Tanjore that once ruled the Coramandel
and beyond, the awe-inspiring Brihadisvara Temple and its giant Nandi.
Tara, seeing the faraway look in Madhav's and Mukta's eyes, also fell
into reminiscence. She thought of her mother, waving forlornly at the
pier, and the fabulous Arsa Mahal with its halls of knowledge, its arts

and its philosophies. And its secret horrors.

Into the thoughts of all the three, Nilkanth crept dourly. So did memories of the recent unpleasantries in their neighbourhood. It pained them to think that Nilkanth had failed to attend his father's funeral. He, being the eldest son, should have lit Ramdas' pyre. The last they heard of Nilkanth was that he was filling his coffers with crores of rupees from the smuggling of ancient statues. But they dismissed these thoughts quickly.

Nilkanth would never change. So, too, their Tanjore neighbourhood. Both were stuck too deeply in their own mire.

"Know something, Tara?" Madhav broke into Tara's thoughts. "I've one great regret. I still haven't been to Killa. My father used to talk so much about it. And now he has died for Killa. I must come back to see the land he so loved. It's the least I can do for his soul to rest in peace."

The SS *Juggernaut* was a brigantine in the service of the British India Steam Navigation Company. Her trademark black funnel had two white bands and her white flag bore the St Andrew's Cross. Like scores of her sister ships plying the Nagapatnam–Penang route during the late nineteenth century, she carried a most precious cargo—Indian immigrants who were the cornerstone of the British Empire.

The *Juggernaut* boasted fifteen first-class cabins (for white officers). Its deck held two thousand immigrant passengers. Another thousand were jam-packed in the converted and fumigated hold. The hold was spiked with the odour of its previous cargo: onions, garlic, potatoes and tomatoes. The deck and hold passengers slept on the floor and queued for meals with their tin plates and mugs. They were given fresh water only for drinking. For bathing and washing, they had to use sea water. In contrast, the cabin passengers had fresh water for all their needs and were served by white-and-blue-uniformed stewards.

Madhav and his family were some of the privileged few who could cough up the extra rupees to travel bunk. It provided a little more comfort than the bare floor.

When not asleep on their straw-matted bunks—sleep did not come easily with the throbbing of the engines in the ship's bowels—the family went above deck to escape the heat. There they waded through the sea of humanity that flooded the deck and went to their favourite spot, the bow.

From high up on the bow, they watched and felt the ship dip and rise, dip and rise, as she mowed the inky-blue waters of the Bay. Before her the waters parted in foam, like white lace curtains. It felt strange (and sometimes claustrophobic) to be surrounded only by water; to see a birdless sky; to taste salt in the air. Had the early Indian sailors felt the same way when they first sailed the high seas, Madhav wondered. For that matter, did the other first-timers on board feel the same way, too?

Like their fellow passengers, the Bhonsles watched with fascination when sharks surrounded the steamer and went on a feeding frenzy. How the predators thrashed about in the water, fighting for the offal disgorged by the vessel. And they kept coming back for more, looking like a fleet of small schooners escorting a man-of-war.

When not watching the predators, the family watched the sunrises and sunsets at sea. They were spectacular. For a few bewitching hours in the morning and evening, the sun, like a groom, claimed the sea as his betrothed, with gifts of gold. And the sea, like a bride, glowed with happiness.

The passengers on board were a mixed lot.

Most were Tamil men and women. The men looked sinewy and strong and the women no less healthy. Some of the women did not wear a sari-blouse. Their well-shaped breasts, toned by years of grinding masala with a grindstone, were covered only by the drape of their saris. A handful of the passengers were Malayalees (they had travelled overland to catch the boat at Nagapatnam Port) and Ceylonese. Madhav and his family were the only Marathas and so were looked upon with curiosity. Tara's beauty did not go unnoticed either.

The passengers were predominantly Hindu while some were Muslims, Christians and Buddhists. They grouped along religious lines.

Prayer times saw the bringing out of dutifully packed holy ash, skull-caps, rosaries and prayer wheels. And the air was filled with fervent whispers of 'Om ...', 'Bismillah ...', 'Our Father ...' and 'Buddham *saranam gachaami ...'.* Wrenched from the bosom of the Motherland, they turned for succour to their gods. Despite the kanganis' reassurances, the prospect of the new land still kindled moments of terror in the immigrants.

As always, there were the incorrigible among these groups who chose to become stone-drunk on palm toddy, fresh when the ship left port and stale later. And having brought along their elongated bronze dice, they played dhayam and gambled away the little savings they had.

But no matter which religion they belonged to, the immigrants had one thing in common: they aimed for a better life in Malaya. The British had made out the country to be flowing with latex and money, where the poverty-stricken could alleviate their suffering or even go from rags to riches. The poor and unschooled would be put to work as rubber tappers and coolies.

But not all on board were poor or unschooled.

Like Madhav, some were middle class, with English education to boot. There were clerks, hospital assistants, compounders, schoolmasters and lawyers. There were rich traders, businessmen and merchants (they went by clan names like Pillai, Mudaliar, Merican, Ali, Menon, Panicker and Hendry) who saw opportunities to set up fledgeling enterprises in the new land. In years to come, theirs would become established names in Malaya.

Following the hot money-trail were the money-lending Chettiar, set apart by the holy ash and vermillion dot on their foreheads. They were a blessing (if you could return their loans with ten per cent interest) and a curse (if you could not). They hugged their money bags throughout the journey.

Everybody noticed a small group of unescorted women. They stood out because of their flaunting gait and painted faces. You did not have to guess their trade. It was rumoured they were rich enough to pay for their own passage. Apparently, they were escaping the British clampdown on their profession and saw ample scope in the new land. The lusty on board were already eyeing them hungrily.

Madhav and Tara made the acquaintance of some of the other

English-speaking passengers. They talked of their respective backgrounds and of the things they had heard about Malaya. They found in each other a common bond of optimism.

There was a particular Ceylonese couple Madhav and Tara found affinity with. The husband and wife, too, were the victims of a caste-ridden, holier-than-thou society.

The man, Ratnam Kandiah, a Jaffna, was darkly handsome with strong jaws and a prominent nose. His wife, Mona, was a chocolate beauty with doe eyes and full lips. Ratnam had done the unthinkable by marrying her. She was Sinhalese. The matter was further complicated because Ratnam was Hindu while his ladylove was Buddhist.

They had boarded the steamer at the Ceylonese port of Trincomalee under the most dramatic circumstances. They were late. The ship's captain had given them half an hour's grace. At last, when they did arrive, they ran into the ship looking back repeatedly as if the Devil himself were after them. And he was: in the form of machete-wielding Jaffna and Sinhalese male relatives who were only thwarted from their murderous intentions by the timely raising of the gangway. When the ship left port, the men were still standing on the pier, waving their machetes and shouting insults at the couple. And at each other.

While the steamer berthed at Trincomalee, Madhav and his family had grabbed the chance to go ashore for a few hours.

The vicinity of the port was a tumult of colours, sounds, smells and tastes. It was in Trincomalee that they had their first taste of the pungent Ceylonese prawn sambol, and the starchy gruel of crabmeat called koolu. The latter was served in cleverly folded banana-leaf cups. In the azure waters near the port, they saw half-naked pearl divers, some of them children, dive from their boats into the water and resurface with their aquatic treasures. They reminded Tara of the Churning of the Ocean in the Puranas.

"Do you remember, I vowed I'd be the one, and not my Ravana-of-a-brother, to bring you to Ceylon?" Madhav asked Tara as they returned to the steamer. "Well, here we are!"

"Oh yes!" Tara answered, remembering. "You're Rama and I'm your Sita."

"Forever?"

"Forever."

It was smooth sailing for most of the seven-day journey. It being July, the south-westerly monsoon wind gently nudged the steamer towards its destination (not that the vessel needed it). The inky-blue waters of the Bay of Bengal gradually turned turquoise as the ship entered the shallower waters of the Andaman Sea.

There was a sudden stirring among the ship's company and passengers when a lone crow circled above the steamer, cawing a loud welcome. The bird could only mean one thing: they were nearing land. Sure enough, in the hazy distance they spotted some islands. The deck hands informed them that they were passing the Andaman and Nicobar Islands. Everybody peered to see the blurred humps of land.

Madhav tried to imagine the Indian convicts banished a thousand miles across the sea to the fortress-like prison on the Andamans. The latest he had heard was that the British were building the cellular jails that were to become the hallmark of their cruelty. Tales told of escaping prisoners (they could not stand the prison torture) sent shivers up his spine. The escapees were either shredded by the razor-sharp corals, or the equally razor-sharp teeth of sharks. It chilled Madhav to think that Nilkanth might well end up on the paradisical yet notorious Andamans if he did not change his ways.

A current of excitement ran through the watchers as they cruised past the nearest island of the chain where the water was still deep and devoid of coral banks. A herd of elephants was swimming across the waters from one island to another. They watched mesmerized as the migrating pachyderms bobbed in the frothy water, looking like floating grey islands. How like us they are, Madhav thought. I wonder what has prompted them to migrate.

Beyond the Andamans, they glimpsed just a hint of the pearl-rich Mergui Islands off the coast of Burma.

On the sixth day of their journey, they entered the wide northern spread of the Strait of Malacca before it narrowed between the Malay Peninsula and the Indonesian island of Sumatra. Here they were to experience the only storm of their crossing, but only a minor one.

It occurred during the night. The steamer was suddenly hit by a Sumatran squall, common to the strait. The screeching winds and battering waves scared the wits out of the passengers, most of whom, like Madhav and his family, were first-time sea travellers. The blackness of the night only served to heighten their fears. Many became seasick and were on the verge of panic, muttering prayers and calling upon their gods to protect them. To the unseasoned, it seemed like the ship would sink into the very next trough between the swells. And there were many troughs. Even the experienced captain's and crewmen's reassurances had no effect.

All the deck-passengers, who were at the mercy of the squall, were herded below deck. There, hugging their possessions, they waited out the storm.

Luckily, the storm abated quickly. Everybody thanked their respective gods. For the rest of the night, they celebrated, not only because they had been unharmed but because the captain announced that they would reach the shores of Malaya the next day.

The Sufis among the passengers broke out into a qwali chorus in praise of Allah. A dervish started to whirl. He whirled a full fifteen minutes, his tunic flaring about him, much to the fascination of the onlookers.

A group of Hindu villagers (all men) used their tin plates as drums and beat out a lively tattoo for the dappang-koothu folk dance. The sprightly among them sprang about to the invigorating rhythm. The beat and dance was so full of verve that even the captain, normally staid, joined in to clap with the revellers. Madhav and his family clapped, too.

The contagious mood had even the prostitutes making merry. They put up an impromptu kummi, clapping right and left, up and down, while rotating all the while in a circle. One of them belted out an accompaniment.

During the wee hours of the morning, the passengers went to sleep, exhausted but happy.

Next morning, the sun was glaring when Madhav, Tara and Mukta took up their favourite spot at the bow. Behind them, there was the din of two thousand deck passengers talking and packing their belongings.

The SS *Juggernaut* was gliding sedately on the satiny waters of the Strait of Malacca. The strategic strait was rich in history. It was the thoroughfare of the seafaring ancient Malays. It saw the arrival of early Indian, Chinese and Arab traders to the peninsula. Centuries later, it was used by the Dutch, Portuegese and British. The Europeans fought great sea battles over the possession of ports like Malacca, Temasik and Palembang along the strait.

Flocks of mynahs, crows and swifts flew past the SS *Juggernaut* in grand salute, signalling land was near. Then they rioted over the ship, looking for pickings. Passengers threw leftover food into the sea for them. White-bellied sea eagles soared high above, their eyes picking out even the smallest fish near the surface of the water. When they sighted a catch, they swooped down and unerringly scooped their prey between their talons. Then they sailed into the air, silent and powerful, like the mythical Garuda.

Madhav's heart started racing when he saw the faint outline of land. He pointed out the land to Tara and Mukta. The mass turned out to be an island which the steamer bypassed. But the family would remember the island: prau-loads of people, dressed in sarongs, were rowing towards it. Through a borrowed handheld telescope, they saw that the men and women were young and unchaperoned, which seemed strange in conservative times. Madhav, always the one for legends, suggested, "There has to be some legend behind this island that draws only young people."

At two in the afternoon, Malaya loomed large before them. All the passengers milled on deck to see the approaching land—a new land, a new home, an El Dorado to the West, Suvarnabhumi to Madhav and the East. Even Ptolemy had called this peninsula Avrea Chersones (The Golden Chersonese) because of its riches.

Madhav's heart thudded in his chest. So did Tara's in hers. Excitement shone in their eyes. They squeezed each other's hands and Madhav gave Tara one of his famous looks.

Penang Island unfurled before them: inlet by inlet, fishing village by fishing village, forest by forest, hill by hill. Possessively called Prince of Wales Island by the colonial masters, Penang cradled Malaya's chief northern port, Georgetown.

It was a lush, verdant island with a central hump of high land. And its forests did kiss the sea, as Madhav had imagined. They were the world's oldest forests. Their giant chengal and meranti soared in tiers, like an emerald crown. Clouds of steam rose from them where it had rained, adding a touch of mystery to the island. What spirits and fairies dwell in these forests, Madhav wondered. He was right. He would soon learn of the penanggalan that had a human head with entrails flying in the air; the langsuyar, a female spirit that sucked blood and could shape-shift into an owl; and the bajang, a cat-man vampire. He would also learn of the Orang Asli (indigenous people) who lived in the forests. They could kill an elephant with a single poison-tipped dart. During sleep, their souls could leave their bodies and travel wherever they wanted. And they possessed magical spears that could fly in the night and kill their enemies.

Beyond Penang, Madhav saw the Malayan mainland. It looked like a long green python having an afternoon nap.

As no one had contracted the pox or suffered from dysentry on board, the ship was not quarantined. At three in the afternoon, the SS *Juggernaut*, her sirens blaring, put in to port at Georgetown.

Georgetown hugged an enclave on the east coast of Penang where the mirror-calm waters of a strait separated it from the mainland. There the ship disgorged her human cargo, the passengers pouring out of her like ants from a nest. Then, like a queen ant, she waited to be pampered and serviced before her return trip to Nagapatnam.

At precisely 3.15 p.m. on 15 July 1896, Madhav set foot in Malaya, the land of his dreams.

In a New Land

Landlubbers that they were, it took Madhav and his family a few minutes to find their legs on land. During those minutes, the world swayed like the SS *Juggernaut*.

For Tara, there was a second reason for swaying: she was in the family way.

Madhav was amazed at the sheer variety of people in the port (he learnt later that the port was named Georgetown after the British monarch, King George III). The place was teeming with Malays, Chinese, Indians, Siamese, Burmese, Javanese, Bugis, Arabs, Moors, Eurasians, Peranakans and Britons.

"I thought Nagapatnam port had a grand mix of races, but look at this place!" Madhav marvelled. "Why, it looks like the meeting place of the whole world!"

He had still not got over the boats of many lands at the harbour: small cockboats, light sampans, long praus, bulky barges, hulk-like junks, cargo-laden tongkang and stately Indiamen and steamers.

Madhav was pushing through the throng of people with Tara and Mukta in tow. They were following the employment agent who had met them at the jetty. Behind them came a group of ten, including Ratnam and his wife. The rest of the immigrants, grouped according to their promised jobs, had been escorted away by other agents.

The Bhonsles heard a strange babble of voices. They could only make out the snatches of English and Tamil they heard. The rest sounded like Sanskrit to them.

The agent led them to a vast compound more than a hundred yards away from the jetty. The compound was overrun by lalang. The coarse blades of the tall weed rasped against their skin and clothes as they headed towards a row of five wooden houses in a corner of the compound. The houses stood on sturdy brick piles, three feet above the ground.

Set apart at a right angle to the row of houses was a long wooden building at ground level. Well behind the houses ran the coolie quarters: three rows of single-room terrace houses built of brick and concrete.

The wooden houses Madhav and company were being herded to were new. They wore a coat of cream paint that was to be the signature colour of all wooden railway quarters in the country. The window and doorframes were dark chocolate and the beams and eaves black with anti-termite treatment. The tile-roofed houses were separated from each other by forty-foot stretches of cow grass. At the moment, the grass looked just about to be invaded by the lalang.

The first house was occupied. Little brown faces peeked over an open window. When the newcomers looked at them, the children ducked, only to slowly creep up again until only the top of their heads and curiosity-filled eyes could be seen. Then they continued staring at the new arrivals.

"This will be your quarters, Mr Bhonsle," the Tamil agent said, showing Madhav the second house and handing him the keys with a toothy smile.

Madhav immediately liked the short dusky man with a crooked nose and kind eyes.

The agent was about to assign a bustling couple with children the third house when Ratnam interrupted. The Ceylonese requested to stay next to the Bhonsles. He thanked the agent profusely when his request was granted. So the couple with children, a Mr and Mrs Arumugam, got the fourth house.

The last house was to be occupied by the remaining three of the group—all young Tamil bachelors with pockets full of emptiness and hearts full of dreams.

"All right, your attention please," the agent said importantly. "For your information, I'm also a liason officer for the Malayan Railways. So it's in your interest to listen to what I'm going to say.

"You're now standing on railway property. It's an extension of the railway premises in Prai on the mainland. All of you will be working in the Railway Jetty Office," here he pointed to the long ground-level building, "and the superintendent will assign you your duties. You'll report for duty at 8 a.m. on 1 August. In the meantime you've got two weeks to get acquainted with each other and familiarise yourselves with the surroundings. You don't have to go far for your needs. There's a row of shops, just after the jetty, that sells provisions and household goods. There's also a market in town. And a dispensary. Any questions?"

"What about our advance? We were promised one on our arrival," Arumugam asked. He was worried. He had four children to feed.

"Yes, I was just coming to that," the agent said as he fished a bundle of notes and a clipboard out of his bag. The bag was stitched from remnant leather strips of the leather upholstery used in the first-class seats on trains.

Licking his fingers, he counted the notes and gave each of the men fifty Malayan dollars.

"Don't look so confused! These aren't rupees you know," he said, seeing the looks on the men's faces. "They may seem a small amount but every note is worth six rupees. The money will see you through till the end of August when you'll receive your first pay packet." He started to make entries in the form on the clipboard. "Now please sign for receipt of the advance." He passed round the clipboard and pen.

When the men finished signing, the agent took leave. "If you need me, I'll be at 6 Coleman Street. It's on the other side of the jetty, next to the Chinese temple. Just ask for Nallathamby."

With a wave, he was off and soon disappeared into the swarm of people outside the jetty.

The newcomers introduced themselves to each other, then went to their new houses.

Madhav and his family went up the five concrete steps to their quarters. A waist-high latched wooden gate opened into the front verandah. A balustrade enclosed the verandah. The front door was set inside the verandah. Madhav unlocked the Vale padlock and they went inside.

They found themselves in a semi-dark room. Tara opened the window facing the verandah and another pair of windows on the left wall. Light poured in to reveal a spacious living room. Two doors were set against the right wall. They led to twin, square bedrooms with a couple of windows each. When the windows were opened, the rooms were bright and airy. Tara already liked the house.

A door at the end of the living room back wall (there was another window on this wall) opened to a short flight of steps to the ground level. A roofed passageway led from the steps to the adjoined kitchen, store and bathroom. On one side of the passage was an open courtyard. For privacy, the courtyard was screened by corrugated zinc sheets. The latrine, of the ubiquitous bucket-system, was at the back, thirty yards from the house. Water had to be drawn from a common well, centrally located behind the third house.

Madhav and Tara decided to use the first room. It faced the front of the house. They deposited their small trunks and mats in the room. Mukta moved into the second room.

"We must boil milk first," Mukta said. "It's customary to boil milk when one first moves into a house. But we have to wash the house before that. Madhav, could you please buy us buckets and brooms? You can buy the milk later. If you buy it now it may turn sour in the heat."

Madhav set off to the nearby shops. He met Ratnam, Arumugam and one of the bachelors, Somasundram, along the way. They, too, were on the same errand as Madhav.

When Madhav returned with a couple of tin buckets and coconut-frond brooms, his wife and mother set about washing the house. Madhav helped for a while, fetching water from the well. They scrubbed, washed and swept the smooth plank flooring of the living room and bedrooms. From the neighbouring houses, came the sploshing sounds of washing, too.

"You can buy the milk now, Madhav," Mukta said as they finished washing the main portion of the house. "Make sure its cow's milk, not buffalo's milk. And while you're at it, buy a small clay pot, a pat of ghee and three measures of rice."

"And don't forget to buy some candles," Tara called after Madhav, "just in case the hurricane lamps in the store don't burn."

Then Tara fetched the water while Mukta washed the back portion of the house. By six thirty, they had finished washing, collecting dry twigs for the stove and bathing.

Madhav returned just before sundown.

"Quick, have your bath before the sun sets, Madhav," Mukta said. "Sunset is an auspicious time to boil the milk and light the oil lamp. The goddess Lakshmi visits homes at that hour."

The woman hurriedly lit the concrete stove with the twigs they had gathered (having learnt from Madhav's first trip to the shops that, in Malaya, they did not sell cow-dung patties for fuel). They boiled the milk in the new pot, added sugar to it, and poured a portion of milk into four tumblers, one for each of them and one for the altar. Into the remaining milk, Mukta added rice, ghee and some cashewnuts, the last ingredient being from the small stock of provisions they had brought from Tanjore. Then she let the rice cook.

Mukta's room would double as the prayer room.

From her trunk, Mukta produced a bronze statuette of the goddess Durga seated on a tiger. This she placed in a corner, facing the direction of the sunrise. She garlanded it with an artificial pearl strand, the mandatory fresh flower garland being unavailable at the moment. She placed a scrubbed brass oil lamp a little in front and to the right of the statue and positioned it so that the wick, when burning, would also face east. There was no end of importance given to the direction of the rising sun. The sun banished the darkness that symbolised evil.

Mukta then set a small salver of the cooked sweet rice and a silver tumbler of the boiled milk in front of the statuette.

"Come, Tara, it's time to light the lamp," Mukta called.

Tara, who was in the kitchen, quickly shut the back door. It was not supposed to be open at lamp-lighting time. If it was, the goddess Lakshmi would not stay: she would just come in by the front door and go out the back. And that would not do as she was the one who brought prosperity to the home.

Tara also made sure the front door was fully open, not just half-open, to let the goddess know how welcome she was.

Madhav came in from the verandah and the lamp-lighting in the new house began.

Full of reverence, Tara lit the oil lamp. The single cotton wick in coconut oil immediately burned bright and made the brass lamp shine. The flame's radiating rays lit up the dark corner and brought into focus the benevolent face of the goddess Durga.

Bringing their palms together, the family bowed and paid homage to the goddess.

Tara lit a couple of joss sticks, stuck them in their holder, then waved flaming camphor around the goddess.

The family said their silent prayers, placing holy ash and vermilion dots on their foreheads. Tara sang a kirtan and Mukta recited the Durga Saptashati from one of her scripture books. Then, they quietly left the room in the belief that the spirit of Durga would emerge and eat and drink, in essence, their offering of sweet rice and milk. She would give them, in return, Her protection from all sorrow and danger in the new land.

After the lamp-lighting, the family sat on the verandah which offered a splendid view of the sea and sky.

They watched Dusk pluck and gather the last stalks of sunbeams to present the golden bouquet to his lover, Dawn.

Tara was suddenly reminded of the Arsa Mahal. At this, the bewitching hour, the courtesans would be beautifying themselves for their night engagements.

Mukta thought of the times she used to sit with Ramdas by the window and follow his gaze towards the sunset and Killa.

Soon, strange noises filled the warm equatorial night. Not sounds of humans or birds but of beasts. For, beyond the fringes of Georgetown lay virgin rainforest, as yet untouched by man. The protagonists were all too familiar with the 'a-a-u-ng' of tigers and the 'mm-a-a-u' of gaurs. But they had not expected to find the animals in such close proximity. They wondered if tigers came prowling into Georgetown in the dead of night.

At dinner, under the stark light of the hurricane lamp, the family ate sweet rice and drank milk. They shared the offering from the altar, too. It was considered a great blessing to eat that which the gods had partaken of.

The remaining rice from the pot Madhav scooped on to banana leaves he had cut from a tree near the coolie lines. He distributed the rice to his Indian neighbours. He left out the Malay neighbour (they occupied the first house) because he was not sure whether the family would accept food prepared by Indians. But Madhav would soon find out.

Later, the family was attacked by hordes of bloodthirsty mosquitoes. In due time, their Malay neighbour would tell them that one of the most effective ways of keeping mosquitoes away was by burning a heap of dry grass, leaves and twigs in the compound at dusk. The smoke would drive away the insects. Indeed, the neighbours themselves had a heap burning outside their house.

The mosquitoes drove the family into the refuge of their bedrooms. There they covered themselves from head to toe with their blankets and, still feeling the buoyancy of the SS *Juggernaut*, fell into a sweaty sleep.

Sweat not withstanding, Madhav had a dream.

He dreamt of Tara dancing on top of the Brihadisvara Temple tower. The tower was floating on the strait between Penang Island and the mainland. Crowds of Chinese, Malays and Europeans were cheering Tara from the waterfront. An elephant was swimming near the tower. On its back sat a blind Nilkanth. He was dressed like a maharajah. And, in his hand, he held high a wooden sword.

What a strange dream, Madhav thought later. The blind Nilkanth puzzled him a bit. But then, Madhav was not the type to seek out interpreters of dreams. So he promptly forgot it.

Next morning, the family was awakened by the loud voices of men talking in Tamil, outside their house.

The men had just alighted from two bullock carts. They turned out to be mandor or overseers and their teams sent by the railway authority to cut grass in the compound. The men wore baggy khaki shorts and white banian. They had thundu, tied turban-style on their heads, for protection from the sun. They set about sharpening their scythes and cutting the lalang, chattering like the birds they frightened from the grass.

Madhav and his family washed and had their morning bath.

But before that, Tara and Mukta had met their Malay neighbour at the well when they went to fetch water. The sarong-clad woman was in the midst of bathing her brood of five, all below the age of six. The two girls and three boys, stark naked, were dripping lather. The youngest peeked through his soapy lashes at Tara and Mukta and immediately screamed as the soap stung his eyes. The woman quickly washed his eyes and face and he quietened down.

She stopped to smile shyly at Tara and Mukta. They returned her smile. She looked twentysomething, sturdy and was olive-skinned like the olive fruit, zaitun, she was named after. Her wavy black hair was combed back tightly and knotted, revealing an intelligent forehead.

"*Apa khabar?*" she asked in a polite and gentle voice. The Malays prized politeness (budi bahasa) and gentleness (lemah lembut). Her gaze was frank.

Tara and Mukta were at a loss. They did not understand a word.

"*Samaj nahin,*" Tara said, gesturing that she did not understand.

They looked at each other in consternation, then burst out laughing.

"*Saya* Zaitun," the woman said, thumping her chest. "Zaitun."

Tara and Mukta understood immediately. They introduced themselves.

"Tara, Mukta," Zaitun repeated, looking at them in turn.

They all nodded at each other in understanding.

Then Tara and Mukta left with their filled water buckets and Zaitun continued bathing her children, pouring dipperfuls of water over them as they jumped and squealed at the touch of the chill well-water.

Later, she would address Tara and Mukta, and they would address her, as Aachee, an accepted local appellation for women.

After their baths, Madhav and family set out for breakfast and a spot of shopping. They were joined by Ratnam and Mona. Along the way, they exchanged notes about the mosquito nuisance. And the ominous nocturnal sounds from the forest.

"You must remember, the British are just beginning to develop the country," Ratnam said. "Give them some time and most of the forests on the island will disappear."

Even as he spoke, gangs of Indian coolies, equipped with axes, changkul and handsaws, were trudging inland, in the direction of the forests. They were dressed in loincloth, just as they were in India. But they held their lean bodies upright, like soldiers. It was as if they knew hundreds of them were going to sacrifice their lives. Not in any war but in wild-animal attacks, rockslides and cave-ins during the early construction of Malayan roads and railways.

Madhav and company jostled their way through the jetty throng. Ratnam and Mona got separated from the family. Ratnam signalled that he and Mona would go ahead on their own. Tara jumped several times at the sudden blaring of sirens on steamships arriving in or leaving the harbour.

Beyond the jetty lay the throbbing heart of Georgetown.

The family was taken by everything they saw: the people, the buildings, the vehicles, the goods.

Indians and Europeans were familiar enough but the others the family found so cosmopolitan and different—each a unique motif in the rich songket-weave of Malaya.

The family caught themselves staring at the wealthy, sallow-skinned Chinese gentlemen in Mandarin robes and long queues; the miserably poor and sunburnt Chinese rickshaw coolies pulling their human loads; the gentle Malay bird-sellers proffering parrots and cockatoos; the fezzed Arabs who had come to spread the Koran; the dark Javanese servants trotting behind their British masters; the fierce-looking Bugis bodyguards who protected the orang puteh (white men); the sun-wrinkled Orang Laut (sea nomads) who came inland to barter their fish for rice and salt; the Siamese peddlers selling potions and charms and the Burmese traders selling pearls and rubies. Madhav and his family were overwhelmed. The Malayan population was as multilayered as a Dutch layer-cake.

All the buildings had sloping roofs to drain year-round equatorial showers. They bore the stamp of both East and West. Some facades were embellished with Neoclassical columns and festoons painted dazzling white. But most had flower motifs of cherry blossoms, peonies, asters and bamboo in vivid hues or in glittering goldleaf. Wooden window and doorframes were intricately carved and exterior walls and floors tiled— Chinese-style. The tiles shone with floral and geometric designs that took your breath away. The family was to learn that these beautiful shops and houses belonged to the rich Straits Chinese or Peranakans. The Peranakans were descendents of the Chinese who had settled in Malaya centuries ago. They now spoke Malay and wore a mixture of Chinese and Malay attire. Later, Nallathamby would inform them that the Straits Chinese men were known as Baba and the women, Nyonya. They were another exotic layer in the layer-cake.

Jamming the laterite streets were bullock carts, gharries, rickshaws and hand carts. They kicked up continual eddies of red dust which irritated the eyes and throat. The dust would only settle after the rain. The streets crisscrossed each other and had easy-to-remember names. They were named after the predominant race that lived and worked there or after the race's place of origin: Madras Lane, Malay Street, Achen Street, Rangoon Road, Amoy Lane, Buckingham Street and so on.

Temporarily lost in the variegated charms of their new surroundings, the family forgot about breakfast.

Later, Tara was the first to feel hungry as she had to eat for two. It was ten o'clock.

"Let's go to Madras Lane," Madhav suggested, steering his wife and mother towards the locale they had passed earlier.

Not surprisingly, Madras Lane was teeming with Indians.

There were shopkeepers, traders, Chettiars, syces, dhobies, barbers, stonesmiths, coolies, temple priests, garland weavers, goldsmiths and night-soil carriers. All of them (except for the temple priests) were going about with an air of new-found freedom. The wall of caste segregation of the Motherland was just beginning to crack and crumble in the new land: coolies were being invited into the houses of traders; barbers were giving their daughters' hand in marriage to dhobies' sons; and night-soil carriers were putting their first tentative steps into the temple.

Small shops selling textiles, provisions and utilities were in the majority. Sandwiched between them were 'hotels' which only served food. The arcades outside the shops were clogged with peanut vendors, appam sellers, betel peddlars, fortune-tellers, and beggars with starving children. The last were unable to work because of illnesses contracted in the new land, mainly malaria and dengue.

The air was abuzz with Tamil, Malayalam, Telugu, Bengali, Punjabi, Parsi and Urdu; and suffused with the reek of attar.

"This does feel like home," Mukta declared happily. "I'd never imagined such a place existed outside India!"

"Yes, it's a little India," Madhav said.

The family entered a hotel nostalgically named Bharat Bhavan. It was overflowing with customers, mostly men, who smacked their lips, licked their fingers and belched loudly to show their satisfaction with the food. After a week of bland fare on the SS *Juggernaut*, the family found the dosa, idli and chutney ambrosial. They polished off the meal with coffee with fresh buffalo's milk. The proprietor told them that cow's milk (which the family was used to) was a scarcity as few cows were raised on the island. The buffalo milk came from the inland paddy farms where herds of buffaloes roamed. When there was a shortage, buffalo milk was brought by boat from the mainland.

The family discovered the cosmopolitan nature of Penang was also symbolised in the provisions and toiletries sold in the shops.

In Madras Lane alone the family was able to buy Siamese rice, Punjab atta flour, Bengal gram, Rangoon dhal, Bombay onions, Ceylon tea, Arabian dates, Java coffee, Prai sugar, Canton potatoes, Penang nutmeg, and English Yardley soap and powder. The Dutch cheese and Madeira wines (in the delicatessen for Europeans) were not on their shopping list.

Then they bought a variety of condiments and coconut oil for cooking. They arranged for a stone grinder and pestle and mortar to be sent over to their house the next day. They engaged a woodcutter to deliver stacks of mangrove wood monthly for the kitchen stove. They also arranged with the hotel for a pint of fresh milk to be delivered every morning to their doorstep.

In Malay Street, the domain of Penang Malays, they came upon a different scene. All along the street, shopkeepers and peddlars were selling batik and pulicat sarongs, kapok-stuffed pillows, mengkuang mats, basketware, Malacca canes, keris, vegetables, fresh herbs, and kitchen utensils of clay and coconut shell.

Madhav and company had difficulty in understanding kati and tahil

(Malay terms for weights that would later be incorporated into the English language as 'catty' and 'tael') and ringgit and kupang (monetary units). But they soon learned that the weights were equivalent to the Indian seer and tola and the money to dollars and cents.

Mukta and Tara bought greens, tomatoes and chillies while Madhav shopped for sleeping-mats and a coconut-scraper. He decided to come back in the evening for pillows and a must-have: mosquito nets.

By the time the family had explored Achen Street with Muslim pepper and tobacco traders from North Sumatra, it was past lunchtime. They went to the nearby Chulia Street and had a satisfying meal of Penang nasi kandar—a rice dish with heaps of curried chicken, spicy mutton and vegetables. A drink of coconut juice by a roadside stall refreshed them. The naturally sweet juice countered the effects of the stifling heat of the Malayan midday.

On the way back home, they noticed that the mandor had almost finished cutting the lalang. They had raked the lalang into mounds which they would later burn. The compound was now safe from snakes and other manner of creepy-crawlies.

Once inside the house, the family decided that a nap was in order after the exciting discoveries of the morning. They stretched their tired limbs and drifted into sleep, a smile on their lips. They had fallen completely in love with Georgetown.

The following fortnight was one of more delightful discoveries.

"I found out the meaning of 'apa khabar' from one of the mandor," Madhav said to Tara. She had told him of Zaitun's greeting. "It means, 'What news?'"

"Why, that's almost exactly what we say. Only we use the word 'kaay' instead of 'apa'. *Kaay khabar?*" Tara observed.

"I even heard words like 'tiga', 'jambu' and 'chamcha' in Malay Street," Mukta joined in. "We, too, use the same words."

The words meant 'three', 'rose apple' and 'spoon'.

"Seeing the early comings and goings between India and Malaya, I'm sure we've many more words in common with the Malays. I guess Malay isn't going to be that difficult to learn, after all. We must learn it. It's the lingua franca here," Madhav said.

"Mami, did you notice the Malay women wear jasmines in their hair, just as we do?"

"Yes. And they cover their heads, too, when out in public," Mukta pointed out, glad that they shared some cultural similarities with the Malays.

"And they're such gentle and polite folk," Madhav opined, basing his judgement on his interactions with the shopkeepers and peddlars in Malay Street.

Proof that Malays were kind, too, came from Zaitun when she offered them a plate of pulut and coconut for tea one day. The steamed glutinous rice was sticky and sweet, eaten with a mixture of shredded coconut cooked in brown palm sugar.

The next day, Tara and Mukta reciprocated with a stack of chappatis and dhal curry. Zaitun accepted the food graciously. In the days to come, they would exchange more dishes.

They would also pick up each other's language during sunset get-togethers.

It was during one such session that Tara and Mukta asked Zaitun about the young people rowing to the island that they had passed just before reaching Penang.

"Oh, that's Pulau Dayang Bunting," Zaitun informed them. The name meant Island of the Pregnant Maiden. She went on to acquaint them with the legend behind the name.

"There was once a putri pari-pari, a fairy princess, who fell in love with and married a mortal prince. They were married for many years but were childless.

"One day, the fairy drank the sweet waters from a crystal clear freshwater lake on the island. Immediately after that, she conceived. But sadly, her infant died at childbirth. Full of grief, the fairy buried the child in the lake. But she also blessed the waters of the lake so that any barren woman who bathes in the lake, or drinks of its waters, will conceive. Then the fairy returned to her realm. Until this day, childless couples frequent the island in the hope of conceiving."

Tara and Mukta were fascinated. Later, they related the legend to

Madhav. He was glad to add it to his trove of hitherto only Greek legends.

"Malaya is a land of legends, you know," Zaitun told the family. "There is the legend of 'Mahsuri', those of 'Putri Gunong Ledang', 'Hikayat Merong Mahawangsa', 'Hikayat Hang Tuah' and many, many more."

Whenever an opportunity presented itself, Zaitun narrated the legends to them.

Tara identified with the legend of Mahsuri most.

Mahsuri had lived on the island of Langkawi, north of Penang. Like Tara, too, Mahsuri had been treated unjustly by the society around her. Worse still, Mahsuri had been impaled on suspicion of adultery. Before dying, she had cursed the people on the island so that they would not prosper for seven generations.

The family was delighted to hear they even shared the *Ramayana*. In Malaya, the epic was portrayed through the wayang kulit—a shadow-play accompanied by the drumbeat of gendang, gong, and the soulful melody of the serunai. Zaitun even took the family to see one of the shows.

Meanwhile, Madhav made friends with Zaitun's husband, Fairuz Khan bin Mohamed. The squat, smooth-skinned man (he sported no moustache and had hairless chest, arms and legs) would be working with him. It turned out that Fairuz was one of the few English-educated Malays on the island, having attended the Penang Free School, the first English school in the country. (The school had been built in 1816 by an Anglican missionary—Reverend R.S. Hutchings. Madhav had seen its white Greco-Roman facade from afar.)

Fairuz was a mild-mannered man. He had no vices except that of smoking a pipe in the evenings. He was trusting (like most people of his race) and friendly (like his wife). Mild himself, Madhav sensed that Fairuz and he were going to get along famously.

Over time, the Bhonsles and the Fairuzes were to welcome the similarities between them and accept the differences, without prejudice. For instance, Tara would not offer Zaitun cooked chicken or lamb dishes knowing that Islam forbade Zaitun to eat haram meat (the animals not having been slaughtered with recitation from the Koran); and Zaitun would never dream of offering beef to the Bhonsles. The Fairuzes, realising that Hinduism was just another of the many ways to reach God, accepted that the Bhonsles bowed before images of their gods; more important still, the Fairuzes never pointed at their neighbours and said, "Look! You pray to idols. We don't. Therefore we shall not have anything to do with you."

The Fairuzes would never segregate their children from the Bhonsles' children on account of race or religion. Their children would grow up as one, giving and taking, while all the time learning from each other. During the Diwali and Aidil Fitri festivals, the families would visit each other, bearing gifts of sweetmeat, cakes and fruit.

One morning, Madhav and his family ventured into the Chinatown of Penang, the largest ethnic enclave on the island.

It was a hive of industry such as they had never seen in Tanjore. The overcrowded precinct was full of coolies, contractors, hawkers, barbers, businessmen, traders, merchants, lantern makers, basket weavers, rickshaw pullers, bankers, clog makers, tailors, butchers and shopkeepers, all driving themselves with a centuries-old force that was born with them in China. The family was to discover that only the Chinese worked past midnight when businesses in the other ethnic sectors of town had long closed.

The sharp scent of burning joss and incense pricked their noses as they passed by the red altars outside every house and business premise.

Between the rows of shops were small temples decorated with carvings of dragons and phoenixes, all covered in shard-work. Devotees were shaking joss sticks and burning paper money for good luck. The family found out the temples were painted red because it was the colour of prosperity for the Chinese.

The people spoke garrulously in the Hokkien, Hakka, Cantonese and Hainanese dialects and also in Mandarin. But to Madhav and company, it sounded all the same.

Tara and Mukta were spellbound by the sight of Chinese women with bound feet. Their light, mincing steps made them appear delicate, fairy-like. They looked as if they would fly off on invisible wings any moment. Do the women feel any pain, the newcomers wondered. Their calm looks certainly did not betray any sign of discomfort. The women had to be from rich families, for their three-inch shoes were of silk, and maids in queues and black-and-white suits were always tagging along with them.

The Nyonya apparel was another thing that fascinated Tara and Mukta.

The Straits Chinese women did not wear the sam fu and cheongsam of their China-born sisters. Instead, they wrapped themselves in Javanese batik sarongs and wore kebaya blouses like those worn by Zaitun. The long-sleeved kebaya, sometimes reaching the knees, were fastened down the front with floral gold pins. The women's hair was set in a bun at the crown and decorated with fresh jasmine or gilt hairpins and ornaments. And on their feet the Nyonyas wore the most stunning of slippers, embroidered thickly with shining glass beads and gold thread. I must have a pair of those slippers, Tara decided.

Tara felt a pang as they passed a row of vice dens. It reminded her of the Arsa Mahal and what it stood for. Only here the joints were sleazy. The entrances bore dusty red lanterns with tassels and exuded cheap perfume. The women were coarse and loud as they solicited for clients from the lowest rungs of society. Looking like China dolls, the women lolled about at the doorways or draped themselves over balustrades and windowsills. Seeing that there were many more Chinese men than women on the island, Tara concluded correctly that these prostitutes provided much-needed comfort to the men who had left their wives behind in China.

The area had its share of gambling and opium dens too, the family noticed. The crash of mahjong tiles and the reek of opium were unmistakable, even from the street.

From the hawker stalls lining the roads wafted the smell of roasted pork, steamed fish, char kuey teow or fried rice noodles, sautéed vegetables, cabbage soup and chrysanthemum tea.

They watched mesmerised as adults and children alike shovelled steaming-hot rice into their mouths with chopsticks. Their dexterous picking of even the tiniest morsels of food with the chopsticks was a point of wonder for the family.

At a stall selling Hokkien mee, the family saw customers slurping thick, almost black, soy-coated noodles.

"What's that? Looks like earthworms to me!" Mukta commented. But in months to come, after her first nibble, she would change her mind and Hokkien mee would become her favourite Chinese food. What's more, adventurous as they were, she, Madhav and Tara would try to use chopsticks, with Mukta finally giving up with an exasperated "I have two left hands!" Not so Madhav and Tara.

Within the first two weeks of their arrival, the family acquainted itself with almost every facet of Penang life.

At the waterfront, they watched young Malay boys dive into the sea for coins thrown by British new-arrivals. They saw the Malay and Chinese fishermen come in with their daily catch of spanish mackerel, pomfret, prawns and cuttlefish. Some of the fishermen sold the fish in little piles by the roadside. Tara and Mukta decided that, henceforward, they would buy fish here as it was cheaper than in the market in town.

At the bazaar and hawker stalls, they sampled the delicacies Penang was famous for even then, the food as varied as the people who prepared it. Nutty salads, fish flakes wrapped in coconut fronds, turnip-stuffed rolls and chicken barbecued on hot coals were just a few of the dishes they tried and loved. And the glutinous rice desserts were unforgettable. Full of coconut cream and palm sugar, every mouthful was creamy and as sweet as nectar.

They had a stroll through the groves that produced a spice so coveted that the Portuguese, Dutch and English had fought pitched battles for its possession: a spice called nutmeg. The fruit hung from the trees like small ochre globes, waiting to be split open for their aromatic nuts. The flesh of the fruit, the Chinese preserved—either in wedges steeped in sugar-syrup or julienned strips sun-dried and coated with crystal sugar.

Areca palms—pinang, that gave the island its name, Penang—they saw in abundance in every thicket and on every hillside. The tall, slim palms were so heavy with clusters of their orangey-yellow nuts that it seemed the trunks would snap any minute. (The family was to learn that millennia ago, early Indian sailors had brought the areca, native to Malaya, to be cultivated in India.)

Street entertainers held their attention at street corners. There were Malay men with performing monkeys, Indian snake charmers and Chinese acrobats and python-wrestlers. These people entertained for a paltry few cents.

One night, they saw an open-air Chinese opera with all its vibrant colours, high-pitched singing and clashing cymbals. Another night, they caught a Siamese puppet show enacting the story of the *Ramayana*.

But as much as it delighted, Penang also shocked. The family was nonplussed on seeing dog, cat, snake, bear, civet and pangolin meat for sale.

They visited the various houses of worship with spires, domes, minarets, towers, moon-gates and gilt statues. Delightedly, Tara and Mukta discovered that the Chinese goddess of mercy, Kuan Yin, also wore a dot on her forehead, just like Hindu goddesses and Hindu women. One goddess even had many arms, like Kali. There were even monkey gods, like Hanuman.

"Well, I'm sure that all the great religions of the world are the fruit of the same tree. But man, being what he is, had to put them in different baskets and say, 'This is your religion. This is my religion. *And my religion is greater than yours*'," Madhav said sadly. "Therein lies the woe of the world."

But what made the family marvel during their ramblings was something they had never seen before: at certain locations, the Muslim masjid, the Hindu kovil, the Chinese tokong and the Christian church were all built next to each other. This meant only one thing—the various congregations accepted with goodwill and tolerance the practices of each other: the imam's call to prayer and the slaughtering of cattle in the masjid during the Haj festival; the chanting of mantras, ringing of bells and images of gods being taken in street processions; the beating of gongs and cymbals and lion- and dragon-dance processions and the hymn and carol-singing. This aspect of tolerance, the family hoped, would never change.

The family took time off to admire one of Penang's most elegant mansions, the Cheong Fatt Tze mansion (Mukta could not get her tongue around the name). It had a grand exterior of carved doors, cast-iron railings and shard-work gables. The fleet of jinrickshaws, parked permanently alongside the mansion, spoke of the untold wealth of the inhabitants within.

Later, just for the experience, they took a jinrickshaw in town to their next place of visit, Fort Cornwallis. Tara and Mukta rode in one while Madhav followed in another. They found the ride bumpy. Mukta was afraid Tara would suffer a miscarriage.

The 1804 Fort Cornwallis, at the north-eastern point of the island, marked the spot where Penang's British founder, Captain Francis Light, first landed in 1786. The whole island had been matted with forest and inhabited by some Malays, a few Chinese and even fewer Indians. It was only after the captain opened up the port on the leeward side of the island that people started pouring in from the Malayan mainland and surrounding islands and countries. And what an ingenious way the captain found to clear the forest for Georgetown: he shot gold coins into the forest to induce men to clear it. Urged by the captain, the British East India Company rented Penang Island, and part of the opposite mainland called Province Wellesley, for a sum of ten thousand dollars per annum from Sultan Diyauddin Al-Mukarram Shah of the state of Kedah. The British urbanised Penang into the thriving port Madhav and family now found themselves in. This nugget of history was fed to the family by the knowledgeable Nallathamby, whom they met one day at a Madras Lane food stall. They had talked over tumblers of tea and piping hot vadai.

Everywhere they went, the family was met with warm smiles. But, as in all societies, there were those few who shut themselves inside the confines of their narrow minds and only peeped through hostile eyes at the rest of the world. The slurs of these few, the family ignored.

Harmony prevailed. If anything, they heard of only occasional clashes among the Chinese in the tin-mining kongsi on the mainland, drunken brawls between Indian coolies and petty quarrels among

Malays. There were no racial clashes. That was the magic of the new land.

By the end of their two-week familiarisation tours, the family had absorbed a little of the rich and friendly atmosphere of Malaya.

Britons, Europeans, Eurasians, Chinese, Indians, Malays, Arabs, Burmese, Siamese, Bugis, Javenese, Filipinos: what a potent brew, the family thought, but they all live in peace!

Malaya. It surely must be God's ultimate dream for mankind, Madhav concluded.

An Oversight

Madhav, Fairuz, Ratnam, Arumugam and the three bachelors reported for duty at eight o'clock in the morning on 1 August. Their superior turned out to be an Englishman by the name of Timothy Duncan. They called him Mr Duncan.

Mr Duncan looked like Shakespeare with a handlebar moustache. The smile below his moustache was kind and the group's first impression was that they were going to like him. At forty, he was older than them and knew everything there was to know about Penang. He said he lived further north in a bungalow by the beach (which is why he's as red as a lobster, his subordinates gathered). He also said he was a bachelor.

"We are here to set into motion two very important projects," Mr Duncan announced as he sat bolt upright at the chengal conference table in the office. (During the previous week, office furniture and equipment had arrived by the bullock-cart load. So had coolies who now occupied the quarters behind Madhav's house.)

"The Federated Malay States Railways, which I shall hereafter refer to as FMSR, for which you are now working, plans to build a railway jetty and ferry terminus around the present jetty site. Goods transported by rail to the railway wharf at Prai on the mainland will be ferried, then shipped out from here."

To make himself clearer, Mr Duncan left the table and strode to a large map of the Malay Peninsula pinned on a board.

Pointing to the relevant places on the map with a ruler, he explained, "The FMSR already has in place railway lines linking mainland towns to the coast: Taiping to Port Weld, Ipoh to Teluk Anson, Kuala Lumpur to Klang and Seremban to Port Dickson. The link between Prai and Bukit

Mertajam has also been completed." Here he pointed to Prai, just opposite Penang Island. "We shall be directly linked with Prai. A passenger pontoon jetty is being constructed there for use of the new railway passenger ferries between Prai and Penang. At this end, we will be constructing a new jetty, too, for the railway ferries. A Station Master's Office, a Booking Office and a new wharf are also in the pipeline. The timber jetty and wharf we have now will be demolished later."

Madhav and his colleagues nodded in understanding.

"The other project we are concerned with," Mr Duncan continued, "is the proposed railway bungalow for the staff. It is to be constructed on Penang Hill." He was referring to the highest forest-clad peak on the island, which was dotted with bungalows and mansions used as weekend retreats by colonials wishing to escape the bustle and heat of Georgetown. "Our immediate job is to clear a swathe for the bullock-cart trains to carry building materials. Engineers will be on hand later to handle the infrastructure."

The superintendent returned to his seat at the head of the table. He motioned to the office peon and said something in a low tone. The Malay boy left the office hurriedly.

"Now, getting back to business," Mr Duncan said. "There are one hundred coolies at the quarters at present." He addressed the bachelors. "Mr Somasundram, Mr Palani and Mr Muniandy, I'm putting you in charge of seventy of them. You'll supervise the clearing of the land for the railway bungalow. The tool shed is at the end of this block. Here are the keys." He passed a bunch of keys to Somasundram. "You'll hold the keys, Somasundram. You'll find everything you need in the shed. By the bye, there'll be five armed Gurkhas guarding all of you in the field. Who knows, there may be the odd tiger or two left on the island. Even if there aren't, it's entirely possible that they may swim across the strait from the mainland."

With a chill, Madhav thought of the ominous nocturnal sounds from the forests. So did the others.

Noting their jittery looks, Mr Duncan said, "Don't look so alarmed. As far as I know, there've been no tiger attacks during the past three years. That's how long I've been on this island."

The men, however, had their reservations and continued looking uneasy.

The peon came in with a tray set with a silver-plated tea service for Mr Duncan and eight cups of tea with milk for the staff.

"*Terima kasih*," Mr Duncan thanked the boy. Then, turning to his subordinates, "Join me for char?" His grey eyes twinkled as he started making himself a cup of Darjeeling tea. He loved the aroma and delicate flavour of the brew.

The peon served the others.

The men were pleasantly surprised. English bosses did not, as a rule, invite natives, especially subordinates, to drink or eat with them. But they accepted his invitation graciously and, murmuring their thanks, sipped the tea. They were even more surprised when Mr Duncan signalled the peon to help himself to the remaining cup of tea. The boy looked bewildered at first. Then he understood. He gave a broad smile, collected his cup and went outside to drink.

When they had finished tea, Mr Duncan continued with his briefing.

"Mr Ratnam and Mr Arumugam, you'll be in charge of the consignments that arrive at the wharf. You'll use twenty coolies for the job. Another ten I'm retaining for general labour around the office and quarters. Mr Bhonsle and Mr Fairuz, you'll assist me with the clerical duties in the office. More about that when I see you separately in my office in the afternoon. Any questions?"

The men shook their heads. You didn't question British authority. But they were itching to know one thing—their remuneration. (Though the agent in India had mentioned it, they wanted exact figures straight from the horse's mouth.)

As if reading their minds, Mr Duncan said, "Your salaries have been fixed at a hundred and fifty dollars a month." He paused for effect. "Payday is the last Friday of every month. Your working hours on weekdays will be from eight to four with a tea break from ten to ten thirty and lunch break from one to two. Saturdays' working hours are from eight to one. Sundays are rest days."

He looked at the earnest, trusting faces around the table. These Indians, he thought, in India they soak the earth with their blood for the

Empire, here they soak the earth with their sweat; will the Empire ever be able to repay them?

"For now, you may familiarise yourself with your particular work areas," he heard himself saying after recovering from his stray thought. "Let me know if there's anything else you require besides the equipment already in place. And Somasundram, have the coolies assemble here first thing in the morning. I'd like to have a word with them." More sweat, he thought again as he mentioned the coolies. "That will be all. Thank you, gentlemen."

With a nod and flashing his kind smile, he vanished behind the swing doors of his office.

Madhav and Fairuz checked the stationery and office supplies, filing cabinets, bureaus and the sole Remington typewriter in the office. Finding everything in order, they instructed the peon to dust their desks and equip them for work the next day.

It was stuffy in the office building but the windows were wide and it would be cool when the breeze waltzed in from the sea. And the soothing sound of surf that filtered in would alleviate their stressful jobs.

They adjourned to the tool shed and found the bachelors busy taking inventory of the tools: axes, machetes, saws, scythes, mallets, chisels, hoes, spades, rakes and wheelbarrows.

At the wharf, they helped Ratnam and Arumugam check the godowns. The weathered buildings were variously filled with boilers, cranes, tin ingots and sacks of sugar. Stacked in the open were railway lines, railway sleepers, cranks, locomotive wheels and axles.

Come lunch hour, all the men went home.

Madhav told Tara and Mukta about his job and salary. The women were happy. With a gantang of rice at $1, a kati of sugar at 30 cents and a chupak of Bengal gram at 10 cents, why we'll not spend more than $50 on monthly provisions, they calculated. Even after reserving $30 for miscellaneous expenses, they would be able to put aside a neat $70 as savings every month.

Their financial future was certainly bright.

The following months were filled with work and fun.

Madhav threw himself into his job with vigour, working overtime on Saturdays. (Sundays he reserved for taking his family on enchanting trips around the island; the mainland would have to wait until he had saved a lot of money.) He got to know his colleagues better. They all became good friends, being nextdoor neighbours and all that.

Tara and Mukta lost no time in turning their empty house into a home.

They filled it with a set of cane furniture in the sitting room; a wrought-iron double bed with a cotton mattress in Madhav's and Tara's room; and a single bed with like mattress and a carved wooden headboard in Mukta's room. Both beds they hung with white mosquito nets.

Tara's Arsa Mahal-trained eyes picked out the best bric-a-brac for decorating the house. From this curio shop she bought a wooden antique clock topped with a statuette of a gilt horse; from that bazaar she purchased a pair of decorative turquoise glazed plates with a hand-painted picture of robins perched on a grapevine; and from another emporium she marched home triumphantly with a large silver tray with filigree border. The nooks and corners in the house she brightened with potted ferns on stands and crepe-paper flowers. The crepe-paper flowers she made herself.

Taking centre stage in all this was the Rani Meera Bai, looking out snugly from her new ornate frame. Even the Chinese framemaker had wondered at her noble looks and gaze. When Tara told him about the Rani, he said in broken Malay, which Tara could now speak and understand, "You know, Achee, we too had such a brave one as this in China. She was not a queen but a general's daughter. Her name was Mulan." He went on to tell Tara about Mulan's might and courage in fighting her enemies.

When Zaitun paid her first visit to the house, she also was drawn to the Rani's picture on the sitting room wall. "Your rani's like our Tun Fatimah. She, too, wielded the keris and brought down the evil nobles of her court. She saved her native Melaka state from certain doom," Zaitun said. "The Rani and Tun Fatimah, they're good women who came out of purdah to right wrongs. What's more, they were so powerful and yet did not let power corrupt them."

Mukta put her heart and soul into setting up a grand altar for the goddess Durga. She had a wooden dais with a silk canopy over it made to order. The dais she placed on a table in the east-facing corner of her room. She set the Durga statuette on the dais and hung the adjacent walls with framed pictures of Ganesh, Vishnu, Shiva and Murugan. She embellished the statuette and pictures with strung beads, tassels and garlands.

For their kitchen, Tara and Muta bought woks, idli- and puttu-steamers and more clay pots. Tara chose a glossy, modestly priced crockery set from the only British department store on the island. The white-and-brown items had floral borders with a rustic design in the middle: a stream flanked by trees, a cottage and a windmill. A small pine dining table with four chairs complemented the dining area.

One day, Madhav surprised his wife and mother with a purchase of his own, proving his undying love for Greek mythology. He brought home a foot-high onyx image of Venus de Milo. The Venus, naked above the waist, stood in all her curvaceous glory with the upper drape of her garment gracefully falling over an urn. Madhav put the statue plumb in the middle of the round coffee table.

"She reminds me of you," Madhav whispered naughtily in Tara's ear.

Tara blushed but was delighted with the purchase.

Mukta was embarrassed. "Half-naked women, whether real or onyx, belong to the bedroom," she commented.

"Don't be a prude, Ma!" Madhav chided. "Our Hindu temples have even more voluptuous and explicit sculptures for all to see."

When Zaitun and Arumugam's wife, Malliga, came to visit with their broods, the children crowded around the Venus, pointed at her breasts and giggled.

After decorating their home, the Bhonsles spent more time discovering Penang's varied cultural life and its beaches, especially Ferringhi Beach. At the end of it Mukta said, "This island is like the Milk Ocean of Hindu myth. The more you churn it, the more treasures it produces!"

Madhav bought Tara a pair of the Nyonya beaded slippers she so longed for. He bought her many other things, too, because Mukta said an expectant mother should be pampered, otherwise the baby would not turn out right. Tara got all the clothes she wished for, including a dressing-gown. Madhav was tickled by Tara's new-fangled fancy for the European dressing gown. But he thought she looked great in it, like one of the memsahibs in the European quarter of town.

Come October, the family tasted its first Diwali in the new land. It was a quiet affair with none of the ear-splitting firecrackers and mammoth fireworks let off in India. They sent over home-made laddoo, jelebi, gulab jamun and muruku to the neighbouring families. Zaitun, tasting her first muruku, was in ecstasy over the crisp, rice-flour swirls. She immediately got the recipe from Mukta.

Then came the festival of the Muslims, Hari Raya Aidil Fitri. It was preceeded by the month-long Ramadhan puasa when the Fairuzes and the rest of the Malay population fasted from sunrise to sunset. At sunset, they broke their fast with something sweet like dates or figs.

Christmas came and went quietly with the muted sounds of carolling from St George's Church, the oldest in the land.

Not so the Chinese Lunar New Year in January of the following year, 1897. It came with a bang. Georgetown erupted with firecrackers. They hung everywhere in festoons. From trees, from lampposts and from double-storey rooftops to the ground. And it seemed they would never stop firing. The Bhonsle family was thrilled by the lion-dances in the streets. The great drums accompanying the dance reverberated through the whole town.

And as January drew to an end, the family waited excitedly for the birth of Tara's child.

Madhav and Tara had already agreed on the name of their child before it was born.

"If it's a girl, I'd like to call her Arundhati Bai," Madhav told Tara one day.

"Arundhati?"

"Yes. I want her to have a name similar to yours. Your name, 'Tara', means 'star'. And 'Arundhati' means 'the morning star'. What do you say?"

Tara was touched.

"What if it's a boy?"

"Ashvin."

Tara knew that 'Ashvin' referred to the planet Mercury which shines as a star in the night sky.

"That way, I'll always be surrounded by stars!" Madhav said with a wink. Then he gave her one of his intense looks. "You're my lucky star, Tara. Look what good fortune you've brought me."

True. Madhav was earning beyond his dreams. At this rate, he could return to Tanjore a Lakshathipathy after retirement and live there like a prince on his gratuity, savings and pension.

"But Mami would want to consult an astrologer. He'll read his charts and come up with the initial letters in affinity with the baby's birth star."

"Look, Tara, we're almost at the dawn of the twentieth century. Do we still have to follow age-old traditions in naming a baby?" Madhav was way ahead of his time. "Look at the Europeans. Do they consult astrologers when naming their babies?"

"I know they don't. But Mami will be displeased just the same."

She was.

"It's unheard of, naming a baby all on our own!" Mukta protested. "It's just not done!" Then she plunged into a lengthy explanation for Madhav's benefit.

"The relative positions of the sun, moon, planets and stars during a child's birth are very significant. The astrologer, or even a temple priest, will trace the positions according to the date and time of the child's birth. He'll determine the dominant star. It will be the baby's birth star. Then, he'll suggest starting syllables in affinity with the star. The starting syllables are actually sound vibrations, for example, 'la', 'li', 'go' or 'ke'. So, if you name the baby 'Latha', 'Lila', 'Gomathy' or 'Keshav', the vibrations are supposed to have a good influence on the character and behaviour of the child. Your father and I named you and Nilkanth only after consulting the temple priest."

"And look what happened to Nilkanth!"

"But he's an exception. Not the rule. You turned out all right, didn't you?"

"That's just it! Astrologers don't make any difference. The fault, dear

Ma, is not in our stars but in ourselves!" Madhav parodied the Bard to drive home his point.

Mukta left it at that. She knew it would be futile arguing with Madhav. His mind was made up. Like when he wanted to marry Tara.

The gods could not have been kinder to Madhav and his family. Tara positively glowed with the second heart beating within her. Except for the disagreement about the baby's name, they were all happy. A letter from Sundari Bai, blessing Tara and wishing her a safe childbirth, made them happier. And they were happiest when Arundhati was born.

On the morning of 9 March 1897, Arundhati burst into the world with a lusty cry that said everything was well with her.

Pink as a Penang Hill rose, plump and cuddly, she was every mother's dream. The neighbour women oo-ed and ah-ed over her. Mona rushed back home and told Ratnam she wanted a baby just like Arundhati. "And shall we get started on the job right away?" Ratnam teased. The lonely bachelors jokingly offered to adopt Arundhati. Zaitun and Fairuz exclaimed at her cuteness, *"Amboi, chomelnya!"* And Mr Duncan dubbed her 'Little Miss Muffet'.

Every available moment, the family feasted their eyes on her, almost greedily, marvelling at the furling and unfurling of her fingers, the kicking of her feet, the pouting of her lips, and the fluttering of her eyelashes.

At times, they tiptoed to and stood around her cot and watched her as she slept. It was then that she evoked the most profundity in the family.

There she lay sleeping. So soft. So innocent. So untroubled.

Her eyelids flickered.

"I wonder if she's dreaming," Madhav said.

Her lips twitched in a sleep-smile.

"Is Lord Vishnu twirling his pink lotus in front of your sleep-eyes to make you smile?" Tara wondered aloud.

"Or is He spinning His Sudharshana disc that shoots a million sparks?" Mukta said. "Yes, she is dreaming of Him. My grandmother once told me, 'When babes sleep, God comes, gives dream'."

Which was all the more poignant as they were to soon wonder whether she saw anything, at all, in her dreams.

Arundhati laughed a lot when you cooed at her. When you put your finger in her hand, she held it tight. When you sang her lullabies, she gurgled and tried to focus her eyes on you before falling asleep. She had green eyes, like Tara's. They sparkled like the cut mirrors of the Arsa Mahal. She reminded you of the smoothness of silk, the lustre of pearls and the pureness of milk. Above all, she reminded you of God.

Talking of God, He must have been distracted when He created Arundhati. After all, there was so much upheaval in the world at that time. In South Africa, the British were about to massacre the Boers; in Europe, Serbs were fighting Bulgarians over Rumelia; in the Far East, Japan and China were quarrelling over Korea; in China, the Boxer Rebellion was fermenting, thanks to the Dowager Empress Tz'u-hsi; in West Asia, Muslim Turks were slaughtering Armenian Christians; in the East Indies, the Dutch were oppressing the Indonesians; in India, trouble was brewing, stemming from the actions of a lone crusader stirring up anti-British sentiments in South Africa ...

God must have been so preoccupied that He gave Arundhati the most beautiful eyes but forgot to erase some minuscule lines in them that would turn her blind.

An oversight on God's part, you might say.

No one noticed anything amiss until one evening, four months later.

Madhav doted on his daughter. As with the romantic promises (of a firefly garment and dew drop-studded shawl) he made to Tara when they were newlyweds, so with Arundhati. In his profoundest moments he promised his baby a pinwheel of the stars, a lolly of the moon and candyfloss of the whitest cloud. But what he actually did was buy her something closer to home. It had to be the best. So he bought her a Made-in-England rattle. It was a round, pink rattle with pictures of Jack Rabbit framed by a garland of lilies. And its sound was just right, not too loud and not too soft.

When Madhav and Tara first shook it in front of Arundhati, she laughed, showing her toothless gums. They did not notice that she did not reach out for the toy as she should have. But later, when they held the rattle very near her hand and she did not look at it or try to grasp it, they were puzzled. They tried again and again but their baby would not reach out for the toy.

Alarmed, they called Mukta. When she, too, could not get Arundhati to respond, they decided to take the baby to a doctor first thing in the morning.

Next morning, there was neither lightning nor thunder, neither hurricane nor earthquake when the doctor made his pronouncement.

*   *   *

The doctor pronounces a life sentence on my baby and still the sun shines and the birds sing, Tara thought, her tears exhausted. How can that be?

She had to swallow a bitter pill. No matter how big the personal tragedy, the world would go on as if nothing happened.

Madhav and Mukta did not know how to console her as they themselves were in need of consolation. A thunderbolt had struck them.

All their neighbours' sympathy and the consolatory letter from Sundari Bai buoyed them for a while but, after that, stark reality started pounding them like angry waves pounding a rock. The Milk Ocean of their lives was churning up clods of sorrow, lumps of hopelessness and geysers of tears. Even Mr Duncan's solemn promise to do all he could for Arundhati was of no help. Only a miracle can cure your daughter, the doctor had said.

For some time, life became a succession of 'rounds' to see anyone who offered hope for a cure, even if it was only a glimmer.

With the best of intentions, the Fairuzes took Madhav, Tara and the baby to see a bomoh. The Malay shaman lived in a rickety hut on stilts at the edge of the forest. The location of the hut had to do with easy access to the forest to collect medicinal herbs, bark and roots. The wild-looking but kind man wore a sarong and a batik headdress. He smelled of betel and pennywort. His rheumy eyes full of pity, he faithfully recited holy verses amidst banana, mango, jasmine and hibiscus offerings and burning incense, for Arundhati to gain sight. He also advised the family to give her kachang hijau soup. The green legumes were said to improve eyesight.

Their Chinese fishmonger accompanied them to the sinseh. The sinseh, a proud descendant of Nankin medicine men, wore a long jacket, loose drawers and a queue. His shop throbbed with the odour of tonics. The man was his best own advertisement with his taut muscles and glowing skin. Jars and bottles of preserved ginseng, animal parts and birds' nests stood testimony around him. Dipping into centuries of knowledge, he recommended Arundhati be given sips of the stew made from gou gi zi. Then he opened a drawer from a wall of drawers, measured a chupak of the red sweet berries and sent the family home with high hopes.

The empathetic Nallathamby had them follow him to a Tamil vaidiyer. The vaidiyer shared his shophouse premises with a Chettiar. The latter looked expectantly at the family, hoping they would borrow money for their child's medical expenses. He lived, after all, on the interest of his loans.

The whiskered and betel-chewing vaidiyer was pounding herbs with a pestle and mortar. His white veshti and banian were spotted green with the juice of the herbs. He was surrounded by a profusion of dried ingredients, fresh herbs, oils, and fruits: ginger, garlic, mango seeds, gorachana or dried bull's gall, mint, basil, mango oil, neem oil, amalaka or Java plum and jujube among others. For Arundhati, he rustled up concoctions of ponnanganni herb and Indian orris flower to be administered daily.

Madhav unsuspectingly squandered half his savings on miracle-mongers and magicians who were tall on promises but short on delivery.

Tara, in desperation, even swallowed her childhood phobia of mantravadi, to accompany Madhav to see one. The evil-looking man drew a yantra of circles and interlocking triangles on the floor with coloured powder. He laid the baby beside it. Then, he chanted mantras and threw offerings into a sacred fire.

Mukta, in a bizarre re-enactment of the past, found herself tying the replica of an eye to the branch of a bael tree, in the local Kaliamman temple.

The family even took Arundhati to the church to be blessed by the priest, to the mosque to be blessed by the imam, and to the vihara to be blessed by the abbot.

At the end, there were no cures and no miracles.

Mukta's heart bled seeing Madhav and Tara agonising over their baby. They were asking the same questions she and Ramdas had asked over Nilkanth: Why? Why us? Why our child? What did we do to deserve this?

"Has Kausalya's curse followed us here?" Mukta asked Madhav the inevitable question. "'*May your sons be cursed! May you never live in peace!*' First your father. Then, Nilkanth. And now you ... All because your father didn't succumb to her charms. You know, your Ganga Ajji once revealed to me how people like Kausalya pray for another's ruin."

Mukta told Madhav and Tara. The couple listened and were chilled to the bone. They did not know whether to blame God or Kausalya.

Mukta took a vow to recite a chain of 1,008 mantras—the Om Namah Shivaya—daily, for Shiva to open his Third Eye and perform a miracle.

Tara aged overnight. Her great beauty dimmed. The Arsa Mahal sparkle left her eyes. Her youthful spunk that had fought Arsa Mahal dictates, now bowed to the dictates of Fate. Am I being punished for disobeying my mother and abandoning her, she asked herself, suddenly feeling guilty. Maybe if I'd listened.

"I'm worthless," she said to Madhav as she languished in self-pity, refusing to let him touch her for fear of giving him another blind child.

"No, you're not!" Madhav said as he wrestled her into a tight embrace. "To me, you'll always be more dear then the sparkle in the diamond and the glitter in the gold."

Whenever he went into town, Madhav could not bear to look at the Light Street Convent. It reminded him cruelly of the promise he had made himself in India after visiting Pondicherry: If I have a daughter, I'll educate her at a convent.

While they were expecting Arundhati, Madhav and Tara had both decided that their children would attend the best English schools in Penang—Penang Free School for boys and Light Street Convent for girls.

But now, the Light Street Convent stood for an empty dream. Hundreds of girls would march in and out of its portals every year, but not their Arundhati. She was doomed to be illiterate, at a time when hitherto conservative Asian parents were breaking away from tradition and sending their daughters to school.

As for Madhav's dream of visiting all the ancient and illustrious places on the Malayan mainland and beyond: that dream committed suicide somewhere in the waters off Penang.

When Ashvin was born, the first thing the family did was get his eyesight checked. It was perfect.

Ashvin brought back a little of the lost laughter in their lives. In nurturing and tending him and watching him grow, their burden eased, and their sunken hearts resurfaced, saved by the lifeline God had thrown them.

With their new-found will, they set about teaching Arundhati all she could learn with her sense of hearing, touch, taste and smell.

Arundhati's remaining senses became doubly sharp. She soon learnt the difference between the sound of the crow and the cuckoo, the horse and the hound, the wind and the wave. She could feel the hibiscus and lily and identify them by name. She knew when she was eating rice or corn, apple or papaya. And she knew when her mother and grandmother were cooking fish, mutton or prawn. But her speech was slightly slurred as she could not see how words were formed. But the family allowed her to feel their lips to learn proper pronunciation.

Arudhati loved cuddling Ashvin. But her kisses were mostly misplaced: on his nostrils, eyebrows or earlobes. Then, as she grew older, she would feel his face with her fingers and then plant a kiss smack on his cheek or forehead.

The languages she heard around her she absorbed like a tropical rain cloud absorbing moisture. She prattled in Marathi to her family, in Malay to the Fairuzes, in Tamil to the Tamil neighbours and in English to Mr Duncan.

Mr Duncan presented her with a book of nursery rhymes on her fifth birthday. Madhav would recite and sing to her from the book every day.

Her favourites were 'Goosey Goosey Gander', 'Humpty Dumpty' (she immediately dubbed Ashvin with that name) and 'London Bridge is falling Down'. She also loved 'Ring a Ring o' Roses'.

Zaitun's and Arumugam's children would hold her hands and include her in the circle. The part she loved best was falling down at the end of the rhyme.

One day, the children wanted to play Blind Man's Buff. To play the blind man, their automatic choice was Arundhati. She's blind, we don't even have to blindfold her, they shouted eagerly. Zaitun heard them and broke up the game. That night, Fairuz and Arumugam gave their children a sound lecture. From then on, out of consideration for Arundhati, they did not play Blind Man's Buff in her presence.

Madhav and Tara took Arundhati out for long walks with Ashvin toddling along. When they passed any blind man, woman or child at the jetty or in town, they were glad Arundhati was their child. At least she did not have to beg like them. Or sit by the roadside and play the harmonium for people to throw a few coins, only to have them stolen by street urchins. Everybody who saw Arundhati exclaimed what a beautiful child she was. But when they saw her cloudy eyes, they shook their heads in pity and told Madhav and Tara, "Blame it on God and carry on with your lives."

Once, in 1903, when Arundhati was six and Ashvin three, the family accompanied the Fairuzes to the mainland to witness a special procession. Zaitun and Fairuz were taking their children to see how official letters were delivered from the Malay Court.

They crossed the two-mile strait between Penang and the mainland in one of the new railway ferries that departed from the spanking new railway jetty. Madhav and Fairuz felt proud that they, too, were partly responsible for the leapfrog progress of the railways.

On the mainland, they boarded a steam-engine train for a short ride to Alor Star, the state capital of Kedah, where the procession was to take place.

En route, the train chugged through endless fields of green paddy, for Kedah was the rice bowl of Malaya. Mukta was reminded of Champakapur and the many somnolent afternoons she spent with

Ramdas on the paddies. Madhav remembered running along the bunds with Nilkanth, chasing birds and butterflies during stolen moments from the regimental timetable imposed on them by their father.

The riverine town of Alor Star was festive. It was gaily decorated with flags and buntings. Hundreds of people lined the laterite roads (only the main road was tarmacked). The crowd was talking excitedly and munching kachang puteh, bought from the roadside Indian peanut-vendors. Coconut-juice hawkers competed with the vendors, and balloon sellers fought for the attention of children.

It was the first time the Bhonsles saw such a large gathering of Malays, the sons of the soil. The men wore traditional garb—the baju Melayu—with loose trousers and long-sleeved tunics, a folded strip of sarong around the hips and black songkok on their heads. The women were decked out in baju Kedah, a batik sarong and waist-length blouse peculiar to the state, and embroidered scarves called selendang covering their heads.

A fair number of people of other races were in the crowd, too.

At mid-morning, the procession appeared around the corner of the main street where Madhav and his family stood. Madhav quickly hoisted Ashvin on his shoulders to give him a better view. Arundhati stood between Tara and Mukta, busy feeling a balloon they had bought her. She was listening intently to all the sounds around her, cocking her head at every new sound. The children held a candyfloss each, a treat from Fairuz when he bought his children the confection.

A traditional Malay pancharagam led the procession. The finely dressed musicians made pleasant music with their drums, pipes and gongs. Behind the musicians came graceful court dancers followed by four elephants bearing court officials.

Then came the *pièce de résistance*: a mammoth royal elephant draped in gold-coloured shawls, gold being the colour of Malay royalty. The elephant was carrying a very important letter from the palace.

On the howdah atop the elephant sat a court official dressed in black and gold songket finery. In his hands he held a gold platter with a scroll on it. The scroll announced the birth of a Kedah prince. The royal announcement was to be delivered to the British Resident at his Residency.

Behind the elephant came more musicians, and silat exponents demonstrating the Malay art of self-defence.

Suddenly, one of the elephants trumpeted and all the children were scared out of their wits. Arundhati, doubly frightened, clung to Tara. She would remember the sound for the rest of her life: it was the loudest sound she had ever heard during her childhood. Later, she wanted to touch an elephant and pouted when told she could not.

As the regal procession went by, the crowd surged forward, waved and roared, "*Daulat Tuanku! Daulat Tuanku!*" ("Sovereignty to the Sultan!") Their voices held a new verve, a cry to preserve the native states that were ominously coming under total British rule: gold-rich Pahang, tin-rich Perak, rubber-rich Selangor, silver-rich Kelantan and timber-rich Johor.

The adults, including Fairuz and Zaitun, went home hoping that this newborn prince's generation, at least, would be able to wean the country off the British. It was not right that the land of Parameswara, Muzaffar Shah, Tun Perak and Hang Tuah be taken over by pith-helmeted colonisers who sapped the sultans' powers. They also ruled by division. The colonisers did not know then they had set a time bomb ticking. They kept the Malays in the villages for farming, assigned the Indians to rubber tapping, manual labour and the civil service, and designated the Chinese to tin mining, commerce and industry. The time bomb would explode in bloody riots on 13 May 1969.

Madhav, Tara and Mukta left with nostalgic memories of the grand royal processions in Tanjore and Killa.

Arundhati would remember not only the elephant's trumpet but also the vibrations on the ground that shot up her legs as the pachyderms lumbered by.

Prospects

The years, like the sultans, looked around regally, nodded and passed by.

They were bitter-sweet years marred by the ever-present spectre of Arundhati's blindness.

Every time she cried in frustration, knocked against furniture, stumbled or groped, the family would be reminded of their sorrow. It was even more painful, later, when Ratnam's daughter and Fairuz's daughters started getting married, one by one. Tara cried her heart out after attending each wedding. Madhav, though he loved it at other times, could not stand the cloying scent of daun pandan wafting from Fairuz's house. The pandanus leaves were an integral part of Malay weddings. All night long, women would shred the sword-like leaves as fine as hair. They would place the shredded leaves in little woven palm-leaf cups so that the cups became nests. Then they would place a boiled egg in each nest. These would be given as fragrant gifts to all the wedding guests. When the pandanus scent reached him, Madhav wished he would stop breathing. So tormented was he by the thought that he could never marry off his daughter.

Madhav became very protective. Especially after some rascals threw stones at her, calling her "*Kurudi! Kurudi!*" He went after them, caught one by the collar, and, quite out of character, slapped the rascal right and left. By the time he finished, the others had done a vanishing act. When loafers loitered near the house, leering at Arundhati, he instructed that she was not to stand at the open windows or doors. Then he reported the loafers to the mata-mata or policemen. He had heard too many stories of blind girls being sweet-talked and raped. They were easy game.

The mata-mata came in their crisp khaki uniforms and marched the loafers away.

When Arundhati broke out with the odd pimple or two, Madhav was most concerned. He harried Tara to distraction, telling her to apply this lotion and that on Arundhati's cheeks. He was afraid the pimples would mar his darling's alabaster complexion. When Arundhati had chicken pox, he almost had a fit. Tara's and Mukta's assertion, that the Indian herbal baths of turmeric and neem were sufficient to clear the skin, went in one ear and out the other. As soon as the scales started falling off, he enlisted Zaitun's help to buy jamu, the traditional skincare used by Malays of Indonesian origin. Tara had her hands full massaging Arundhati with creams of cinnamon, tangerine and jasmine. And she had to give her lulur baths steeped with rice powder, bark, and a variety of herbs and flowers. Only then was Madhav satisfied.

Arundhati blossomed like the wild orchids in the forests of Penang Hill: exotic, soft, enticing (Mukta liked to compare her to a Champakapur magnolia). Like her mother, she made heads turn everywhere she went. Her cool temperament drew all to her. Her easy laughter made people wonder whether she grieved over her fate in private. The younger of Fairuz's and Arumugam's children, and Ratnam's daughter (alas, the dark and snub-nosed girl did not resemble Arundhati, much to Mona's disappointment) loved to gather around and hear the yarns Arundhati spun about the grey world she lived in. That world was always inhabited by her family, friends, dolls, toy animals, and the cats, dogs, birds, butterflies and flowers that she touched. The fresh fish her mother let her feel in the kitchen occasionally flavoured her yarns.

As she grew into adulthood, her other senses grew extra sharp. She could hear a snake rustle deep in the lalang when others could not; she could hear the distant whining of a dog; she could sniff the air and tell that it was going to rain; she could taste and tell the difference between pure honey and sugar syrup; and she could even tell the exact number of veins on the underside of a leaf.

Her informal education continued through the years, her educators being her family, the neighbours and Mr Duncan. Mr Duncan still fondly called her his Little Miss Muffet though she was almost a woman.

The clothes Arundhati wore were a bit like Miss Muffet's, too. Tara loved to parade her in frilled skirts, lacey blouses with puffed sleeves and Peter Pan collars, and shoes and socks. Tara even teased her wavy black hair into a mass of locks that framed her face.

"You ought to get her used to wearing the sari, too, Tara," Mukta would say, afraid that her granddaughter would lose her Indian identity. Especially since she was so influenced by Mr Duncan.

Confirmed bachelor though he was, Mr Duncan could not suppress his fatherly instincts. Arundhati was the child he would never have. Full of empathy, he would visit during weekends with gifts of chocolates, marshmallows and coconut candies. This consternated his new deputy and other compatriots. They wanted him to join them for a game of lawn tennis, croquet or gin rummy at the Railway Club. Or to just sling a 'stengah' with them. But he preferred Arundhati's company. 'Oddball', they called him.

During such visits, Arundhati would ask him over and over again to tell her about his birthplace in England. And Mr Duncan would oblige, never tiring. Madhav and Ashvin would join Arundhati and be just as thrilled.

Mr Duncan said he was born in Wiltshire, north-west of England's southern port of Southampton. Wiltshire lay in the rolling Salisbury Plains. Here stood one of the world's most ancient temples: Stonehenge. He described the magical circles of giant stones and spoke of the legend that said Merlin, the wizard, had spirited Stonehenge out of Ireland and planted it on the Salisbury Plains. Mr Duncan even built a scaled-down model of it in the verandah, using bits of discarded timber from the railway yard.

Arundhati felt the circles with their uprights and lintels with wonder. She was filled with even more wonder when Mr Duncan told her tales of the Celts who had built the Stonehenge structures: the druid priests who, like the Hindu Shaktas, offered human sacrifices to their gods in Stonehenge; King Arthur and his Knights of the Round Table; and the mythical gods and goddesses who could change into animals or plants.

But the story that gripped Arundhati was that of King Arthur's magical sword, Excalibur. He had found the dazzling sword half-buried in a rock. Others tried to pull it out. They did not succeed. Only King Arthur was destined to free the sword and possess it. He fought and won countless battles with it. Then Mr Duncan told Arundhati of the misty Vale of Avalon with its lake. Beneath the lake was the kingdom of the Lady of the Lake, Lady Avalon. Lady Avalon was the keeper of Excalibur. When King Arthur died, Excalibur was thrown into the lake. Lady Avalon's hand shot out of the water and caught the blazing sword and she has kept Excalibur in the lake ever since.

"I hope Lady Avalon will rise out of the lake one day with Excalibur," Arundhati said.

"Why?"

"Maybe if she touches me with Excalibur I'll be able to see."

Mr Duncan remained silent, full of pity.

Sometimes, Mr Duncan would bring along his portable gramophone. It had a shiny brass horn. Arundhati would crank the gramophone and he would play his collection of records. Very soon, Arundhati was singing 'Over The Sea To Skye', 'Santa Lucia', 'The Blue Danube' and 'The Merry Widow Waltz'. Mr Duncan taught her to dance, too. She had no problem progressing from the jig to the polka to the waltz. She loved the waltz. So much so, when Mr Duncan was kept away a weekend or two by important matters, she would fret till he visited again. Then she would beg him for a dance.

The family looked upon all this with benevolence. They were willing to put up with anything that made Arundhati happy, provided it was within the bounds of decency. But Mukta sometimes tutted when they danced too closely.

"Do you think they are in love?" she asked once, alarmed.

"Hush Mami!" Tara said. "He's old enough to be her grandfather. Maybe she just reminds him of someone at home."

But Mukta tutted all the same.

After his storytelling or dance sessions, the Bhonsles always invited him to stay for lunch. And he accepted. He had a passion for Tara's mutton curry and pineapple pachari.

Mr Duncan became so much a part of the family that when he retired and left for England, they all cried. Arundhati cried the most.

When not waltzing, Arundhati still danced. For Tara had done the impossible. She had taught Arundhati the Bharathanatyam.

Some evenings, the neighbours would be invited over for tea and vadai to give Arundhati a chance to show off her talents. Tara would sing and Arundhati would perform the Mudras and Adavus flawlessly, gaining generous applause. "Your daughter's an achiever," the neighbours would tell Madhav.

Ashvin, meanwhile, finished his schooling at the Penang Free School when he was seventeen. As expected, he passed with distinction and scored highest in English literature. He did what was then in vogue for many youths of his generation: he joined his father in the Malayan Railways and became a clerk in the same office. (The office, by then, had expanded into a brick complex bustling with forty staff members.)

After Mr Duncan returned to England, Ashvin became his substitute. He acquainted Arundhati with all the aspects of English life he had gleaned from his reading. He even waltzed with her. But she was always crying "Ouch!" and complaining he was stepping on her toes.

He got his parents and grandmother a little worried by growing more and more to resemble his Uncle Nilkanth: fair, curly haired, well built and handsome. "Pray God he'll not inherit his uncle's traits," Mukta said, wondering why Ashvin was so secretive sometimes. But Georgetown was a small place and everyone knew everyone else, at least by sight. So the family would have heard of misdemeanours, if any.

Mukta imbued in Arundhati and Ashvin a strong sense of their heritage even while they were children. She told them about Killa, Rani Meera Bai and her legacy. And she told them about the flight of the swans.

"The Hamsa swan is not only famous in India but in faraway lands, too," Mukta said. "A traveling storyteller in Champakapur once told me so. He had been to the borders of India and beyond."

The storyteller had revealed that in Burma the Hamsa was called Hintha. The Burmese revered it because the Buddha was born a swan in one of his previous births. Now the Hintha is used in royal insignia, crowns and atop pagoda flagstaffs.

In Siamese lore, the Hamsa is called Subana-hongsa (The Golden Hamsa). Only the King of Siam is permitted to use it as a symbol. And use it he does. Splendidly. The King's royal barge is shaped to represent the Hamsa. It has a Hamsa figurehead decorated in gold and embedded with precious stones and mirrors. And the fifty oarsmen row the barge with such style and synchronisation that it appears the barge is a soaring Hamsa.

"Our good name should soar like the Hamsa," Mukta said. "Not only in life but in death, too. Like the Rani's."

Arundhati asked Madhav for a swan.

"There are no swans in Penang. But perhaps we'll go to Kuala Lumpur some day and you can hold a swan," he said. "I hear there are some on the lake in the Kuala Lumpur Lake Gardens." He did not guess then that Arundhati was destined to go elsewhere.

Madhav and Tara started greying young (Mukta's hair was already a thatch of silk-cotton). But Madhav did not lose that special look he always reserved for Tara. When he looked at her that way, Tara would feel like a girl all over again, her great sorrow over Arundhati forgotten. They worried. Having an unmarried daughter over twenty was bad enough, but an unmarried, blind daughter? What would her future be without them? Would Ashvin and his future wife take care of her the way they did, after the elders were all gone? Times were changing and so were daughters-in-law.

One day, Madhav came home from town, highly excited. He was waving a copy of *The Hindu*, an English-language newspaper from India. It was a month-old copy given to him by Nallathamby. The agent had just returned from one of his regular trips to India.

"Tara! Ma! Come here quickly!" Madhav called.

Tara dropped the curry puff she was making. Hearing the urgency in Madhav's voice, she came running from the kitchen to the sitting room where he was. Mukta shuffled as fast as she could from her room, ignoring the arthritic pain in her knees.

"Look at this!" Madhav cried stabbing his finger at the headlines.

Staring back at them were the words 'Braille Comes To India'.

Madhav read the words aloud.

"Do you know what this means?"

"No," the women chorused. 'Braille' was a new word to them.

Madhav explained.

"Braille is a system of reading and writing for the blind, using letters in the form of raised dots." Madhav himself had just learnt what the word meant from the newspaper article. "The blind person reads by feeling the dots. Isn't that magnificent?"

"Our Arundhati can learn to read then?" Tara was wide-eyed. "How wonderful! Did you hear that, Arundhati?" She went to her daughter, who was sitting nearby with ears cocked, and gave her a hug.

"I can learn how to read?" Arundhati asked, the full implication of the good news still not having sunk in.

"Yes! And write. And ... and ... study language. Study any subject!" Madhav felt a zest he had not felt in many years.

"Where in India do they have this 'Braille'?" Mukta asked.

"In Delhi, Calcutta, Bombay and Madras."

"Madras? How convenient! We're only a week's journey away," Tara enthused. "We can go there during your next annual leave."

They lost themselves in their own euphoria for a minute, conjuring all kinds of pleasant images in their minds. Then sobriety took over.

"What about expenses?" Mukta asked. "I'm sure such education is going to be as expensive as buying elephants and horses."

"You're right there, Ma. It's going to cost us the earth. That's why we can't go now."

Tara's face fell. So did Arundhati's.

"Don't look so crestfallen," Madhav said. "I've got everything planned. Here's what we'll do. As you know, my retirement is only a year away. I'll be receiving at least twenty thousand dollars in gratuity. That amount can go toward Arundhati's formal education. My monthly pension will cover our other expenses. What do you say, Tara?"

Tara's face lit up.

"Sounds sensible to me. Do you agree, Mami?"

Just then, Ashvin returned after a game of badminton. The badminton courts in the new Railway Club (there was another club exclusively for whites) was the haunt of Ashvin and his colleagues. He came in whistling his favourite Boy Scouts song: 'The Happy Wanderer'. His flushed looks contrasted with his white tailor-made shorts, white banian and Bata shoes and socks.

The family told him the good news and their plans for returning to India. Ashvin was overjoyed and almost squeezed the breath out of Arundhati with a bear hug.

"Don't worry about finances," Ashvin reassured his parents. "I'll remit you part of my salary every month. Anything for Arundhati!"

"What do you mean, 'remit'?" Madhav looked shocked. "You're supposed to go with us to India! We're a family, you know."

"Return to India?" It was Ashvin's turn to look shocked. "I've been born and bred here. I like living here. And there's my job. Do you expect me to leave my good job? Forget it, Bah!"

"You can get a good job in India, too, son."

"But will the remuneration be the same?"

The question stumped Madhav.

"Money shouldn't be the first consideration, Ashvin," Tara said. "We should stay together as a family."

"What would you do here alone, anyway?" Mukta asked. "You're not even married yet. Who'll take care of you?"

"And I'll miss you terribly," Arundhati complained. "Who's going to sing and dance with me, tell me jokes and buy me chocolates every day?"

"It's not that I don't want to, Arundhati. Thambi, Kannan and Appu write and tell me how much they regret returning to India." Ashvin was referring to Arumugam's sons who had returned with their parents to India. "They don't have the jobs they like. They don't have the money they were earning here. And they don't have the lifestyle they're used to."

"But you're our only son. And we don't leave young men of your age to live alone. It's unconventional. What happens if you get snared by some … undesirable woman? There are many of those around." He was referring to the burgeoning redlight districts in Georgetown, their brazen hussies openly soliciting on the streets. "And you, won't you worry about us, too? Or don't you love us enough?" Madhav was surprised to see dissent in his usually obedient son.

"Bah, don't make me feel guilty, as if I'm abandoning all of you. It's just that I'm happy here and I don't want to end up frustrated, like Arumugam's sons."

It's happening all over again, Tara thought. She was reminded of the time when she had stood alone against the opinion of the Arsa Mahal. Now, her son was in a similar predicament. Should we stand in the way of his happiness, she asked herself.

"Maybe he's right," Tara came to Ashvin's rescue, inwardly afraid of Madhav's displeasure.

"What! You take his side, too?" Disappointment changed Madhav's face.

"I think what he says make sense. If he's happy here, we shouldn't drag him to India to satisfy our notions. Besides, his remittance will come in handy. You never know when you'll need extra cash. Especially since all your gratuity will be used for Arundhati's education and we'll have to depend solely on your pension."

It was the first time Madhav heard Tara's dissenting voice in their twenty-four years of marriage. All the same, he turned her words over in his mind.

"Why don't we do this? As soon as we go to India, we can find Ashvin a suitable girl. Then he can come over, marry her and bring her back to Malaya," Mukta suggested. "That way, we don't have to worry about his well-being." She had not expected Madhav to be so conventional suddenly. After all, he had gone against all convention. He had love-married, had married a courtesan, had left his Motherland, had not consulted the astrologer when naming his children, had allowed Arundhati to wear skirts and gowns and dance with Mr Duncan.

Madhav arrived at a decision.

"All right. All of you win. Ashvin, you can stay. But make sure you come to India at least to light my funeral pyre." The bitterness in his voice was plain.

"Hush, nawra! Don't talk like that. Nothing's going to happen to you now. You're going to live to be a hundred!"

Later, in private, he told his wife and mother, "I didn't mean to force Ashvin. It's just that I didn't expect us to have differing opinions. I thought we agreed on everything."

"Which just goes to show, do we ever really know our children?!" Mukta said.

The following year flew by with Madhav making preparations for their return to India.

He had Nallathamby find them a modest house for rent in the Tambaram suburb of Madras. He transferred his savings through the Penang branch of the Mercantile Bank of India to its branch in Madras, and arranged to have his gratuity transferred, too. He got his friends visiting India to bring back information about the School for the Blind in Madras. He allowed Tara, Arundhati and Mukta to buy anything they liked and could possibly carry on the steamer. He got permission for Ashvin to continue occupying the railway quarters they lived in, with the assurance to the FMSR that Ashvin would soon bring back a wife from India. Otherwise, the FMSR had the right to order Ashvin to vacate, in favour of a married couple.

Amidst this sea of preparations and contemplation of Arundhati's prospects was an exciting thought that bobbed up now and then: here, at last, was his chance to see Nilkanth again. It troubled him that he had not heard of him for more than twenty years. (It troubled his mother, too. Though staunchly casting him out of her mind when she was younger, she talked of him increasingly as she grew old. "No matter what he's done, he's still my son," she said, feeling a wrench in the pit of her belly every time she thought of him.) Madhav blamed himself for allowing Arundhati's affliction to get the better of him. But I'll make amends to him when I return to India, he promised himself.

The day Madhav retired, the office staff threw a tea party in his honour at the plush Eastern & Oriental Hotel in Penang. The seafront hotel with its swaying palms and fresh breezes was once the haunt of Kipling. It had a European chef who whipped up a spread of smoked salmon sandwiches, puff pastry with chicken filling, raisin scones, fairy cakes, jam tarts and chocolate éclairs. He served the spread with Earl Grey and Darjeeling teas. Madhav was presented with a Swiss Rado watch by his new superintendent, Mr Duncan having long retired.

Two months before the Bhonsles left, something happened that, though calamitous, endeared Malaya to the family even more.

The Indians have their kutty saitan, the Malays their toyol and the Chinese their jing.

They are mischievous little imps that love to play pranks on humans. Everybody said what happened must have been their doing.

There was a fire. No one knew exactly how it started. But by the time the Port Authority fire brigade and the neighbours doused the flames, Madhav's quarters was an empty shell of smoking timber.

The family escaped unhurt. Mukta, being a light sleeper, was the first to awake amidst choking smoke. Her screams alerted the others. But there was no time to save belongings. Everything went up in smoke. Except Rani Meera Bai's picture. It miraculously fell through the burning floorboards and plopped into a trough of water under the house. The family had placed the water there for stray dogs, cats and chickens that sought shade underneath. "She will never die," Mukta said. They salvaged the picture and restored it lovingly.

The family was given temporary accommodation in newly built quarters nearby.

Within a month, another house rose out of the ashes like a phoenix, thanks to the efficiency of the Malayan Railways. The Bhonsles returned to it. Ashvin, especially, insisted they stay there. He was born in that house and vowed he would bring back its old ambience. He started off by hanging the Rani's picture on the wall.

Madhav lost five thousand dollars in the fire. He thanked his lucky stars his gratuity and savings were already safely in India. But losing so much money was a big setback all the same. It was like losing an arm. The money was supposed to be used for immediate expenses and to buy their passage to Madras. What was he to do?

That was when true Malayan spirit came to the fore.

Everyone the family knew, and even those they did not know, chipped in to help.

Fairuz and Zaitun were the first. They planned to go on the once-in-a-lifetime Haj pilgrimage to Mecca. They had put aside money for the trip. Now they postponed the Haj trip and donated part of their savings to the Bhonsles. Not only that. They got their children to donate as well.

Ratnam and Mona owned a piece of land in Bukit Mertajam on the mainland. They had rented it out to a rubber planter. They gave all of a month's rent to the Bhonsles.

The Lims (they lived in Arumugam's vacated quarters) sacrificed a favourite food. The couple and their brood of six loved to eat out weekly at the esplanade hawker stalls. There they tucked into ikan bakar—spice and chilli-coated fish wrapped in banana leaves and roasted over a hot griddle. The Lims stopped eating out for a month and pressed the saved money into Madhav's hands.

The bachelors, all about to be married, pooled some of their savings to give to the Bhonsles.

The hat was passed around at the Railway Office. The new boss was generous. Even the old Malay peon gave what he could afford.

So they all gave: the committees of Kapitan Kling Mosque, Kek Lok See Buddhist Temple, St George's Church, Kuan Yin Temple, the Sikh Gurdwara, Sri Mariamman Temple, Khoo Kongsi, the Penang Malays association, the Babas and the Indian merchant houses.

That was what being Malayan was all about.

On a cool September morning in 1921, the family set sail on the SS *Trishul* for Madras.

In retrospect, Madhav regretted that he was leaving without seeing most of what he had set out to see from India, twenty-five years ago. The gods had seen to that, by bestowing upon him a sightless child. After her birth, every cent he could hoard, he hoarded—all for Arundhati's sake. If and when a medical breakthrough presented Arundhati with a chance to see, he wanted to be able to pay the medical bills. (When he was an adolescent, Ashvin was most affected by this hoarding: he was denied fishing rods, butterfly nets and kites, and had to either make them himself or borrow them from friends; and the Raleigh bicycle he pestered his father for he never got, until he started earning for himself.) Madhav was glad he had substantial savings besides his gratuity.

The ruins of the city-kingdom of Kadahram at the mouth of the Merbok and Muda Rivers; the Hindu-Buddhist chandi ruins in the

Bujang Valley; the ancient Kuala Kedah Fort built by Indian masons; the ruins of the old capital of Siam, Ayuthia; and much, much more Madhav did not see. They were all on the mainland. So near and yet so far.

It was difficult, parting from the neighbours.

"May Allah always watch over you," a balding and rotund Fairuz said, taking Madhav's hands in his.

How well Hindu and Muslim get along here, Madhav thought, if only it were the same in India. He held Fairuz's hands wordlessly.

Zaitun, turned grandmother, hugged the women in turn. She and Fairuz were a lonely couple, all their children having married and left home.

"I'll be staying in my kampong on the mainland after my retirement, but I promise I'll look up Ashvin whenever I come to Penang to visit my children. So don't worry about him," Fairuz reassured Madhav.

Ratnam and Mona had decided to put down their roots in Malaya. They would be staying with their married daughter in Alor Star after Ratnam's retirement.

"I'm sorry you've to leave, Madhav. I wish you'd stay. But I understand Arundhati comes first," Ratnam said. It would be difficult to forget their nightly rendezvous, together with Fairuz, at the Railway Club where they enjoyed a game of cards, chess or billiards. Or an occasional peg of brandy and soda.

The bachelors, now married and living in the new row of quarters nearby, also wished the family well. They, too, promised to keep an eye on Ashvin.

"I'll miss all of you. To tell you the truth, when I left India twenty-five years ago, circumstances were such that coming to Malaya was easy," Madhav said. "But leaving Malaya is difficult. Malaya entraps you like the lianas entrap the trees in the forest. You're entrapped by the goodwill, the understanding and the tolerance. It's a wonderful entrapment."

It was even more difficult parting from Ashvin.

They kept their goodbyes short, lest they gave way to their emotions.

Even then, Mukta cried.

"We'll notify you as soon as we've found you a suitable girl," she sniffled, looking at him through horn-rimmed spectacles "Make sure you come to India then." As an afterthought she added, wagging her finger at him as if he were a small boy, " And no nonsense about marrying English or Eurasian girls, you hear? It seems to be the new fad among English-educated Asians."

"Have your meals regularly and make sure you take your oil bath every Saturday. Let us know if there's anything you want and we'll send it through Nallathamby," Tara managed to say.

Patting Ashvin on the back, Madhav said, "You've got a good name here, Ashvin. Keep it up. I'll be writing to you soon."

"And be sure to reply to Bah's letters," Arundhati thought it proper to give some sisterly advice. She was leaving with great expectations. And her family sensed it. "You know, when I see you next, I'll be able to read and write. I'm sure I'll be able to answer all your questions then. And read to you from the English classics!" She sighed. "Only thing is, I still won't be able to see you."

"Don't give up," Ashvin said. "Who knows, like Ajji says, maybe Shiva will open his Third Eye some day, and *voila!* you'll be able to see."

PART FIVE

The Third Eye Opens

A lone man stood silhouetted against the sky on the tip of a rocky promontory. The weather was rough. Below him, the sea, in its eternal quest to conquer land, was battering the rocks that stood in its way.

The man looked like a Hindu ascetic with his flowing beard, matted shoulder-length hair and the briefest of clothes. A whistling wind swept his beard, hair and his tattered clothes to one side. He was hunched. He must have been very tall once. His wizened face was a mask. It betrayed nothing of the storm within his breast. His hooded and half-blind eyes squinted at the ship passing by to anchor at the port. He made out the words 'SS *Trishul*'. A feeling of déjà vu swept through him. Had he arrived in the port on a grand ship like this? Or on a rusty tin can where humanity had been packed like sardines in the hold and breathed the stench of their own filth? He could not remember. When had he arrived? Blank. Why had he arrived? What was his name? Blank. Blank.

Kala Pani did that to you. The notorious British India penal colony in Port Blair made you forget. It also made you deaf, from beatings. It made you dumb, from tongue cutting. It made you blind, from malnutrition. And it made you crippled, from precision joint breaking.

After staring at the ship for a long time, the man started hobbling back to the prison, tripping and falling every few yards, grimacing, and picking himself up again with great effort.

He reached the three-storey prison complex. Only the prison was no longer one. Its doors and gate were wide open. After more than twenty years, the British admitted to the atrocities committed by its officers in the prison and closed it down. They were now shipping the convicts back to the mainland.

The man entered the cellular jail, on the second floor, where he had been incarcerated. Solitary confinement, for he knew not how many years. But poor though his memory was, he instinctively found his cell, like a homing pigeon.

The cell was twelve feet long and half as wide. The slit of a window, ten feet above, did not offer him any view. And the barred door faced the back wall of the next block. The stench and dinginess of his cell he was used to. He felt comfortable in it. But the pain was killing him. His Kala Pani-shattered knees and elbows caused some of the pain. But most of it was caused by the disease that ravaged his body.

The strain of climbing the stairs to the cell was too much. Gasping, he collapsed on the floor. A warden, supervising the few convicts who were still about, caught sight of him in the cell.

"What, man. Aren't you going home? You're a free man now."

The man only dragged himself, like a wounded animal, into a corner. This was home. He did not want to leave. He curled up in pain and faced the brick wall. If pain had colour, it would be the colour of bricks.

As the weather cleared, a ray of morning sunlight illumined a word in front of him. It was his name. He had once scratched it on the wall. Now he looked at it uncomprehendingly.

*   *   *

Madras
4 October 1921

My dear Ashvin

We arrived in Madras a week after setting sail from Penang. But there was a small diversion on the way. On the morning of the third day, we had to put in for six hours at Port Blair on the Andamans. One of the ship's boilers had sprung a leak and had to be repaired urgently.

As usual, I was all excited at the sight of a new land. Remember me telling you how I borrowed a telescope to look at

Pulau Dayang Bunting, as the SS *Juggernaut* reached Malaya? Well, history repeated itself. I borrowed the captain's telescope to view Port Blair. And what I saw was unforgettable: pristine beaches guarded by sentinal coconut palms, lush forests throbbing with birdlife, and a couple of giant green turtles crawling back into the emerald waters after laying their eggs on shore (rather late, I am told, as they usually leave the shores before daylight).

I was on the lookout for the Jarawa and Onges tribesmen the ship's crew talked so much about but I did not even catch a glimpse of them. Instead, I saw a solitary man on a rock. He was old. The telescope was powerful enough for me to see his matted hair and shrivelled looks. He was too fair to be a native (they tell me the natives are negroid). And he could not have been a vagabond or an ascetic. There is no place for such people in the penal colony. So he must have been an ex-convict. He would have slipped my mind if not for the way he walked: a strange, disjointed walk that made him collapse every few steps. It was as if his legs and hands had been taken apart and then fixed back at grotesque angles. I have never seen anyone like that. Poor man. He reminded me of a sick stallion I once saw tottering on its legs before it died.

But to other matters now.

The first thing your grandmother did on reaching Madras was fall on her knees and kiss the ground. She thought she would never see India again!

Your mother and I have mixed feelings. We are torn between India and Malaya. The first gave us birth. The second gave us refuge. And much more.

For Arundhati, India is a whole new experience.

She says her ears tell her there are infinitely more people here ("It sounds like a thousand beehives," she said). She can also feel the change in climate from the humidity of the equator to the sizzle of the tropics and pick out a completely new range of sounds. Her palate, too, is on an epicurean adventure. It reminds me of the time your mother, grandmother and I first came to Malaya: the sheer variety of food knocked us off our feet.

Already, your grandmother is missing Hokkien mee. Your mother is yearning for popiah as I am for nasi lemak. Arundhati dreams of chendol and char kuey teow. We also miss the babble of Malay, Chinese and the host of other Malayan voices. It seems strange now, hearing just one language after all these years.

Madras is like an amoeba. From the nucleus of the main business district, it multiplies into numerous suburbs with interesting names like Mylapore, Triplicane, Saidapet, Kodampakkam, Royapuram ... I could go on and on. To put it consicely, Madras city has no boundaries.

And here is a surprise for you. Georgetown, Penang, has a twin here—Georgetown, Madras! There is Madras Harbour, Madras Beach, Fort St George, Railway Office and St Mary's Cathedral. There are also missionary schools, fishing villages and markets. Only thing missing is the eclectic mix of races, cultures and religions of Penang.

Here, you see Tamils everywhere. Only once in a blue moon do you see a Northerner. And the British presence is minimal.

Our house in Tambaram is one in a row of terraced houses. By local standards, it is spacious (with four rooms). It has piped water (from a communal pump) and electricity. We have hired a water carrier who sees to our daily supply of water. Compared to our neighbours, we are well off, thanks to the Malayan dollar.

Talking of the Malayan dollar, I find we are still very Malayan. We keep saying, "How many kupang?", "Give me a kati of rice", or "Bring down your price lah!", much to the confusion of local shopkeepers. And, sometimes, we are downright mean. When people offend us and we do not want them to know our remarks, we speak in Malay: "*orang kedekut!*", "*tipu!*" or "*bodoh lah!*" May God forgive us!

I am happy to say that last week, Arundhati joined the School for the Blind. It is run by an Englishman, a Mr Ian Fergus. I am told the school strives to attain the standards set by Helen Keller.

In case you have not heard of her, Helen Keller is the famous blind and deaf American who, despite her handicaps, is a scholar and an author. She is also a source of great inspiration to the blind all over the world.

I send Arundhati to school by rickshaw every day. I also fetch her home in the evenings. Her teachers tell me she is a quick learner. That is very good. I want so much for her. We all want so much for her, don't we?

Before I end this letter, there is a piece of sad news I have to convey to you. Your maternal grandmother, Sundari Bai, has passed away. The unhappy event occurred while we were en route to Madras. The Arsa Mahal sends word that she held out bravely on her death bed, knowing that she would be seeing your mother soon. But God decided otherwise. She was a good woman, although her hereditary profession made a villainess of her. May she attain nirvana.

Your mother, grandmother and sister send you their love and blessings. Please convey our regards to the Fairuzes, Ratnams, Somasundrams, Palanis, and Muniandys. We miss all of you.

Take care of your health and be good. We may be far away but the picture of Rani Meera Bai we left behind should always remind you of who you are and inspire you to be noble in everything you do.

Yours affectionately
R. Madhav Rao Bhonsle

*   *   *

Madras
1 November 1921

My dear Ashvin

Your mother thanks you for your letter of condolence to her on the demise of her mother. The only regret your mother has is that Sundari Bai never got to meet you and Arundhati.

Apart from that sad note, we are all happy here though we can never be really happy in the true sense of the word, as long as Arundhati remains blind.

Arundhati is making excellent progress in school. She is already reading in Braille. (She had no problem with letters; our teaching her the Braille ABCs with modelling clay has paid off!) The reading materials are very expensive but we can afford them.

Your mother and grandmother have not lost any time in looking for a bride for you. Right now, they have the horoscopes ('horror'-scopes as far as I am concerned) of three candidates. (I say 'horror'-scopes because if the astrologer says the stars are not compatible, then couples in love are forever doomed to pine for each other. Or to commit suicide.)

Now about the candidates.

Candidate No.1 lives in Madras. She is ivory-fair and pretty, can cook, can sing Carnatic songs but is slightly hunched. Candidate No.2 is from Palani. She, too, is fair and pretty, can cook and sew but cannot sing and is illiterate. And candidate No.3 is from Pudhukotai. She can sing, dance, draw elaborate rangoli but cannot cook.

Your mother and grandmother cannot decide which girl to pick as all three have shortcomings. As far as they are concerned, a suitable girl would be one who is fair, pretty, literate, can cook, play the veena, sing Carnatic songs, dance the Bharathanatyam, sew, draw rangoli and be of good deportment. Of course having a good reputation goes without saying.

Just where do we find a girl with all these qualities, they ask, sighing.

I wish they were not so fussy. As long as a girl is of good character, literate, healthy, can cook and carry out household duties efficiently, she is suitable. What do you say, son? Anyway, I shall keep you informed of any further developments.

The agent, Nallathamby, is now in Madras. He had been to

Tanjore after a long interval and has just returned. And he has some disturbing news about your Uncle Nilkanth. He says the British captured your uncle (as I feared) in 1896, just after we left for Malaya. He was convicted on charges of smuggling and thuggery and sentenced to twenty-five years in the penal colony on the Andamans. But, to atone for his sins, he has requested his wealth be distributed among the poor. People are always flocking to his mansion for handouts, Nallathamby says. He has even left us ten lakhs. I am touched by your uncle's gesture. But I will not accept his money. I have enough. As long as he is helping others, I am happy for him. I am sorry we were wrong about him. We thought he would never change. What a pity he changed too late! But the prison facility has closed now. He has been given the choice of either staying on the Andamans or leaving. I wonder which choice he will make.

And now for some brighter news. I hear your mother set a precedent for Tanjore courtesans. Nallathamby says a whole generation of them has broken with tradition and found a new life outside the Arsa Mahal. And society, after much debate, has accepted it.

(That is another thing we were wrong about. About society never changing.) Right now, no one could be happier than your mother. "It's well worth the hell I went through," she says.

Back to Nallathamby. Through him we will be sending you some sweetmeats and preserves. Please expect a visit from him in early December. You may give him a small tip. I have already tipped him generously here.

Tell the neighbours I thank them for their good wishes and wish them well, too.

Yours affectionately
R. Madhav Rao Bhonsle

*   *   *

Madras

2 December 1921

My dear Ashvin

The die is cast. A suitable girl has been found and your marriage date has been set: 5 February 1922.

You will please apply immediately for a month's leave and, on its approval, book your passage to Madras. It would be ideal if you could sail during the last week of January, get married and stay here during the first two weeks of February, and return during the third week. At this end, we have already started making the wedding arrangements.

As it turns out, the girl is not any one of the three candidates I wrote you about earlier. She happens to be the granddaughter of a distant cousin of your grandmother. We met at a temple function. The family is domiciled in Madras.

The bride's father is a retired police inspector by the name of Vittal Rao Shinde. His wife's name is Sumathi Bai. Your intended goes by the name of Jija Bai. She is eighteen. And yes, she has all the required qualifications except that she is tawny, cannot sing and cannot dance the Bharathanatyam. I am glad your mother and grandmother have scaled down their Himalayan standards. Otherwise, you will be a doddering old man before you get married!

I shall be forwarding a batch of wedding invitation cards soon. We have to invite all our friends in Penang although we know they will not be able to attend the wedding. It is a matter of courtesy.

You mother says take Somasundram and Menaka in our stead to distribute the cards. And let Menaka present them. According to custom, it is imperative that a shrimati [a woman whose husband is still living] delivers the wedding invitations. It is supposed to auger well for the marriage. Frankly, I do not understand all this nonsense about only shrimati bringing good luck. What is so wrong with a widow, like your grandmother, delivering a wedding invitation? Does losing her husband mean that a good, God-fearing woman turns into a she-devil and bad omen overnight? Can a widow not wish her own children well, too?

Regarding your proposal to join the about-to-be-formed Indian National Army in Malaya, I urge you to rethink the idea.

I have read a lot about the INA from the backdated copies of the *Straits Echo* of Penang (thanks to Nallathamby). It is clear that many Indian youths in Malaya want to join the INA to fight for India's Independence. How commendable! But should you not be joining an effort to fight for Malaya's Independence? I am sure I do not have to tell you that you owe your loyalties to Malaya. Perhaps those of you whose young blood is crying for freedom should get together and form a congress along the lines of the Indian National Congress. I have read that Malayan nationalists like Onn bin Jaafar and Tan Cheng Lock are already sowing the seeds of Malayan independence in their Malay and Chinese communities. For the Indians, the young E.E.C. Thuraisingham, John Thivy and V.T. Sambanthan seem good choices as leaders. If anything, you should join their efforts in fighting for Malayan Independence. Give it a thought.

Coming back to your marriage, your mother requests that you purchase a dozen of those floral, gilt brooches worn by the Nyonya women. She wants to be different. She insists that her daughter-in-law-to-be should clip her wedding sari drape with one of those brooches. Your mother will be wearing one and so, too, will Arundhati. The rest she intends to distribute to the bride's close relatives as novel gifts. Leave it to your mother to come up with ideas like that.

I close with a bit of advice (?!) from your grandmother. She urges you to gorge yourself on as much mutton briyani, laddoo and jelebi as possible during the next two months so that, I quote, "he will look rounded and presentable and not like a scrawny chicken."

Yours affectionately
R. Madhav Rao Bhonsle

*   *   *

Madras
10 April 1922

My dear Ashvin

We are all taking a well-earned rest after the hectic schedule of your marriage.

"At last, we can sleep in peace," say your mother and grandmother, meaning they do not have to worry about you, since you now have a wife to take care of you. I must admit I feel the same way, too.

Your in-laws have heaped praises on us for the grandeur of the pre-nuptial and post-nuptial rites we conducted for your marriage. They apologise that they were not able to reciprocate. But we do not hold it against them. We have the advantage of the Malayan dollar. They do not.

Arundhati looked heavenly in a sari during your wedding, did she not? Your mother once looked like that.

It would please you to know that a few families have shown interest in and proposed marriage for Arundhati. But we are against the idea, even if we long to see her married. In these times when in-laws are setting fire to their normal daughters-in-law because of dowry problems, what guarantee is there that our handicapped Arundhati will not be abused? We have reconciled ourselves to the fact that we will never see Arundhati in a bridal outfit. By the way, she is at the top of her class in school.

We are happy to learn from your letter that Fairuz and all the other neighbours and friends attended the wedding reception you gave them. They are a good lot. Don't lose touch with them.

How are political developments over there? Here, the country is still reeling from the shock of the Amritsar Massacre. Things are beginning to hot up, what with Gandhi-ji, Nehru, Patel and Jinnah making no bones about throwing off British rule. Not a day passes without a political rally, a strike, a demonstration or arrests. And the Raj is coming down hard on nationalists. I pray that Independence, when it comes, will be a peaceful process.

I am glad that Jija Bai is taking well to Malaya. I remember how your mother, grandmother and I fell immediately under its spell the moment we set foot in Penang.

Yours affectionately
R. Madhav Rao Bhonsle

*   *   *

Madras
21 May 1922

My dear Ashvin

First let me congratulate you on becoming a father-to-be. You have no idea how happy we all are. Your mother is already smocking little vests and grandmother is busy preparing mango pickle, ginger-tamarind pickle and every other spicy-sour condiment Jija Bai may fancy during the coming months. As usual, Nallathamby (I do not know what we will do without him!) will deliver the condiments to you. (The good man has even gone out of his way to find news of Champakapur for us: it seems it is once again like before, a purple paradise. Some places, like some people, never die. I must visit it one day. After all, it is my birthplace.)

Your mother requests that you fulfill Jija Bai's every wish during her pregnancy. I enclose a packet of vibhuti [holy ash] from the Mylapur Temple. Grandmother offered special prayers there on hearing the good news and sends the vibhuti for both of you. She also suggests you enlist Mak Chik Zaitun's and Auntie Mona's help to have a midwife come over regularly to give Jija Bai pre-natal checks.

I have already thought of a name for your child!

As you are aware, I named you and your sister after the stars, as is your mother. I would like to continue the trend with my grandchildren, too, if it is all right with you.

These are the names that tickle my fancy: 'Mithun' for a boy, and 'Mina' for a girl. Mithun refers to the star, Gemini, just as Ashvin does. Mina is the Pisces constellation. Just imagine: Tara, Arundhati, Ashvin, Mithun, Mina. A galaxy of stars in my life! How about it? Will you humour your old man?

Your grandmother is already rumbling like distant thunder. I did not consult astrologers before naming you and Arundhati. Grandmother says that could be the reason why Arundhati is blind. According to her, the name has no rasi, affinity, with your sister. If that is the case, how is it that so many people with astrology-determined names are handicapped in later life, I ask. ("I really don't know where your stubbornness is going to lead you," she grumbles.) In the meantime, if you have any star-name suggestions, let me know. They may be better than the names I have thought of.

I am afraid I have to sign off now. There is someone at the door with an urgent message from Arundhati's school.

Yours affectionately
R. Madhav Rao Bhonsle

*   *   *

Madras
2 August 1922

My dear Ashvin

I am sorry if I got you worried by not replying your letters for the past two months. But when know the reason, you will forgive me. It has to do with Arundhati.

It has happened, Ashvin: the miracle we have been waiting for!

Here is how it came about.

In May, on the 21st to be exact (while I was writing to you), Arundhati had a fall in school. She was knocked unconscious. Her teachers rushed her to hospital. On being informed, we, too, rushed there. We went through some very tense moments before she regained consciousness. And when she did, we almost fainted with joy.

She said she could see shadowy images moving about. It meant she was no longer totally blind as in these past years. It meant there was hope! Even the doctors were baffled. They, too, said it was a miracle. But wait till you hear what I am about to tell you next. That is the real miracle.

I immediately set about searching for a specialist in ophthalmology. I found the best—one Dr Sridhar Lachmanan. He practices in Bangalore where he has a private clinic.

All of us went to Bangalore and took Arundhati to see the doctor. He conducted many tests on her. Then he confirmed what we have known since she was tested on entrance to the School for the Blind: that she suffers from a condition known as corneal dystrophy. He went further to say that the type of corneal dystrophy Arundhati had was 'dominant lattice-like corneal dystrophy'. According to the doctor, an afflicted person has a lattice-like pattern of fine lines in the cornea, making him or her blind. Dr Sridhar, too, was just as baffled as the other doctors about how she could see shadowy, moving images. We all agreed that there was an invisible hand at work here; that is why some things cannot be explained by medical science.

And the doctor's prognosis: "Arundhati will not see beyond the images she sees now. But her chances are good if …".

The proposition he made after 'if' is unheard-of, stupendous,

God-defying, considering that we are just emerging from the Dark Ages of Medicine. In order that you understand his proposition. I must tell you more about Dr Sridhar and his work. But first, you must remember to keep everything I am going to tell you a secret, otherwise, we will land the good doctor, and ourselves, in trouble.

Dr Sridhar is a brilliant ophthalmologist, and an eye surgeon aspiring to fame, with degrees from medical colleges in London. He returned to India only a year ago and so is well-acquainted with the latest medical breakthroughs and innovations in the West. He is also very ambitious and hopes to make a name for himself as *the* ophthalmologist in India.

Have you heard of the American surgeon, Michael E. De Bakey? He successfully implanted on his patient an artificial heart to help the deceased heart pump blood. Dr Sridhar says that ever since then, his peers in London started experimenting with transplanting entire hearts, using monkeys as guinea pigs. They took out the faulty hearts and put in healthy ones. Then, they started experimenting on humans.

Following their example, other surgeons started experimenting with transplanting different organs and even limbs. That was when Dr Sridhar asked himself why he should not experiment with eye transplants.

So he set up a secret surgery a few miles out of Bangalore city. To the casual observer, it looks like any other country home with its sprawling garden, fountains and fish pond.

And now for the crux: the doctor's corneal transplant experiments.

They were all clandestine operations, of course, with corneas obtained criminally from newly dead vagabonds. He conducts the experiments with the help of his wife who is a nurse. He says the first few transplants were unsuccessful. But his latest attempt was a thumping success. The man regained one hundred per cent vision. The doctor had to pay him a hefty sum to disappear from the state and keep the operation a secret.

Coming to Arundhati, the doctor says he is willing to operate on her. But we face some problems:

1. Donor: even the most beggarly of dying beggars refuse to donate their eyes upon death, even in exchange for the fortune I have offered their families. "I don't want to be born blind during my next incarnation, even if I'm born a pig," they say.

2. Uncertainty: assuming we have a donor, there is still no guarantee that Arundhati will see. The doctor has warned us not to get our hopes too high. His success may have been a fluke. If the operation gets botched up, Arundhati stands to lose seeing even the shadowy images she sees now.

3. Finance: the transplant fees are exorbitant. My gratuity will disappear overnight. (Your mother was right. This is where your remittance will come in handy.)

Of course there is a fifty-fifty chance that the operation will be a success since Arundhati is young and strong. So says the doctor (his confidence frightens me). In the event the transplant is successful, the doctor will not be able to claim any glory for himself, as the operation is illegal. And he has asked that we leave Madras immediately and move to a faraway address where nobody knows that Arundhati was once blind. This is to safeguard the doctor and us.

Should such a situation arise, we have decided to settle in Killa.

I know what you must be thinking, Ashvin: 'He tells me to guard my good name and there he is risking his!' But then, as you yourself once said, anything for Arundhati! You have no idea how far I am willing to go for her.

In the meantime, the doctor has given Arundhati various boosters to fortify her and we commute to Bangalore regularly for her checkups.

So there you are. What do you think?

Your mother is skeptical at best. Your grandmother is convinced the doctor is God. As for me, I want him to play God, but ...

Arundhati cannot wait for the transplant. She is so excited she cannot even sleep. (Neither can I.) A great change has come over her. She talks a lot. Her lips are no longer pursed but stretched in a Mona Lisa smile. She looks so ethereal when she smiles that way. And she keeps on humming 'The Merry Widow Waltz'. Since Mr Duncan is not around, she grabs me and we shuffle about. She is in a bubble of happiness and I cringe at the thought of bursting it.

Many questions still bother us. Will we ever find a donor? The poor here die like flies but does that mean we can plunder their corpses? I could never bear to see your sister looking at me through stolen eyes. Would we be doing the right thing, abetting a doctor in an illegal operation? Which is more important: giving Arundhati a chance to see or bowing to our moral convictions?

We are in limbo.

I remember once, long ago in Tanjore, when your mother, grandmother and I were in a terrible crisis, God showed us a way out of it.

Will He show us a way now?

Yours affectionately
R. Madhav Rao Bhonsle

*   *   *

Madras
10 October 1922

My dear Ashvin

Don't be too shocked, but this is your Ma writing to you with the services of an English interpreter.

There is something wrong with your Bah.

He is going over the top with this corneal transplant question and causing us much alarm. Ever since the doctor offered hope for Arundhati, he has become obsessed with the idea of getting someone to donate his or her eyes to Arundhati.

Armed with a thick wad of rupees, he has been going from one beggar colony to another (there are countless in Madras), trying to buy a donor. He tells us about each of his trips: the rat infested hovels, the skeletal beggars, the hostile reactions (one threw a begging-bowl at him and another, an amputee, even asked for Bah's leg in exchange for an eye).

Bah has visited scores of the dying: the starvation-wasted, the TB-racked, the cancer-ridden, the coma-stricken ... but without success. He sets out fresh and optimistic every morning and returns droopy-shouldered and edgy every evening.

Can you believe your Bah, who can hold his own in any discourse on Greek Mythology, is now reduced to the daily litany of 'Is anyone dying in this hovel?' So much so the beggars have dubbed him 'The Dying Man'. He even touches their feet in a desperate attempt to gain favour.

With each unsuccessful attempt, he has grown more and more depressed. Sometimes, he looks at us vacantly and your grandmother and I are reminded of the way his father was. We and Dr Sridhar have tried to reason with him but he will not see. His blindness is worse than Arundhati's.

"Arundhati must see," he insists.

"Then you should give your consent to the doctor to go ahead with the transplant," we tell him.

You should hear the way he raves against the dying beggars. "The bastards know they have no hope of living, so why can't they do one last good deed and gain a place in Heaven?" he says. "I feel like throttling them!" Can you imagine your mild-mannered Bah talking that way?

We understand he loves Arundhati very much. If there is any

truth in the belief that fathers are closer to their daughters than to their sons, then your father is living proof. He is even closer to Arundhati than he is to me, especially because she is blind.

"She deserves so much more," he keeps on saying. "What dreams she must dream, now that she knows sight is within reach."

Sometimes I wish we had never met Dr Sridhar. But that is selfish of me, is it not? I know Arundhati comes first. Still, I do not approve of the way your Bah is going about doing things. As I see it, it is best we let the doctor do things his way, corpse-plundering or not.

Write to your father, Ashvin. Try to make him see sense. Maybe he will listen to you.

Your worried Ma
Tara Bai

*　　*　　*

A week later, Ashvin received a telegram:

TELECOMMUNICATIONS DEPARTMENT, MALAYA
Receiving Form
OFFICE OF ORIGIN   Bangalore   **DATE** 17/10/22 **TIME** 1600
To: Ashvin Rao Bhonsle, Esq.
Regret to inform Bah passed away Stop 9 a.m. today Stop Car accident Stop Cremated afternoon Stop **Sent by:** Tara Bai Bhonsle

Six hours later:

Ashvin, I know you will never hear what I am saying. But hell, I have to tell someone! (Sorry about the expletive, but of late I have been driven to spewing them.)

I have arrived in Deathland. It has taken me more than the stipulated time as I was delayed at the start.

I am now at the gates of Yamapura—Death City. The city is walled and has only one gate. Obese and ugly buffalo-horned men are guarding it. They are bare chested and wear only kilt-like black wraps. Their arms, wrists and ankles are encircled with thick rings the colour of the moon. Maces are their main weapons. They hold them against their shoulders like sepoys hold rifles. With them are Yama's two hounds. They are diabolical. The wolverine-looking beasts have four eyes each. They gore me with their red eyes and snarl as if they want to tear me to shreds. How they strain against their leash!

Death City is milling with the recently dead. But silence pervades it. The dead do not talk, once they have entered the gates. The evil look worried. The good look serene. Yama will be passing judgement on them soon. They will either be sent to suffer in naraka or to taste paradise in swarga.

Earlier, after I arrived, one of the guards brought another man to the gate. He was dressed in black and powdered with ash. He resembled Dracula, with fangs peeping from the corners of his lips. In his hands he clutched a thick, heavy book that looked like a register.

"I'm Chitragupta," he announced grandly. Chitragupta is the Registrar of the Dead. He has pouches under his eyes as he is on call twenty-four hours a day. He looked me up and down and said, "Now what do we have here? An early bird?"

He asked me my name. I gave it.

Opening his register, he ran a gnarled finger down a list of names. "Nope. You're not on the Death List for today," he said, banging shut the register. "And what makes you think you can come any time you like?" His lips curled back in anger. He hissed and bared his fangs. I jumped back in fear. But he quickly subdued his anger and rearranged his features. "Here the early bird does not catch the worm. It only catches pneumonia waiting outside the gates."

"How long do I have to wait?" I asked, my voice a mew.

"Until Yama returns."

"Returns? From where?"

"California."

"California?"

"Yes. There's been an earthquake in San Francisco."

"So, how long will he take to return?"

"As long as it takes to collect all the souls. Could be a few hours. Or a few days if the death toll is high."

"Don't you have the authority to let me in?"

"No. I'm sorry. You'll just have to stick it out here. See you!" He lugged his register and bustled off. He had to record all the good and bad deeds of the dead in the city.

So here I am, still waiting at the gates. I am bracing myself for the cold and the punishment I am about to receive.

While waiting, I might as well tell you what happened immediately after I died.

*　　*　　*

The instant my heart stops, I rise out of my mortal body cage. I sense another spirit next to me. He is Yamaduta, Yama's messenger. He is Chitragupta's twin, minus the fangs. He escorts the dead to Deathland. Understanding my plight, he allows me to hover and watch events unfold below.

Everything and everybody moves slowly, as if time has slowed down.

Your mother screams. She faints beside my dead body. Dr Sridhar and his wife help revive her. Revived, she turns hysterical and faints again. Poor Tara. Once so strong.

Arundhati is confused. She runs here and there like a frightened chicken, asking what is happening. But nobody answers her. Then your grandmother becomes aware of her, runs up and hugs her. She tells Arundhati the news. Arundhati stiffens with shock.

Your grandmother weeps. She weeps for all the lost men in her life: me, my father, my grandfather and my brother. There is no consoling her.

Between them, the doctor and his wife carry my body into the surgery. I float in behind them. Yamaduta waits outside, like a jail warden waits for a prisoner to finish saying goodbye to his family. Your mother (now conscious but weak) and grandmother lead Arundhati in. They whisper words of encouragement to her and leave to wait outside.

Dr Sridhar and his wife are efficient. They prepare my body and Arundhati for surgery. Before Yamaduta has time to become impatient with me, they have already carried out the transplant. It is a success. I see my baby sleeping peacefully. I plant a fatherly kiss on her forehead. I love her so much it hurts. But I leave knowing she is about to start living a brand new life—a life dazzling with light and colour. Never mind that it cost me nirvana.

I pass through the surgery door and Yamaduta takes my hand. His hand feels like an iron cuff.

Then I begin the ultimate of journeys.

Epilogue

December 1922

The family was standing among the ruins of Killa Fort.

Mukta, Tara and Arundhati were present. They were on their long-awaited visit to the fort. Ashvin and Jija Bai, visiting from Malaya, were in their company. So, too, was their baby, named Mithun after Madhav's wish. Though Ashvin could not light his father's funeral pyre, he compensated by sprinkling milk at the cremation site and scattering his ashes in a river.

Around them, mist was swirling in the air in a rising, twisting, ghostly Bharathanatyam of welcome. The sound of silence gripped them as ageless Death slept in the fort.

The victorious British, after trouncing Prince Dilip and his army, had long moved to the rebuilt palace in Killa. The fort now stood as a monument to a brave queen and her loyal subjects. Some of its battlements were missing like a child's milk teeth. But the towers, including those that housed the Megh Garjana and Agni Astra stood solid. And the rusty cannons still sat in defiance. The moat surrounding the fort had disappeared under choking weeds.

Mukta glimpsed a black snake slithering for cover behind a heap of stones. She was immediately reminded of the legend behind the fort.

The morning sky was red. Memories of the other red morning flooded Mukta: fifty-two years ago, when her husband had set out for the decisive battle and she and her in-laws had reported for duty in the fort's sickbay.

Mukta listened and she could hear them again: the roar of Killa *ka*

Jai!, the earth-shattering cannon booms, the staccato gunfire, the thundering hoofs, the piercing screams, the agonised groans, the screeching lammergeiers. And she could feel the swoosh of the wind as the swans flew by. She swayed and Ashvin caught her in his arms.

"I'm sorry, Ashvin," Mukta said, "the memory is too much for me. For a moment, it was as if the whole fort had come to life."

When she regained her composure, she pointed at the Saraswathi Mandir tower. "Look! That's where Rani Meera Bai was standing with her advisors when I last saw her. Oh! You could feel the courage emanating from her like the heat from the sun! And there," she pointed at the rotting North Gate, "that was where your grandfather Ramdas fought so gallantly but in vain against the traitors."

Mukta shook off Ashvin's hands, treaded carefully over the uneven ground and stopped to sweep the fort with her gaze. Then she recounted all the stories they had heard about the fort.

They wandered around, scattering the morning dew. They touched the fort's mossy, weeping walls and entered its silent, screaming buildings. Mukta even showed them the trap door in the palace kitchen through which she had escaped. At the haathi tal—the sparkling pond where temple elephants once bathed—Mukta froze. There, on the placid water sat a lone white swan. It cruised, stopped to nestle its beak under one wing, then cruised again. "She still haunts Killa!" Mukta whispered in awe. "How close to her heart Killa must have been!"

The others nodded in agreement, not wanting to hurt Mukta.

Mukta took a handful of sweet rice from the tiffin they had packed. She placed it reverently at the edge of the tank, whispering a prayer. Remnants of other people's offerings still dotted the tank's edge. Visitors had offered rice, wheat, corn, mango and banana the previous day.

Mukta would not be alive to see it, but at the stroke of midnight on 15 August 1947, the great swan would soar out of the fort and fly into the night, never to be seen again. And the jubilant people of Killa, looking up at the Independence Day fireworks, would see the swan become a speck in the sky and say, "At last, she will rest in peace."

Mukta led the family to the spot the Rani had been cremated.

Bent on erasing the Rani from the memory of her people, the British had not allowed the spot to be marked. But a rain tree had grown on the hallowed ground. It was rumoured that every time the British tried to cut it down, the tree bled. They finally gave up, frightened off by reports of their own countrymen being cursed by spirits when they disturbed sacred tombs in Egypt. The tree had grown to maturity and now had spreading, sheltering branches.

"A sheltering tree for a sheltering queen. How appropriate!" Tara exclaimed.

They all sat under the tree, happy that they had, at last, come to the one place on earth they had all wanted to visit; either to relive old memories, to satisfy their curiosity, or to live someone else's dream.

"If only my nawra were here," Mukta said and sighed, thinking of Ramdas. "How he longed to see Killa again."

"And my husband, too. He did so much want to come in memory of his father. For him, coming to Killa would have been a pilgrimage," Tara said. "If only he hadn't died so soon!"

Both women had aged since Madhav's death. Mukta stooped. Tara was hollow-cheeked and had a haunted look about her.

The hit-and-run accident was still fresh in Tara's memory: stepping out of Dr Sridhar's clinic, the speeding Austin, the sickening thud. Death had been instantaneous.

"But he has come, Ma. He is here with us!" Arundhati said, glorying in the family she saw around her with her new, seeing eyes. The green orbs sparkled again like the cut mirrors of the Arsa Mahal, like Tara's had once.

"Oh Arundhati! I don't know whether to be sad for your father or to be happy for you."

"Be happy, Ma. Bah would have wanted it this way."

"Yes, he would. More than you'll ever know ..." Tara's voice trailed off as a gnawing vision came back to her.

She and only she had seen Madhav walk deliberately into the path of the car ...

Acknowledgements

My heartfelt thanks to:

Philip Tatham, the kind of publisher writers dream about, for giving my words flight.

The team at Monsoon Books.

B. Jayachandra Rao Chavan, M. Saroja Bai Bhonsle, M. Yeshwant Rao Bhonsle and A. Kasturi Bai Waaghmare of Tanjore (Thanjavur) and Chennai, for clearing the path.

H. Shanta Bai Rathode and S. Rama Devi Jagtap for showing the light.

Eric C. Forbes, Rose Ismail, Aishah Ali, M. King, S. Uma Bai King, Azizah Idris and Moo Pen Nie who, in their own little ways, made this book possible.

My relatives and friends for their blessings.

And ...

Sukhanya, Diwakar and Pritika, I could not have done it without you.

Bibliography

Danielou, Alain, *The Complete Kama Sutra*. Vermont: Park Street Press, 1994.

Desai, K.N., Vinod Chandra Pande and L.N. Mukherjee, *History of the Marathas*. Lucknow: Prakash Kendra, 1983.

Federated Malay States Railways, *Fifty Years of Railways in Malaya 1885–1935*. Kuala Lumpur: 1935.

Knappart, Jan, *Indian Mythology*. London: Diamond Books, 1995.

Morgan, W.S., *The Story of Malaya*. Singapore: Malaya Publishing House Limited, 1950.

Sarkar, Sir Jadunath, *Shivaji And His Times*. New Delhi: Orient Longman Ltd, 1973.

Sinha, Shyam Narain, *Rani Lakshmi Bai of Jhansi*. Allahabad: Ghugh Publications, 1980.

Tate D.J.M., *Straits Affairs, The Malay World and Singapore*. Hong Kong: John Nicholson Ltd., 1989.